"HE PUT HIS FACE CLOSE TO HERS, AND STARED INTO HER EYES"

The Awakening of Helena Richie

By MARGARET DELAND

Author of
"Dr. Lavendar's People," "Old Chester Tales," Etc.

With Four Illustrations
By WALTER APPLETON CLARK

A. L. BURT COMPANY
PUBLISHERS ∴ NEW YORK

Copyright, 1905, 1906, by HARPER & BROTHERS.

All rights reserved.

Published July, 1906.

TO
LORIN DELAND

MAY 12, 1906

THE AWAKENING OF HELENA RICHIE

CHAPTER I

DR. LAVENDAR and Goliath had toiled up the hill to call on old Mr. Benjamin Wright; when they jogged back in the late afternoon it was with the peculiar complacency which follows the doing of a disagreeable duty. Goliath had not liked climbing the hill, for a heavy rain in the morning had turned the clay to stiff mud, and Dr. Lavendar had not liked calling on Benjamin Wright.

"But, Daniel," said Dr. Lavendar, addressing a small old dog who took up a great deal more room on the seat of the buggy than he was entitled to, "Daniel, my boy, you don't consult your likings in pastoral calls." Then he looked out of the mud-spattered window of the buggy, at a house by the roadside—"The Stuffed Animal House," Old Chester children called it, because its previous owner had been a taxidermist of some little local renown. "That's another visit I ought to make," he reflected, "but it can wait until next week. G'long, Goliath!"

Goliath went along, and Mrs. Frederick Richie, who lived in the Stuffed Animal House, looking listlessly from an upper window, saw the hood of the buggy jogging by and smiled suddenly. "Thank Heaven!" she said.

Benjamin Wright had not thanked Heaven when Dr. Lavendar drove away. He had been as disagreeable as usual to his visitor, but being a very lonely old man he enjoyed having a visitor to whom to be disagreeable. He lived on his hilltop a mile out of Old Chester, with his "nigger" Simmons, his canary-birds, and his temper. More than thirty years before he had quarrelled with his only son Samuel, and the two men had not spoken to each other since. Old Chester never knew what this quarrel had been about; Dr. Lavendar, speculating upon it as he and Goliath went squashing through the mud that April afternoon, wondered which was to blame. "Pot and kettle, probably," he decided. "Samuel's goodness is very irritating sometimes, and Benjamin's badness is—well, it's not as distressing as it should be. But what a forlorn old critter he is! And this Mrs. Richie is lonely too—a widow, with no children, poor woman! I must call next week. Goliath wouldn't like to turn round now and climb the hill again. Danny, I fear Goliath is very selfish."

Goliath's selfishness carried them home and landed Dr. Lavendar at his own fireside, rather tired and full of good intentions in regard to calls. He confided these intentions to Dr. William King who looked in after supper to inquire about his cold.

"Cold? I haven't any cold! You can't get a job here. Sit down and give me some advice. Hand me a match first; this ragamuffin Danny has gone to sleep with his head on my foot, and I can't budge."

The doctor produced the match; "I'll advise you

THE AWAKENING OF HELENA RICHIE

not to go out in such weather. Promise me you won't go out to-morrow."

"To-morrow? Right after breakfast, sir! To make calls on the people I've neglected. Willy, how can I find a home for an orphan child? A parson up in the mountains has asked me to see if I can place a little seven-year-old boy. The child's sister who took care of him has just died. Do you know anybody who might take him?"

"Well," said Willy King, "there's Mrs. Richie."

Dr. Lavendar looked at him over his spectacles. "Mrs. Frederick Richie?—though I understand she calls herself Mrs. Helena Richie. I don't like a young female to use her own name, William, even if she is a widow! Still, she may be a nice woman I suppose. Do you think a little boy would have a good home with her?"

"Well," the doctor demurred, "of course, we know very little about her. She has only been here six months. But I should think she was just the person to take him. She is mighty good-looking, isn't she?"

"Yes," Dr. Lavendar said, "she is. And other things being equal I prefer a good-looking woman. But I don't know that her looks are a guarantee that she can train up a child in the way he should go. Can't you think of anybody else?"

"I don't see why you don't like Mrs. Richie?"

"I never said I didn't like her," protested Dr. Lavendar; "but she's a widow."

"Unless she murdered the late Richie, that's not against her."

"Widows don't always stay widows, Willy."

"I don't believe she's the marrying kind," William

said. "I have a sort of feeling that the deceased Richie was not the kind of husband who receives the compliment of a successor—"

"Hold on; you're mixing things up! It's the bad husband and the good wife that get compliments of that kind."

William laughed as he was expected to, but he stuck to his opinion that Mrs. Richie had had enough of husbands. "And anyway, she's devoted to her brother—though he doesn't come to see her very often."

"There's another point," objected Dr. Lavendar; "what kind of a man is this Mr. Pryor? Danny growled at him once, which prejudiced me against him."

"I don't take to him much myself," William King confessed; "though I must say he seems a decent man enough. He doesn't cultivate acquaintances in Old Chester, but that only shows bad taste."

"She says he is not very well," Dr. Lavendar explained; "she says he likes to keep quiet when he comes down here."

"I don't see anything wrong with him."

"Hasn't taken any of your pills? Maybe he doesn't believe in doctors. I don't myself."

"Thank you," said William King.

"There's too much fuss anyway over our precious carcasses! And you fellows encourage it," Dr. Lavendar grumbled. Then he said he wished he knew more about Mrs. Richie. "I ask you for information and all you say is that she's good-looking, and her brother doesn't take your pills."

William laughed.

"She doesn't come to church very regularly, and she never stops afterwards to talk," Dr. Lavendar ruminated.

THE AWAKENING OF HELENA RICHIE

"Well, she lives 'way up there on the hill road—"

"Yes, she does live pretty far out of town," Dr. Lavendar admitted, "but that's not a reason for not being neighborly after church."

"She's shy," said William King, "that's all. Shyness isn't anything very wrong. And she's mighty pleasant when she does talk to you. I tell you Dr. Lavendar, pleasantness goes a good way in this world. I'd say it was better than goodness—only they are the same thing."

"No, they're not," said Dr. Lavendar.

"I grant she doesn't belong to the sewing society," William said grinning. "Martha says that some of the ladies say she doesn't show proper grief for her husband. She actually smiles sometimes! They say that if the Lord were to remove *their* beloved husbands, they would never smile again."

"William," said Dr. Lavendar chuckling, "I begin to like your widow."

"She's not my widow, thank you! But she's a nice woman, and she must be pretty lonely up there all by herself."

"Wish I had gone in to see her this afternoon," the old man said thoughtfully. "As you say she may be a suitable person to take this little boy. I wonder if she's going to stay in Old Chester?"

"Sam Wright says she has spoken to him of buying the house. That looks as if she meant to settle down. Did you know that Sam's Sam is casting sheep's eyes at her?"

"Why, she's old enough to be his mother!" said Dr. Lavendar.

"Oh, no. Sam's Sam is twenty-three, and one of **my** patients says that Mrs. Richie will never see forty-five again. Which leads me to conclude that she's about thirty."

"Of course she doesn't encourage him?" Dr. Lavendar said anxiously.

"She lets him come to see her, and she took him out once in that wicker-work vehicle she has—looks like a clothes-basket on wheels. And she provides the clothes to put into it. I'm told they're beautiful; but that no truly pious female would be willing to decorate poor flesh and blood with such finery. I'm told—"

"William! Is this the way I've brought you up? To pander to my besetting sin? Hold your tongue!" Dr. Lavendar rose chuckling, and stood in front of the fireplace, gathering the tails of his flowered cashmere dressing-gown under his arms. "But Willy I hope Sam isn't really smitten? You never can tell what that boy will do."

"Yes, he's a hair-trigger," the doctor agreed, "a hair-trigger! And his father understands him about as well as—as Danny there understands Hebrew! I think it's a case of Samuel and his father over again. Dr. Lavendar, do you suppose anybody will ever know what those two quarrelled about?"

"Probably not."

"I suppose," William King ruminated, "that you'd call Sam a genius?"

"No, I wouldn't; he has no patience. You can't have genius without patience. Sam hasn't a particle."

"Well," the doctor explained, "he hasn't the slightest sense of responsibility; and I notice that when people have no sense of responsibility, you call them either criminals or geniuses."

"I don't," said Dr. Lavendar dryly, "I call 'em poor critters, either way. But Willy, about this little boy;

the great point is who needs him? I expect he'll be here on Saturday."

"What! This week? But you haven't found anybody to take him."

"Oh, he'll stay with me for a while. Mary 'll look after him. And I'll play marbles with him. Got any white alleys? Gimme six, and I'll give you an agate."

"But Dr. Lavendar, that will be a nuisance to you," William King protested. "Let me take him. Or, at least — I'll ask Martha; she's house-cleaning now, and she says she's very tired; so I'm not sure—" William ended weakly.

"No, no; I want him myself," said the old minister.

"Well," Dr. King said with evident relief, "shall I speak to Mrs. Richie about him? I'm going up there to-morrow; she's got a sick cook, and she asked me to call. What's his name?"

"David Allison. You might sound her William, but don't be definite. Don't give her any chance to say yes or no. I want to know her a little better before I make up my mind. When the boy comes I'll happen along in my buggy with him, and then we'll see. And meantime Willy, keep your eye on Sam's Sam. He mustn't get too much interested up there. A little falling in love with an older woman doesn't hurt most boys; in fact, it's part of their growing up and likely as not it does 'em good. But Sam's Sam isn't like most boys."

"That's so," said William King, "he may not be a genius and he certainly isn't a criminal, but he has about as much stability as a sky-rocket."

CHAPTER II

"YOU can't think of anybody who might like to take this little David Allison, can you, my dear?" William King asked his wife at breakfast the next morning.

"I certainly cannot," Martha said decidedly. "I think it's a very dangerous thing to take unknown children into your family. I suppose you think I ought to offer to do it? But in the first place, I'm very tired, and in the second place, I don't like boys. If it was a girl it might be different."

"No doubt we could find a girl," William began, but she interrupted him.

"Girls are a great expense. And then, as I said—unknown children!—they might turn into anything. They might have evil tendencies; they probably have. If the parents die early, it's a sign of weakness of some sort. I've no doubt this boy's father drank. I don't want to seem unkind, but I must say flatly and frankly that considering how hard it is for us to make both ends meet—as you keep up a sort of free practice—I don't think it's prudent to suggest any new responsibilities and expenses."

"Oh, I wasn't making suggestions," William King said. "I guess we're not the people to bring up a child. I'd spoil him, I've no doubt."

"I'm sure you would!" Martha said, greatly relieved.

THE AWAKENING OF HELENA RICHIE

"It would be the worst possible thing for him. But Willy, there's that Mrs. Richie?"

"You think his evil tendencies wouldn't hurt her?" the doctor said dryly.

"I think she's a rich woman, so why shouldn't she do a thing like that? I'll go and see her if you want me to—though she never makes you feel welcome; and tell her about the boy?"

"You needn't bother; Dr. Lavendar will see her himself."

"I don't understand that woman," Mrs. King said. "She keeps herself to herself too much. It almost looks as if she didn't think we were good enough to associate with her!"

William made no reply.

"Willy, does she use perfumery?"

"How in the world should I know!"

"Well, there's a sort of fragrance about her. It isn't like cologne, it's like—well, orris-root."

William made no comment.

"It's a kind of sachet, I guess; I'd like to know what it is. Willy, Sam Wright's Sam went out walking with her yesterday. I met them on the River Road. I believe the boy is in love with her!"

"He's got eyes," William agreed.

"*Tck!*" said Martha, "the idea of calling her good-looking! And I don't think it speaks well for a woman of her age—she's forty if she's a day—to let a boy trail round after her like that. And to fix herself up with sachet-powders and things. And her Sarah told the Draytons' Jean that she had her breakfast in bed every morning! I'd like to know how my housekeeping would go on if *I* had breakfast in bed, though dear knows I'm very tired and it would be pleasant enough.

THE AWAKENING OF HELENA RICHIE

But there's one thing about me: I may not be perfect, but I don't do lazy things just because they are pleasant."

The doctor made no defence of Mrs. Richie. Instead he asked for another cup of coffee and when told that it would not be good for him, got up, then paused patiently, his hand on the door-knob, to hear his Martha out.

"William, what do you suppose is the last thing Sam Wright's Sam has done?"

The doctor confessed his ignorance.

"Well, his father sent him to Mercer on Monday to buy supplies for the bank. He gave him seventy-five dollars. Back comes my young gentleman with— what do you suppose? A lot of pictures of actors and actresses! And no supplies."

"What! you don't mean he spent the money on the pictures?"

"Every bit of it! His mother came in and told me about it last night. She said his father was frantic. She was dreadfully upset herself. As for Sam, he kept saying that the 'prints,' as he called them, were very valuable. Though I'm sure I can't see why; they were only of actor people, and they had all died sixty or seventy years ago."

"Actors!" the doctor said. "Poor Samuel! he hates the theatre. I do believe he'd rather have pictures of the devil."

"Oh, but wait. You haven't heard the rest of it. It appears that when the boy looked at 'em yesterday morning he found they weren't as valuable as he thought—I don't understand that part of it," Martha acknowledged—"so what does he do but march downstairs, and put 'em all in the kitchen stove! What do you think of that?"

THE AWAKENING OF HELENA RICHIE

"I think," said William King, "that he has always gone off at half-cock ever since he was born. But Martha, the serious thing is his spending money that didn't belong to him."

"I should think it was serious! If he'd been some poor little clerk in the bank, instead of Mr. Samuel Wright's only son, he would have found it was serious! Willy, what do you make of him?"

"He is queer," William said; "queer as Dick's hatband; but that's all. Sam wouldn't do a mean thing, or a dirty thing, any more than a girl would."

"And now he thinks he's in love with this Richie woman," Martha went on—but William made his escape. He had to go and hitch up, he said.

Before he took Jinny out of her stall he went into the harness-room and hunted about on a shelf until, behind a rusty currycomb and two empty oil-bottles, he found a small mirror. It was misty and flecked with clear spots where the quicksilver had dropped away, but when he propped it against the cobwebbed window he could see himself fairly well. Staring into its dim depths he retied his necktie; then he backed the buggy out of the carriage-house. But after he had put his mare between the shafts he hesitated. . . . The buggy was very shabby; it sagged badly on the right side and there was a rent in the faded cushion. The doctor looked at his watch. . . . Then, hurriedly, led Jinny back to her stall, got a bucket of water and a sponge, and washed off the dashboard and wheels. After that he fumbled along a dusty beam to find a bottle of oil with which he touched up the harness. But when all was done he shook his head. The buggy was hopeless. Nevertheless, when he climbed in and slapped Jinny's flank with the newly oiled rein he was careful to sit in the middle of the seat to make the springs truer, and he avoided the mud-puddles on the road up to the Stuffed Animal House. There were a good many puddles, for it had rained the day before. To-day the clouds had gathered up behind the hills into white domes, but the sky was that faint April blue that dims easily into warm mists. There was the smell of earth, the fainter scent of unopened buds, and from the garden borders of the Stuffed Animal House came the pungent odor of box.

Helena Richie, standing by a bed of crown-imperials, bareheaded, a trowel in her gloved hand, her smooth cheek flushed with the unwonted exertion of planting seeds, caught the exquisite breath of the box, and sighed; then, listlessly, she turned to walk back towards the house. Before she reached it the gate clicked and Dr. King came up the path. She saw him and looked hurriedly about, as if seeking a way of escape, but it was too late.

"Gardening?" he called to her.

"Yes," she said, and her smile like reluctant sunshine did not betray to the doctor that he was not welcome.

"Don't work too hard," he cautioned her. It seemed to William King, looking at her with wondering admiration, that she was too delicate a creature to handle a trowel. There was a certain soft indolence in the way she moved that was a delight to his eye. It occurred to him that he would ask his Martha why she didn't wear gardening-gloves. Mrs. Richie wore them, and as she pulled one off he saw how soft and white her hand was. . . .

"How's the patient?" he asked.

"Poor Maggie? Oh, she's pretty uncomfortable I'm afraid."

THE AWAKENING OF HELENA RICHIE

They had gone together to the front porch, and as she stood on the lower step looking up at him, the sunshine suddenly filled her eyes with limpid brown light. "Maggie is in her room in the ell—the first door on the left. Shall I show you the way?"

"I know the way," he said.

Mrs. Richie sat down on the porch step to wait for him. She had nothing else to do. She never had anything to do. She had tried to be interested in the garden, and bought a trowel and some seeds and wandered out into the borders; but a manufactured interest has no staying quality—especially if it involves any hard work. She was glad when William King came back and sat down beside her; sickness was not an agreeable topic, but it was a topic.

"Maggie will be all right in two or three days, but don't let her go into the kitchen before Monday. A bad throat pulls you down. And she's had a good deal of pain."

"Oh, poor Maggie!" she said wincing.

"A sore throat is nothing so very dreadful," William assured her with open amusement.

She drew a breath of relief. "Oh, I'm glad! I can't bear to think of pain." Then she looked at him anxiously. "Don't you think she can cook before Monday? I'm so tired of scrappy dinners."

"I'm afraid not," William King said. "I'm very sorry." But that his sorrow was not for Maggie was evident.

"Oh, dear!" said Mrs. Richie; and then her eyes crinkled with gayety at his concern. "I don't really mind, Dr. King."

"I shouldn't blame you if you did. Nobody likes scrappy dinners. I wish you would come down and have dinner with us?"

"Oh, thank you, no," she said. And the sudden shy retreat into her habitual reserve was followed by a silence that suggested departure to the doctor. As he got up he remembered Dr. Lavendar and the little boy, but he was at a loss how to introduce the subject. In his perplexity he frowned, and Mrs. Richie said quickly:

"Of course she sha'n't do any work. I'm not so bad-tempered as you think; I only meant that I don't like discomfort."

"*You* bad-tempered?" he said. "No, indeed! You're just the opposite. That's why I suggested you when I heard about this boy."

"What boy?"

"Why, a little fellow of seven—David his name is—that Dr. Lavendar is trying to find a home for. And I thought perhaps you—"

"—would take him?" cried Mrs. Richie in astonishment, and then she laughed. "*I!*"

"Why, it occurred to me that perhaps you might be lonely, and—"

Helena Richie stopped laughing; she pulled off her other glove and looked down at her white hands. "Well, yes, I'm lonely. But—I don't like children, Dr. King."

"You don't?" he said blankly, and in his surprise he sat down again. "Oh, I'm sure that's only because you don't know them. If you had ever known a child—"

"I have," Mrs. Richie said, "one." Her voice was bleak; the gayety had dropped out of it; for an instant she looked old. William King understood.

"It died?"

She nodded. She began to pull her gloves on

THE AWAKENING OF HELENA RICHIE

again, smoothing down each finger carefully and not looking at him.

"A little girl?"

"Boy." She turned her face away, but he saw her chin tremble. There was a moment's silence; then the doctor said with curious harshness.

"Well, anyhow, you know what it means to have owned your own."

"Better not have known!"

"I can't feel that. But perhaps I don't understand."

"You don't understand." Her head, with its two soft braids wound around it like a wreath, was bent so that he could not see her face. "Dr. King, his father — hurt him. Yes; hurt a little baby, eight months and twelve days old. He died seven weeks later."

William drew in his breath; he found no words.

"That was twelve years ago, but I can't seem to — to get over it," she said with a sort of gasp.

"But how—" Dr. King began.

"Oh, he was not himself. He was—happy. I believe you call it 'happy'?"

"How did you bear it!"

"I didn't bear it I suppose. I never have borne it!"

"Did he repent before he died?" William King said passionately.

"Before he—?" Her voice suddenly shook; she made elaborate pretence of calmness, fastening her gloves and looking at them critically; then she said: "Yes, Dr. King; he repented. He repented!"

"If there ever was excuse for divorce, you had it!"

"You don't think there ever is?" she asked absently.

"No," William said. "I suppose you'll think I'm

very old-fashioned, but I don't, unless—" he stopped short; he could not have put his qualifying thought into words to any woman, especially not to this woman, so like a girl in spite of her thirty-odd years. "You see," he said, awkwardly, "it's such an unusual thing. It never happened in Old Chester; why, I don't believe I ever saw a—a divorced person in my life!"

"Well," she said, "anyhow, I didn't get a divorce."

"Mrs. Richie!" he said, blushing to his temples, "you didn't think I thought of such a thing?"

But it was plain that she regretted her confidence; she rose with the evident purpose of changing the subject. "I must go and put in some more seeds. Why doesn't Dr. Lavendar keep this little boy? After all, he's lonely himself."

"Well, he's an old man you know, and—"

"Dr. King," she broke in, "I don't mind having the child here for a week while Dr. Lavendar is looking for somebody to take him. Not longer. It wouldn't do. Really it wouldn't. But for a week, perhaps, or maybe two—"

"That would be a great help," William King said. "Then Dr. Lavendar can have plenty of time to find a home for him. I would have been glad to take him myself, but just at present it happens that it is not— I should say, Mrs. King is very tired, and—"

"It is perfectly convenient for me," Mrs. Richie said, "if you'll only cure Maggie! You must cure Maggie, so that she can make cookies for him."

"I'll cure Maggie," the doctor assured her smiling, and went away much pleased with himself. But when he got into his shabby old buggy he sighed.

"Poor soul!" he said. "Poor soul!"

CHAPTER III

WILLIAM KING reported the result of his call to Dr. Lavendar, and when he told the tragic story of the dead baby the old man blinked and shook his head.

"Do you wonder she doesn't call herself Mrs. *Frederick* Richie?" William demanded. "I don't!"

"No; that's natural, that's natural," Dr. Lavendar admitted.

"I suppose it was a dreadful thing to say," said William, "but I just burst out and said that if ever there was an excuse for divorce, she had it!"

"What did she say?"

"Oh, of course, that she hadn't been divorced. I was ashamed of myself the next minute for speaking of such a thing."

"Poor child," said Dr. Lavendar, "living up there alone, and with such memories! I guess you're right; I guess she'd like to have little David, if only for company. But I think I'll keep him for a week or two myself, and let her get sort of acquainted with him under my eye. That will give me a chance to get acquainted with her. But to think I haven't known about that baby until now! It must be my fault that she was not drawn to tell me. But I'm afraid I wasn't drawn to her just at first."

THE AWAKENING OF HELENA RICHIE

Yet Dr. Lavendar was not altogether at fault. This newcomer in Old Chester was still a stranger to everybody, except to Sam Wright's Sam and to William King. To be sure, as soon as she was settled in her house Old Chester had called and asked her to tea, and was confused and annoyed because its invitations were not accepted. Furthermore, she did not return the calls. She went to church, but not very regularly, and she never stopped to gossip in the vestibule or the church-yard. Even with Dr. Lavendar she was remote. The first time he went to see her he asked, with his usual directness, one or two questions: Did Mr. Pryor live in Mercer? No; he had business that brought him there occasionally. Where did he live? In Philadelphia. Had she any relatives in this part of the world—except her brother? No, none; none anywhere. Was Mr. Pryor married? Yes. Had he any family? One daughter; his wife was dead. "And you have lost your husband?" Dr. Lavendar said, gently. "This is a lonely life for you here, I am afraid."

But she said oh, no; not at all; she liked the quiet. Then, with faint impatience as if she did not care to talk about her own affairs, she added that she had always lived in the East; "but I find it very pleasant here," she ended vaguely.

Dr. Lavendar had gone away uneasy and puzzled. Why didn't she live with her brother? Family differences no doubt. Curious how families fall out! "You'd think they'd be glad to hang together," the solitary old man thought; "and they are not necessarily bad folk who quarrel. Look at Sam and his boy. Both of 'em good as gold. But it's in the blood there," he said to himself sighing.

THE AWAKENING OF HELENA RICHIE

Sam and his son were not bad folk. The boy had nothing bad about him; nothing worse than an unexpectedness that had provided Old Chester with smiles for many years. "No; he is not bad; I have seen to *that*," his father used to say. "He's hardly been out of my sight twenty-four hours at a time. And I put my foot down on college with all its temptations. He's good — if he's nothing else!" And certainly Samuel Wright was good too. Everybody in Old Chester said so. He said so himself. "I, my dear Eliza, have nothing with which to reproach myself," he used to tell his wife ponderously in moments of conjugal unbending. "I have done my duty. I always do my duty; under all circumstances. I am doing my duty now by Sam."

This was when he and his son fell out on one point or another, as they had begun to do as soon as young Sam learned to talk; and all because the father insisted upon furnishing the boy with his own most excellent principles and theories, instead of letting the lad manufacture such things for himself. Now when Sam was twenty-three the falling-out had become chronic. No doubt it was in the blood, as Dr. Lavendar said. Some thirty years before, Sam senior, then a slim and dreamy youth, light-hearted and given to writing verses, had fallen out with his father, old Benjamin Wright; fallen out so finally that in all these years since, the two men, father and son, had not spoken one word to each other. If anybody might have been supposed to know the cause of that thirty-year-old feud it was Dr. Lavendar. He certainly saw the beginning of it. . . .

One stormy March evening Samuel Wright, then twenty-four years old, knocked at the Rectory door;

Dr. Lavendar, shielding his lamp from the wind with one hand, opened it himself.

"Why, Sam, my boy," he said and stopped abruptly. He led the way into his study and put the lamp down on the table. "Something is the matter?"

"Yes."

"What is it, Samuel?"

"I can't tell you, sir."

"Does your father know?"

"My father knows. . . . I will tell you this, Dr. Lavendar—that so help me God, I will never speak to my father again."

The young man lifted one hand; his face was dreadful to look upon. Then trying to speak in a natural voice he asked if he might stay at the Rectory for that night.

Dr. Lavendar took two turns about his study, then he said, "Of course you may, Samuel, but I shall feel it my duty to acquaint your father with the fact."

"Just as you please, sir."

"And Sam—I hope the night will bring wisdom."

Sam was silent.

"I shall see your father in the morning and try to clear this thing up."

"Just as you please, sir. I would like to go to my room now if you have no objection."

And that was all Dr. Lavendar got out of the son.

He lighted a lamp and silently preceded his guest up-stairs; then he went back to his study and wrote a line to the father. He sent it out to the Wright house and sat up until midnight waiting for an answer. None came. "Well," said Dr. Lavendar at last trudging up to bed, "the boy comes by his obstinacy honestly." The next morning he went early to see

Mr. Benjamin Wright. But as far as any straightening out of the trouble went or any enlightenment as to its cause, he might as well have stayed at home.

"Sam send you?"

"No; I came to see what I could do for you both. I take it for granted that Sam is at fault in some way? But he is a good boy, so I am sure he can be made to see his error."

"Did he tell you what was the trouble?"

"No; will you?"

"Let him come back and behave himself!" the older man said.

Dr. Lavendar thrust out his lower lip with a thoughtful frown. "It would expedite things, Wright, if you could tell me a little about the affair?"

Mr. Wright hesitated. He thrust his hand down into a blue ginger-jar for a piece of dried orange-skin and bit at it as if to steady his lips. "Sam can tell you if he wants to. He has perhaps informed you that he wishes to see the world? That he thinks life here very narrow? No? Well, I sha'n't quote him. All I shall say, is that I am doing my duty to him. I've always done my duty to him. If he sees fit to set up his own Ebenezer, and say he won't speak to me— I suppose he conveyed that filial sentiment to you?— he can do so. When he gets hungry he can speak. That's what other puppies do when they are hungry."

And that was all Dr. Lavendar got out of the father. . . .

This was thirty-two years ago. Sam Wright may have been hungry, but he never spoke. Instead, he worked. Old Chester seethed with curiosity for a while—to see Benjamin Wright pass his son with a contemptuous stare, to see Sam pass his father without a glance was very exciting. But excitement ebbs in thirty-two years. For one thing, old Mr. Wright came less often into town—because he could not bear to meet his son, people said; and Samuel never took the hill road out of Old Chester for a corresponding reason. Furthermore, it was hard to connect Samuel with anything so irrational as a quarrel, for every year he grew in solemn common sense. Benjamin Wright's growth was all in the way of temper; at least so his boy Simmons, a freckled mulatto of sixty years, informed Old Chester.

"He 'ain't got no human feelin's, 'cept for them there canaries," Simmons used to say in an aggrieved voice; "he'll stand and look at 'em and chirp to 'em by the hour—an' 'en he'll turn round and swear at you 'nough to take your leg off," Simmons said, bitterly. Simmons did his best for the canaries which he detested, cleaning out the cages and scraping the perches and seeing that the seed-trays and bath-tubs were always full; he did his best conscientiously, and it was hard to be "swore at when you 'ain't done nothin'." Perhaps Benjamin Wright had some "human feelings" for his grandson, Sam; but certainly Simmons's opinion was justified by his treatment of his granddaughters. When by their father's orders the little girls came up to the lonely house on the hill, the old man used to pitch small coins to them and tell them to go and look at the canaries,—"and then clear out. Simmons, give 'em some cake or something! Good-by. Good-by. Clear out." Long before he had settled into such dreary living, the son with whom he had quarrelled had made a life of his own. His slimness and gayety had disappeared as well as his dreaminess and versifying instincts. "Poetry?" he had been heard to say, "why, there isn't a poem that was ever written that I'd take five minutes out of my business to read!" It seemed as if the quarrel had wrenched him from the grooves, physical and spiritual, in which Nature had meant him to run and started him on lines of hard common sense. He was intensely positive; heavy and pompous and painfully literal; inclined to lay down the law to everybody; richer than most of us in Old Chester, and full of solemn responsibilities as burgess and senior warden and banker. His air of aggressive integrity used to make the honestest of us feel as if we had been picking pockets! Yes; a good man, as Old Chester said.

Years ago Dr. Lavendar had given up trying to reconcile the two Wrights; years ago Old Chester's speculations languished and died out. Once in a while some one remembered the quarrel and said, "What in the world could it have been about?" And once in a while Samuel's own children asked awkward questions. "Mother, what was father's row with grandfather?" And Mrs. Wright's answer was as direct as the question. "I don't know. He never told me."

When this reply was made to young Sam he dropped the subject. He had but faint interest in his father, and his grandfather with whom he took tea every Sunday night was too important a person to connect with so trivial an affair as a quarrel.

This matter of offspring is certainly very curious. Why should the solid Samuel Wright and his foolish, obedient Eliza have brought into the world a being of mist and fire? A beautiful youth, who laughed or wept or sung aloud, indifferent to all about him! Sometimes Sam senior used to look at his son and shake his head in bewildered astonishment; but often he was angry, and oftener still—though this he never admitted—hurt. The boy, always impersonally amiable, never thought it worth while to explain himself; partly because he was not interested in his father's opinion of his conduct, and partly because he knew he could not make himself understood.

"But who, my dear Eliza," Samuel would say to his wife—"who could understand such a boy? Look at this last performance of his! Purchasing pictures of *actors!* Where does he get such low tastes?—unless some of your family were interested in such things?"

"Oh no, Samuel; no, indeed," Mrs. Wright protested nervously.

"And to use money not his own! Do you know what that is called, my dear Eliza? It is called—"

"Oh don't, Samuel," whimpered the poor mother.

"And to think how carefully I have trained him! And all I have done for him. I let him buy that skiff he said he wanted. Absolute waste of money! Our old rowboat is good enough for the girls, so why isn't it good enough for him? And I never laid a hand on him in punishment either; not many fathers can say that."

As for the bank supplies young Sam had explained to his mother that they had been ordered and charged, so what *was* the matter? And Mrs. Wright kneading her tear-soaked handkerchief into a ball, cried some more and said:

"Oh, Sam dear, why do you act so?"

Sam looked at her attentively, wondering why her little nose always reddened when she cried. But he waited patiently, until she finished her rambling reproaches. It occurred to him that he would tell Mrs.

THE AWAKENING OF HELENA RICHIE

Richie all about this matter of the prints. "She will understand," he thought.

Sam's acquaintance with Mrs. Richie had begun when she was getting settled in her new house. Sam senior, having no desire to climb the hill road, sent his various communications to his tenant by his son, and afterwards Sam junior had communications of his own to make. He fell into the habit of stopping there on Sunday afternoons, quite oblivious of the fact that Mrs. Richie did not display any pleasure at seeing him. After one of these calls he was apt to be late in reaching "The Top," as his grandfather's place was called, and old Benjamin Wright, in his brown wig and moth-eaten beaver hat, would glare at him with melancholy dark eyes.

"Gad-a-mercy, what do you mean,—getting here at six-five! I have my tea at six, sir; at six sharp. Either get here on time or stay away. I don't care which. Do you hear?"

"Yes, sir," young Sam would murmur.

"Where have you been? Mooning after that female at the Stuffed Animal House?"

"I had to leave a message, sir, about the lease."

"How long does it take to leave a message about a lease?"

"She was not down-stairs and I had to wait—"

"*I* had to wait! That's more to the point. There, don't talk about it. You drive me crazy with your chatter."

Then they would sit down to supper in a black silence only broken by an occasional twitter from one of the many cages that hung about the room. But afterwards young Sam had his reward; the library, a toby, long before he was old enough to smoke, and his grandfather reading aloud in a wonderful voice, deep, sonorous, flexible—Shakespeare, Massinger, Beaumont and Fletcher. To be sure, there was nothing personal in such reading—it was not done to give pleasure to young Sam. Every night the old man rumbled out the stately lines, sitting by himself in this gloomy room walled to the ceiling with books, and warmed by a soft-coal fire that snapped and bubbled behind the iron bars of the grate. Sometimes he would burst into angry ecstasy at the beauty of what he read "There! What do you think of that?"

"Oh, it's splendid!"

"Hah! Much you know about it! There is about as much poetry in your family as there is in that coal-scuttle."

It was when he was eighteen that once the old man let his grandson read *The Tempest* with him. It was a tremendous evening to Sam. In the first place, his grandfather swore at him with a fury that really attracted his attention. But that night the joy of the drama suddenly possessed him. The deed was done; the dreaming youth awoke to the passion of art. As Benjamin Wright gradually became aware of it delight struggled with his customary anger at anything unexpected. He longed to share his pleasure with somebody; once he mentioned to Dr. Lavendar that "that cub, Sam, really has something to him!" After that he took the boy's training seriously in hand, and his artless pride concealed itself in a severity that knew no bounds of words. When Sam confessed his wish to write a drama in blank verse, his grandfather swore at him eagerly and demanded every detail of what he called the "fool plot of the thing."

"What does that female at the Stuffed Animal

House say to the idea of your writing a drama?" he asked contemptuously.

"She says I may read it to her."

"Knows as much about dramatic poetry as you do I suppose? When you finish the first act bring it to me. I'll tell you how bad it is."

His eager scoffing betrayed him, and every Sunday night, in spite of slaughtering criticism the boy took courage to talk of his poem. He had no criticism from Mrs. Richie.

When he first began to call at the Stuffed Animal House she had been coldly impatient, then uneasy, then snubbing. But nothing can be so obtuse as a boy; it never occurs to him that he is not wanted. Sam continued to call and to tell her of his play and to look at her with beautiful, tragic eyes, that by and by openly adored. Inevitably the coldness to which he was so calmly impervious wore off; a boy's innocent devotion must touch any woman no matter how self-absorbed she may be. Mrs. Richie began to be glad to see him. As for his drama, it was beautiful, she said.

"No," Sam told her, "it isn't—yet. You don't know. But I like to read it to you, even if you don't." His candor made her laugh, and before she knew it in spite of the difference in their years they were friends. As William King said, she was lonely, and Sam's devotion was at least an interest. Besides, she really liked the boy; he amused her, and her empty days were so devoid of amusement! "I can't read novels *all* the time," she complained. In this very bread-and-butter sort of interest she had no thought of possible consequences to Sam. A certain pleasant indolence of mind made it easy not to think of consequences at all. But he had begun to love her—with that first passion of youth so divinely tender and ridiculous! After a while he talked less of his play and more of himself. He told her of his difficulties at home, how he hated the bank, and how stupid the girls were.

"Lydia is the nicest, but she has no more imagination than a turnip. They are very uninteresting—my family," he said meditatively. "I don't like any of them—except mother. Mother hasn't any sense, but she's good," Sam ended earnestly.

"Oh, but you mustn't say things like that!"

"Why not? They're true," he said with a surprised look.

"Well, but we don't always tell the truth right out," she reminded him.

"I do," said Sam, and then explained that he didn't include his grandfather in his generalization. "Grandfather's bully; you ought to hear him swear!"

"Oh, I don't want to!" she said horrified.

"I told him that I burned the prints up," Sam went on. "And he said, 'good riddance to bad rubbish.' That was just like grandfather! Of course he did say that I was a d—I mean, a fool, to buy them in the first place; and I knew I was. But having bought them, the only thing to do was to burn them. But father!—"

Mrs. Richie's eyes crinkled with mischievous gayety. "Poor Mr. Wright!"

Sam dropped his clasped hands between his knees. "It's queer how I always do the wrong thing. Though it never seems wrong to me. You know father would not let me go to college for fear I'd go to the devil?" he laughed joyously. "But I might just as well, for

he thinks everything I do in Old Chester is wrong."
Then he sighed. "Sometimes I get pretty tired of
being disapproved of;—especially as I never can understand why it is. The fact is people are not reasonable," he complained. "I can bear anything but
unreasonableness."

She nodded. "I know. I never could please my
grandmother—she brought me up. My mother and
father died when I was a baby. I think grandmother
hated me; she thought everything I did was wrong.
Oh, I was so miserable! And when I was eighteen I
got married—and that was a mistake."

Sam gazed up at her in silent sympathy.

"I mean my—husband was so much older than I,"
she said. Then with an evident effort to change the
subject she added that one would think it would be
simple enough to be happy; "all my life I only wanted to be happy," she said.

"You're happy now, aren't you?" he asked.

She looked down at him—he was sitting on a stool
before the fire near her feet—and laughed with a
catching of the breath. "Oh, yes, yes; I'm happy."

And Sam caught his breath too, for there were tears
in her eyes.

But instantly she veered away from personalities.
"What is that scar on your wrist?"

Sam looked down at his hands clasped about his
knees, and blushed faintly. "Oh, nothing; I was very
young when that happened."

"How did it happen?" she asked absently. It
was often possible to start Sam talking and then think
her own thoughts without interruption.

"Why, I was about twelve, I believe," Sam said,
"and Miss Ellen Bailey—she used to teach school here;

then she got married and went out West;—she gave me a little gold image of Pasht; at least I thought it was gold. It was one of those things you ladies wear on your watch-chains, you know."

"Yes?" she said indolently.

"Well, I took a tremendous fancy to it. But it seems it wasn't gold, it was brass, and somebody told me so; I think it was Miss Ellen herself. I was so disappointed, I didn't want to live—queer! I can remember now just how I felt; a sort of sinking, here;" Sam laid his hand on his breast. "So I decided to throw myself out of the window. I did; but unfortunately—"

"You threw yourself out of the window!" she interrupted horrified.

Sam laughed. "Oh, well, I wasn't successful; I continued to live. Unfortunately my trousers caught on the grape trellis under the window, and there I hung! It must have been pretty funny—though I didn't think so at the time. First place, I tore my wrist on a nail—that's the scar; and then father caught me and sent me to bed for being a fool; so I didn't gain anything." His lip drooped. His feeling for his father was a candid mixture of amusement and contempt.

"But do you always act on the spur of the moment?" she said astonished.

Sam laughed and said he supposed so. "I am a good deal of a fool," he added simply.

"Well," she said sighing, "it's dangerous to be like that. I know, because I—I am a good deal of a fool myself." Then again, abruptly, she changed the subject. "What do you think? I'm going to have some company!"

Sam frowned. "Your brother?"

THE AWAKENING OF HELENA RICHIE

"No, oh no; not—Mr. Pryor." Then she told him that Dr. Lavendar had asked her if she would look after a little boy for him for a few weeks.

Sam was not responsive. Little boys were a great deal of trouble, he said.

"Come now; how long since—"

Sam's limpid deer's-eyes reproached her silently.

"How shall I amuse him?" she said.

And Sam eager to serve her promised to find a pair of rabbits for the child. "I used to like rabbits when I was young," he explained.

At last, after his hostess had swallowed many yawns, Sam reluctantly said good night. He went bounding down the hill in the darkness, across the fields, through the woods. In the starlight, the great world lay dim and lovely before him—it belonged to him! He felt the joyous buffet of the night wind upon his face, the brush of boughs against his shoulder, the scent of young ferns, and the give of the spongy earth under his feet; he sprang in long leaps over the grass, the tears were wet upon his fresh cheeks, he sang aloud. But he did not know what he sang; in his young breast, Love, like some warm living thing, stirred, and lifted glorious wings and drove his voice throbbing and exultant to his lips! As he came down Main Street, the church clock struck eleven. But it might have struck twelve and he would not have been disturbed.

Standing in the doorway of the Wright house in thunderous silence the senior warden, lamp in hand awaited his son. As Sam entered, the silence broke into a flash of crackling and scathing contempt.

"It does not occur to you, sir, I suppose, that a lady may find your society tiresome? It is after eleven!"

Sam smiling to himself hung up his hat. He was reflecting that he must see about those rabbits at once.

"You will understand, sir, if you please, that while you do me the honor to live under my roof you will return to it at night at a respectable hour. I will not sit up for you in this way. You will be in at ten o'clock. Do you hear?"

"Yes, sir," said Sam; and added with sudden awakening of interest, "if you would let me have a key, father, I—"

"I will not let you have a key! I will have no boy entering my house at midnight with a key! Do you understand?"

"Yes, sir," Sam murmured falling back into his own thoughts.

Mr. Wright, still talking, stood at the foot of the stairs so that his son could not pass him. Sam yawned, then noticed how in oratorical denunciation his father's long upper lip curved like the beak of a bird of prey; behind his hand he tried to arch his own lip in the same manner. He really did not hear what was said to him; he only sighed with relief when it was over and he was allowed to go up-stairs and tumble sleepily into bed.

As for his long-suffering hostess, when she was alone Helena Richie rubbed her eyes and began to wake up. "That boy never knows when to go!" she said to herself with amused impatience. Then her mind turned to her own affairs. This little boy, David Allison, would be in Old Chester on Saturday; he was to stay with Dr. Lavendar for a while, and then come to her for a week or two. But she was beginning to regret the invitation she had sent through Dr. King. It would be pleasant to have the little fellow, but—

THE AWAKENING OF HELENA RICHIE

"I can't keep him, so why should I take him even for a week? I might get fond of him! I'm afraid it's a mistake. I wonder what Lloyd would think? I don't believe he really loves children. And yet—he cared when the baby died."

She pulled a low chair up to the hearth and sat down, her elbows on her knees, her fingers ruffling the soft locks about her forehead. "Oh, my baby! my little, little baby!" she said in a broken whisper. The old passion of misery swept over her; she shrank lower in her chair, rocking herself to and fro, her fingers pressed against her eyes. It was thirteen years ago, and yet even now in these placid days in Old Chester, to think of that time brought the breathless smother of agony back again—the dying child, the foolish brute who had done him to death. . . . If the baby had lived he would be nearly fourteen years old now; a big boy! She wondered whether his hair would still have been curly? She knew in her heart that she never could have had the courage to cut those soft curls off—and yet, boys hated curls, she thought; and smiled proudly. He would have been so manly! If he had lived, how different everything would have been, how incredibly different! For of course, if he had lived she would have been happy in spite of Frederick. And happiness was all she wanted.

She brushed the tears from her flushed cheeks, and propping her chin in her hands stared into the fire, thinking—thinking. . . . Her childhood had been passed with her father's mother, a silent woman who with bitter expectation of success had set herself to discover in Helena traits of the poor, dead, foolish wife who had broken her son's heart. "Grandmamma hated me," Helena Richie reflected. "She begrudged

THE AWAKENING OF HELENA RICHIE

me the least little bit of pleasure." Yet her feeling towards the hard old woman now was not resentment; it was only wonder. "*Why* didn't she like me to be happy?" she thought. It never occurred to her that her grandmother who had guarded and distrusted her had also loved her. "Of course I never loved her," she reminded herself, "but I wouldn't have wanted her to be unhappy. She wanted me to be wretched. Curious!" Yet she realized that at that time she had not desired love; she had only desired happiness. Looking back, she pondered on her astounding immaturity; what a child she had been to imagine that merely to get away from that gray life with her grandmother would be happiness, and so had married Frederick. Frederick.... She was eighteen, and so pretty. She smiled remembering how pretty she was. And Frederick had made such promises! She was to have every kind of happiness. Of course she had married him. Thinking of it now, she did not in the least blame herself. If the dungeon doors open and the prisoner catches a glimpse of the green world of sunshine, what happens? Of course she had married Frederick! As for love, she never thought of it; it did not enter into the bargain—at least on her part. She married him because he wanted her to, and because he would make her happy. And, oh, how glad her grandmother had been! At the memory of that passionate satisfaction, Helena clasped her hands over the two brown braids that folded like a chaplet around her head and laughed aloud, the tears still glittering on her lashes. Her prayers, her grandmother said, had been answered; the girl was safe—an honest wife! "Now lettest Thou Thy servant—" the old woman murmured, with dreadful gratitude in her voice.

THE AWAKENING OF HELENA RICHIE

Thinking of that gratitude, the tears dried upon Helena's cheeks, hot with the firelight and with her thoughts. "Suppose she had lived just a little longer? —just three years longer? Where would her gratitude have been then?" Helena's face overflowed with sudden gay malice, but below the malice was weariness. "You are happy now—aren't you?" Sam Wright had said. . . . Why, yes, certainly. Frederick had "repented," as Dr. King expressed it; she had seen to his *"repentance"!* That in itself was something to have lived for—a searing flame of happiness. Enough one might think to satisfy her—if she could only have forgotten the baby. At first she had believed that she could forget him. Lloyd had told her she would. How young she had been at twenty-one to think that any one could forget! She smiled dryly at her childish hope and at Lloyd's ignorance; but his tenderness had been so passionately convincing,—and how good he had been about the baby! He had let her talk of him all she wanted to. Of course, after a while he got a little tired of the subject, and naturally. It was Frederick's baby! And Lloyd hated Frederick as much as she did. How they used to talk about him in those first days of his "repentance"! . . . "Have you heard anything?" "Yes; running down-hill every day." "Is there any news?" "Yes, he'll drink himself into his grave in six months." Ah, that was happiness indeed!—"his *grave*, in six months!" . . . She flung herself back in her chair, her hands dropping listlessly into her lap. "Oh—my little, dead baby!" . . .

It was nearly midnight; the fire had burned quite out; the room had fallen into shadows. Oh, yes, as she told Sam Wright, she was happy. Her face fell into lines of dull indifference.

THE AWAKENING OF HELENA RICHIE

She got up, wearily, rubbing her eyes with her knuckles, as a child does; then suddenly remembered that she had reached no conclusion about this little boy Dr. Lavendar was interested in. Suppose she should get fond of him and want to keep him—how would Lloyd feel about it? Would he think the child might take her thoughts from him? But at that she smiled; he could not be so foolish! "I'll write and ask him, anyhow. Of course, if he objects, I wouldn't dream of it. I wonder what he will think?"

CHAPTER IV

MR. LLOYD PRYOR thought very deeply after he read Mrs. Richie's letter. He sat in his office and smoked and reflected. And as he reflected his face brightened. It was a handsome face, with a mouth that smiled easily. His heavy-lidded eyes behind astonishingly thick and curling lashes were blue; when he lifted them the observer felt a slight shock, for they were curiously motionless; generally, however, the heavy lids drooped, lazily good-humored. He read Mrs. Richie's letter and tapped the edge of his desk with strong, white fingers.

"Nothing could be better," he said.

Then suddenly he decided that he would go to Old Chester and say so in person. "I suppose I ought to go, anyhow; I haven't been there for six weeks. Yes; this child is just what she needs."

And that was how it came about that when he went home he pulled his daughter Alice's pretty ear and said he was going away that night. "I shall take the ten-o'clock train," he said.

His girl — a pleasant, flower-like young creature — scolded him affectionately. "I wish you wouldn't take so many journeys. Promise to be careful; I worry about you when I'm not with you to take care of you," she said, in her sweet, anxious young voice. Her father, smiling, promised prudence, and for the mere joy of watching her let her pack his bag, lecturing him as she did so about his health. "Now that you have undertaken all this extra business of the Pryor-Barr people, you owe it to your stockholders to be careful of your health," she told him, refusing to notice his smile when he solemnly agreed with her.

"What would happen to the Company if anything happened to you?" she insisted, rubbing her soft cheek against his.

"Ruin, of course."

But she would not laugh. "And what would happen to *me*?"

"Ah, well, that's a different matter," he admitted, and kissed her and bade *her* be careful. "What would happen to me if anything happened to you?" he teased.

She hung about him, brooding over him like a little mother dove with a hundred questions. "Are you going anywhere except to Mercer?"

"Well, yes; possibly."

"Where?"

"Oh, to a place called Old Chester."

"Who are you going to see there?"

"Nobody you know, Gas-bag! I never heard of such curiosity!"

"Ah, but I like to think about you when you are away, and know just where you are and what you are doing every minute of the time."

At which he laughed and kissed her, and was off to take the night train for Mercer, which made it possible for him to catch the morning stage for Old Chester.

There was one other passenger in the stage—a little boy with a soft thatch of straight, yellow hair that had been chopped short around the bowl of some domestic barber. He sat on the opposite seat and held a bundle in his arms, peering out over the top of it with serious blue eyes.

"Well, young man, where are you bound?" inquired Mr. Pryor. When the child said "Old Chester," Lloyd Pryor tossed a quarter out of the window to a hostler and bade him go into the stage-house and buy an apple. "Here, youngster," he said, when the man handed it up to him, "take that.—Keep the change, my man."

When it did not involve any personal inconvenience, Mr. Lloyd Pryor had a quick and cordial kindliness which most people found very attractive. The child, however, did not seem much impressed; he took the apple gravely, and said, "Thank you, sir;" but he was not effusive. He looked out of the window and hugged his bundle. Half-way to Old Chester he began to nibble the apple, biting it very slowly, so that he might not make a noise, and thrusting it back into his pocket after each bite with an apprehensive glance at the gentleman in the corner. When he had finished it and swallowed the core, he said, suddenly:

"Mister, have you any little boys and girls?"

His companion, who had quite forgotten him, looked over the top of his newspaper with a start. "What? What did you say? Oh—boys and girls? Yes; I have a girl." He smiled as he spoke.

"Is she as big as me?"

Lloyd Pryor put down his paper and twitched his glasses off. "About twice as big I should think," he said kindly.

"Twice as big! And twice as old?"

"How old are you?"

"I'm seven, going on eight."

"Well, then, let's see. Alice is—she is twice and

five years more as old. What do you make of that?"

The child began to count on his fingers, and, after looking at him a minute or two with some amusement, Mr. Pryor returned to his paper. After a while the boy said, suddenly, "In the flood the ducks couldn't be drowned, could they?"

But Lloyd Pryor had become interested in what he was reading. "You talk too much, young man," he said coldly, and there was no further conversation. The old stage jogged along in the uncertain sunshine; sometimes Mr. Pryor smoked, once he took a nap. While he slept the little boy looked at him furtively, but by and by he turned to the window, absorbed in his own affairs.

As the stage pulled into Old Chester, Mr. Pryor roused himself. "Well, my boy, here we are," he said.

The child quivered and his hands tightened on his bundle, but he said nothing. When they drew up at the tavern, there was Danny and Goliath and Dr. Lavendar.

"Mary gave me some gingerbread for him," Dr. Lavendar was saying to Van Horn. "I've got it tied up in my handkerchief. Why," he interrupted himself, screwing up his eyes and peering into the dusk of the old coach—"why, I believe here's Mrs. Richie's brother too!"

As the horses came to a standstill, Dr. Lavendar was in quite a flutter of eagerness. But when the very little boy clambered out, the old minister only shook hands with him, man fashion, with no particular display of interest.

"I'm glad to see you, David. I am Dr. Lavendar." Then he turned to say "How do you do?" to Mr.

Pryor. "Why, look here," he added in a cheerful after-thought, "I'm going up your way; get out and come along in my buggy. Hey! Danny! Stop your snarling. The scoundrel's temper is getting bad in his old age. Those snails Jonas drives can't keep up with my trotter."

"But you have one passenger already," Mr. Pryor protested. "I'll just go on up in the stage, thank you."

"Oh," Dr. Lavendar said, "David's bundle is the biggest part of him, isn't it, David? We'll leave it with Van Horn and get it as we come back. Come along, Mr. Pryor. There, David, tuck yourself down in front; Danny can tag behind." There was a moment's hesitation, and then Mr. Pryor did as he was bid. Dr. Lavendar climbed in himself and off they jogged, while Jonas remarked to Van Horn that the old gentleman wasn't just the one to talk about snails, as he looked at it. But Mr. Pryor, watching the April sunshine chased over the hills by warm cloud shadows and bursting into joy again on the low meadows, reflected that he had done well for himself in exchanging the dark cavern of the stage for Dr. Lavendar's easy old buggy and the open air. They stopped a minute on the bridge to look at the creek swollen by spring rains; it was tugging and tearing at the branches that dipped into it, and heaping up rocking lines of yellow froth along the banks.

"In summer that's a fine place to wade," Dr. Lavendar observed. David glanced up at him and then down at the water in silence.

"Well, Goliath! at this rate Jonas could beat us," said Dr. Lavendar, and smacked a rein down on the shaggy old back. David looked around at Mr. Pryor with sudden interest.

"Is your name Goliath?" he asked.

Lloyd Pryor was greatly amused. "I hope you haven't such a thing as a sling with you, David?" he said.

The little boy grew very red, but made no reply.

"It's my horse's name," Dr. Lavendar told him, so kindly that David did not hear the chuckle in his voice. But the color was hot in the child's face for many minutes. He had nothing to say for the rest of the pull up the hill, except briefly, "'Bye," when Mr. Pryor alighted at the green gate of a foot-path that led up to the Stuffed Animal House.

"I'm very much obliged for the lift, Dr. Lavendar," he said in his coldly courteous voice, and turned quickly at an exclamation behind him.

"Lloyd!"

"I've brought your brother home, Mrs. Richie," said Dr. Lavendar.

Helena Richie was standing inside the hedge, her face radiant.

"Oh, Lloyd!" she said again breathlessly.

Mr. Pryor laughed and shook hands with her in somewhat formal greeting.

"Do you see my other passenger?" Dr. Lavendar called out. "He came with your brother. David, suppose you shake hands with Mrs. Richie? I generally take my hat off, David, when I shake hands with a lady."

"I don't, sir," said David, gently, putting a hand out across the wheel. Mrs. Richie had not noticed the little boy; but when she took his hand her eyes lingered on his face, and suddenly she drew him forward and kissed him.

David bore it politely, but he looked over her head at Mr. Pryor. "Mister, Alice is nineteen."

THE AWAKENING OF HELENA RICHIE

"*What?*" Mr. Pryor said, his heavy-lidded eyes opening with a blue gleam; then he laughed. "Oh yes, I'd forgotten our sum in arithmetic; yes, Alice is nineteen."

"Well," Dr. Lavendar said, "g'long, Goliath!" and the buggy went tugging on up the hill. "David, if you'll look in my pocket you'll find some gingerbread."

David thrust a hand down into the capacious pocket and brought up the gingerbread, wrapped in a red silk handkerchief. He offered it silently to Dr. Lavendar.

"I don't believe I'll take any. Suppose you eat it, David?"

"No, thank you, sir."

Dr. Lavendar shook his head in a puzzled way.

David swallowed nervously. "Please, sir," he said, "was that lady that gentleman's sister?"

"Yes," Dr. Lavendar told him cheerfully.

"But if she is his sister," the little boy reasoned, "why didn't she kiss him? Janey, she—she always gave me forty kisses."

"Just forty?" Dr. Lavendar inquired, looking at the child over his spectacles.

David was silent for a moment, then he said, earnestly: "I never counted. But Janey, she always said 'forty kisses.'" His whole face quivered. A very large tear gathered, trembled, then rolled over; he held his hands together under the lap-robe and looked the other way; then he raised one shoulder and rubbed his cheek against it.

"I guess Janey was a pretty nice sister," Dr. Lavendar said.

David's hands tightened; he looked up speechless into the kind old face.

"David," said Dr. Lavendar in a business-like way, "would you mind driving for me? I want to look over my note-book."

"Driving?" said David. "Oh, *my!*" His cheeks were wet but his eyes shone. "I don't mind, sir. I'd just as lieves as not!"

CHAPTER V

"SO that's the youngster we're going to adopt, is it?" Mr. Pryor said; then he looked at Helena through his curling brown lashes, with open amusement. Her eyes were full of tears.

"It has been—so long," she said faintly.

"I've been very busy," he explained.

She nodded and smiled. "Anyhow, you are here now. But, oh, Maggie has a sore throat. I don't know what we're going to have for dinner. Oh, how glad I am you're here!" Her face was glowing, but her chin trembled.

"Why, this is very flattering, I'm sure; I thought you were so taken up with your orphan that you wouldn't care whether I came or not."

"You know that isn't true," she said gayly, brushing her cheek against his arm; "but isn't he a dear little fellow?—though I'm sorry his hair isn't curly." Then her face changed. "What did he mean about Alice being nineteen?"

"Oh, Alice? Why, he asked me in the stage if I had any children, and I put Alice's age as a sum in mental arithmetic for him. And he asked me if my name was Goliath."

But she had forgotten David. "Lloyd! To think you are here!"

"Yes, I'm here, and a hamper is here, too. I hope

THE AWAKENING OF HELENA RICHIE

the stage will bring it up pretty soon. I don't believe I could stand an Old Chester bill of fare. It's queer about women; they don't care what they eat. I don't believe you've got anything on hand but bread and jam and tea?"

"I care a great deal!" she assured him laughing, and then looked worried. "Yes, I really have been living on bread and jam." She was hanging on his arm, and once she kissed his hand. "Will you go upstairs? And I'll see what we can do about food. That dreadful Maggie! She's sick in bed."

Mr. Pryor looked annoyed. "Can't she get us something to eat? Ask her, Nelly; I don't believe it will hurt her. Here; give her that," and he took a crumpled bill out of his waistcoat pocket.

She did not take the money, but her eyes shone. "You are the most generous being!" she said. Then, sobering, she thought of Maggie's throat—hesitated —and Maggie was lost. For when she opened the woman's door, and in her sweet, appealing voice declared that Mr. Pryor had come unexpectedly, and was so hungry—what *should* they do?—Maggie, who adored her, insisted upon going down to the kitchen.

"Oh, Maggie, you oughtn't to! I oughtn't to let you. Maggie, look here: you will be careful, won't you?"

"Now, you go right along back to your brother," the woman commanded smiling. "I'm goin' to get into my clothes; 'twon't do me a bit of harm."

And Helena, protesting and joyous, fled to her room and to her mirror. She flung off her cambric morning dress and ran to hunt in her wardrobe for something pretty. With girlish hurry she pulled her hair down, braided it afresh, and fastened the burnished plats around her head like a wreath; then she brushed the soft locks in the nape of her neck about her finger, and let them fall into loose curls. She dressed with breathless haste, and when she finished, stood for a minute, her lip between her teeth, staring at herself in the glass. And as she stared her face fell; for as the color and sparkle faded a little, care suddenly looked out of the leaf-brown eyes—care and something like fright. But instantly drawing in her breath, she flung her head up as one who prepares for battle. When she went down-stairs and found Mr. Pryor waiting for her in the parlor, the sparkle had all come back. She had put on a striped silk dress, faint rose and green, made very full in the skirt; her flat lace collar was fastened by a little old pin—an oval of pearls holding a strand of hair like floss-silk.

"Why, Nelly," her visitor said, "you look younger every time I see you."

She swept him a great courtesy, making her dress balloon out about her; then she clasped her hands at her throat, her chin resting on the fluff of her white undersleeves, and looked up at him with a delighted laugh. "We are not very old, either of us; I am thirty-three and you are only forty-six—I call that young. Oh, Lloyd, I was so low-spirited this morning; and now—you are here!" She pirouetted about the room in a burst of gayety.

As he watched her through half-shut eyes, the bored good humor in his face sharpened into something keener; he caught her hand as she whirled past, drawing her close to him with a murmured caress. She, pausing in her joy, looked at him with sudden intentness.

"Have you heard anything of—*Frederick?*"

At which he let her go again and answered curtly:

"No; nothing. Perfectly well, the last I heard. In Paris, and enjoying himself in his own peculiar fashion."

She drew in her breath and turned her face away; they were both silent. Then she said, dully, that she never heard any news. "Mr. Raynor sends me my accounts every three months, but he never says anything about—Frederick."

"I suppose there isn't anything to say. Look here, Nelly, hasn't that stage-driver brought the hamper yet? When are we going to have something to eat?"

"Oh, pretty soon," she said impatiently.

They were standing at one of the long windows in the parlor; through the tilted slats of the Venetian blinds the April sunshine fell in pale bars across her hair and dress, across the old Turkey carpet on the floor, across the high white wainscoting and half-way up the landscape-papered walls. The room was full of cheerful dignity; the heavy, old-fashioned furniture of the Stuffed Animal House was unchanged, even the pictures, hanging rather near the ceiling, had not been removed — steel-engravings of Landseer's dogs, and old and very good colored prints of Audubon's birds. The mantel-piece of black marble veined with yellow was supported by fluted columns; on it were two blown-glass vases of decalcomania decoration, then two gilt lustres with prisms, then two hand-screens of wool-work, and in the middle an ormolu clock—"Iphigenia in Aulis"—under a glass shade. In the recess at one side of the fireplace was a tall bookcase with closed doors, but a claw-footed sofa stood out from the wall at an angle that prevented any access to the books. "I can't read Stuffed Animal books," Helena had long ago confided to Lloyd Pryor. "The British Classics, if you please! and Baxter's *Saint's Rest*, and *The Lady of the Manor*." So Mr. Pryor made a point of providing her with light literature. He pulled a paper-covered volume out of his pocket now, and handed it to her.

"Not improving, Nelly, I assure you; and there is a box of candy in the hamper."

She thanked him, but put the book down. "Talk to me, Lloyd. Tell me—everything! How are you? How is Alice? Are you very busy with politics and things? Talk to me."

"Well," he said good naturedly, "where am I to begin? Yes; I'm very well. And very busy. And unusually poor. Isn't that interesting?"

"Oh, Lloyd! Are you in earnest? Lloyd, you know I have a lot of money, and of course, if you want it, it is yours."

He was lounging lazily on the sofa, and drew her down beside him, smiling at her through his curling lashes. "It isn't as bad as that. It is only that I have shouldered the debts of the old Pryor-Barr Co., Limited. You know my grandfather organized it, and my father was president of it, and I served my 'prenticeship to business in it."

"But I thought," she said, puzzled, "you went out of it long ago, before—before—"

"The flood? Yes, my dear, I did. I've only been a silent partner for years—and that in a very small way. But I regret to say that the young asses who have been running it have got into trouble. And they propose going into bankruptcy, confound them! It is very annoying," Lloyd Pryor ended calmly.

"But I don't understand," she said; "what have you to do with it?"

"Well, I've got to turn to and pay their damned debts."

"Pay their debts? But why? Does the law make you?"

"The law?" he said, looking at her with cold eyes. "I suppose you mean statute law? No, my dear, it doesn't."

"Then I can't understand it," she declared laughing.

"It's nothing very abtruse. I can't have stockholders who trusted our old firm cheated by a couple of cousins of mine. I've assumed the liabilities—that's all."

"But you don't *have* to, by law?" she persisted, still bewildered.

"My dear Nelly, I don't do things because of the *law*," he said dryly. "But never mind; it is going to give me something to do. Tell me about yourself. How are you?"

"I'm—pretty lonely, Lloyd," she said.

And he answered, sympathetically, that he had been afraid of that. "You are too much by yourself. Of course, it's lonely for you. I am very much pleased with this idea of the little boy."

She shook her head. "I can't take him."

"Why not?" he protested, and broke off. "Nelly, look! You are going to have company."

He had caught sight of some one fumbling with the latch of the green gate in the hedge. Helena opened her lips in consternation.

"Lloyd! It's old Mr. Benjamin Wright. He lives in that big house with white columns on the top of the hill. Do you suppose he has come to *call?*"

"Tell your woman to say you are out."

THE AWAKENING OF HELENA RICHIE

But she shook her head, annoyed and helpless. "Don't you see how tired he is?—poor old man! Of course, he must come in. Go and help him, Lloyd." She put her hands on his arm. "Please!" she said.

"No, thank you; I have no desire to help old gentlemen." And as she left him and ran impetuously to open the door herself, he called after her, "Nelly, don't have dinner held back!"

Mr. Benjamin Wright stood, panting, at the foot of the porch steps; he could hardly lift his head to look up at the figure in the doorway. "You—Mrs. Richie?" he gasped.

"Yes, sir," she said. "May I help you? These steps are so steep."

"No," he snarled. "Do you think I'm so decrepit that I have to have a female help me up-stairs?" Then he began toiling up the steps. "My name is Wright. You know my grandson? Sam? Great fool! I've come to call on you." On the porch he drew a long breath, pulled off his mangy old beaver hat, and, with a very courtly bow, held out his hand. "Madam, permit me to pay my respects to you. I am your neighbor. In fact, your only neighbor; without me,

> 'Montium domina ut fores
> silvarumque virentium
> saltuumque reconditorum
> amniumque sonantum.'

Understand that? No? Good. I don't like learned females."

She took his hand in a bewildered way, glancing back over her shoulder at Mr. Pryor, uncertain what she ought to do. Mr. Wright decided for her.

"I know this house," he said, pushing past her into

the dusky hall; "friend of mine used to live here. Ho! This is the parlor. Well; who's this?" He stood chewing orange-skin and blinking up at Lloyd Pryor, who came forward reluctantly.

"My name is Pryor, sir. I—"

"Oh! Yes. *I* know. *I* know. The lady's brother. Here! Push that chair out for me."

And Mr. Lloyd Pryor found himself bringing a chair forward and taking the hat and stick from the trembling old hand. Helena had gone quickly into the dining-room, and came back with a decanter and glass on a little tray. She gave a distressed glance at her other guest as though to say, "I can't help it!"

Benjamin Wright's old head in its brown wig was still shaking with fatigue, but under the prickle of white on his shaven jowl the purplish color came back in mottled streaks. He sipped the sherry breathlessly, the glass trembling in his veined and shrunken hand. "Well," he demanded, "how do you two like this God-forsaken place?"

Mr. Pryor, looking over their visitor's head at Helena, shrugged his shoulders.

"It is very nice," she said vaguely.

"It's a narrowing place," he demurred, "very narrowing; sit down, sit down, good people! I'll take some more sherry. My grandson," he went on, as Helena filled his glass, "is always talking about you, madam. He's a great jackass. I'm afraid he bothers you with his calls?"

"Oh, not at all," Helena said nervously. She sat down on the other side of the big rosewood centre-table, glancing with worried eyes at Lloyd Pryor.

"Move that lamp contraption," commanded Mr. Wright. "I like to see my hostess!"

And Helena pushed the astral lamp from the centre of the table so that his view was unobstructed.

"Is he a nuisance with his talk about his drama?" Mr. Wright said, looking across at her with open eagerness in his melancholy eyes.

"Why, no indeed."

"Do you think it's so very bad, considering?"

"It is not bad at all," said Mrs. Richie.

His face lighted like a child's. "Young fool! As if he could write a drama! Well, madam, I came to ask you to do me the honor of taking supper with me to-morrow night, and then of listening to this wonderful production. Of course, sir, I include you. My nigger will provide you with a fairly good bottle. Then this grandson of mine will read his truck aloud. But we will fortify ourselves with supper first."

His artless pride in planning this distressing festivity was so ludicrous that Lloyd Pryor's disgust changed into involuntary mirth. But Helena was plainly nervous. "Thank you; you are very kind; but I am afraid I must say no."

Mr. Pryor was silently retreating towards the dining-room. As for the visitor, he only had eyes for the mistress of the house.

"Why should you say no?"

She tried to answer lightly. "Oh, I like to be quiet."

"Quiet?" cried Benjamin Wright, rapping the table with his wine-glass. "At your age? Nonsense!" He paused, cleared his throat, and then sonorously:

"'Can you endure the livery of a nun,
  For aye to be in shady cloister mew'd,
  To live a barren sister all your life,
  Chanting faint hymns to the cold, fruitless moon?'

Give me some more sherry. Of course you must come. No use being shy—a pretty creatur' like you! And you said you liked the play," he added with childlike reproach.

Helena, glad to change the subject, made haste to reassure him. "I do, I do!" she said, and for a few minutes she kept the old face beaming with her praise of Sam and his work. Unlike his grandson, Mr. Wright was not critical of her criticism. Nothing she could say seemed to him excessive. He contradicted every statement, but he believed it implicitly. Then with a sigh of satisfaction, he returned to his invitation. Helena shook her head decidedly.

"No; thank you very much. Mr. Pryor couldn't possibly come. He is only here over Sunday, and—" She looked towards the dining-room for protection, but the door had been gently closed.

"Hey?" Benjamin Wright said blankly. "Well, I won't insist; I won't insist. We'll wait till he goes. Come Monday night."

"Oh," she said, her voice fluttering, "I am sorry but I really can't."

"Why can't you?" he insisted. "Come, tell the truth! The advantage of telling the truth, young lady, is that neither God nor the devil can contradict you!" He laughed, eying her with high good humor.

"Oh, it's merely—" she hesitated, and he looked affronted.

"What! Some female airs about coming to an unmarried man's house?" Her involuntary mirth disarmed him. "No? Well, I'm glad you've got some sense. Then you'll come?"

"If I went to your house, it would seem unfriendly not to go to other houses."

THE AWAKENING OF HELENA RICHIE

"Why shouldn't you go to other houses? Done anything you're ashamed of?" He laughed uproariously at his own wit. "Come now; don't be finikin and ladylike!"

"I don't make visits," she explained, the color rising angrily in her cheeks.

"Gad-a-mercy! Why not?" he interrupted. "Do you think you're too good for us here in Old Chester?"

"Oh, Mr. Wright!"

"Or perhaps Old Chester is too good for you?"

His face had softened wonderfully; he was looking at her with the same quizzical delight with which he would look at one of his canaries when he caught it, and held it struggling in his hand. "Are we too good for you?" he jeered, "too—"

He stopped abruptly, his laugh breaking off in the middle. Then his mouth fell slowly open in blank amazement; he leaned forward in his chair and stared at her without a word.

"I don't care for society," she said, in a frightened way, and rose as if to bring the visit to an end.

But Benjamin Wright sat still, slowly nodding his head. "You don't care for society? I wonder why."

"Oh, because I am—a very quiet person," she stammered.

The dining-room door opened and Sarah came in, looked about, found the decanter, and withdrew.

"Where is — that gentleman?" the old man demanded.

"Mr. Pryor went in to dinner," she said faintly. "Please excuse him; he was tired."

The silence that fell between them was like a blow. ... Mr. Wright pulled himself to his feet, and with one shaking hand on the table felt his way around until he stood directly in front of her; he put his face close to hers and stared into her eyes, his lower lip opening and closing in silence. Then, without speaking, he began to grope about on the table for his hat and stick.

"I will bid you good day," he said.

Without another word he went shuffling out into the dark hall. At the front door he turned and looked back at her; then, slowly, shook his head.

CHAPTER VI

POOR Maggie paid for her good nature. On Sunday morning she was so decidedly worse that William King, to the disgust of his Martha, was summoned from his breakfast-table.

"Women who can't look after a simple sore throat without bothering their doctors, are pretty inefficient creatures," she said coldly.

William thought of women who were so efficient that they did not hesitate to advise their doctors; but he only agreed with proper seriousness to Martha's declaration that it was too bad, for he would be late for church—"unless you hurry, William!" she called after him.

Perhaps he hurried when he was with Maggie, but certainly he displayed no haste when giving his directions to Mrs. Richie, nor even later when just as he was about to drive off, Mr. Pryor hailed him from the garden.

"How's your patient, doctor?"

"Pretty sick. She didn't obey your sister's orders and keep in bed yesterday. So, of course, she's worse to-day."

Mr. Pryor leaned a comfortable elbow on the green gate. "That's a nice prospect! What am I going to have to eat?" he said, good-humoredly.

Yet behind the good humor there was annoyance.

It came into William King's mind that this fellow would not spare his sister his irritation, and with a sudden impulse of concern for her, he said, "Well now, look here; why don't you and Mrs. Richie come in this evening and take tea with us? I don't know what you'll get, but come and take pot-luck."

"Thank you," Lloyd Pryor said, "but—"

"Oh, come now," interrupted the doctor, gathering up his reins; "you good people are not neighborly enough. We'll expect you both at six."

"You are very kind, but I think—"

But William would not listen. He was in great spirits. "It will be pot-luck, and my wife will be delighted—" then, his voice dragged—"I hope you'll come," he said uncertainly.

Mr. Pryor began to protest, but ended with a laugh. "Well, we'll come! Thank you very much."

"That's good," the doctor said a little less cordially. Indeed, as he drove away he looked distinctly less cordial, and once he sighed. . . . Now, how should he put it? "Oh, Martha, by the way, Mr. Pryor and his sister will drop in to tea to-night. I suggested it, and—" No, that would not do. . . . "Martha, it occurred to me it would be neighborly—" No. "Confound it," William King muttered to himself, "what did I do it for, anyhow? 'Martha, my dear, I know you like to do a kindness, so I asked Mrs. Richie and her brother'"—that was better. "But I hate a circumbendibus!" William said, irritably, to himself. Then he drew a long breath, and set his lips as a man may who is about to face the domestic cannon's mouth.

After he had driven on, screwing up his courage, it appeared that Mr. Pryor also had a cannon to face.

THE AWAKENING OF HELENA RICHIE

Helena Richie came out into the garden, and found him sitting on a bench built round a great silver poplar. Her face was worried. "I ought not to have made poor Maggie get up yesterday," she said; "but I was so distressed not to have a good dinner for you."

"Well, at least you need have no anxieties about supper; we've had an invitation."

"An invitation! From Dr. King? Well, that's very nice in him. But, of course—"

"I told him we would come."

"You told him we would come!"

"I couldn't help it, Nelly. People who invite you face to face are perfect nuisances. But, really, it's no great matter—for once. And I knew it would be a convenience for you. Besides, I wanted a good supper."

"Well, we must make some excuse."

"There isn't any excuse to make," he explained, good-naturedly; I tried to find one and couldn't. We've got to go."

"*I* sha'n't go."

He looked at her from under his heavy eyelids; then blew two smoke wreaths slowly. "You're a queer creature."

She turned on him hotly. "Queer? Because I won't go out to supper with you? I'd be queer if I did! I'm entirely satisfied with myself, Lloyd; I consider that I have a perfect right to be happy in my own way. You know I don't care a copper for what you call 'morality'! it's nothing but cowardly conventionality. But I won't go out to supper with you."

"Please don't let us have a tirade," he said. "I thought it would be more convenient for you. That's always the way with your sex, Helena, you do a thing to help them out, and they burst into tears."

"I haven't burst into tears," she said sullenly, "but I won't go."

"Come, now! don't be a goose. I wouldn't make a practice of accepting their invitations; but for once, what does it matter?"

"Can't you understand?" she said passionately; "*they are kind to me!*"

She turned quickly and ran into the garden, leaving him to call after her: "Well, you've got to go to-night, because I've accepted."

"I won't go to-night!" she flung back, her voice breaking.

Lloyd Pryor shook his head. "And she wonders I don't come oftener," he said to himself.

So the sleepy Sunday morning passed. Mr. Pryor roamed about the garden, looking furtively over his shoulder now and then—but Helena had disappeared. "Sulking in her room, I suppose," he thought.

He had come at some inconvenience, to spend Sunday and talk over this project of the child; "for I'd like to see her happier," he told himself; and now, instead of sitting down, sensibly, to discuss things, she flared out over this invitation to supper. Her intensity fatigued him. "I must be getting old," he ruminated, "and Helena will always be the age she was ten years ago. Ten? It's thirteen! How time flies; she was twenty. How interested I was in Frederick's health in those days!"

He stretched himself out on the bench under the poplar, and lit another cigar. "If *I'm* willing to go, why is she so exercised? Women are all alike—except Alice." He smiled as he thought of his girl, and instantly the hardness in his face lifted, as a cloud shadow lifts and leaves sunshine behind it. Then some obscure sense of fitness made him pull himself together, and put his mind on affairs that had nothing in common with Helena; affairs in which he could include his girl without offending his taste.

After a while he got up and wandered about between the borders, where the clean, bitter scent of daffodils mingled with the box. Once he stood still, looking down over the orchard on the hill-side below him, at the bright sheen of the river edged with leafless maples; on its farther side were the meadows, and then the hills, smoky in their warm haze. Over all was the pale April sky with skeins of gray cloud in the west. He wondered what Alice was doing at this moment, and looked at his watch. She must be just coming back from church. When he was at home Mr. Pryor went to church himself, and watched her saying her little prayers. This assumption of the Pryor-Barr liabilities would be a serious check to the fortune he was building up for her; he set his jaw angrily at the thought, but of course it couldn't be helped. Furthermore, Alice took great pride in the almost quixotic sense of honor that had prompted the step; a pride which gave him a secret satisfaction, quite fatuous and childlike and entirely out of keeping with certain other characteristics, also secret.

There was a gleam of humor in his eyes, as he said to himself that he hoped Alice would not ask him how he had spent his Sunday morning. Alice had such a feeling about truth, that he did not like to tell her even little lies, little ones that she could not possibly find out. It was the sentiment of fibbing to his girl, that offended him, not the fib; for Mr. Lloyd Pryor had no doubt that, in certain matters, Truth must be governed by the law of benefit.

Thinking of his daughter, and smiling to himself, he lounged aimlessly about the garden; then it occurred to him to go into the stable and look at Helena's pony. After that he strolled over to the carriage-house where were stored a number of cases containing stuffed creatures—birds and chipmunks and small furry things. Some larger animals were slung up under the beams of the loft to get them out of the way; there was a bear in one corner, and a great crocodile, and a shark; possessions of the previous owner of the Stuffed Animal House, stored here by her executor, pending the final settlement of the estate.

Lloyd Pryor stood at the doorway looking in. Through a grimed and cobwebbed window at the farther end of the room the light filtered down among the still figures; there was the smell of dead fur and feathers, and of some acrid preservative. One box had been broken in moving it from the house, and a beaver had slipped from his carefully bitten branch, and lay on the dusty boards, a burst of cotton pushing through the splitting belly-seam. Lloyd Pryor thrust it into its case with his stick, and started as he did so. Something moved, back in the dusk.

"It's I, Lloyd," Helena Richie said.

"You? My dear Nelly! Why are you sitting in this gloomy place?"

She smiled faintly, but her face was weary with tears. "Oh, I just—came in here," she said vaguely.

She had said to herself when, angry and wounded, she left him in the garden, that if she went back to the house he would find her. So she had come here to the dust and silence of the carriage-house, and sitting down on one of the cases had hidden her face in her hands. Little by little anger ebbed. Just misery remained. But still she sat there, looking absently at these dead creatures about her, or at a thin line of sunshine falling through a heart-shaped opening in a shutter, and moving noiselessly across the floor. A mote dipped into this stream of light, zigzagged through it, then sank into the darkness. She followed it with dull eyes, thinking, if she thought at all, that she wished she did not have to sit opposite Lloyd at dinner. But, of course, she would have to; the servants would think it strange if she did not come to table with him. Suddenly the finger of sunshine vanished, and all the motes were gone. Raising her head with a long sigh she saw him in the doorway, his tall figure black against the smiling spring landscape outside. Her heart came up into her throat with a rush of delight. He was looking for her! Ah, this was the way it had been in those first days, when he could not bear to let her out of his sight!

He put his arm around her with careless friendliness, and helped her to her feet. "What a place this will be for your boy to play. He can be cast away on a desert island and surrounded by wild animals every day in the week." His voice was so kind that her anger of two hours ago seemed impossible—a mistake, a misunderstanding! She tried in a bewildered way to get back to it in her own mind; but he was so matter of fact about the stuffed animals and the little boy and the desert island, that she could only say vaguely, "Yes, it would be nice; but of course I'm not going to take him."

"Well now, that's just what I want to talk to you about," he said, watching her through his long, curling eyelashes. "That's why I came down to Old Chester—"

"Oh, is it?"

He checked an impatient exclamation, and then went on: "When I got your letter about this boy, I was really delighted.—Let's go out into the sunshine; the smell of this place is very disagreeable.—I think you would find the child company; I really hope you will take him." His voice was sincere and she softened.

"It's kind of you, Lloyd, to urge it. But no; it won't do."

"My dear, of course it will do! You'll give him a good home, and—"

"No, no, I can't; you know I can't."

"My dear Nelly! What possible harm could you do the child?"

She drew away from him sharply. "*I* do him any harm! I! Oh—you wouldn't have said such a thing, once!" She pressed the back of her hand against her lips, and Lloyd Pryor studiously looked in another direction.

"What have I said? That you wouldn't do him any harm! Is there anything unkind in that? Look here, Nell, you really mustn't be so unreasonable. There is nothing a man hates so much as a fool. I am merely urging something for your pleasure. He would be company for you; I thought him quite an attractive youngster."

"And you wouldn't have me so much on your mind? You wouldn't feel you had to come and see me so often!"

"Well, if you want to put it that way," he said coldly. "I'm a very busy man. I can't get off whenever I feel like it."

"And you can't leave your beloved Alice."

He shot a blue gleam at her from under his heavy eyelids. "No; I can't."

She quivered. But he went on quietly: "I know you're lonely, Helena, and as I can't come and see you quite so often as I used to, I want you to take this little fellow, simply to amuse you."

She walked beside him silently. When they reached the bench under the poplar, she sat looking into the April distance without speaking. She was saying to herself, miserably, that she didn't want the child; she didn't want to lessen any sense of obligation that brought him to her;—and yet, she did not want him to come from a sense of obligation!

"You would get great fun out of him, Nelly," he insisted.

And looking up, she saw the kindness of his face and yielded. "Well, perhaps I will; that is, if Dr. Lavendar will let me have him. I'm afraid of Dr. Lavendar somehow."

"Good!" he said heartily; "that's a real weight off my mind."

Her lip curled again, but she said nothing. Lloyd Pryor yawned; then he asked her whether she meant to buy the house.

"I don't know; sometimes I think there is less seclusion in the country than there is in town." She drew down a twig, and began to pull at the buds with aimless fingers. "I might like to come to Philadelphia and live near you, you know," she said. The sudden malice in her eyes was answered by the shock in his; his voice was disturbed when he spoke, though his words were commonplace:

"It's a pleasant enough house."

THE AWAKENING OF HELENA RICHIE

Then he looked at his watch, opening the case under the shelter of his hand—but she saw the photograph in the lid.

"Is that a good picture of Alice?" she said with an effort.

"Yes," he answered, hastily snapping the lid shut. "Helena, what are we going to have for dinner?"

"Oh, nothing very much, I'm afraid," she told him ruefully. Then rising, she held out her hand. "Come! We mustn't quarrel again. I don't know why we always squabble!"

"I'm sure I don't want to," he said. "Nelly, you are prettier every time I see you." He put a finger into one of the loose curls in the nape of her neck, and she looked up at him, her lip trembling.

"And do you love me?"

"Of course I do!" he declared, slipping his arm around her waist. And they walked thus between the box borders, back to the house.

CHAPTER VII

BUT she would not go to the Kings' to tea.

"No," she said, her eyes crinkling with fun, "I'm not going; but you've got to; you promised! And remember, I have 'a very severe headache.'"

He laughed, with a droll look, and then explained that at home he was never allowed to tell tarradiddles. "Alice has a perfect mania about truth," he said ruefully; "it is sometimes very inconvenient. Yes; I'll enlarge upon your headache, my dear. But why in thunder did I say yes to that confounded doctor? I'd like to wring your cook's neck, Nelly!"

"You'll have a good supper," she consoled him, "and that's what you want. They say Mrs. King is a great housekeeper. And besides, if you stayed at home you would probably have to entertain Mr. Sam Wright."

"I'll be darned if I would," he assured her, amiably, and started off.

He had the good supper, although when the doctor broke to his wife that company was coming, Mrs. King had protested that there was nothing in the house to eat. "And there's one thing about me, I may not be perfect, but I am hospitable, and—"

"Just give them what we were going to have ourselves."

"Now, William! I must say, flatly and frankly—"

"There's the office bell," murmured the doctor, sidling away and hearing the reproachful voice lessening in the distance—"how hard I try—nothing fit—"

The office door closed; the worst was over. There would be a good supper—William had no misgivings on that point. Mrs. Richie would talk to him, and he would tease her and make her laugh, and laugh himself. The doctor did not laugh very much in his own house; domestic virtue does not necessarily add to the gayety of life. During the afternoon Willy tried on three different neckties, and twice put cologne on his handkerchief. Then appeared Mr. Pryor to say that Mrs. Richie had one of her headaches! He was so sorry, but Mrs. King knew what a bad headache was?

"Indeed I do," Martha said, "only too well. But *I* can't give way to them. That's what it is to be a doctor's wife; the patients get all the prescriptions," Martha said; and William, out of the corner of his eye, saw that she was smiling! Well, well; evidently Mrs. Richie's defection did not trouble her; the doctor was glad of that. "But I didn't bargain on entertaining the brother," he said to himself crossly; and after the manner of husbands, he left the entertaining to Martha.

Martha, however, did her duty. She thought Mr. Pryor a very agreeable gentleman; "far more agreeable than his sister," she told William afterwards. "I don't know why," said Martha, "but I sort of distrust that woman. But the brother is all right; you can see that—and a very intelligent man, too. We discussed a good many points, and I found we agreed perfectly."

Mr. Pryor also had an opinion on that supper-table talk. He said to himself grimly, that Nelly's bread and jam would have been better. But probably bread and jam, followed by young Sam Wright, would have seemed less desirable than Mrs. King's excellent supper.

It was about seven when the boy appeared at the Stuffed Animal House. Had Mr. Pryor been at home, Helena would, no doubt, have found some way of dismissing him; as it was, she let him stay. He was bareheaded; he had seen a bird flapping painfully about in the road, and catching it in gentle hands had discovered that its wing was broken, so put it tenderly in his cap and brought it to Mrs. Richie's door.

"Poor little thing!" she cried, when he showed it to her. "I wish Mr. Pryor would come back; he would tell us what to do for it."

"Oh, is he here?" Sam asked blankly.

"Well, not at this moment. He has gone to take tea at Dr. King's."

Sam's face lightened with relief.

"You mustn't tell anybody you saw me this evening," she charged him gayly. "I didn't go to Mrs. King's because—I had such a very bad headache!"

"Is it better?" he asked, so anxiously that she blushed.

"Oh, yes, yes. But before tea I—didn't want to go."

"I'm glad you didn't," he said, and forgot her in caring for the bird. He ordered a box and some cotton batting—"and give me your handkerchief." As he spoke, he took it from her surprised hand and tore it into strips; then, lifting the broken wing with exquisite gentleness, he bound it into place. She looked at the bandages ruefully, but Sam was perfectly matter-of-course. "It would have been better without lace," he said; "but it will do. Will you look at him sometimes? Just your touch will cure him, I think."

Mrs. Richie laughed.

"Well, you can laugh, but it's true. When I am near you I have no pain and no worry; nothing but happiness." He sat down beside her on the old claw-footed sofa near the fire, for it was cool enough these spring evenings to have a little fire. He leaned forward, resting his chin on his fist, and staring into the blaze. Once he put his hand out and touched her dress softly, and smiled to himself. Then abruptly, he came out of his reverie, and spoke with joyous excitement:

"Why! I forgot what I came to tell you about — something extraordinary has happened!"

"Oh, what?" she demanded, with a sweet eagerness that was as young as his own.

"You could never guess," he assured her. "To-night, at supper, grandfather suddenly told me that he wanted me to travel for a while—he wanted me to go away from Old Chester. I was perfectly amazed. 'Go hunt up a publisher for your truck,' he said. He always calls the drama my 'truck,'" Sam said snickering; "but the main thing, evidently, was to have me get away from home. To improve my mind, I suppose. He said all gentlemen ought to travel. To live in one place all the time was very narrowing, he said. I told him I hadn't any money, and he said he'd give me some. He said, 'anything to get you away.' It wasn't very flattering, was it?"

Helena's face flashed into suspicion. "Why did he want to get you away?" she asked coldly. There was an alarmed alertness in her voice that made the boy look at her.

"He said he wanted me to 'be able to know cakes and ale when I saw them,'" Sam quoted. "Isn't that just like grandfather?"

"Know cakes and ale!" she stammered, and then looked at him furtively. She took one of the little hand-screens from the mantel, and held it so that he could not see her face. For a minute the pleasant firelit silence fell between them.

"Oh, listen," Sam said in a whisper; "do you hear the sap singing in the log?" He bent forward with parted lips, intent upon the exquisite sound—a dream of summer leaves rustling and blowing in the wind. He turned his limpid stag's eyes to hers to feel her pleasure.

"I think," Mrs. Richie said with an effort that made her voice hard, "that it would be an excellent thing for you to go away."

"And leave you?"

"Please don't talk that way. Your grandfather is quite right."

The boy smiled. "I suppose you really can't understand? It's part of your loveliness that you can't. If you could, you would know that I can't go away. I told him I was much obliged, but I couldn't leave Old Chester."

"Oh, please! you mustn't be foolish. I don't like you when you are foolish. Will you please remember how much older I am than you? Let's talk of something else. Let's talk about the little boy who is coming to visit me—his name is David."

"I would rather talk about you, and what you mean to me—beauty and poetry and good—"

"Don't!" she said sharply.

"Beauty and poetry and goodness."

"I'm not beautiful, and I'm not—poetical."

"And so I worship you," the young man went on in a low happy voice.

"Do please be quiet! I won't be worshipped."

"I don't see how you are going to help it," he said calmly. "Mrs. Richie, I've got my skiff; it came yesterday. Will you go out on the river with me some afternoon?"

"Oh, I don't think I care about boating," she said.

"You don't!" he exclaimed blankly; "why, I only got it because I thought you would go out with me!"

"I don't like the water," she said firmly.

Sam was silent; then he sighed. "I wish I'd asked you before I bought it. Father is so unreasonable."

She looked puzzled, for the connection was not obvious.

"Father always wants things used," Sam explained. "Do you really dislike boating?"

"You absurd boy!" she said laughing; "of course you will use it; don't talk nonsense!"

Sam looked into the fire. "Do you ever have the feeling," he said in an empty voice, "that nothing is worth while? I mean, if you are disappointed in anything? A feeling as if you didn't care, at all, about anything? I have it often. A sort of loss of appetite in my mind. Do you know it?"

"Do I know it?" she said, and laughed so harshly that the boy drew back. "Yes, Sam; I know it."

Sam sighed; "I hate that skiff."

And at that she laughed again, but this time with pure gayety. "Oh, you foolish boy!" she said. Then she glanced at the clock. "Sam, I have some letters to write to-night—will you think I am very ungracious if I ask you to excuse me?"

Sam was instantly apologetic. "I've stayed too long! Grandfather told me I ought never to come and see you—"

"*What!*"

"He said I bothered you."

"You don't bother me," she protested; "I mean, when you talk about your play you don't bother me. But to-night—"

"Of course," said Sam simply, and took himself off after one or two directions about the bird.

When the front door closed behind him she went back to her seat by the lamp, and took up her novel; but her eyes did not see the printed page. Suddenly she threw the book down on the table. It was impossible to read; Sam's talk had disturbed her to the point of sharp discomfort. What did old Mr. Wright mean by "knowing cakes and ale"? And his leer yesterday had been an offence! Why had he looked at her like that? Did he—? Was it possible—! She wished she had spoken to Lloyd about it. But no; it couldn't be; it was only his queer way; he was half crazy, she believed. And it would do no good to speak to Lloyd. The one thing she must not do, was to let any annoyance of hers annoy him. Yet below her discomfort at Sam's sentimentality and his grandfather's strange manner lay a deeper discomfort—a disturbance at the very centres of her life. . . . *She was afraid.*

She had been afraid for a long time. Even before she came to Old Chester she was a little afraid, but in Old Chester the fear was intensified by the consciousness of having made a mistake in coming. Old Chester was so far away. It had seemed desirable when she first thought of it; it was so near Mercer where business very often called him. Besides, New York, with its throngs of people, where she had lived for several years, had grown intolerable; in Old Chester she and Lloyd had agreed she would have so much more privacy. But how differently things had turned out! He did not have to come to Mercer nearly so often as he had expected. Those visions of hers— which he had not discouraged—of weekly or certainly fortnightly visits, had faded into lengthening periods of three weeks, four weeks—the last one was more than six weeks ago. "He can't leave his Alice!" she said angrily to herself; "*I* remember the time when he did not mind leaving her." As for privacy, the great city, with its hurrying indifferent crowds, was more private than this village of insistent friendliness.

She leaned back in her chair and pressed her hands over her eyes; then sat up quickly—she must not cry! Lloyd hated red eyes. But oh, she was afraid!— afraid of what? She had no answer; as yet her fear was without a name. She picked up her book, hurriedly; "I'll read," she said to herself; "I won't think!" But for a long time she did not turn a page.

However, by the time Mr. Pryor came back from the tea-party she was outwardly tranquil, and looked up from her novel to welcome him and laugh at his stories of his hostess. But he was instant to detect the troubled background of her thoughts.

"You are lonely," he said, lounging on the sofa beside her; "when that little boy comes you'll have something to amuse you;" he put a caressing finger under her soft chin.

"I didn't have that little boy, but I had another," she said ruefully.

"Did your admirer call?"

She nodded.

"What!" he exclaimed, for her manner told him.

"He tried to be silly," she said. "Of course I snubbed him. But it makes me horribly uncomfortable somehow."

Lloyd Pryor got up and slowly scratched a match under the mantel-piece; he took a long time to light his cigar. Then he put his hands in his pockets, and standing with his back to the fire regarded his boots. Helena was staring straight ahead of her with melancholy eyes.—("Do you ever have the feeling," the boy had said, "that nothing is worth while?")

Lloyd Pryor looked at her furtively and coughed. "I suppose," he said—and knocked the ashes from his cigar with elaborate care—"I suppose your adorer is a good deal younger than you?"

She lifted her head sharply, "Well, yes;—what of it?"

"Oh, nothing; nothing at all. In the first place, the health of our friend, Frederick, is excellent. But if this fellow were not younger; and if apoplexy or judgment should—well; why, perhaps—"

"Perhaps what?"

"Of course, Helena, my great desire is for your happiness; but in my position I—I am not as free as I once was to follow my own inclinations. And if—"

"Oh, my *God!*" she said violently.

She fled out of the room with flying feet. As he followed her up the stairs he heard her door slam viciously and the bolt slip. He came down, his face flushed and angry. He stood a long while with his back to the fire, staring at the lamp or the darkness of the uncurtained window. By and by he shook his head and set his jaw in sullen determination; then he went up-stairs and knocked softly at her door. There was no answer. Again, a little louder; silence.

"Nelly," he said; "Nelly, let me speak to you—just a minute?"

Silence.

"Nelly!"

Silence.

"Damn!" said Lloyd Pryor, and went stealthily back to the parlor where the fire was out and the lamp flickering into smoky darkness.

A quarter of an hour later he went up-stairs again.

"How *could* you say it!"

"I didn't mean it, Nelly; it was only a joke."

"A joke! Oh, a cruel joke, a cruel joke!"

"You know I didn't mean it. Nelly, dearest, I didn't mean it!"

"You do love me?"

"I love you. . . . Kiss me. . . ."

CHAPTER VIII

"WELL, now," said Dr. Lavendar that Sunday evening when he and David came into the study after tea; "I suppose you'd like me to tell you a story before you go to bed?"

"A Bible story?"

"Why, yes," Dr. Lavendar admitted, a little taken aback.

"No, sir," said David.

"You don't want a Bible story!"

The little boy shook his head.

"David," said Dr. Lavendar chuckling, "I think I like you."

David made no response; his face was as blank as an Indian's. He sat down on a stool by the fire, and once he sighed. Danny had sniffed him, slowly, and turned away with a bored look; it was then that he sighed. After a while he got up and wandered about the room, his hands gripped in front of him, his lips shut tight. Dr. Lavendar watched him out of the tail of his eye, but neither of them spoke. Suddenly David climbed up on a chair and looked fixedly at a picture that hung between the windows.

"That is a Bible picture," Dr. Lavendar observed.

"Who," said David, "is the gentleman in the water?"

Dr. Lavendar blew his nose before answering. Then

he said that that was meant to be our Saviour when He was being baptized. "Up in the sky," Dr. Lavendar added, "is His Heavenly Father."

There was silence until David asked gently, "Is it a good photograph of God?"

Dr. Lavendar puffed three times at his pipe; then he said, "If you think the picture looks like a kind Father, then it is. And David, I know some stories that are not Bible stories. Shall I tell you one?"

"If you want to, sir," David said. Dr. Lavendar began his tale rather doubtfully; but David fixed such interested eyes upon his face that he was flattered into enlarging upon his theme. The child listened breathlessly, his fascinated eyes travelling once or twice to the clock, then back to the kind old face.

"You were afraid bedtime would interrupt us?" said Dr. Lavendar, when the tale was done. "Well, well; you are a great boy for stories, aren't you?"

"You've talked seven minutes," said David, thoughtfully, "and you've not moved your upper jaw once."

Dr. Lavendar gasped; then he said, meekly, "Did you like the story?"

David made no reply.

"I think," said Dr. Lavendar, "I'll have another pipe."

He gave up trying to make conversation; instead, he watched the clock. Mary had said that David must go to bed at eight, and as the clock began to strike, Dr. Lavendar, with some eagerness, opened his lips to say good night — and closed them. "Guess he'd rather run his own rig," he thought. But to his relief, at the last stroke David got up.

"It's my bedtime, sir."

"So it is! Well, it will be mine after a while.

Good night, my boy!" Dr. Lavendar blinked nervously. Young persons were generally kissed. "I should not wish to be kissed," he said to himself, and the two shook hands gravely.

Left alone, he felt so fatigued he had to have that other pipe. Before he had finished it his senior warden looked in at the study door.

"Come in, Samuel," said Dr. Lavendar. "Samuel, I feel as if I had driven ten miles on a corduroy road!"

Mr. Wright looked blank; sometimes he found it hard to follow Dr. Lavendar.

"Sam, young persons are very exciting."

"Some of them are, I can vouch for that," his caller assured him grimly.

"Come, come! They are good for us," said Dr. Lavendar. "I wish you'd take a pipe, Sam; it would cheer you up."

"I never smoke, sir," said Samuel reprovingly.

"Well, you miss a lot of comfort in life. I've seen a good many troubles go up in smoke."

Mr. Wright sat down heavily and sighed.

"Sam been giving you something to think about?" Dr. Lavender asked cheerfully.

"He always gives me something to think about. He is beyond my comprehension! I may say candidly, that I cannot understand him. What do you think he has done now?"

"Nothing wicked."

"I don't know how you look at it," Samuel said, "but from my point of view, buying prints with other people's money is dangerously near wickedness. This present matter, however, is just imbecility. I told him one day last week to write to a man in Troy, New York, about a bill of exchange. Well, he wrote. Oh, yes—he wrote. Back comes a letter from the man, enclosing my young gentleman's epistle, with a line added"—Mr. Wright fumbled in his breast pocket to find the document—"here it is: '*Above remarks about ships not understood by our House.*' Will you look at that, sir, for the 'remarks about ships'?"

Dr. Lavendar took the sheet stamped "Bank of Pennsylvania," and hunted for his spectacles. When he settled them on his nose he turned the letter over, and read in young Sam's sprawling hand:

"Was this the face that launched a thousand ships,
And burnt the topless towers of Ilium?"

"What's this? I don't understand."

"Certainly you do not; no sensible person would. I showed it to my young gentleman, and requested an explanation. 'Oh,' he said, 'when you told me to write to Troy, it made me think of those lines.' He added that not wishing to forget them, he wrote them down on a sheet of paper, and that probably he used the other side of the sheet for the Troy letter—'by mistake.' 'Mistake, sir!' I said, 'a sufficient number of *mistakes* will send me out of business.'"

"Samuel," said Dr. Lavendar thoughtfully, "do you recall whose face it was that 'launched the thousand ships' on Troy?"

Samuel shook his head.

"*Helen's*," said Dr. Lavendar.

The senior warden frowned, then suddenly understood. "Oh, yes, I know all about that. Another evidence of his folly!"

"I've no doubt you feel like spanking him," Dr. Lavendar said sympathetically, "but —" he stopped short. Sam Wright was crimson.

THE AWAKENING OF HELENA RICHIE

"I! *Spank* him? I?" He got up, opening and shutting his hands, his face very red. The old minister looked at him in consternation.

"Sam! what on earth is the matter with you? Can't a man have his joke?"

Mr. Wright sat down. He put his hand to his mouth as though to hide some trembling betrayal; his very ears were purple.

Dr. Lavendar apologized profusely. "I was only in fun. I'm sure you know that I meant no disrespect to the boy. I only wanted to cheer you up."

"I understand, sir; it is of no consequence. I—I had something else on my mind. It is of no consequence." The color faded, and his face fell into its usual bleak lines, but his mouth twitched. A minute afterwards he began to speak with ponderous dignity. "This love-making business is, of course, most mortifying to me; and also, no doubt, annoying to Mrs. Richie. To begin with, she is eleven years older than he—he told his mother so. He added, if you please! that he hoped to marry her."

"Well! Well!" said Dr. Lavendar.

"I told him," Mr. Wright continued, "that in my very humble opinion it was contemptible for a man to marry and allow another man to support his wife."

Dr. Lavendar sat up in shocked dismay. "Samuel!"

"I, sir," the banker explained, "am his father, and I support him. If he marries, I shall have to support his wife. According to my poor theories of propriety, a man who lets another man support his wife had better not have one."

"But you ought not to have put it that way," Dr. Lavendar protested.

"I merely put the fact," said Samuel Wright.

81

"Furthermore, unless he stops dangling at her apronstrings, I shall stop his allowance. I shall so inform him."

"You surely won't do such a foolish thing!"

"Would you have me sit still? Not put up a single barrier to keep him in bounds?"

"Samuel, do you know what barriers mean to a colt?"

Mr. Wright made no response.

"They mean something to jump over."

"Possibly," said Mr. Wright with dignity, "you are, to some extent, correct. But a man cannot permit his only son to run wild and founder."

"Sam won't founder. But he may get a bad strain. You'd better look out. He is his father's son."

"I do not know, sir, to what you refer."

"Oh, yes, you do," Dr. Lavendar assured him easily; "and you know that no man can experience unforgiving anger, and not be crippled. You didn't founder, Sam, but you gave yourself a mighty ugly wrench. Hey? Isn't that so?"

The senior warden looked perfectly deaf; then he took up the tale again.

"If he goes on in his folly he will only be unhappy, and deservedly so. She will have nothing to do with him. In stopping him, I shall only be keeping him from future unhappiness."

"Samuel," said Dr. Lavendar, "I never begrudge unhappiness to the young."

But Mr. Wright was too absorbed in his own troubles to get any comfort out of that.

"By the way," said Dr. Lavendar, "speaking of Mrs. Richie—do you think she'd be a good person to take this little David Allison?"

"I don't know why she shouldn't be, sir," Samuel

said. "I have no fault to find with *her*. She pays her rent and goes to church. Yes; a very good person to take the boy off your hands."

"The rent is important," Dr. Lavender agreed nodding; "but going to church doesn't prove anything."

"All good people go to church," the senior warden reproved him.

"But all people who go to church are not good," Dr. Lavendar said dryly.

"I am afraid she lets Sam talk poetry to her," Sam's father broke out. "Stuff! absolute stuff! His mother sometimes tells me of it. Why," he ended piteously, "half the time I can't understand what it's about; it's just bosh!"

"What you don't understand generally *is* bosh, isn't it, Sam?" said Dr. Lavendar thoughtfully.

"I am a man of plain common sense, sir; I don't pretend to anything but common sense."

"I know you don't, Samuel, I know you don't," Dr. Lavendar said sadly; and the banker, mollified, accepted the apology.

"On top of everything else, he's been writing a drama. He told his mother so. Writing a drama, instead of writing up his ledgers!"

"Of course, he ought not to neglect his work," Dr. Lavendar agreed; "but play-writing isn't one of the seven deadly sins."

"It is distasteful to me!" Sam senior said hotly; "most distasteful. I told his mother to tell him so, but he goes on writing—so she says." He sighed, and got up to put on his coat. "Well; I must go home. I suppose he has been inflicting himself upon Mrs. Richie this evening. If he stays late, I shall feel it my duty to speak plainly to him."

THE AWAKENING OF HELENA RICHIE

Dr. Lavendar gave him a hand with his coat. "Gently does it, Samuel, gently does it!"

His senior warden shook his head. The sense of paternal helplessness, felt more or less by all fathers of sons, was heavy upon him. He knew in a bewildered way, that he did not speak the boy's language. And yet he could not give up trying to communicate with him,—shouting at him, so to speak, as one shouts at a foreigner when trying to make oneself understood; for surely there must be some one word that would reach Sam's mind, some one touch that would stir his heart! Yet when he brought his perplexity to Dr. Lavendar, he was only told to hold his tongue and keep his hands off. The senior warden said to himself, miserably, that he was afraid Dr. Lavendar was getting old. "Well, I mustn't bother you," he said; "as for Sam, I suppose he will go his own gait! I don't know where he gets his stubbornness from. I myself am the most reasonable man in the world. All I ever ask is to be allowed to follow my own judgment. I asked his mother if obstinacy was a characteristic of her family, and she assured me it was not. Certainly Eliza herself has no will of her own. I don't think a good woman ever has. And, as I say, I never insisted upon my own way in my life—except, of course, in matters where I knew I was right."

"Of course," said Dr. Lavendar.

CHAPTER IX

THE parting at the Stuffed Animal House the next morning was dreary enough. The day broke heavy with threatening rain. The man, after that brief flaming up of the embers of burned-out passion, had fallen into a weariness which he did not attempt to conceal. But the woman—being a woman—still tried to warm herself at the poor ashes, wasting her breath in a sobbing endeavor to blow them into some fitful ardor. There was a hurried breakfast, and while waiting for the stage the desultory talk that skims over dangerous topics for fear of getting into discussions for which there is no time. And with it the consciousness of things that burn to be said—at least on one side.

"I'm sorry I was cross last night," she murmured once, under her breath.

And he responded courteously, "Oh, not at all."

But she pressed him. "You know it was only because I—love you so? And to make a joke of—"

"Of course! Helena, when is that stage due? You don't suppose the driver misunderstood, and expects to take me on at the Tavern?"

"No; he was told to call here. . . . Lloyd, it's just the same? You haven't—changed?"

"Certainly not! I do hope he hasn't forgotten me? It would be extremely inconvenient."

She turned away and stood looking out of the window into the rain-sodden garden. Mr. Pryor lighted a cigar. After a while she spoke again. "You'll come soon? I hope you will come soon! I'll try not to worry you."

"Of course," he assured her; "but I trust your cook will be well next time, my dear."

"Give me a day's notice, and I will have another cook if Maggie should be under the weather," she answered eagerly.

"Oh, that reminds me," he said, and thrusting his hand into his pocket he went out to the kitchen. When he came back he went at once to the window. "I'm afraid that stage-driver has forgotten me," he said, frowning. But she reassured him — it really wasn't time yet; then she leaned her cheek on his shoulder.

"Do you think you can come in a fortnight, Lloyd? Come the first of May, and everything shall be perfect. Will you?"

Laughing, he put a careless arm around her, then catching sight of the stage pulling up at the gate, turned away so quickly that she staggered a little.

"Ah!" he said in a relieved voice;—"beg your pardon, Nelly;—There's the stage!"

At the door he kissed her hurriedly; but she followed him, bareheaded, out into the mist, catching his hand as they went down the path.

"Good-by!" he called back from the hinged step of the stage. "Get along, driver, get along! I don't want to miss my train in Mercer. Good-by, my dear. Take care of yourself."

Helena standing at the gate, followed the stage with her eyes until the road turned at the foot of the hill.

Then she went back to the bench under the silver poplar and sat down. She said to herself that she was glad he was gone. His easy indifference to the annoyance to her of all these furtive years, seemed just for a moment unbearable. He had not showed a glimmer of sympathy for her position; he had not betrayed the slightest impatience at Frederick's astonishing health, so contrary to every law of probability and justice; he had not even understood how she felt at taking the friendship of the Old Chester people on false pretences—oh, these stupid people! That dull, self-satisfied, commonplace doctor's wife, so secure, so comfortable, in her right to Old Chester friendships! Of course, it was a great thing to be free from the narrowness and prejudice in which Old Chester was absolutely hidebound. But Lloyd might at least have understood that in spite of her freedom the years of delay had sometimes been a little hard for her; that it was cruel that Frederick should live, and live, and live, putting off the moment when she should be like —other people; like that complacent Mrs. King, even; (oh, how she detested the woman!) But Lloyd had shown no spark of sympathy or understanding; instead he had made a horrid joke. . . . Suddenly her eyes, sweet and kind and shallow as an animal's, clouded with pain, and she burst out crying—but only for one convulsive moment. She could not cry out here in the garden. She wished she could get into the house, but she was sure that her eyes were red, and the servants might notice them. She would have to wait a while. Then she shivered, for a sharp wind blew from across the hills where in the hollows the snow still lingered in grimy drifts, icy on the edges, and crumbling and settling and sinking away with every day of pale sunshine. The faint fragrance of wind-beaten daffodils reached her, and she saw two crocuses, long gold bubbles, over in the grass. She put the back of her hand against her cheek—it was hot still; she must wait a little longer. Her chilly discomfort made her angry at Lloyd, as well as hurt. . . . It was nearly half an hour before she felt sure that her eyes would not betray her and she could go into the house.

Somehow or other the empty day passed; she had Lloyd's novel and the candy. It was cold enough for a fire in the parlor, and she lay on the sofa in front of it, and read and nibbled her candy and drowsed. Once, lazily, she roused herself to throw some grains of incense on the hot coals. Gradually the silence and perfume and warm sloth pushed the pain of the last twenty-four hours into the background of her mind, where it lay a dull ache of discontent. By and by even that ceased in physical well-being. Her body had her in its grip, and her spirit sunk softly into the warm and satisfied flesh. She bade Sarah bring her dinner into the parlor; after she had eaten it she slept. When she awoke in the late afternoon, she wished she could sleep again. All her thoughts ran together in a lazy blur. Somewhere, back of the blur, she knew there was unhappiness; so this was best—to lie warm and quiet by the fire, eating candy and yawning over her book.

The next few days were given up to indolence and apathy. But at the end of the week the soul of her stirred. A letter from Lloyd came saying that he hoped she had the little boy with her, and this reminded her of her forgotten promise to Dr. Lavendar.

But it was not until the next Monday afternoon

that she roused herself sufficiently to give much thought to the matter. Then she decided to go down to the Rectory and see the child. It was another dark day of clouds hanging low, bulging big and black with wind and ravelling into rain along the edges. She hesitated at the discomfort of going out, but she said to herself, dully, that she supposed she needed the walk. As she went down the hill her cheeks began to glow with the buffet of the wind, and her leaf-brown eyes shone crystal clear from under her soft hair, crinkling in the mist and blowing all about her smooth forehead. The mist had thickened to rain before she reached the Rectory, and her cloak was soaked, which made Dr. Lavendar reproach her for her imprudence.

"And where are your gums?" he demanded. When she confessed that she had forgotten them, he scolded her roundly.

"I'll see that the little boy wears them when he comes to visit me," she said, a comforted look coming into her face.

"David? David will look after himself like a man, and keep you in order, too. As for visiting you, my dear, you'd better visit him a little first. I tell you—stay and have supper with us to-night?"

But she protested that she had only come for a few minutes to ask about David. "I must go right home," she said nervously.

"No, no. You can't get away,—oh!" he broke off excitedly—"here he is!" Dr. Lavendar's eagerness at the sight of the little boy who came running up the garden path, his hurry to open the front door and bring him into the study to present him to Mrs. Richie, fussing and proud and a little tremulous, would have touched her, if she had noticed him. But she did not notice him,—the child absorbed her. She could not leave him. Before she knew it she found herself taking off her bonnet and saying she would stay to tea.

"David," said Dr. Lavendar, "I've got a bone in my leg; so you run and get me a clean pocket-handkerchief."

"Can I go up-stairs like a crocodile?" said David.

"Certainly, if it affords you the slightest personal satisfaction," Dr. Lavendar told him; and while the little boy crawled laboriously on his stomach all the way up-stairs, Dr. Lavendar talked about him. He said he thought the child had been homesick just at first; he had missed his sister Janey. "He told me 'Janey' gave him 'forty kisses' every night," said Dr. Lavendar; "I thought that told a story—" At that moment the crocodile, holding a handkerchief between his teeth, came rapidly, head foremost, down-stairs. Dr. Lavendar raised a cautioning hand;—"Mustn't talk about him, now!"

There was a quality in that evening that was new to Helena; it was dull, of course;—how very dull Lloyd would have found it! A childlike old man asking questions with serious simplicity of a little boy who was full of his own important interests and anxieties;—the feeding of Danny, and the regretful wonder that in heaven, the little dog would not be "let in."

"Who said he wouldn't?" Dr. Lavendar demanded, fiercely, while Danny yawned with embarrassment at hearing his own name.

"You read about heaven in the Bible," David said, suddenly shy; "an' it said outside were dogs;—an' some other animals I can't remember the names of."

THE AWAKENING OF HELENA RICHIE

Dr. Lavendar explained with a twinkle that shared with his visitor the humor of those "other animals" itemized in the Revelations. It was a very mild humor; everything was mild at the Rectory; the very air seemed gentle! There was no apprehension, no excitement, no antagonism; only the placid commonplace of goodness and affection. Helena could not remember such an evening in all her life. And the friendship between youth and age was something she had never dreamed of. She saw David slip from his chair at table, and run around to Dr. Lavendar's side to reach up and whisper in his ear;—oh, if he would but put his cheek against hers, and whisper in her ear!

The result of that secret colloquy was that David knelt down in front of the dining-room fire, and made a slice of smoky toast for Dr. Lavendar.

"After supper you might roast an apple for Mrs. Richie," the old minister suggested. And David's eyes shone with silent joy. With anxious deliberation he picked out an apple from the silver wire basket on the sideboard; and when they went into the study, he presented a thread to Mrs. Richie.

"Tie it to the stem," he commanded. "You're pretty slow," he added gently, and indeed her white fingers blundered with the unaccustomed task. When she had accomplished it, David wound the other end of the thread round a pin stuck in the high black mantel-shelf. The apple dropped slowly into place before the bars of the grate, and began—as everybody who has been a child knows—to spin slowly round, and then, slowly back again. David, squatting on the rug, watched it in silence. But Mrs. Richie would not let him be silent. She leaned forward, eager to touch him—his shoulders, his hair, his cheek, hot with the fire.

"Won't you come and sit in my lap?"

David glanced at Dr. Lavendar as though for advice; then got up and climbed on to Mrs. Richie's knee, keeping an eye on the apple that bobbed against the grate and sizzled.

"Will you make me a little visit, dear?"

David sighed. "I seem to visit a good deal; I'd like to belong somewhere."

"Oh, you will, one of these days," Dr. Lavendar assured him.

"I'd like to belong to you," David said thoughtfully.

Dr. Lavendar beamed, and looked proudly at Mrs. Richie.

"Because," David explained, "I love Goliath."

"Oh," said Dr. Lavendar blankly.

"It's blackening on one side," David announced, and slid down from Mrs. Richie's knee to set the apple spinning again.

"The red cheek is beginning to crack," said Dr. Lavendar, deeply interested; "smells good, doesn't it, Mrs. Richie?"

"Have you any little boys and girls?" David asked, watching the apple.

"Come and climb on my knee and I'll tell you," she bribed him.

He came reluctantly; the apple was spinning briskly now under the impulse of a woolly burst of pulp through the red skin.

"Have you?" he demanded.

"No, David."

Here his interest in Mrs. Richie's affairs flagged, for

the apple began to steam deliciously. Dr. Lavendar, watching her with his shrewd old eyes, asked her one or two questions; but, absorbed in the child, she answered quite at random. She put her cheek against his hair, and whispered, softly: "Turn round, and I'll give you forty kisses." Instantly David moved his head away. The snub was so complete that she looked over at Dr. Lavendar, hoping he had not seen it. "I once knew a little baby," she said, trying to hide her embarrassment, "that had curly hair the color of yours."

"It has begun to drip," said David briefly. "Does Alice live at your house?"

"*Alice!*"

"The gentleman — your brother — said Alice was nineteen. I thought maybe she lived at your house."

"No, dear. Look at the apple!"

David looked. "Why not?"

"Why, she lives at her own house, dear little boy."

"Does she pay you a visit?"

"No. David, I think the apple is done. Why didn't you roast one for Dr. Lavendar?"

"I had to do it for you because you're company. Why doesn't she pay you a visit?"

"Because — oh, for a good many reasons. I'm afraid I must go home now."

The child slipped from her knee with unflattering haste. "You've got to eat your apple first," he said, and ran to get a saucer and spoon. With great care the thread was broken and the apple secured. Then David sat calmly down in front of her to watch her eat it; but after the first two or three mouthfuls, Dr. Lavendar had pity on her, and the smoky skin and the hard core were banished to the dining-room.

While the little boy was carrying them off, she said eagerly, that she wanted him.

"You'll let me have him?"

"I'm going to keep him for a while."

"Oh, do give him to me!" she urged.

"Not yet. You come here and see him. I won't make ye eat a roast apple every time." He smiled at her as he spoke, for she was clasping her hands, and her eyes were eager and shining.

"I must have him! I *must!*"

"No use teasing—here comes Dr. King. He'll tell you I'm an obstinate old man. Hey, Willy, my boy! Ain't I an obstinate old man?"

"You are," said William. He had walked in unannounced, in good Old Chester fashion, and stood smiling in the doorway.

"Oh, plead my cause!" she said, turning to him.

"Of course I will. But it isn't much use; we are all under his heel."

They were standing, for Mrs. Richie had said she must go, when Dr. Lavendar had an idea: "Would you mind seeing her home, Willy?" he said, in an aside. "I was going to send Mary, but this is a chance to get better acquainted with her—if you're not too tired."

"Of course I'm not too tired," the doctor said eagerly, and went back to the fireside where Mrs. Richie had dropped on her knees before David. "I'm going to walk home with you," he announced. She looked up with a quick protest, but he only laughed. "If we let you go alone, your brother will think we have no manners in Old Chester. Besides I need the walk." And when she had fastened her cloak, and kissed David good night, and thrown Dr. Lavendar an appealing look, William gave her his hand down the two steps from the front door, and then made her take his arm. Dr. Lavendar had provided a lantern, and as its shifting beam ran back and forth across the path the doctor bade her be careful where she stepped. "These flag-stones are abominably rough," he said; "I never noticed it before. And one can't see in the dark."

But what with the lantern and the stars, there was light enough for William King to see the stray curl that blew across her forehead—brown, was it? And yet, William remembered that in daylight her hair was too bright to be called brown. He was solicitous lest he was making her walk too fast. "I don't want your brother to think we don't take care of you in Old Chester," he said; and in the starlight he could see that her face flushed a little. Then he repeated some Old Chester gossip, which amused her very much—and held his breath to listen to the delicious gayety of her laugh.

"There ought to be a better path for you up the hill," he said; "I must speak to Sam Wright about it." And carefully he flung the noiseless zigzag of light back and forth in front of her, and told some more stories that he might hear that laugh again.

When he left her at her own door she said with a sudden impetuous timidity, "Dr. King, *please* make Dr. Lavendar give me the little boy!"

"I will!" he said, and laughed at her radiant face.

It seemed to the doctor as he went down the hill, that he had had a most delightful evening. He could not recollect what they had talked about, but he knew that they had agreed on every point. "A very intelligent lady," he said to himself.

"William," said Martha, looking up from her mend-ing as he entered the sitting-room, "did you remember to tell Davis that the kitchen sink leaks?"

"Oh!" said the doctor blankly; "well—I'll tell him in the morning." Then, smiling vaguely, he dropped down into his shabby old easy-chair, and watched Martha's darning-needle plod in and out. "Martha," he said after a while, "what shade would you call your hair if it was—well, kind of brighter?"

"*What?* said Martha, looking at him over her spectacles; she put up her hard capable hand and touched her hair softly, as if she had forgotten it. "My hair used to be a real chestnut. Do you mean chestnut?"

"I guess I do. It's a pretty color."

Martha looked at him with a queer shyness in her married eyes, then tossed her head a little and thrust her darning-needle into the gray stocking with a jaunty air. "That's what you used to say," she said. After a while, noticing his tired lounge in the old chair, she said kindly, "Why did you stay so long at Dr. Lavendar's, Willy? You look tired. Do go to bed.'

"Oh," William explained, "I didn't stay very long; he asked me to see Mrs. Richie home. She had taken tea with him."

Martha's face suddenly hardened. "Oh," she said coldly. Then, after a short silence: "Mrs. Richie's hair is too untidy for my taste."

When Dr. Lavendar went back into the study he found David curled up in an arm-chair in profound meditation.

"What are you thinking about so hard?" Dr. Lavendar said.

"Yesterday. After church."

"Thinking about yesterday?" Dr. Lavendar repeated puzzled. David offered no explanation, and the old minister searched his memory for any happening of interest after church . . . but found none. He had come out of the vestry and in the church David had joined him, following him down the aisle to the door and waiting close behind him through the usual Sunday greetings: "Morning, Sam!" "Good morning, Dr. Lavendar." "How are you, Ezra? How many drops of water make the mighty ocean, Ezra?" "The amount of water might be estimated in tons, Dr. Lavendar, but I doubt whether the number of minims could be compu—" "Hullo! there's Horace; how d'ye do, Horace? How's Jim this morning?"—and so on; the old friendly greetings of all the friendly years. . . . Surely nothing in them to make the child thoughtful?

Suddenly David got up and came and stood beside him.

"What is your name?"

"N. or M.," Dr. Lavendar replied.

"What, sir?" said David, in a troubled voice; and Dr. Lavendar was abashed.

"My name is Edward Lavendar, sir. Why do you want to know?"

"Because, yesterday everybody said 'Dr. Lavendar.' I didn't think Doctor could be your front name. All the other people had front names."

"Well, I have a front name, David, but you see, there's nobody in Old Chester to call me by it." He sighed slightly, and then he smiled. "The last one who called me by my front name is dead, David. John was his name. I called him Johnny."

David looked at him with wide eyes, silent. Dr. Lavendar took his pipe out of his mouth, and stared for a minute at the fire.

"I should think," David said sadly, "God would be discouraged to have *everybody* He makes, die."

At that Dr. Lavendar came quickly out of his reverie. "Oh, it's better that way," he said, cheerfully. "One of these days I'll tell you why. What do you say to a game of dominoes?"

David squeaked with pleasure. Then he paused to say: "Is that lady, Alice's aunt?" and Dr. Lavendar had to recall who "Alice" was before he could say "yes." Then a little table was pulled up, and the dominoes were poured out upon it, with a joyful clatter. For the next half hour they were both very happy. In the midst of it David remarked, thoughtfully: "There are two kinds of aunts. One is bugs. She is the other kind." And after Dr. Lavendar had stopped chuckling they discussed the relative merits of standing the dominoes upright, or putting them on their sides, and Dr. Lavendar built his fence in alternate positions, which was very effective. It was so exciting that bedtime was a real trial to them both. At the last stroke of eight David clenched both hands.

"Perhaps the clock is fast?"

Dr. Lavendar compared it with his watch, and shook his head sympathetically. "No; just right. Tumble 'em back into the box. Good night."

"Good night, sir," David said, and stood hesitating. The color came and went in his face, and he twisted the top button of his jacket with little nervous fingers.

"Good night," Dr. Lavendar repeated, significantly.

But still David hesitated. Then he came and stood close beside Dr. Lavendar. "Lookee here," he said tremulously, "*I'll* call you Edward. I'd just as lieves as not."

There was a full minute's silence. Then Dr. Lavendar said, "I thank you, David. That is a kind thought. But no; I like Dr. Lavendar as a name. So many boys and girls have called me that, that I'm fond of it. And I like to have you use it. But I'm much obliged to you, David. Now I guess we'll say good night. Hey?"

The child's face cleared; he drew a deep breath as if he had accomplished something. Then he said good night, and trudged off to bed. Dr. Lavendar looked after him tenderly.

CHAPTER X

APRIL brightened into May before David came to live at the Stuffed Animal House. Dr. Lavendar had his own reasons for the delay, which he did not share with anybody, but they resulted in a sort of intimacy, which Helena, eager for the child, could not refuse

"He needs clothes," Dr. Lavendar put her off; "I can't let him visit you till Mary gets his wardrobe to rights."

"Oh, let me get his little things."

—Now, who would have supposed that Dr. Lavendar was so deep! To begin with, he was a man, and an old man, at that; and with never a chick or a child of his own. How did he know what a child's little clothes are to a woman?—"Well," he said, "suppose you make him a set of night-drawers."

Helena's face fell. "I don't know how to sew. I thought I could buy what he needed."

"No; he has enough bought things, but if you will be so kind, my dear, as to make—"

"I will!" she promised, eagerly, and Dr. Lavendar said he would bring David up to be measured.

Her sewing was a pathetic blunder of haste and happiness; it brought Dr. Lavendar and David up to the Stuffed Animal House very often, "to try on." David's coming was always a delight, but the old man

"HER SEWING WAS A PATHETIC BLUNDER OF HASTE AND HAPPINESS"

THE AWAKENING OF HELENA RICHIE

fretted her, somehow;—he was so good. She said so to William King, who laughed at the humor of a good woman's objection to goodness. The incongruity of such a remark from her lips was as amusing as a child's innocently base comment.

William had fallen into the habit of drawing up and calling out "good morning" whenever he and his mare passed her gate. Mrs. Richie's lack of common sense seemed to delight the sensible William. When he was with her, he was in the frame of mind that finds everything a joke. It was a demand for the eternal child in her, to which, involuntarily, she responded. She laughed at him, and even teased him about his shabby buggy with a gayety that made him tingle with pleasure. She used to wonder at herself as she did it—conscious and uneasy, and resolving every time that she would not do it again. She had none of this lightness with any one else. With Dr. Lavendar she was reserved to the point of coldness, and with young Sam Wright, matter-of-fact to a discouraging degree.

But she did not see Sam often in the next month. It had occurred to Sam senior that Adam Smith might cure the boy's taste for 'bosh'; so, by his father's orders, his Sunday afternoons were devoted to *The Wealth of Nations*. As for his evenings, his grandfather took possession of them. Benjamin Wright's proposal that the young man should go away for a while, had fallen flat; Sam replying, frankly, that he did not care to leave Old Chester. As Mr. Wright was not prepared to give any reasons for urging his plan, he dropped it; and instead on Sunday nights detained his grandson to listen to this or that drama or poem until the boy could hardly hide his impatience. When he was free and could hurry down the hill road, as often as not the lights were out in the Stuffed Animal House, and he could only linger at the gate and wonder which was her window. But when he did find her, he had an evening of passionate delight, even though occasionally she snubbed him, lazily.

"Do you go out in your skiff much?" she asked once; and when he answered, "No; I filled it with stones and sunk it, because you didn't like rowing," she spoke to him with a sharpness that surprised herself, though it produced no effect whatever on Sam.

"You are a very foolish boy! What difference does it make whether I like rowing or not?"

Sam smiled placidly, and said he had had hard work to get stones enough to fill the skiff. "I put them in," he explained, "and then I sculled out in mid-stream, and scuttled her. I had to swim ashore. It was night, and the water was like flowing ink, and there was a star in every ripple," he ended dreamily.

"Sam," she said, "if you don't stop being so foolish, I won't let you come and see me."

"Am I a nuisance about my drama?" he asked with alarm.

"Not about your drama," she said significantly; but Sam was too happy to draw any unflattering deductions.

When old Mr. Wright discovered that his stratagem of keeping his grandson late Sunday evenings had not checked the boy's acquaintance with Mrs. Richie, he tried a more direct method. "You young ass! Can't you keep away from that house? She thinks you are a nuisance!"

"No, grandfather," Sam assured him earnestly, "she doesn't. I asked her, and she said—"

"Asked her?" roared the old man. "Do you expect a female to tell the truth?" And then he swore steadily for a minute. "I'll have to see Lavendar," he said despairingly.

But Mr. Wright's cause was aided by some one stronger than Dr. Lavendar. Helena's attention was so fixed on the visitor who was coming to the Stuffed Animal House that Sam's conversation ceased to amuse her. Those little night-drawers on which she pricked her fingers interested her a thousand times more than did his dramatic visions. They interested her so much that sometimes she could almost forget that Lloyd Pryor's visit was delayed. For though it was the first of May, he had not come again. "I am so busy," he wrote; "it is impossible for me to get away. I suppose David will have his sling all ready for me when I do arrive?"

Helena was sitting on the porch with her clumsy needlework when Sarah brought her the letter, and after she had read it, she tore it up angrily. "He was in Mercer a week ago; I know he was, because there is always that directors' meeting on the last Thursday in April, so he must have been there. And he wouldn't come!" Down in the orchard the apple-trees were in blossom, and when the wind stirred, the petals fell in sudden warm white showers; across the sky, from west to east, was a path of mackerel clouds. It was a pastel of spring—a dappled sky, apple blossoms, clover, and the river's sheen of gray-blue. All about her were the beginnings of summer — the first exquisite green of young leaves, oaks, still white and crumpled from their furry sheaths; horse-chestnuts, each leaf drooping from its stem like a hand bending at the wrist; a thin flicker of elm buds, still distrustful of the sun. Later, this delicate dance of foliage would thicken so that the house would be in shadow, and the grass under the locusts on either side of the front door fade into thin, mossy growth. But just now it was overflowing with May sunshine. "Oh, he *would* enjoy it if he would only come," she thought. Well, anyhow, David would like it; and she began to fell her seam with painstaking unaccustomed fingers.

The child was to come that day. Half a dozen times she dropped her work to run to the gate, and shielding her eyes with her hand looked down the road to Old Chester; but there was no sign of the jogging hood of the buggy. Had anything happened? Was he sick? *Had Dr. Lavendar changed his mind?* Her heart stood still at that. She debated whether or not she should go down to the Rectory and find out what the delay meant? Then she called to one of the servants who was crossing the hall, that she wondered why the little boy who was to visit her, did not come. Her face cleared at the reminder that the child went to school in the morning.

"Why, of course! I suppose he will have to go every morning?" she added ruefully.

"My," Maggie said smiling, "you're wan that ought to have six!"

Mrs. Richie smiled, too. Then she said to herself that she wouldn't let him go to school every day; she was sure he was not strong enough. She ventured something like this to Dr. Lavendar when, about four o'clock, Goliath and the buggy finally appeared.

"Strong enough?" said Dr. Lavendar. "He's strong enough to study a great deal harder than he does, the little rascal! I'm afraid Rose Knight will spoil him; she's almost as bad as Ellen Bailey. You didn't know our Ellen, did ye? No; she'd married Spangler and gone out West before you came to us. Ah, a dear woman, but wickedly unselfish. Rose Knight took the school when Spangler took Ellen." Then he added one or two straight directions: Every school-day David was to come to the Rectory for his dinner, and to Collect Class on Saturdays. "You will have to keep him at his catechism," said Dr. Lavendar; "he is weak on the long answers."

"Oh!" Helena said, rather startled; "you don't want me to teach him—things like that, do you?"

"Things like what?"

"The catechism, and—to pray, and—"

Dr. Lavendar smiled. "You can teach folks to say their prayers, my dear, but nobody can teach them to pray. Only life does that. But David's been taught his prayers; you just let him say 'em at your knee, that's all."

David, dismissed to the garden while his elders talked, had discovered the rabbit-hutch, and could hardly tear himself away from it to say good-by. But when Dr. Lavendar called out that he was going, the little boy's heart misgave him. He came and stood by the step of the buggy, and picked with nervous fingers at the dry mud on the wheel—for Dr. Lavendar's buggy was not as clean as it should have been.

"Well, David?" Dr. Lavendar said cheerfully. The child with his chin sunk on his breast said something. "What?" said Dr. Lavendar.

David mumbled a word or two in a voice that seemed to come from his stomach; it sounded like,

"Like you best." But Dr. Lavendar did not hear it, and David ran swiftly back to the rabbits. There Helena found him, gazing through two large tears at the opal-eyed pair behind the wooden bars. Their white shell-like ears wavered at her step, and they paused in their nibbling; then went on again with timid, jewel-like glances in her direction.

Helena, at the sight of those two tears, knelt down beside the little boy, eager to be sympathetic. But he did not notice her, and by and by the tears dried up. After she had tried to make him talk;—of Dr. Lavendar, of school, of his old home;—without drawing anything more from him than "yes ma'am," or "no ma'am," she gave it up and waited until he should be tired of the rabbits. The sun was warm, the smell of the crushed dock leaves heavy in the sheltered corner behind the barn; it was so silent that they could hear the nibbling of the two prisoners, who kept glancing at them with apprehensive eyes that gleamed with pale red fires. David sighed with joy.

"What are their names?" he said at last in a low voice.

"They haven't any names; you can name them if you like."

"I shall call them Mr. and Mrs. Smith," he said with decision. And then fell silent again.

"You came to Old Chester in the stage with Mr. Pryor," she said after a while; "he told me you were a very nice little boy."

"How did he know?" demanded David.

"He is very nice himself," Helena said smiling.

David meditated. "Is that gentleman my enemy?"

"Of course not! he isn't anybody's enemy," she told him reprovingly.

THE AWAKENING OF HELENA RICHIE

David turned silently to his rabbits.

"Why did you think he was your enemy?" she persisted.

"I only just hoped he wasn't; I don't want to love him."

"What!"

"If he was my enemy, I'd have to love him, you know," David explained patiently.

Helena in her confused astonishment knew not what to reply. She stammered something about that being wrong; of course David must love Mr. Pryor!

"They ought to have fresh water," David interrupted thoughtfully; and Helena had to reach into the hutch for a battered tin pan.

She watched him run to the stable and come back, holding the pan in both hands and walking very slowly under the mottled branches of the buttonwoods; at every step the water splashed over the rusty brim, and the sunshine, catching and flickering in it, was reflected in a rippling gleam across his serious face.

All that afternoon he permitted her to follow him about. He was gently polite when she spoke to him, but he hardly noticed her until, as they went down through the orchard, his little hand tightened suddenly on hers, and he pressed against her skirts.

"Are there snakes in this grass?" he asked timorously. "A snake," he added, looking up at her confidingly, "is the only insect I am afraid of."

She stooped down and cuddled him reassuringly, and he rewarded her by snuggling up against her like a friendly puppy. She was very happy. As it grew dusk and cool, and all the sky was yellow behind the black line of the hills, she lured him into the house, and watched him eat his supper, forgetting to eat her own.

When she took him up-stairs to bed, Dr. Lavendar's directions came back to her with a slight shock—she must hear him say his prayers. How was she to introduce the subject? The embarrassed color burned in her cheeks as she helped him undress and tried to decide on the proper moment to speak of—prayers. But David took the matter into his own hands. As he stepped into his little night-clothes, buttoning them around his waist with slow precision, he said:

"Now I'll say my prayers. Sit by the window; then I can see that star when I open my eyes. It's hard to keep your eyes shut so long, ain't it?" he added confidentially.

Helena sat down, her heart fluttering in her throat. David knelt beside her, shutting first one eye and then the other. "'Now I lay me—'" he began in a businesslike voice. At the Amen he opened his eyes and drew a long breath. Helena moved slightly and he shut his eyes again; "I've not done yet.

"'Jesus, tender Shepherd, hear me,
Bless Thy little lamb to-night—'"

He paused and looked up at Mrs. Richie. "Can I say colt?" Before she could reply he decided for himself. "No; colts don't have shepherds; it has to be lamb."

Her silent laughter did not disturb him. He finished with another satisfied Amen. Helena put her arms about him to raise him from the floor, but he looked up, aggrieved.

"Why, I've not done *yet*," he reproached her. "You've forgot the blessings."

"The blessings?" she asked timidly.

"Why, of course," said David, trying to be patient; "but I'm most done," he encouraged her. "God bless everybody— Dr. Lavendar taught me the new blessings," he interrupted himself, his eyes snapping open, "because my old blessings were all gone to heaven. God bless everybody; Dr. Lavendar, an' Mary, an' Goliath—" Helena laughed. "He said I could," David defended himself doggedly — "an' Danny, an' Dr. King, an' Mrs. Richie. And make me a good boy. For Jesus' sake Amen. Now I'm done!" cried David, scrambling happily to his feet.

"And—Mr. Pryor, too? Won't you ask God to bless Mr. Pryor?"

"But," said David, frowning, "I'm *done*."

"After this, though, it would be nice—"

"Well," David answered coldly, "God can bless him if He wants to. But He needn't do it just to please me."

CHAPTER XI

WHEN Dr. Lavendar left David at the Stuffed Animal House, he didn't feel, somehow, like going home; the Rectory would be so quiet. It occurred to him that, as he was on the hill, he might as well look in on Benjamin Wright.

He found the old gentleman in his beaver hat and green serge dressing-gown, tottering up and down the weedy driveway in front of his veranda, and repeating poetry:

> "O great corrector of enormous times,
>   Shaker of o'er rank states, thou grand decider
>   Of dusty and old titles, that healest with blood—

Hello! 'Bout time you came to see me. I suppose you want to get some money out of me for something?"

"Of course; I always want money out of somebody for something. There's a leak in the vestry roof. How are you?"

"How do you suppose I am? At eighty-one, with one foot in the grave! Ready to jump over a five-barred gate?"

"I'm seventy-two," said Dr. Lavendar, "and I played marbles yesterday."

"Come in and have a smoke," the older man said, hobbling on to the veranda, where four great white columns, blistered and flaked by time, supported a roof that darkened the shuttered windows of the second story.

He led the way indoors to the dining-room, growling that his nigger, Simmons, was a fool. "He *says* he closes the shutters to keep the flies out; makes the room as dark as a pocket, and there ain't any flies this time of year, anyhow. He does it to stop my birds from singing; he can't fool me! To stop my birds!" He went over to one of the windows and pushed the shutters open with a clatter; instantly a twitter ran from cage to cage, and the fierce melancholy of his old face softened. "Hear that?" he said proudly.

"I ought to come oftener," Dr. Lavendar reproached himself; "he's lonely."

And, indeed, the room with its mammoth sideboard black with age and its solitary chair at one end of the long table, was lonely enough. On the walls, papered a generation ago with a drab paper sprinkled over with occasional pale gilt medallions, were some time-stained engravings: "The Destruction of Nineveh"; "The Trial of Effie Deans"; "The Death-bed of Washington." A gloomy room at best; now, with the shutters of one window still bowed, and the faint twitter of the canaries, and that one chair at the head of the table, it was very melancholy.

"Sit down!" said Benjamin Wright. Still in his moth-eaten high hat, he shuffled about to fetch from the sideboard a fat decanter with a silver chain and label around its neck, and two tumblers.

"No," said Dr. Lavendar; "I'm obliged to you."

"What, temperance?" snarled the other.

"Well, I hope so," Dr. Lavendar said, "but not a

teetotaler, if that's what you mean. Only I don't happen to want any whiskey at five o'clock in the afternoon."

At which his host swore softly, and lifting the decanter poured out two good fingers.

"Mr. Wright," said Dr. Lavendar, "I will be obliged if you will not swear in my presence."

"You needn't talk to me," cried Benjamin Wright, "I despise this damned profanity there is about; besides, I am always scrupulously particular in my language before females and parsons. Well;—I wanted to see you, because that jack-donkey, Sam, my grandson, is causing me some anxiety."

"Why, Sam is a good boy," Dr. Lavendar protested.

"Too good. I like a boy to be human at twenty-three. He doesn't know the wickedness of the world."

"Thank God," said Dr. Lavendar.

"Dominie, ignorance ain't virtue."

"No; but it's a fair substitute. I wouldn't want one of my boys to be able to pass an examination on wrong-doing."

"But you want him to recognize it when he sees it, don't you?"

"If he knows goodness, you can trust him to recognize the other thing. Teach 'em goodness. Badness will label itself."

"Doesn't follow," Benjamin Wright said. "But you're a parson; parsons know about as much as females—good females. Look here! I have reasons for saying that the boy ought to get out of Old Chester. I want your assistance."

"Get out of Old Chester!—to see how wicked the world is?"

Mr. Wright shook his head. "No; he could see that here—only the puppy hasn't got his eyes open yet. A little knocking about the world, such as any boy ought to have, will open 'em. Living in Old Chester is narrowing; very narrowing. Besides, he's got—well, he's got some truck he's written. It isn't entirely bad, Lavendar, and he might as well try to get it published, or, maybe, produced in some theatre. So let him go and hunt up a publisher or a manager. Now, very likely, his—his *mother* won't approve. I want you to urge—her, to let him go."

"Travelling might be good for Sam," said Dr. Lavendar; "I admit that—though not to learn the wickedness of the world. But I don't know that it would be worth while to take a journey just on account of his writing. He could put it in an envelope and mail it to a publisher; he'd get it back just as soon," Dr. Lavendar said chuckling. "Look here, what's the matter? I can see you're concerned about the boy."

"Concerned?" cried Benjamin Wright, pounding the table with his tumbler and chewing orange-skin rapidly. "I'm damned concerned."

"I will ask, sir, that you will not swear in my presence."

Mr. Wright coughed. "I will endeavor to respect the cloth," he said stiffly.

"If you will respect yourself, it will be sufficient. As for Sam, if there's anything wrong, his father ought to know it."

"Well then, tell his—*mother*, that there is something wrong."

"What?"

Mr. Wright got up, and clasping his hands behind him, shuffled about the room. Instantly one of the canaries began to sing. "Stop that!" he said. The bird quivered with shrill music. "Stop! You! . . . There's no such thing as conversation, with these creatures about," he added in a proud aside. "Did you ever hear such singing?"

Dr. Lavendar, unable to make himself heard, shook his head.

"If you don't stop," said Mr. Wright, "I'll wring your neck!" and as the bird continued, he opened the door. "Simmons! You freckled nigger! Bring me the apron." Then he stamped, and cursed the slowness of niggers. Simmons, however, came as fast as his old legs could carry him, bearing a blue gingham apron. This, thrown over the cage, produced silence.

"There! Now, perhaps, you'll hold your tongue? . . . Lavendar, I prefer not to say what is wrong. Merely tell Sam's—*mother*, that he had better go. If —she is too mean to provide the money, I will."

"Sam's father is not too mean to do anything for Sam's welfare; but of course, a general accusation is not convincing; should not be convincing— Why!" said Dr. Lavendar, interrupting himself, "bless my heart! I believe you mean that the boy is making sheep's-eyes at your neighbor here on the hill? Is that it? Why, Benjamin, the best way to cure that is to pay no attention to it."

"Sir," said Mr. Wright, sinking into his chair breathlessly, and tapping the table with one veined old finger; "when I was a young man, it was not thought proper to introduce the name of a female into a discussion between gentlemen."

"Well," Dr. Lavendar admitted, "maybe not— when you were young. But all of us young folks in

Old Chester know perfectly well that Sam is smitten, and we are ignoring it."

"What! His—*mother* knows it?"

"His father knows it perfectly well," said Dr. Lavendar smiling.

Mr. Wright got up again, his fingers twitching with impatience. "Lavendar," he began — another bird trilled, and snarling with annoyance, he pulled the blue apron from the first cage and threw it over the second. "These creatures drive me distracted! . . . Lavendar, to get Sam out of Old Chester, I might almost consent to see his—*mother*, if there was no other way to accomplish it."

At that Dr. Lavendar stopped smiling. "Benjamin," he said solemnly, "if any foolishness on the part of the boy brings you to such wisdom, the hand of the Lord will be in it!"

"I don't want to see—his relations!" cried Benjamin Wright; "but Sam's got to get away from this place for a while, and if you won't persuade his—*mother* to allow it, why I might be driven to seeing—her. But why shouldn't he try to get his truck published?"

Dr. Lavendar was very much moved. "If you'll only see your son," he said, "this other business will straighten itself out somehow. But—" he paused; "getting Sam's play published isn't a very good excuse for seeing him. I'd rather have him think you were worried because the boy had an attack of calf-love. No; I wouldn't want you to talk about theatrical things," Dr. Lavendar ended thoughtfully.

"Why not?"

"Well, the fact is, Samuel has no sympathy with dramas or playhouses. I do not myself approve of the theatre, but I am told respectable persons have adopted the profession. Samuel, however, can't find any good in it."

"He can't, can't he? Well, well; it was efficacious—it was efficacious!"

"What was efficacious?"

Benjamin Wright laughed loudly. "You don't know? He never told you?"

"You mean what you and he quarrelled about? No; he never told me."

"He was a fool."

"Benjamin, if you were not a fool at twenty-four, you missed a good deal."

"And now he objects to theatrical things?"

"He objects so intensely," said Dr. Lavendar, "that, anxious as I am to have you meet and bring this foolish and wicked quarrel to an end, I should really hesitate to have you do so, if you insisted on discussing that subject."

Benjamin Wright lifted one trembling fist. "It was efficacious!"

"And you would give your right hand to undo it," said Dr. Lavendar.

The very old man lowered his shaking right hand and looked at it; then he said sullenly, "I only wanted his own good. You ought to see that—a parson!"

"But you forget; I don't know what it was about."

Mr. Wright's face twitched. "Well," he said spasmodically, "I'll—tell you. I—"

"Yes?"

"I—" his voice broke, then he coughed, then he tried to laugh. "Simple enough; simple enough. I had occasion to send him to Mercer. He was to come back that night." Mr. Wright stopped; poured some whiskey into his glass, and forgetting to add any water, drank it at a gulp. "He didn't come back until the next afternoon."

"Yes. Well?"

"In those days I was of—of somewhat hasty temper."

"So I have heard," said Dr. Lavendar.

Benjamin Wright glared. "When I was young, listening to gossip was not thought becoming in the cloth. When he came, I learned that he had stayed over in Mercer—without my consent, mark you—*to go to the theatre!*"

"Well?" said Dr. Lavendar. "He was twenty-four. Why should he have your consent?"

Mr. Wright waved this question aside. "When he came home, I spoke with some severity."

"This quarrel," said Dr. Lavendar, "is not built on such folly as that."

Benjamin Wright shook his head, and made a careless gesture with his trembling hand. "Not—entirely. I reproved him, as I say. And he was impertinent. Impertinent, mind you, to his father! And I—in those days my temper was somewhat quick—I—"

"Yes?"

But Mr. Wright seemed unable to proceed, except to say again, "I—reproved him."

"But," Dr. Lavendar protested, "you don't mean to tell me that Samuel, just for a reproof, an unkind and unjust reproof, would—why, I cannot believe it!"

"It was not unjust!" Benjamin Wright's melancholy eyes flamed angrily.

"I know, Samuel," said Dr. Lavendar. "He is obstinate; I've told him so a hundred times. And he's conceited—so's everybody, more or less; if in nothing else, we're conceited because we're not conceited. But he's not a fool. So, whether he is right or not, I am sure he thinks he had something more to complain of than a good blowing-up?"

"In a way," said the old man, examining his ridgy finger-nails and speaking with a gasp, "he had. Slightly."

Dr. Lavendar's stern lip trembled with anxiety. "What?"

"I—chastised him; a little."

"You—*what?*"

Benjamin Wright nodded; the wrinkled pouches under his eyes grew dully red. "My God!" he said plaintively; "think of that—a hasty moment! Thirty-two years; my God! I—spanked him."

Dr. Lavendar opened his lips to speak, but found no words.

"And he was offended! Offended? What right had he to be offended? *I* was the offended party! He went to a low theatre. Apparently you see nothing wrong in that? Well, I've always said that every parson had the making of an actor in him. It's a toss-up—the stage or the pulpit. Same thing at bottom. But perhaps even you won't approve of his staying away all night? Smoking! Drinking! He'd been drunk. He confessed it. And there was a woman in it. He confessed that. Said they'd all 'gone to supper together.' Said that he was 'seeing the world' —which a man ('*man*,' if you please!) of his years had a right to do. Well; I suppose you'd have had me smile at him, and tuck him up in bed to sleep off his headache, and give him a stick of candy? That wasn't my way. I reproved him. I—chastised him. Perfectly proper. Perhaps—unusual. He was twenty-four, and I laid him across my knee, and—well; I got over it in fifteen minutes. I was, perhaps, hasty.

My temper in those days was not what it is now. But I forgave him in fifteen minutes; and he had gone! He's been gone—for thirty-two years. My God!"

He poured out another finger of whiskey, but forgot to drink it. A canary-bird chirped loudly, then lapsed into a sleepy twitter.

"I was well rid of him! To make a quarrel out of a thing like that—a joke, as you might say. I laughed, myself, afterwards, at the thought of it. A fellow of twenty-four—spanked! Why didn't he swear and be done with it? I would have reproved him for his profanity, of course. Profanity in young persons is a thing I will not tolerate; Simmons will tell you so. But it would have cleared the air. If he had done that, we'd have been laughing about it, now;—he and I, together." The old man suddenly put both hands over his face, and a broken sound came from behind them.

Dr. Lavendar shook his head, speechlessly.

"What's the matter with you?" cried Benjamin Wright, pulling off his hat and banging it down on the table so fiercely that the crown collapsed on one side like an accordion. "Good God! Can't you see the tomfoolery of this business of thirty-two years of hurt feelings?"

Dr. Lavendar was silent.

"What! You excuse him? When I was young, parsons believed in the Ten Commandments; 'Honor thy father and thy mother—'"

"There is another scripture which saith, 'Fathers, provoke not your children to wrath.' And when it comes to the Commandments, I would commend the third to your attention. As for Samuel, you robbed him."

"Robbed him?"

"You took his self-respect. A young man's dignity, at twenty-four, is as precious to him as a woman's modesty. You stole it. Yes; you robbed him. Our Heavenly Father doesn't do that, when He punishes us. We lose our dignity ourselves; but He never robs us of it. Did ye ever notice that? Well; you robbed Samuel. My—my—*my!*" Dr. Lavendar sighed wearily. For, indeed, the matter looked very dark. Here was the moment he had prayed for—the readiness of one or the other of the two men to take the first step towards reconciliation. Such readiness, he had thought, would mean the healing of the dreadful wound, whatever it was; forgiveness on the father's part of some terrible wrong-doing, forgiveness on the son's part of equally terrible hardness of heart. Instead he found a cruel and ridiculous mortification, made permanent by thirty-two unpardoning years. Here was no sin to command the dreadful dignity of repentance, with its divine response of forgiveness. The very lack of seriousness in the cause made the effect more serious. He looked over at the older man, and shook his head. . . . How could they pay their debts to each other, this father and son? Could Benjamin Wright return the self-respect he had stolen away? Could Samuel offer that filial affection which should have blessed all these empty years? A wickedly ludicrous memory forbade the solemnity of a reconciliation: below any attempt the father might make, there would be a grin, somewhere; below any attempt the son might make, there would be a cringe, somewhere. The only possible hope was in absolute, flat commonplace. Play-writing, as a subject of conversation, was out of the question!

THE AWAKENING OF HELENA RICHIE

"Benjamin," he said with agitation, "I thank God that you are willing to see Samuel; but you must promise me not to refer to Sam's play. You must promise me this, or the last end of the quarrel will be worse than the first."

"I haven't said I was willing to see him," Mr. Wright broke out; "I'm *not* willing! Is it likely that I would hanker after an interview? All I want is to get the boy away from Old Chester; to 'see the world.' His—father ought to sympathize with that! Yes; to get him away, I would even— But if you will tell his—relatives, that in my judgment, he ought to go away, that is all that is necessary."

"No! You must urge it yourself," Dr. Lavendar said eagerly. "Put it on the ground of calf-love, if you want to. I'll tell Samuel you want to get Sam out of town because you're afraid he's falling in love with Mrs. Richie; and you'd like to consult him about it."

But the old man began a scrabbling retreat. "No! No!" he said, putting on his hat with shaking hands. "No; don't tell anybody anything. I'll find some other way out of it. Let it go. Seeing his—relatives is a last resource. If they are so virtuous as to object to plays, I'll try something else. Object?" he repeated. "Gad-a-mercy! My discipline was successful!" He grinned wickedly.

Dr. Lavendar made no reply. The interview had been a strain, and he got up a little feebly. Benjamin Wright, as he saw him to the door, swore again at some misdemeanor on the part of Simmons, but was not rebuked.

The old minister climbed into his buggy, and told Goliath to "g'long." As he passed the Stuffed Animal House, he peered through the little dusty window of the hood; but David was not in sight.

CHAPTER XII

"I THINK," said Dr. Lavendar, as he and Goliath came plodding into Old Chester in the May dusk, "I think I'll go and see Willy. He'll tell me how much Sam's love-making amounts to."

His mind was on the matter to such an extent that he hardly heard Mary's anxious scolding because he looked tired; but his preoccupation lifted at supper, in the consciousness of how lonely he was without David. He really wanted to get out of the house and leave the loneliness behind him. So after tea he put on his broad-brimmed felt hat and tied a blue muffler around his throat—Dr. Lavendar felt the cold a good deal; he said it was because the seasons were changing —and walked wearily over to Dr. King's house. That talk with Benjamin Wright had told on him.

"Well," he said, as the doctor's wife opened the door; "how are you, Martha?"

"Very tired," said Mrs. King. "And dear me, Dr. Lavendar, you look tired yourself. You're too old to do so much, sir. Come in and sit down."

"I'll sit down," said Dr. Lavendar, dropping into a chair in the parlor; "but don't flatter yourself, Martha, that you'll ever be as young as I am!" ("He *is* failing," Mrs. King told her husband afterwards. "He gets his words all mixed up. He says 'young' when he means 'old.' Isn't that a sign of something,

William?" "It's a sign of grace," said the doctor, shortly.)

"I want Willy to come over and give my Mary a pill," Dr. Lavendar explained. "She is as cross as a bear, and cross people are generally sick people—although I suppose that's Mary's temperament," he added sighing.

Martha shook her head. "In my judgment *temperament* is just another word for temper! I don't believe in making excuses for it. That's a great trick of William's, I'm sorry to say."

"I should have thought you'd have cured him of it by this time?" Dr. Lavendar murmured; and then he asked if the doctor was out.

"Oh, yes," said Mrs. King, dryly; "Willy always manages to get out in the evening on one excuse or another. You'd think he'd be glad of a restful evening at home with me, sometimes. But no; William's patients need a surprising amount of attention, though his bills don't show it. When Mrs. Richie's cook was sick—just as an instance—he went six times to see her. I counted."

"Well; she got well?" said Dr. Lavendar.

"Got well? She'd have got well if he hadn't gone near her." Martha began to stroke the gathers on a bit of cambric with a precise needle that suddenly trembled. "The woman herself was not to blame; it's only just to say that.—And there's one thing about me, Dr. Lavendar; I may not be perfect, but I am always just. No; she was not to blame; it was Mrs. Richie who sent for William. She is the most helpless woman I ever saw, for her years;—she is at least forty, though she uses sachet-powders, and wears undersleeves all trimmed with lace, as if she were sixteen! I don't want to find fault, Dr. Lavendar, but I must say that *I* wouldn't have trusted that little boy to her."

"Oh," said Dr. Lavendar, "I trusted *her* to the little boy! She'll be so busy looking after his sleeves, she'll forget her own."

Mrs. King sniffed, doubtfully. "I'm sure I hope you are right; but in my opinion, she's a very helpless and foolish woman;—if nothing worse. Though according to my ideas, the way she lets Sam Wright's Sam behave is worse!"

Dr. Lavendar was suddenly attentive. "How does she let him behave?"

"Well, he is so daft over her that he neglects his work at the bank to write verses. Why doesn't she stop it?"

"Because," said William King, appearing in the doorway, smelling honestly of the barn and picking off a straw here and there from his sleeve; "she knows nothing about it."

Dr. Lavendar and Martha both looked up, startled at his tone.

"Women," said the doctor, "would gossip about a —a clam!"

"I am not gossiping!" Martha defended herself; but Dr. Lavendar interrupted her, cheerfully.

"Well, I am. I came over to gossip with William on this very subject.—Martha, will you let him put a match to that grate? I declare, the seasons are changing. When I was your age it wasn't cold enough to have a fire in May.—Look here, Willy, what do you mean by saying Mrs. Richie doesn't know Sam's sentiments?"

"I mean that women like Mrs. Richie are so unconscious, they don't see things like that. She's as unconscious as a girl."

"*Tck!*" said Martha.

"A girl!" said Dr. Lavendar.—"Say a tree, or a boy; but don't say a girl. Why, William, everybody sees it. Even Benjamin Wright. Of course she knows it."

"She doesn't; she isn't the kind that thinks of things like that. Of course, some women would have discovered it months ago; one of your strong-minded ladies, perhaps—only Sam wouldn't have been spoony on that kind."

"Well!" said Martha, "I must say, flat—"

But William interrupted her—"To prove what I say: she lets him come in and bore her to death, just out of kindness. Do you suppose she would do that if she knew he was such an idiot as to presume to—to—"

"Well," said Dr. Lavendar, "as there is so much ignorance about, perhaps Sam doesn't know he's lost his heart?"

But at that William laughed. "*He* knows! Trust a young fellow! That's just the difference between a man and a woman, sir; the man always knows; the woman, if she's the right kind, doesn't—until she's told."

"*Tck!*" said Martha.

Dr. Lavendar looked down at the bowl of his pipe; then he said meekly, "I was under the impression that Eve ate her apple before Adam had so much as a bite. Still, whether Mrs. Richie knows the state of Sam's affections or not, I do wish she would urge him to put his mind on his work. That's what I came in to speak to you about. His father is all on edge about it, and now his grandfather has taken it into his head to be worried over it, too. But you know her better than the rest of us do, and I thought perhaps you'd drop a hint that she would be doing missionary work if she'd influence the boy to be more industrious."

"I'll go and talk it over with her," Martha volunteered. "I am always ready to advise any one."

William King got up and kicked at a lump of coal in the grate. "I am sure you are," he said dryly; "but no talking over is necessary. I shall probably be going up the hill in a few days, and I'll say a word if Dr. Lavendar wants me to. Nothing definite; just enlist her sympathy for his father—and get her to protect herself, too. He must be an awful nuisance."

"That's it!" said Dr. Lavendar. "I'd do it myself, but you know her better than I do. I'm getting acquainted with her through David. David is really a remarkable child! I can't tell you how I miss him." And then he began to relate David's sayings, while Martha sewed fiercely, and William stared at the hearth-rug. "The little rascal is no Peter Grievous," Dr. Lavendar declared, proudly; and told a story of a badly barked knee, and a very stiff upper-lip; "and the questions he asks!" said the old man, holding up both hands; "theological questions; the House of Bishops couldn't answer 'em!" He repeated some of the questions, watching the husband and wife with swift glances over his spectacles; when he had wrung a reluctant laugh from the doctor, and Mrs. King was not sewing so fast, he went home, not much rested by his call.

But the result of the call was that at the end of the week Dr. King went up to the Stuffed Animal House.

"We are shipwrecked!" cried Mrs. Richie, as she

THE AWAKENING OF HELENA RICHIE

saw him coming down the garden path towards the barn. Her face was flushed and gay, and her hair, shaken from its shining wreath around her head, hung in two braids down her back. She had had a swing put up under the big buttonwood beside the stable, and David, climbing into it, had clung to the rigging to be dashed, sidewise, on to the rocks of the carriageway, where Mrs. Richie stood ready to catch him when the vessel should drive near enough to the shore. In an endeavor to save himself from some engulfing sea which his playmate had pointed out to him, David had clutched at her, breaking the top hook of her gown and tearing her collar apart, leaving her throat, white and round, open to the hot sun. Before the doctor reached her, she caught her dress together, and twisted her hair into a knot. "You can't keep things smooth in a shipwreck," she excused herself, laughing.

David sighed, and looked into the carriage-house. In that jungle—Mrs. Richie had called it a jungle—were wild beasts; there were also crackers and apples—or to be exact, breadfruit and citrons—hanging from what George called "harness-racks," though of course, as thoughtful persons know, they were trees; David was to gather these tropical spoils, and then escape from the leopard, the shark, the crocodile! And now here was Dr. King, spoiling everything.

The doctor sat down on a keg and looked at the two, smiling. "Which is the younger of you?" he said. It came over him, in a gust of amusement, what Martha would say to such a scene, and he laughed aloud.

"Dr. King," said David, in a small distinct voice, "won't Jinny run away, if you leave her so long at the gate?"

"Oh, David!" cried Mrs. Richie, horrified. But the visitor threw back his head with a shout.

"That's what my wife would call speaking 'flatly and frankly'! Well, Mrs. Richie, I never wrote a better prescription in my life. You look like a different woman, already."

And, indeed, the youth in her face was as careless as David's own. But it flagged when he added that he hoped her brother would not think the care of David would be too much for her.

"Oh, no," she said, briefly.

"I feel like saying 'I told you so'! I knew you would like to have a child about."

"I do, but he is a tyrant. Aren't you, David? I have to get up for breakfast!"

"Terrible," said William delightedly.

"Why, but it *is*. I don't know when I've done such a thing! At first I thought I really couldn't. But I couldn't leave him all by himself, down-stairs —could I, David?"

"I'd just as lieves," said David, gently.

"Oh, how like your sex!" Helena cried.

"What do you suppose I've come for?" Dr. King began in the bantering tone one uses to a child. "I've come to get you to exert your influence to improve business. *Business!*" he repeated, delighted at his own absurdity; "a lady who finds it hard to get up in the mornings."

She looked at him ruefully; "I'm lazy, I am afraid."

"No, you're not—it's a very sensible thing to do, if you are not strong. Well, I must tell you what we want; Sam Wright is anxious, because young Sam neglects his work at the bank, and—"

"But he doesn't like business," she explained with a surprised look; and William laughed with pleasure.

THE AWAKENING OF HELENA RICHIE

"So that's a reason for not attending to it? Unfortunately, that's the young man's own point of view. He's a queer youngster," William added in his kind voice.

"I don't think it's queer not to like disagreeable things," Helena said.

"Well, no; but all the same, we've got to stand them. Sam has no patience with anything disagreeable. Why, when he was a little fellow—let me see, he was younger than David; about four, I think—he scratched his finger one day pretty severely; it smarted, I guess, badly. Anyway, he roared! Then he picked up a pair of scissors and ran bawling to his mother; 'Mamma, cut finger off! It hurts Sam—cut finger off!' That's been his principle ever since: 'it hurts—get rid of it.'"

"I don't blame him in the least," Helena protested gayly; "I'm sure I've wanted to 'cut finger off.' And I have done it, too!"

"Well," said the doctor with great pretence of gravity, "I suppose, then, we'll have to tell old Mr. Wright that nobody must ever do anything he doesn't want to do? It appears that he's worried, too, because the young gentleman isn't industrious. The fact is, he thinks Sam would rather come up here than work over his ledgers," he teased.

Helena sprung to her feet, nervously. "But I wish he wouldn't come! I don't want him to come. I can't help it; indeed I—I can't help it!" She spoke with a sort of gasp. Instantly David, who had been lounging in the swing, slipped down and planted himself directly in front of her, his arms stretched out at each side. "I'll take care of you," he said protectingly.

THE AWAKENING OF HELENA RICHIE

William King caught his breath. No one could have heard the frightened note in her voice without understanding David's impulse. The doctor shared it. Evidently Sam had been making love to her, and her very innocence made her quick to feel herself rebuked! William felt an ardent desire to kick Sam Wright's Sam.

But Mrs. Richie was herself again; she laughed, though not quite naturally, and sat down in the swing, swaying slightly back and forth with an indolent push of her pretty foot. David lounged against her knee, eying the doctor with frank displeasure. "I am sure," she said, "I wish Sam would attend to his ledgers; it would be much better than making visits."

"Dr. King," David said, gently, "I'll shake hands now, and say good-by."

The laugh that followed changed the subject, although warm in William's consciousness the thought remained that she had let him know what the subject meant to her: he shared a secret with her! She had told him, indirectly perhaps, but still told him, of her troubles with young Sam. It was as if she had put out her hand and said, "Help me!" Inarticulately he felt what David had said, "I'll take care of you!" And his first care must be to make her forget what had distressed her. He said with the air of one imparting interesting information, that some time in the next fortnight he would probably go to Philadelphia on business. "Can I do any errands for you? Don't you ladies always want ribbons, or something."

"Does Mrs. King let you buy ribbons for her?" Helena asked.

"Ribbons! I am to buy yarn, and some particular brand of lye for soap."

"Lye! How do you make soap out of lye?"

"You save all the"—William hesitated for a sufficiently delicate word—"the—fat, you know, in the kitchen, and then you make soft soap."

"Why! I didn't know that was how soap was made."

"I'm glad you didn't," said William King. "I mean — it's disagreeable," he ended weakly. And then, to David's open joy, he said good-by and jogged off down the hill, leaving Mrs. Richie to her new responsibilities of discipline.

"Now, David, come here. I've got to scold you."

David promptly climbed up into the swing and settled himself in her lap. Then he snuggled his little nose down into her neck. "I'm a bear," he announced. "I'm eating you. Now, you scream and I'll roar."

"Oh, David, you little monkey! Listen to me; you weren't very polite to Dr. King."

"O-o-o-o-o-o!" roared the bear.

"You should make him feel you were glad to see him."

"I wasn't," mumbled David.

"But you must have manners, dear little boy."

"I have," David defended himself, sitting up straight. "I have them in my head; but I only use them sometimes."

Upon which the disciplinarian collapsed; "You rogue!" she said; "come here, and I'll give you 'forty kisses'!"

David was instantly silent; he shrank away, lifting his shoulder against his cheek and looking at her shyly. "I won't, dear!" she reassured him, impetuously; "truly I won't."

But she said to herself she must remember to repeat the speech about manners to the doctor; it would make him laugh.

William laughed easily when he came to the Stuffed Animal House. Indeed, he had laughed when he went away from it, and stopped for a minute at Dr. Lavendar's to tell him that Mrs. Richie was just as anxious as anybody that Sam Wright should attend to his business. "*Business!*" said the doctor, "much she knows about it!" And then he added that he was sure she would do her part to influence the boy to be more industrious. "And you may depend upon it, she won't allow any love-making," said William.

He laughed again suddenly, out loud, as he ate his supper that night, because some memory of the afternoon came into his head. When Martha, starting at the unusual sound, asked what he was laughing at, he told her he had found Mrs. Richie playing with David Allison. "They were like two children; I said I didn't know which was the younger. They were pretending they were shipwrecked; the swing was the vessel, if you please!"

"I suppose she was trying to amuse him," Mrs. King said. "That's a great mistake with children. Give a child a book, or put him down to some useful task; that's my idea."

"Oh, she was amusing herself," William explained. Mrs. King was silent.

"She gets up for breakfast now, on account of David; it's evidently a great undertaking!" the doctor said humorously.

Martha held her lips hard together.

"You ought to hear her housekeeping ideas," William rambled on. "I happened to say you wanted some lye for soap. She didn't know soap was made with lye! You would have laughed to hear her—"

But at that the leash broke: "*Laughed?* I hope not! I hope I wouldn't laugh because a woman of her age has no more sense than a child. And she gets up for breakfast, does she? Well, why shouldn't she get up for breakfast? I am very tired, but I get up for breakfast. I don't mean to be severe, William, and I never am; I'm only just. But I must say, flatly and frankly, that ignorance and laziness do not seem *funny* to me. Laugh? Would you laugh if I stayed in bed in the mornings, and didn't know how to make soap, and save your money for you? I guess not!"

The doctor's face reddened and he closed his lips with a snap. But Martha found no more fault with Mrs. Richie. After a while she said in that virtuous voice familiar to husbands, "William, I know you don't like to do it, so I cleaned all the medicine-shelves in your office this morning."

"Thank you," William said, curtly; and finished his supper in absolute silence.

CHAPTER XIII

DR. LAVENDAR was not sleeping very well that spring. He fell into the habit of waking at about three, just when the birds begin the scattered twittering that swells into full clamor and then dies suddenly into silence. In that gray stillness, broken by bird-calls, he used to occupy himself by thinking of his people.

"The name of the large upper chamber, facing the east, was Peace." And so this old pilgrim found it, lying in his four-poster, listening to the cries and calls in the jargonelle pear-tree in the corner of the garden, and watching the ghostly oblong of the window that faced the east, glimmer and brighten into the effulgence of day. It was then, with his old hands folded on his breast, that he thought about the Wrights—all three of them. . . .

It was a relief to know that Mrs. Richie would influence Sam to put his mind on his work; if the boy would do that, his father would be less irritated with him. And William's assurance that she would not allow any love-making ought to end his grandfather's worry. But while that worry lasted it must be utilized. . . .

The room was slipping out of the shadows. Dr. Lavendar could see the outline of the window distinctly. The bureau loomed up in the grayness like a rock; opposite the bed, under a high wooden mantel, was the cavernous blackness of the chimney. Dr. Lavendar reflected that it must be nearly four. . . .

The question was, when should he use this weapon of Benjamin Wright's worry, on the two hard hearts? He had made several attempts to use it, only to feel the blade turn in his hand: He had asked Mr. Wright when he was going to talk things over with Samuel, and the old man had instantly declared that he had changed his mind. He had mentioned to his senior warden that Benjamin was troubled about his grandson's sheep's-eyes, and Samuel's studied deafness had put an end to conversation. So Dr. Lavendar had made up his mind that a matter of this kind cannot be forced. A thirty-two-year-old wound is not to be healed in a day. He took any chance that offered to drop a suggestive word; but he did not try to hurry his Heavenly Father. For it was Dr. Lavendar's belief that God was more anxious about that reconciliation than he was. . . .

A line of light threaded its way under the window-curtain, and fell in a spot of fluid gold upon the mirror. He watched it move silently across the powdery surface; suddenly another dimpling pool appeared on the soot of the chimney-back, and his eye followed the tremulous beam to its entrance over the top of the shutter. The birds were shouting now in full voice. How fond Benjamin was of his poor caged creatures! Well, he had so little else to be fond of; "and I have so much," thought Dr. Lavendar, shamefacedly;— "all my people. And David, the rascal!" Then he chuckled; Dr. Lavendar was under the delusion that he was unprejudiced in regard to David; "a very unusual child!" he assured himself, gravely. No wonder

Mrs. Richie liked to have him.—And he would be the making of her! he would shake her out of her selfishness. "Poor girl, I guess, by the way she talks, she has never known anything but self. David will wake her up. But I've got to look out that she doesn't spoil him." It was this belief of what David might do for Mrs. Richie that had reconciled him to parting with the little boy.

His eyes wandered to the window; a glittering strip of green light between the bowed shutters meant that the sun was in the trees. Yes; to be sure, for the birds had suddenly stopped singing.

Dr. Lavendar yawned and looked at his watch; five o'clock. He would have liked to get up, but Mary would be worried if she knew he was awake so long before breakfast. Well; he must try to have a nap; no, the room was too light for that. He could see all the furniture; he could count the pleats in the sunburst of the tester; he could, perhaps, see to read? He put his hand out for *Robinson Crusoe*, and after that he possessed his soul in patience until he knew that Mary would allow him to come down-stairs.

It was in one of those peaceful dawns early in June that he decided that the moment had come to strike a decisive blow: he would go and talk to Benjamin of Sam's Sam, and though truth demanded that he should report Mrs. Richie's good sense he did not mean to insist upon it too much; Benjamin's anxiety was the Lord's opportunity—so Dr. Lavendar thought. He would admit Sam's sentimentality and urge putting the matter before his father. Then he would pin Benjamin down to a date. That secured, he would present a definite proposal to Samuel. "He is the lion in the way," he told himself anxiously; "I am pretty sure I can manage Benjamin." Yet surely if he could only put it properly to Samuel, if he could express the pitiful trouble in the old father's soul, the senior warden's heart would soften. "It must touch him!" Dr. Lavendar thought, and closed his eyes for a moment. . . .

When he said *Amen*, the bird-calls were like flutes of triumph.

On his way up the hill that morning, he paused under a great chestnut to talk to David Allison, who, a strapful of books over his shoulder, was running down the path to school. David was willing to be detained; he pulled some grass for Goliath and told Dr. Lavendar that Mrs. Richie had bought him a pair of suspenders. "And I said a bad word yesterday," he ended proudly.

"Well, now, I'm sorry to hear that."

"It's been in me a good while," David explained, "but yesterday I said it. It was 'damn.'"

"It's a foolish word, David; I never use it."

"You *don't?*" David said blankly, and all his pride was gone. They parted with some seriousness; but Dr. Lavendar was still chuckling when he turned in at Benjamin Wright's neglected carriage road where burdocks and plantains grew rank between the wheeltracks. As he came up to the house he saw Mr. Wright sitting out in the sun on the gravel of the driveway, facing his veranda. A great locust was dropping its honey-sweet blossoms all about—on his bent shoulders, on his green cashmere dressing-gown, on his shrunken knees, even one or two on the tall beaver hat. A dozen bird-cages had been placed in a row along the edge of the veranda, and he was nibbling orange-skin and watching the canaries twittering and hopping on their perches. As he heard the wheels of the buggy, he looked around, and raised a cautioning hand:

"Look out! You scare my birds. Rein in that mettlesome steed of yours! That green cock was just going to take a bath."

Goliath stopped at a discreet distance, and Dr. Lavendar sat still. There was a breathless moment of awaiting the pleasure of the green cock, who, balancing on the edge of his tub, his head on one side, looked with inquisitive eyes at the two old men before deciding to return to his perch and attack the cuttle-fish stuck between the bars of his cage. Upon which Mr. Wright swore at him with proud affection, and waved his hand to his visitor.

"Come on! Sorry I can't take you indoors. I have to sit out here and watch these confounded fowls for fear a cat will come along. There's not a soul I can trust to attend to it, so I have to waste my valuable time. Sit down."

Dr. Lavendar clambered out of the buggy, and came up to the porch where he was told to "*'Sh!*" while Mr. Wright held his breath to see if the green cock would not bathe, after all.

"That nigger of mine is perfectly useless. Look at that perch! Hasn't been cleaned for a week."

"Yes, suh; cleaned yesterday, suh," Simmons murmured, hobbling up with a handful of chickweed which he arranged on the top of one of the cages, its faint faded smell mingling with the heavy fragrance of the locust blossoms.

"Whiskey!" Mr. Wright commanded.

"Not for me," said Dr. Lavendar; and there was the usual snarl, during which Simmons disappeared. The whiskey was not produced.

"Lavendar, look at that cock—the scoundrel understands every word we say."

"He does look knowing. Benjamin, I just dropped in to tell you that I think you needn't worry so about Sam's Sam. Your neighbor has promised Willy King that she will help us with him. But I want you to talk the matter over with Samuel, and—"

"My *neighbor?*" the older man interrupted, his lower lip dropping with dismay. "Ye don't mean—the female at the Stuffed Animal House?"

"Yes; Mrs. Richie. She will snub him if it's necessary, William says; but she'll help us, by urging him to attend to his business. See?"

"I see—more than you do!" cried Benjamin Wright. "Much Willy King has accomplished! It's just what I've always said;—if you want a thing done, do it yourself. It's another case of these confounded canaries. If they are not to be eaten up by some devilish cat, I've got to sit out here and watch over 'em. If that boy is not to be injured, I've got to watch over him. My neighbor is going to help? Gad-a-mercy! Help!"

Dr. Lavendar took off his broad-brimmed felt hat and wiped his forehead with his big red bandanna. "Benjamin, what's got into you? A little being in love won't hurt him. Why, before I was his age I had lost my heart to my grandmother's first cousin!"

But the older man was not listening. His anger had suddenly hardened into alarm; he even forgot the canaries. "She's going to help? Lavendar, this is serious; it is very serious. He's got to be sent away! —if I have to see"—his voice trailed into a whisper; he looked at Dr. Lavendar with startled eyes.

The green cock hopped down into his glass tub and

began to ruffle and splash, but Benjamin Wright did not notice him. Dr. Lavendar beamed. "You mean you'll see his father?"

The very old man nodded. "Yes; I'll have to see —my son."

"Thank God!" said Dr. Lavendar.

"Dominie," said Mr. Wright, "it's better to 'make your manners when you've got your 'baccy.' Yes; I'll have to see—his father; if there's no other way of getting him out of town?"

"Of course there's no other way. Sam won't go without his father's consent. But you mustn't make play-writing the excuse; you mustn't talk about that."

"I won't talk about anything else," said Benjamin Wright.

Dr. Lavendar sighed, but he did not encourage perversity by arguing against it. "Benjamin," he said, "I will tell Samuel of your wish to see him—"

"My *wish!*"

Dr. Lavendar would not notice the interruption. "Will you appoint the time?"

"Oh, the sooner the better; get through with it! Get through with it!" He stared at his visitor and blinked rapidly; a moment later he shook all over. "Lavendar, it will kill me!" He was very frail, this shrunken old man in the green dressing-gown and high beaver hat, with his lower lip sucked in like a frightened child's. The torch of life, blown so often into furious flame by hurricanes of rage, had consumed itself, and it seemed now as if its flicker might be snuffed out by any slightest gust. "He may come up to-night," he mumbled, shivering in the hot sunshine and the drift of locust blossoms, as if he were cold.

"It can't be to-night; he's gone out West. He gets back Saturday. I'll send him up Sunday evening—if I can."

"Gad-a-mercy, Lavendar," Benjamin Wright said whimpering, "you've got to come, too!" He looked at his old friend with scared eyes. "I won't go to the gate with you. Can't leave these birds. I'm a slave to 'em."

But Dr. Lavendar saw that shaking legs were the real excuse; and he went away a little soberly in spite of his triumph. Would there be any danger to Benjamin from the agitation of the interview? He must ask Willy King. Then he remembered that the doctor had started for Philadelphia that morning; so there was nothing to do but wait. "I'm afraid there's some risk," he thought. "But Benjamin had better die in peace than live in anger. Oh, this play-writing business! If I could only depend on him to hold his tongue about it; but I can't." Then as he and Goliath trudged along in the sun, he gave himself up to his own rejoicings. "To think I was afraid to let him know that Mrs. Richie could be depended upon to help us!" He looked up as if in smiling confession to some unseen Friend. "Yes, indeed; 'He taketh the wise in their own craftiness.' It was the promise of Mrs. Richie's help that scared him into it! I won't be so crafty next time," he promised in loving penitence.

CHAPTER XIV

IN the stage, the day he started for Philadelphia, William King read over his Martha's memorandum with the bewildered carefulness peculiar to good husbands: ten yards of crash; a pitcher for sorghum; samples of yarn; an ounce of sachet-powder, and so forth.

"Now, what on earth does she want sachet-powder for?" he reflected. But he did not reflect long; it suddenly came into his mind that though Mrs. Richie had not given him any commission, he could nevertheless do something for her. He could go, when he was in Philadelphia, and call on her brother. "How pleased she'll be!" he said to himself. Naturally, with this project in mind, he gave no more thought to sachet-powders. He decided that he would turn up at Mr. Pryor's house at six o'clock; and Pryor would ask him to supper. It would save time to do that, and he needed to save time, for this one day in Philadelphia was to be very busy. He had those errands for Martha, and two medical appointments, and a visit to the tailor,—for of late William thought a good deal about his clothes and discovered that he was very shabby. He wished he had asked Mrs. Richie for her brother's address; it took so long to look it up in the Directory! Happily, the first name was unusual; there was only one Lloyd, or he would have given up the search. He could not have called on all the Johns or Thomases!

What with matching the yarn, and getting his drugs, and being terribly cowed by the tailor, William had a hurried day. However, he managed to reach Mr. Lloyd Pryor's house as the clock struck six. "Just in good time," he said to himself, complacently. Indeed, he was ahead of time, for it appeared that Mr. Pryor had not yet come home.

"But Miss Alice is in, sir," the smiling darky announced.

"Very well," said Wiliam King; "tell her 'Dr. King, from Old Chester.'" He followed the man into a parlor that seemed to the country doctor very splendid, and while he waited, he looked about with artless curiosity, thinking that he must tell Martha of all this grandeur. "No wonder she thinks we are stupid people in Old Chester," he thought. Now, certainly Martha had never had so disloyal a thought! At that moment he heard a girlish step, and Lloyd Pryor's daughter came into the room, — a pretty young creature, with blond hair parted over a candid brow, and sweet, frank eyes.

"Dr. King?" she said smiling.

"Doesn't resemble her in the least," the doctor thought, getting on his feet, and putting out a friendly hand. "I am just in from Old Chester," he said, "and I thought I'd come and say how-do-you-do to your father, and tell you the latest news of Mrs. Richie—"

The front door banged, and Lloyd Pryor pushed aside the curtain. — William had wondered what Martha would say to a curtain instead of a door! His blank panic as he heard the doctor's last word, turned his face white. ("Bad heart?" William asked himself.)

"*Dr. King!* Alice, you needn't wait."

Alice, nodding pleasantly, left them, and her father, setting his teeth, looked out through his curling eyelashes with deadly intentness.

"Thought I'd come in and say how-do-you-do?" William King said, hungry and friendly, but a little bewildered.

"Oh," said Mr. Pryor.

William put out his hand; there was a second's hesitation, then Lloyd Pryor took it — and dropped it quickly.

"All well?" the doctor asked awkwardly.

"Yes; yes. All well. Very well, thank you. Yes."

"I was just passing. I thought perhaps your sister would be pleased if I inquired; she didn't know I was coming, but—"

"You are very kind, I'm sure," the other broke in, his face relaxing. "I am sorry that just at this moment I can't ask you to stay, but—"

"Certainly not," William King said shortly; "I was just passing. If you have any message for Mrs. Richie—"

"Oh! Ah;—yes. Remember me to her. All well in Old Chester? Very kind in you to look me up. I am sorry I—that it happens that—good-by—"

Dr. King nodded and took himself off; and Lloyd Pryor, closing the door upon him, wiped the moisture from his forehead. "Alice, where are you?"

"In the dining-room, daddy dear," she said. "Who is Dr. King?"

He gave her a furtive look and then put his arm over her shoulder. "Nobody you know, Kitty."

"He said something about 'Mrs. Richie';—who is Mrs. Richie?"

"Some friend of his, probably. Got anything good for dinner, sweetheart?"

As for William King, he walked briskly down the street, his face very red. "Confound him!" he said. He was conscious of a desire to kick something. That evening, after a bleak supper at a marble-topped restaurant table, he tried to divert himself by going to see a play; he saw so many other things that he came out in the middle of it. "I guess I can get all the anatomy I want in my trade," he told himself; and sat down in the station to await the midnight train.

It was not until the next afternoon, when he climbed into the stage at Mercer and piled his own and Martha's bundles on the rack above him, that he really settled down to think the thing over. . . . What did it mean? The man had been willing to eat his bread; he had shown no offence at anything; what the deuce—! He pondered over it, all the way to Old Chester. When Martha, according to the custom of wives, inquired categorically concerning his day in Philadelphia, he dragged out most irritatingly vague answers. As she did not chance to ask, "Did you hunt up Mr. Lloyd Pryor? Did you go to his house? Did you expect an invitation and not receive it?" she was not informed on these topics. But when at last she did say, "And my sachet-powder?" he was compelled to admit that he had forgotten it.

Martha's lip tightened.

"I got the lye and stuff," her husband defended himself. "And what did you want sachet-powder for, anyway?"

But Martha was silent.

THE AWAKENING OF HELENA RICHIE

After supper William strolled over to Dr. Lavendar's, and sat smoking stolidly for an hour before he unbosomed himself. Dr. Lavendar did not notice his uncommunicativeness; he had his own preoccupations.

"William, Benjamin Wright seems to be a good deal shaken this spring?"

Silence.

"He's allowed himself to grow old. Bad habit."

Silence.

"Got out of the way of doing things. Hasn't walked down the hill and back for three years. He told me so himself."

"Indeed, sir?"

"For my part," Dr. Lavendar declared, "I have made a rule about such things, which I commend to you, young man: *As soon as you feel too old to do a thing*, DO IT!"

William gave the expected laugh.

"But he does seem shaken. Now, would it be safe, do you think, for him to—well, very much excited? Possibly angered?"

"It wouldn't take much to anger Mr. Wright."

"No, it wouldn't," Dr. Lavendar admitted. "William, suppose I could induce Samuel and his father to meet—"

"What!" The doctor woke up at that; he sat on the edge of his chair, his hands on his knees, his eyes starting in his head. "*What!*"

"Well, suppose I could?" Dr. Lavendar said. "I have a notion to try it. I don't know that I'll succeed. But suppose they met, and things shouldn't run smoothly, and there should be an explosion—would there be danger to Benjamin?"

William King whistled. "After all these years!"

THE AWAKENING OF HELENA RICHIE

Then he reflected. "Well, of course, sir, he is an old man. But he is like iron, Dr. Lavendar. When he had quinsy two years ago, I thought he had come to the end. Not a bit of it! He's iron. Only, of course, anger is a great drain. Better caution Sam not to cross him."

"Then there would be some danger?"

"I shouldn't like to see him get into a rage," the doctor admitted. "But why should he get into a rage, if they are going to patch things up? Good Lord!" said William King, gaping with astonishment; "at last!"

"I haven't said they would patch things up. But there is a chance that I can get 'em to talk over Benjamin's anxiety about Sam's Sam. Fact is, Benjamin is disturbed about the boy's sheep's-eyes. Sam thinks, you know, that he is in love with Mrs. Richie, and—"

"In love with Mrs. Richie!" William broke in angrily. "The idea of his bothering Mrs. Richie! it's outrageous. I don't wonder Mr. Wright is concerned. It's disgraceful. He ought to be thrashed!"

Dr. Lavendar drew a quick breath and let his pipe-hand fall heavily on the table beside him. "No, William, no; not thrashed. Not thrashed, William."

"Well, I don't know," the doctor said, doggedly; "it might do him good; a squirt of a boy!"

Dr. Lavendar sighed. They smoked silently for a while, and, indeed, it was not until it was almost time to go home that William burst out with his own wrongs.

"Confound him!" he ended, "what do you make of it, sir? Why, Dr. Lavendar, he sent his girl out of the room—didn't want her to talk to me! You'd have thought I was a case of measles. His one idea was to get rid of me as quickly as possible."

THE AWAKENING OF HELENA RICHIE

Dr. Lavendar thrust out his lower lip; then he scratched a match on the bottom of his chair, and held it out to Danny, who came forward with instant curiosity, sniffed, sneezed, and plainly hurt, retired to the hearth-rug.

"William, 'a moral, sensible and well-bred man will not affront—'"

"I'm not feeling affronted."

"Oh, aren't you?"

"No," William declared boldly, "not at all; not in the least! He's not worth it. But I'm all mixed up."

"Daniel," said Dr. Lavendar, "how dare you lie on the rug? Willy, when I was young—I mean when I was younger—we children were never allowed to come nearer the fire than the outside edge of the hearth-rug. I feel wicked now, whenever I come over that edge. But look at that scoundrel Danny!"

Danny opened one eye and beat his stub of a tail softly on the rug. William King was silent. Dr. Lavendar began to sing:

> "Queen Victoria's very sick;
> Napoleon's got the measles.
> Why don't you take Sebastopol?
> Pop goes the weasel!"

"Dr. Lavendar, why do you keep trying to change the subject? What do you think about Mrs. Richie's brother?"

"Well, Willy, my boy, I think he's not given to hospitality."

"Ah, now, no shenanigan!" poor William pleaded. "Do you suppose he's up to some monkey-shines? Do you suppose I took him unawares, and he was afraid to entertain me?"

Dr. Lavendar chuckled. "'Fraid he might entertain a Recording Angel unawares?"

William shook his head. "There was something wrong, or I don't know human nature."

"Willy, if you do know human nature, you are the only living man who does. But, perhaps, now, it really wasn't convenient?"

"Convenient!" William burst out. "In Old Chester we don't talk about *convenience* when a man knocks at the door at supper-time!"

"But Philadelphia isn't Old Chester," Dr. Lavendar reminded him, mildly. "When you've seen as much of the world as I have, you'll realize that. I once was short of my railroad fare in New York. I—well, a poor creature asked me for some money to buy a coat. It was a dreadfully cold day. It left me just three dollars short of my fare home; so I stepped into the Bible House—you know the Bible House?—and just stated the case to the head clerk, and said I would be obliged if he would lend me the amount. Willy," Dr. Lavendar got very red; "I assure you—"

"You don't say so, sir!" said William King respectfully; but he bent down and pulled Danny's ear.

"Yes," said Dr. Lavendar; "yes, indeed! I will not repeat what he said; you would be indignant. I just mention the circumstance to show you how differently people look at things. If any gentleman got into such a fix in Old Chester, of course he would just speak to Sam Wright, or you, or me. Or take your own case; if any stranger came on business at dinner-time, you would say, 'Sit down, sir'!"

William thought of Martha and moved uneasily in his chair.

"But," proceeded Dr. Lavendar, "it is not so everywhere. Convenience is considered. It isn't hospitable; but you can't say it's wicked?"

"Dr. Lavendar," said William King, "you don't believe that was the reason."

The old minister sighed. "I'm afraid I don't, my boy; but I thought maybe you might."

"No, sir! There's something wrong with that fellow. I don't mean to judge, but somehow, instinctively, I don't trust him."

"Well," said Dr. Lavendar; "I wouldn't judge; but —I'd trust my instincts."

William grinned; then he sighed. "I won't tell Mrs. Richie about seeing him. She'd be mortified at his behavior. If she knew as much of the wickedness of the world as we do, she might even be suspicious! But, thank God, she's not that kind of a woman. I don't like worldly-wise ladies."

Dr. Lavendar nodded. "Black sheep can pull the wool over people's eyes better than white ones can. Do you know, one reason why I hesitated about letting her have David, was just because I didn't take to her brother? For that matter, David doesn't take to him either; — and Danny can't abide him. And William, I have a great respect for the judgment of my betters in such matters! Yes; I almost kept the little monkey myself; but I suppose it's better for him to be with a woman?"

"Of course it is," said William King, and Dr. Lavendar's face fell. "I think she wants to adopt him," William added.

Dr. Lavendar shook his head. "I haven't made up my mind about that yet. Not only because of the brother;—he comes so rarely he doesn't count. But I want to make sure she can be trusted to bring a child up."

"I don't think there could be a better person," the doctor declared, warmly. "She has a lovely nature."

"A pretty creature," Dr. Lavendar ruminated; "Martha fond of her?"

"Oh, yes indeed," William said enthusiastically;—"at least, I don't know that I ever happened to hear her speak of it; but of course she is. Nobody could help it. She is a sweet woman, as you say."

"Well," said Dr. Lavendar, "get Martha to be neighborly with her. She needs neighboring. And Martha could teach her so many things—she's such a sensible woman."

"Yes; Martha is sensible," William agreed. "Dr. Lavendar, did you ever notice how, when she laughs, she has a way of putting her hands on the top of her head, and sort of drawing them down over her eyes like a girl? It's as pretty!"

Dr. Lavendar tried to remember. "Why, no," he said; "I don't know that I ever noticed it. Martha doesn't laugh very often."

"Martha?" William repeated puzzled. "Oh—I was speaking of Mrs. Richie."

"Oh," said Dr. Lavendar.

CHAPTER XV

EVERY Sunday morning Mr. Samuel Wright and Mr. Thomas Dilworth — the one pale and pompous, the other rosy and smiling—took up the collection in St. Michael's. A mahogany pole with a black velvet pouch on one end, was thrust solemnly into each pew, then drawn back with very personal pauses —which were embarrassing if you had forgotten to put some change into your glove before starting for church. When these poles had raked every pew, they were carried up the aisle to Dr. Lavendar, who, taking hold of the purple tassel on the bottom of each bag, turned the contents into a silver plate. The change came out with a fine clatter; we children used to keep awake on purpose to hear it. Once in a while a bill would rustle out with the silver and balance on the top of the little heap in such an exciting way that Dr. Lavendar had to put his hand over it to keep it from blowing off as he carried the plate to the communion-table—we did not say "altar" in Old Chester. This done, Mr. Wright and Mr. Dilworth would tiptoe solemnly back to their respective pews. When the service was over the senior warden always counted the money. On this summer Sunday morning, when he went into the vestry for that purpose, he found Dr. Lavendar just hanging up his black gown behind the door.

THE AWAKENING OF HELENA RICHIE

"Dr. Lavendar," said the senior warden, "you will, I am sure, be pleased when I inform you that there is a good collection. Mrs. Richie put in a five-dollar bill."

"Well," said Dr. Lavendar, "we need it. Your father sent me a check the other day; but we need some more."

Mr. Wright did not comment upon his father's generosity; instead, he slid the money from the silver plate on to the table and began to count it. Dr. Lavendar looked at him over his spectacles; when only half a dozen coppers were left, he said suddenly:

"Samuel!"

The senior warden looked up; "Yes, sir?"

"Samuel, your father has spoken to me of you."

Mr. Wright looked down; then he slowly picked up the last penny.

"Yes; he spoke of you. Samuel, I have something to say to you of a very serious nature."

"We have nine dollars and seventy-seven cents," said the senior warden.

"Your father," said Dr. Lavendar, "has expressed a willingness to see you."

Mr. Wright put the money into a small canvas bag, and pulling the drawing-string up, wound it round and round the top; his hands trembled.

"He has some concern about your Sam—as you have yourself. He is disturbed because the boy has lost his heart to your tenant, Mrs. Richie."

"Call it twelve dollars," Samuel said, embarrassed to the point of munificence. He put the canvas bag in his pocket, and rose. "I'll deposit this to-morrow, sir," he added, as he had added every Sunday morning for the last twenty years.

"Samuel," said Dr. Lavendar, sternly, "sit down!"

With involuntary haste the senior warden sat down, but he would not look at Dr. Lavendar. "It is not my purpose or desire," he said, "to be disrespectful, but I must request you, sir—"

"To mind my own business? I will, Sam, I will! My business is to admonish you: *Leave there thy gift before the altar, and go thy way. First, be reconciled to thy brother, and then come and offer thy gift.*"

Samuel Wright cleared his throat. "I cannot, Dr. Lavendar, discuss this matter with you. I must be my own judge."

"I have heard that a man might be his own lawyer," said Dr. Lavendar, smiling; "but you can't be your own judge. The Christian religion judges you, Samuel, and convicts you. Your father is willing to see you; he has taken the first step. Think what that means to a man like your father! Now listen to me; I want to tell you what it's all about."

"I have no desire, sir, to be informed. I—"

Dr. Lavendar checked him gently: "I am sure you will listen, Samuel, no matter what your decision may be." Then, very cautiously, he began about young Sam. "Your father thinks he ought to get away from Old Chester; he's worried because of Mrs. Richie."

"You know my sentiments, sir, in regard to my son's idiocy."

"Oh, come, come! Falling in love is a harmless amusement," said Dr. Lavendar; "but your father does take it a good deal to heart. He wants to get him out of town. However, to send him away without letting him know why, is difficult; and the last thing would be to let him think we take his love-making seriously! Therefore your father thinks some kind of excuse has to be made."

THE AWAKENING OF HELENA RICHIE

Here Dr. Lavendar became elaborately casual; he had decided that he must prepare his senior warden for a possible reference to a dangerous topic. "He mustn't be taken unawares," Dr. Lavendar had told himself. But he quailed, now that the moment of preparation had come. "Your father thinks the excuse might be the finding a publisher for some poetry that Sam has written."

Samuel Wright's large pallid face suddenly twitched; his dull eyes blazed straight at Dr. Lavendar; "Finding a publisher — for poetry! Dr. Lavendar, rather than have my son encouraged in making what you call 'poetry,' I'd let him *board* at Mrs. Richie's!"

"Well," said Dr. Lavendar, easily, "never mind about his poetry; your father has an idea that life in a small place with only your own interests, is narrowing; and I guess he's right to some extent. Anyway this project of a journey isn't a bad one. Sam has never been further from his mother's apron-string in his life, than Mercer."

"My dear Dr. Lavendar," said Samuel, pompously, "a boy attached to that string will never have the chance to fall into temptation."

"My dear Samuel," said Dr. Lavendar, "a boy attached to that string may never have the chance to overcome temptation — which would be almost as serious. I tell you, Sam, safety that depends on an apron-string is very unsafe!"

"My son is not to be trusted, sir."

"Samuel!" Dr. Lavendar protested with indignation, "how can he become worthy of trust without being trusted? You have no more right to shut up a grown man in Old Chester for fear of temptation, than you would have to keep a growing boy in his first pair of trousers! Why, Sam, there isn't any virtue where there has never been any temptation. Virtue is just temptation, overcome. Hasn't that ever struck you? However, that's not the point. The point is, that your father has expressed a willingness to meet you."

Mr. Wright made no answer.

"He will talk over with you this matter of Sam's falling in love. Whether you agree with him that the boy should go away, is not important. What is important is his desire to see you."

"I said," Samuel Wright broke out, with a violence that made Dr. Lavendar start—"I said I would never speak to him again! I took my oath. I cannot break my oath. 'He that sweareth to his own hurt, and changeth not—'"

"Yes," said Dr. Lavendar; "'to his own hurt,' but not to somebody else's hurt. You swore to your father's, to your children's, to the community's hurt. Change as quickly as you can. Come up the hill with me to-night."

"I can't," Samuel Wright said hoarsely, and into his hard eyes came the same look of childish terror that the old minister had seen in Benjamin Wright's face when he sat in the hot sunshine watching the canaries.

Then Dr. Lavendar began to plead. . . .

It was a long struggle. Sometimes it really seemed as if, as the senior warden had said, he "could not" do it; as if it were a physical impossibility. And there is no doubt that to change a habit of thought which has endured for thirty-two years involves a physical as well as a spiritual effort, which may cause absolute anguish. Mr. Wright's face was white; twice he wiped the perspiration from his forehead; half a dozen times he said in an agonized tone, "I cannot do it; I *cannot*."

"Samuel, your father is very old; he is very feeble; but he has had the strength to take the first step. Haven't you the strength to take the second? Will you carry your wicked quarrel to his grave? No, Sam, no! I am sure you won't." ...

An hour later, when Dr. Lavendar sat down to a dinner of more than ordinary Sunday coldness, his old face was twinkling with pleasure. Samuel had promised to go with him that night to The Top! Perhaps as the still afternoon softened into dusk his joy began to cast a shadow of apprehension. If so, he refused to notice it. It was the Lord's business, and "He moves in a mysterious way," he hummed to himself, waiting in the warm darkness for Samuel to call for him,—for both the quailing men had made Dr. Lavendar's presence a condition of the interview.

At half-past seven Mr. Wright arrived. He was in a shiny box-buggy, behind a smart sorrel. He was dressed in his black and solemn best, and he wore his high hat with a flat brim which only came out at funerals. His dignity was so tremendous that his great bulk seemed to take even more than its share of room in the buggy. When he spoke, it was with a laboriousness that crushed the breath out of any possible answer. As they drove up the hill he cleared his throat every few minutes. Once he volunteered the statement that he had told Sam not to stay late at— at—

"Oh," said Dr. Lavendar, "your father will pack him off;—he will probably take the opportunity to call on Mrs. Richie," he added smiling. But Sam's father did not smile. And, indeed, Dr. Lavendar's own face was sober when they turned in between the sagging old gate-posts at The Top.

When the moment came to get out of the buggy, Samuel looked at his companion dumbly; a sort of paralysis seemed to hold him in his seat. When he did move, Dr. Lavendar heard him gasp for breath, and in the darkness, as he hitched the sorrel to a staple in one of the big locusts, his face went white. The large manner which had dominated Old Chester for so many years was shrinking and shrivelling; the whole man seemed, somehow, smaller. . . .

Benjamin Wright, in his mangy beaver hat, sitting quaking in his library, heard their steps on the veranda. As soon as supper was over, he had dismissed his rejoicing grandson, and long before it was necessary, had bidden Simmons light the lamps; but as night fell, it occurred to him that darkness would make things easier, and in a panic, he shuffled about and blew them all out. A little later, he had a surge of terror; he couldn't bear *that voice* in the dark!

"You! Simmons!" he called across the hall. "Light the lamps!"

"I done lit 'em, suh—" Simmons expostulated from the pantry, and then looked blankly at the black doorway of the library. "I 'clare to goodness, they's gone out," he mumbled to himself; and came in, to stand on one leg and scratch a match on the sole of his carpet slipper.

"Don't light all four, you stupid nigger!" the old man screamed at him.

When Simmons left him he lit a cigar, his fingers trembling very much; it went out almost at once, and he threw it away and took another. Just as he heard that ponderous step on the veranda, he took a third—

but only to throw it, too, still smouldering, into the empty fireplace.

Dr. Lavendar came in first. His face was very grave; he made no conventional pretence of ease. Behind him, in the doorway, loomed the other figure. Out in the hall, Simmons, his bent old back flattened against the wall, his jaw chattering with amazement, stood, clutching at the door-knob and staring after the visitors.

"Come in!" said Benjamin Wright. "Hello, Lavendar. Hello—"

Alas! at that moment Samuel's cracked and patched-up self-respect suddenly crumbled;—his presence of mind deserted him, and scrambling like an embarrassed boy into a marked discourtesy, he thrust both hands into his pockets. Instantly he realized his self-betrayal, but it was too late; his father, after a second's hesitation, occupied both his hands with the decanter and cigar-box.

"Well; here we are, Benjamin!" said Dr. Lavendar.

"Take a cigar," said the very old man; he held the box out, and it shook so that the loose cigars jarred within it. Dr. Lavendar helped himself. "Have one—" Benjamin Wright said, and thrust the box at the silent standing figure.

"I—do not smoke." Samuel slid into a seat near the door, and balancing his hat carefully on his knees twisted one leg about the leg of his chair.

His father bustled around to the other side of the table. "That doggoned nigger brought up Kentucky instead of Monongahela!" He lifted the decanter and began to fill the glasses.

"Hold on! hold on! Don't swamp us," said Dr. Lavendar. He leaned over to rescue his tumbler, and

his good-natured scolding made an instant's break in
the intensity.

"Have some?" said Mr. Wright, turning to his son.

"I—do not drink." The banker uncoiled his leg,
and put his hat on the floor.

His father pounded the decanter down on the table.
"Simmons!" he called out; "light the rest of these
lamps, you—you freckled nigger! Gad-a-mercy! niggers
have no sense."

Simmons came stumbling in, the whites of his yellow
eyes gleaming with excitement. While he was
fumbling over the lamps, his lean brown fingers all
thumbs, Benjamin Wright insisted upon filling Dr.
Lavendar's tumbler with whiskey until it overflowed
and had to be sopped up by the old minister's red
bandanna.

As soon as Simmons could get out of the room, Dr.
Lavendar settled himself to the business which had
brought them together. He said to his senior warden,
briefly, that his father was concerned about Sam's attentions
to Mrs. Richie; "he thinks it would be an especially
good time to have the boy see a little of the
world, if you will consent? He says it's 'narrowing
to live in Old Chester,'" said Dr. Lavendar, slyly
jocose;—but Samuel refused to smile, and the old
minister went on with determined cheerfulness. "I
think, myself, that it would be good for Sam to travel.
You know

> 'Home-keeping youths
> Have ever homely wits.'"

"A boy," said the senior warden, and stopped; his
voice cracked badly and he cleared his throat; "a boy
—Dr. Lavendar;—is better at home."

"SAMUEL SLID INTO A CHAIR NEAR THE DOOR"

THE AWAKENING OF HELENA RICHIE

The old minister gave him a quick look—his senior warden was trembling! The cloak of careful pomposity with which for so many years this poor maimed soul had covered its scars, was dropping away. He was clutching at it—clearing his throat, swinging his foot, making elaborate show of ease; but the cloak was slipping and slipping, and there was the man of fifty-six cringing with the mortification of youth! It was a sight from which to turn away even the most pitying eyes. Dr. Lavendar turned his away; when he spoke it was with great gentleness.

"I don't know that I quite agree with you, Sam, any more than with your father; but still, if you don't want the boy to go away, can't we convince your father that he is in no real danger of a broken heart? If he goes too far, I am sure we can trust Mrs. Richie to snub him judiciously. You think so, don't you, Samuel?"

"Yes;—Dr. Lavendar."

"Do you hear that, Wright?"

Benjamin Wright took off his hat and banged it down on the table. Then he threw away another barely lighted cigar, put his hand into the blue ginger-jar for some orange-skin, and looked closely at his son; his agitation had quite disappeared. "I hear," he said calmly.

But as he grew calm, Mr. Samuel Wright's embarrassment became more agonizing, nor was it lessened by the very old man's quite obvious interest in it; his head, in its brown wig, was inclined a little to one side, like a canary's, and his black eyes helped out the likeness—except that there was a carefully restrained gleam of humor in them. But he said nothing. To cover up the clamorous silence between

THE AWAKENING OF HELENA RICHIE

father and son, Dr. Lavendar talked a good deal, but rather at random. He was confounded by the situation. Had he made a mistake, after all, in insisting upon this interview? In his own mind he was asking for wisdom, but aloud he spoke of the weather. His host gave no conversational assistance except an occasional monosyllable, and his senior warden was absolutely dumb. As for the subject which brought them together, no further reference was made to it.

"Take some more whiskey, Dominie," said Mr. Wright. His eyes were glittering; it was evident that he did not need any more himself.

Dr. Lavendar said, "No, thank you," and rose. Samuel shot up as though a spring had been released.

"Going?" said Benjamin Wright; "a short call, considering how long it is since we've met;—Lavendar."

Samuel cleared his throat. "'Night," he said huskily. Again there was no hand-shaking; but as they reached the front door, Benjamin Wright called to Dr. Lavendar, who stepped back into the library. Mr. Wright had put on his hat, and was chewing orange-skin violently. "It ain't any use trying to arrange anything with— So I'll try another tack." He came close to Dr. Lavendar, plucking at the old minister's black sleeve, his eyes snapping and his jaws working fast; he spoke in a delighted whisper. "But, Lavendar—"

"Yes."

"He wouldn't take a cigar."

"Samuel never smokes," Dr. Lavendar said shortly.

"And he wouldn't take a drink of whiskey."

"He's a very temperate man."

"Lavendar—"

"Yes?"

"Lavendar—*it was efficacious!*"

CHAPTER XVI

"THE play is my life—next to you," Sam Wright's Sam was saying to his father's tenant. He had left The Top before the two visitors arrived, and as Dr. Lavendar had foreseen, had gone straight to the Stuffed Animal House. . . .

Helena was in a low chair, with David nestling sleepily in her arms; Sam, looking up at her like a young St. John, half sat, half knelt, on the step at her feet. The day had been hot, and evening had brought no coolness; under the sentinel locusts on either side of the porch steps the night was velvet black; but out over the garden there were stars. A faint stirring of the air tilted the open bowls of the evening-primroses, spilling a heavy sweetness into the shadows. The house behind them was dark, for it was too hot for lamps. It was very still and peaceful and commonplace—a woman, a dozing child, and the soft night. Young Sam, so sensitive to moods, had fallen at once into the peace and was content to sit silently at Helena's feet. . . . Then David broke in upon the tranquillity by remarking, with a sigh, that he must go to bed.

"I heard the clock strike," he said sadly.

"I think you are a very good little boy," Helena declared with admiration.

"Dr. Lavendar said I must," David explained

crossly. "You're misbehavious if you don't do what Dr. Lavendar says. Mrs. Richie, is heaven up in the sky?"

"Why, I suppose so," she said hesitating.

"What do they stand on?" David inquired. "There isn't any floor," he insisted doggedly, for she laughed under her breath.

Helena looked over at Sam, who was not in the least amused. Then she kissed the top of David's head. "I wish I could make his hair curl," she said. "I knew a little boy once—" she stopped and sighed.

She took the sleepy child up-stairs herself. Not for many guests would she have lost the half-hour of putting him to bed. When she came back her mind was full of him: "He hates to go to bed early," she told Sam, "but he always walks off at eight, without a word from me, because he promised Dr. Lavendar he would. I think it is wonderful."

Sam was not interested.

"And he is so funny! He says such unexpected things. He told me yesterday that Sarah 'slept out loud';—Sarah's room is next to his."

"What did he mean?" Sam said, with the curious literalness of the poetic temperament, entirely devoid of humor. But he did not wait for an answer; he locked his hands about his knee, and leaning his head back, looked up through the leaves at the stars. "How sweet the locust blossoms are!" he said. One of the yellow-white flakes fell and touched his cheek.

"They are falling so now," she said, "that the porch has to be swept twice a day."

He smiled, and brushing his palm along the step, caught a handful of them; "Every night you sit here all alone; I wish—"

THE AWAKENING OF HELENA RICHIE

"Oh, I like to be alone," she interrupted. As the balm of David's presence faded, and the worship in the young man's eyes burned clearer, that old joke of Lloyd's stabbed her. She wished he would go. "How does the drama get on?" she asked, with an effort.

Sam frowned and said something of his father's impatience with his writing. "But I am only happy whe I am writing; and when I am with you. The play is my life,—next to you."

"Please don't!" she said; and then held her breath to listen. "I think I hear David. Excuse me a minute." She fled into the house and up-stairs to David's room. "Did you want me, precious?" she said, panting.

David opened dreaming eyes and looked at her. He had called out in his sleep, but was quiet again, and did not need her eager arms, her lips on his hair, her voice murmuring in his ear. But she could not stop cuddling the small warm body; she forgot Sam and his play, and even her own dull ache of discontent,—an ache that was bringing a subtle change into her face, a faint line on her forehead, and a suggestion of depth, and even pain, in the pleasant shallows of her leaf-brown eyes. Perhaps the discontent was mere weariness of the whole situation; if so, she did not recognize it for what it was. Her fellow-prisoner, straining furtively against the bond of the flesh which was all that held him to her, might have enlightened her, but he took her love so for granted, that he never suspected the discontent. However, watching David, Helena was herself unconscious of it; when she was sure the little boy was sound asleep she stole the "forty kisses," which as yet he had not granted; folded the sheet back lest he might be too hot; drew a thin

THE AWAKENING OF HELENA RICHIE

blanket over his feet, and then stood and looked at him. Suddenly, remembering Sam Wright, she turned away; but hesitated at the door, and came back for one more look. At last, with a sigh, she went downstairs.

"He loves your rabbits," she told Sam; "he has named them Mr. George Rufus Smith and Mrs. Minnie Lily Smith."

"It is all finished," said Sam.

"What is finished?"

"The drama," the young man explained.

"Oh," she said, "do forgive me! My mind is so full of David, I can't think of anything else."

He smiled at that. "You couldn't do anything I wouldn't forgive."

"Couldn't I?"

He looked up at her, wistfully. "I love you, you know."

"Oh, please, please—"

"I love you," he said, trembling.

"Sam," she said—and in her distress she put her hand on his shoulder—"you don't really care for me. I am so much older; and—there are other reasons. Oh, *why* did I come here!" she burst out. "You displease me very much when you talk this way!" She pushed her chair back, and would have risen but for his detaining hand upon her arm.

"Will you marry me?"

"No! of course I won't!"

"Why?"

"Because—" she stopped; then, breathlessly: "I only want to be let alone. I came to Old Chester to be alone. I didn't want to thrust myself on you,— any of you!"

THE AWAKENING OF HELENA RICHIE

"You never did," he said wonderingly. "You? Why, there never was anybody so reserved, so—shy, almost. That's one reason I love you, I guess," he said boyishly.

"You mustn't love me."

"Will you marry me?" he repeated. "Oh, I know; it is like asking an angel to come down out of heaven—"

"An angel!"

"Mrs. Richie, isn't it possible for you to care, just a little, and marry me?"

"No, Sam; indeed it isn't. Please don't think of it any more."

"Is it because you love him, still?"

"Love—*him?*" she breathed.

"He is dead," Sam said; "and I thought from something you once said, that you didn't really love him. But if you do—"

"My—husband, you mean? No! I don't. I never did. That's not the reason; oh, why did I come here?" she said in a distressed whisper.

At that he lifted his head. "Don't be unhappy. It doesn't matter about me." His eyes glittered. "'All is dross that is not Helena'! I shall love you as long as I live, even if you don't marry me. Perhaps —perhaps I wouldn't if you did!"

He did not notice her involuntary start of astonishment; he rose, and lifting his arms to the sky, stood motionless, rapt, as if in wordless appeal to heaven. Then his arms dropped. "No," he said, speaking with curious thoughtfulness: "no; you would be human if you could marry a fool like me." Helena made a protesting gesture, but he went on, quietly: "Oh, yes; I am a fool. I've been told so all my life; but I knew it, anyhow. Nobody need have told me.

Of course you couldn't marry me! If you could, you would be like me. And I would not want that. No; you are God to me. Stay divine."

Helena put her hands over her ears.

"But please, can't you love me? We needn't be married, if you'd rather not. If you'll just love me a little?"

The innocence of the plea for love without marriage struck her with a dull humor that faded into annoyance that she should see the humor. It was an uncomfortable sensation; and she hated discomfort; in her desire to escape from it, she spoke with quick impatience. "No, Sam, of course not,—not the way you want me to. Why, you are just a boy, you know!" she added, lightly.

But Sam threw himself on his knees beside her, and pressed his head against her skirts. "Oh, are you *sure*, Mrs. Richie? Why, it seems to me you might— just a little? Can't you? You see, I'm so lonely," he ended pitifully. His innocent solemn eyes were limpid with tears, and he looked at her with terrified beseeching, like a lost child.

The tears that sprang to her eyes were almost motherly; for an impetuous instant she bent over him, then drew back sharply, and the tears dried in a hot pang of shame. "No, Sam; I can't. Oh, I am so sorry! Please forgive me—I ought not to have let you—but I didn't know—yes; I did know! And I ought to have stopped you. It's my fault. Oh, how selfish I have been! But it's horrible to have you talk this way! Won't you please not say anything more?" She was incoherent to the point of crying.

Sam looked out over the dark garden in silence. "Well," he said slowly, "if you can't, then I don't want to see you. It would hurt me too much to see you. I'll go away. I will go on loving you, but I will go away, so that I needn't see you. Yes; I will leave Old Chester—"

"Oh, I wish you would," she said.

"You don't love me," he repeated, in a sort of hopeless astonishment; "why, I can't seem to believe it! I thought you must—I love you so. But no, you don't. Not even just a little. Well—"

And without another word he left her. She could not hear his step on the locust flowers on the porch.

CHAPTER XVII

"*I WISH your confounded Old Chester people would mind their own affairs! This prying into things that are none of their business is—*"

Lloyd Pryor stopped; read over what he had written, and ground his teeth. No; he couldn't send her such a letter. It would call down a storm of reproach and anger and love. And, after all, it wasn't her fault; this doctor fellow had said that she did not know of his call. Still, if she hadn't been friendly with those people, the man wouldn't have thought of "looking him up"! Then he remembered that he had been the one to be friendly with the "doctor fellow"; and that made him angry again. But his next letter was more reasonable, and so more deadly.

"*You will see that if I had not happened to be at home, it might have been a very serious matter. I must ask you to consider my position, and discourage your friends in paying any attention to me.*"

This, too, he tore up, with a smothered word. It wouldn't do; if he wounded her too much, she was capable of taking the next train—! And so he wrote, with non-committal brevity:

"*I have to be in Mercer Friday night, and I think I can get down to Old Chester for a few hours between stages on Saturday. I hope your cook has recovered, and we can have some dinner? Tell David he can get his sling ready; and do, for Heaven's sake, fend off visitors!*" Then he added a postscript: "*I want you all to myself.*" He smiled as he wrote that, but half shook his head. He did not (such was his code) enjoy being agreeable for a purpose. "But I can't help it," he thought, frowning; "she is so very difficult, just now."

He was right about the postscript; she read the letter with a curl of her lip. "'A few hours,'" she said; then—"'I want you all to myself.'" The delicate color flooded into her face; she crushed the letter to her lips, her eyes running over with laughing tears.

"Oh, David," she cried,—"let's go and tell Maggie —we must have such a dinner! He's coming!"

"Who?" said David.

"Why, Mr. Pryor, dear little boy. I want you to love him. Will you love him?"

"I'll see," said David; "is Alice coming?"

Instantly her gayety flagged. "No, dear, no!"

"Well; I guess she's too old to play with;" David consoled himself; "she's nineteen."

"I must speak to Maggie about the dinner," Helena said dully. But when she talked to the woman, interest came back again; this time he should not complain of his food! Maggie smiled indulgently at her excitement.

"My, Mrs. Richie, I don't believe no wife could take as good care of Mr. Pryor—and you just his sister!"

For the rest of that glowing afternoon, Helena was very happy. She almost forgot that uncomfortable scene with Sam Wright. She talked eagerly of Mr. Pryor to David, quite indifferent to the child's lack of interest. She had many anxious thoughts about what she should wear. If it was a very hot day, how would her white dimity do? Or the thin sprigged blue and white? it was so pretty—bunches of blue flowers on a cross-barred muslin, and made with three flounces and a bertha. She was wandering about the garden just before tea, trying to decide this point, when David came to say that a gentleman wanted to see her. David did not know his name;—he was the old tangled gentleman who lived in the big house on the hill.

"*Oh!*" Helena said; she caught her lip between her teeth, and looked at David with frightened eyes. The child was instantly alert.

"I'll run and tell him to go home," he said protectingly.

But she shook her head. "I've got to see him—oh, David!"

The little boy took hold of her skirt, reassuringly; "I'll not let him hurt you," he said. She hardly noticed that he kept close beside her all the way to the house.

Mr. Benjamin Wright was sitting on the lowest step of the front porch. His trembling head was sunk forward on his breast; he did not lift it at her step, but peered up from under the brim of his dusty beaver hat; then seeing who it was, he rose, pushing himself up by gripping at the step behind him and clutching his cane first in one hand, then in the other. His face, like old ivory chiselled into superb lines of melancholy power, was pallid with fatigue. On his feet, with exaggerated politeness, he took off his hat with a sweeping bow.

"Madam; your very obedient!"

"Good afternoon," she said breathlessly.

THE AWAKENING OF HELENA RICHIE

Benjamin Wright, tottering a little, changed his cane from his left to his right hand, and chewed orange-skin fiercely. "I have called, madam—"

But she interrupted him. "Won't you come in and sit down, sir? And pray allow me to get you a glass of wine."

"Come in? No, madam, no. We are simple rustics here in Old Chester; we must not presume to intrude upon a lady of such fashion as you. I fear that some of us have already presumed too much"—he paused for breath, but lifted one veined old hand to check her protest—"too much, I say! Far too much! I come, madam, to apologize; and to tell you—" Again he stopped, panting; "to tell you that I insist that you forbid further intrusion—at least on the part of my grandson."

"But," she said, the color hot in her face, "he does not intrude. I don't know what you mean. I—"

"Oh, madam, you are too kind; I am sure you know what I mean; it is your excessive kindness that permits the visits of a foolish boy—wearying, I am sure, to a lady so accustomed to the world. I will ask you to forbid those visits. Do you hear me?" he cried shrilly, pounding the gravel with his cane. "Gad-a-mercy! Do you hear me? You will forbid his visits!"

"You are not very polite, Mr. Old Gentleman," said David thoughtfully.

"David!" Helena protested.

Benjamin Wright, looking down at the little figure planted in front of her, seemed to see him for the first time.

"Who is this? Your child?"

"A little boy who is visiting me," she said. "David, run away."

THE AWAKENING OF HELENA RICHIE

Benjamin Wright made a sneering gesture. "No, no; don't dismiss him on my account. But that a child should visit you is rather remarkable. I should think his parents—"

"Hush!" she broke in violently. "Go, David, go!"

As the child went sulkily back to the garden, she turned upon her visitor. "How dare you! Dr. Lavendar brought him to me; I will not hear another word! And—and I don't know what you mean, anyhow. You are a cruel old man; what have I ever done to you? I have never asked your grandson to come here. I don't want him. I have told him so. And I never asked you!"

Benjamin Wright cackled. "No; I have not been so far honored. I admit that. You have kept us all at arm's length,—except my boy." Then, bending his fierce brows on her, he added, "But what does Lavendar mean by sending a child—to you? What's he thinking of? Except, of course, he never had any sense. Old Chester is indeed a foolish place. Well, madam, you will, I know, *protect yourself*, by forbidding my grandson to further inflict his company upon you? And I will remove my own company, which is doubtless tiresome to you."

He bowed again with contemptuous ceremony, and turned away.

The color had dropped out of Helena's face; she was trembling very much. With a confused impulse she called to him, and even ran after him for a few steps down the path. He turned and waited for her. She came up to him, her breath broken with haste and fear.

"Mr. Wright, you won't—" Her face trembled with dismay. In her fright she put her hand on his arm and shook it; "you won't—?"

174

THE AWAKENING OF HELENA RICHIE

As he looked into her stricken eyes, his own suddenly softened. "Why—" he said, and paused; then struck the ground with his stick sharply. "There, there; I understand. You think I'll tell? Gad-a-mercy, madam, I am a gentleman. And my boy Sam doesn't interest you? Yes, yes; I see that now. Why, perhaps I've been a trifle harsh? I shall say nothing to Lavendar, or anybody else."

She put her hands over her face, and he heard a broken sound. Instantly he reddened to his ears.

"Come! Come! You haven't thought me harsh, have you? Why, you poor—*bird!* It was only on my boy's account. You and I understand each other—I am a man of the world. But with Sam, it's different; now, isn't it? You see that? He's in love with you, the young fool! A great nuisance to you, of course. And I thought you might—but I ask your pardon! I see that you wouldn't think of such a thing. My dear young lady, I make you my apologies." He put his hand out and patted her shoulder; "Poor bird!" he said. But she shivered away from his touch, and after a hesitating moment he went shuffling down the path by himself.

On the way home he sniffled audibly; and when he reached the entrance to his own place he stopped, tucked his stick under his arm, and blew his nose with a sonorous sound. As he stuffed his handkerchief back into his pocket, he saw his grandson lounging against the gate, evidently waiting for him. . . . The dilapidation of the Wright place was especially obvious here at the entrance. The white paint on the two square wooden columns of the gateway had peeled and flaked, and the columns themselves had rotted at the base into broken fangs, and hung loosely upon their inner-posts; one of them sagged sidewise from the weight of the open gate which had long ago settled down into the burdocks and wild parsley that bordered the weedy driveway. What with the canaries, and the cooking, and the slovenly housework, poor old Simmons had no time for such matters as repairing or weeding.

Sam, leaning on the gate, watched his grandfather's toiling progress up the hill. His face was dull, and when he spoke all the youth seemed to have dropped out of his voice.

"Grandfather," he said, when Mr. Wright was within speaking distance, "I want to go away from Old Chester. Will you give me some money, sir?"

Benjamin Wright, his feet wide apart, and both hands gripping the top of his stick, came to a panting standstill and gaped at him. He did not quite take the boy's words in; then, as he grasped the idea that Sam was agreeing to the suggestion which he had himself made more than a month before, he burst out furiously. "Why the devil didn't you say so, *yesterday?* Why did you let me—you young jackass!"

Sam looked at him in faint surprise. Then he proceeded to explain himself: "Of course, father won't give me any money. And I haven't got any myself—except about twelve dollars. And you were kind enough, sir, to say that you would help me to go and see if I could get a publisher for the drama. I would like to go to-morrow, if you please."

"Go?" said Benjamin Wright, scowling and chewing orange-skin rapidly; "the sooner the better! I'm glad to get rid of you. But, confound you! why didn't you tell me so yesterday? Then I needn't have— Well, how much money do you want? Have you told your—your mother that you are going? Come on up to the house, and I'll give you a check. But why didn't you make up your mind to this yesterday?" Snarling and snapping, and then falling into silence, he began to trudge up the driveway to his old house.

Sam said briefly that he didn't know how much money he wanted, and that he had not as yet told his family of his purpose. "I'll tell mother to-night," he said. Then he, too, was silent, his young step falling in with his grandfather's shuffling gait.

When Mr. Wright left her, Helena stood staring after him, sobbing under her breath. She was terrified, but almost instantly she began to be angry....

That old man, creeping away along the road, had told her that he would not betray her; but his knowledge was a menace, and his surprise that she should have David, an insult! Of course, her way of living was considered "wrong" by people who cannot understand such situations—old-fashioned, narrow-minded people. But the idea of any harm coming to David by it was ridiculous! As for Sam Wright, all that sort of thing was impossible, because it was repugnant. No married woman, "respectable," as such women call themselves, could have found the boy's love-making more repugnant than she did. And certainly her conduct in Old Chester was absolutely irreproachable: she went to church fairly often; she gave liberally to all the good causes of the village; she was kind to her servants, and courteous to these stupid Old Chester people. And yet, simply because she had been forced by Frederick's cruelty into a temporary unconventionality, this dingy, grimy old man despised her! "He looked at me as if I were—I don't know what!"

Anger swept the color up into her face, her hands clenched, and she ground her heel down into the path as if she were grinding the insolent smile from his cruel old face. Horrible old man! Dirty, tremulous; with mumbling jaws chewing constantly; with untidy white hairs pricking out from under his brown wig; with shaking, shrivelled hands and blackened nails; this old man had fixed his melancholy eyes upon her with an amused leer. He pretended, if you please! to think that she was unworthy of his precious grandson's company — unworthy of David's little handclasp. She would leave this impudent Old Chester! She would tell Lloyd so, as soon as he came. She would not endure the insults of these narrow-minded fools. . . .

"Hideous! Hideous old wretch!" she said aloud furiously, between shut teeth. "How dared he look at me like that, as if I were— Beast! I hate—I hate—I *hate* him." Her anger was so uncontrollable that for a moment she could not breathe. It was like a whirlwind, wrenching and tearing her from the soil of contentment into which for so many years her vanity and selfishness had struck their roots.

"But the Lord was not in the wind."

CHAPTER XVIII

WHEN Helena went back to the house, her face was red, and her whole body tingling; every now and then her breath came in a gasp of rage. At that moment she believed that she hated everybody in the world—the cruel, foolish, arrogant world!—even the thought of David brought no softening. And indeed, when that first fury had subsided, she still did not want to see the little boy; that destroying wind of anger had beaten her complacency to the dust, and she could not with dignity meet the child's candid eyes. It was not until the next day that she could find any pleasure in him, or even in the prospect of Lloyd's visit; and when these interests began to revive, sudden gusts of rage would tear her, and she would fall into abrupt reveries, declaring to herself that she would tell Lloyd how she had been insulted! But she reminded herself that she must choose just the right moment to enlist his sympathy for the affront; she must decide with just what caress she would tell him that she meant to leave Old Chester, and come, with David, to live in Philadelphia. (Oh, would Frederick *ever* die?) . . . But, little by little, she put the miserable matter behind her, and filled the days before Lloyd's arrival with plans for the few golden hours that they were to be together, when he was to have her "all to himself." But, alas, the plans were all disarranged by David.

Now Saturday, when you come to think of it, is always a day of joy—even if there must be a visitor. To begin with, there is no school, so you have plenty of time to attend to many important affairs connected with playthings. Then, the gravel paths must be raked and the garden made tidy for Sunday, and so there is brush and refuse to be burned; and that means baking potatoes in the ashes, and (as you will remember), unless you stand, coughing, in the smoke to watch them, the potatoes are so apt to burn. Also, the phaeton is washed with peculiar care to make it fine for church; the wheels must be jacked up, one after the other, and spun round and round; then, if you go about it the right way, you can induce George to let you take the big, gritty sponge out of the black water of the stable bucket, and after squeezing it hard in your two hands, you may wipe down the spokes of one wheel. Besides these things, there are always the rabbits. Right after breakfast, David had run joyously out to see Mr. and Mrs. Smith, but while he poked lettuce leaves between the bars of their hutch, the thought struck him that this was the moment to demonstrate that interesting fact in natural history, so well known to those of your friends who happen to be stablemen, but doubted by Dr. Lavendar, namely, that a hair from the pony's tail will, if soaked in water, turn into a snake. David shuddered at the word, but ran to the stable and carefully pulled two hairs from the pony's silvery-gray tail. The operation was borne with most obliging patience, but when he stooped to pick up another beautiful long hair from the straw— for when you are making snakes you might as well make plenty, alas! the pony was so absent-minded as to step back—and down came the iron-shod hoof on the small, eager hand!

David's shriek and George's outcry brought the feminine household running and exclaiming, and at the sight of the bruised hand, with one hanging, helpless finger, Helena gathered the quivering little body into her arms, and forgot everything but the child's pain. George was rushed off for William King, and Mrs. Richie and the two women hung over the boy with tears and tender words and entreaties "not to cry"! David, in point of fact, stopped crying long before they did; but, of course, he cried again, poor little monkey! during the setting of the tiny bone, though William King was as gentle and determined as was necessary, and David, sitting in Helena's lap, responded to the demand for courage in quite a remarkable way. Indeed, the doctor noticed that Mrs. Richie quivered more than the child did. It was nearly eleven before it was all over, and William went off, smiling at Helena's anxiety, for she accompanied him to the gate, begging for directions for impossible emergencies. When he had driven away, she flew back to the house; but at the door of David's room looked at her watch, and exclaimed. Lloyd was due in half an hour! What should she do?

"Dear-precious," she said, kneeling down beside the little boy, "Sarah shall come and sit with you while Mr. Pryor is here; you won't mind if I am not with you?"

David, who had begun to whimper again, was too interested in himself to mind in the least. Even when she said, distractedly, "Oh, there's the stage!" his unhappiness was not perceptibly increased. Helena, calling Sarah to come and sit with the invalid, ran down-stairs to meet her guest. There had been no time to make herself charming; her face was marked by tears, and her dress tumbled by David's little wincing body. Before she could reach the gate, Lloyd Pryor had opened it, and, unwelcomed, was coming up the path. His surprised glance brought her tumultuous and apologetic explanation.

"Oh, I'm sorry!" he said kindly; "I must console him with a new dollar; don't you think a dollar will be healing?"

She laughed and possessed herself of his hand.

"You run a sort of hospital, Nelly, don't you? I must be a Jonah; it was your cook the last time. How is she? I trust we are to have enough food to sustain life?"

"I meant to have such a fine dinner," she said, "but we've all been so distracted about David, I'm afraid things won't be as extraordinary as I planned. However, it will 'sustain life'!—Though you could go to Dr. King's again," she ended gayly.

The instant irritation in his face sobered her. She began, carefully, to talk of this or that: his journey, the Mercer business, his health—anything to make him smile again. Plainly, it was not the moment to speak of Mr. Benjamin Wright and her purpose of leaving Old Chester.

"Now I must run up-stairs just one minute, and see David," she said in the middle of a sentence. Her minute lengthened to ten, but when she came back, explaining that she had stopped to wash David's face —"it was all stained by tears"—he did not seem impatient.

"Your own would be improved by soap and water,

my dear," he said with an amused look. "No! no—don't go now; I want to talk to you, and I haven't much time."

She knew him too well to insist; instead, she burst into what gayety she could summon, for that was how he liked her. But back in her mind there was a growing tremor of apprehension: — there was something wrong; she could not tell what it was, but she felt it. She said to herself that she would not speak of Mr. Benjamin Wright until after dinner.

Little by little, however, her uneasiness subsided. It became evident that the excitement of the morning had not been too much for Maggie; things were very good, and Lloyd Pryor was very appreciative, and Helena's charm more than once touched him to a caressing glance and a soft word. But as they got up from the table he glanced at his watch, and she winced; then smiled, quickly. She brought him his cigar and struck a light; and he, looking at her with handsome, lazy eyes, caught the hand which held the flaming match, and lit his cigar in slow puffs.

"Now I must go and give a look at David," she said.

"Look here, Nelly," he protested, "aren't you rather overdoing this adopted-mother business?"

She found the child rather flushed and in an uneasy doze. Instantly she was anxious. "Don't leave him, Sarah," she said. "I'll have Maggie bring your dinner up to you. Oh, I *wish* I didn't have to go downstairs!"

"I'm afraid he is worse," she told Lloyd Pryor with a worried frown.

"Well, don't look as if it were an affair of nations," he said carelessly, and drew her down on the sofa beside him. He was so gracious to her, that she forgot

David; but she quivered for fear the graciousness should cease. She was like a thirsty creature, drinking with eager haste, lest some terror should drive her back into the desert. But Lloyd Pryor continued to be gracious; he talked gayly of this or that; he told her one or two stories that had been told him in a directors' meeting or on a journey, and he roared with appreciation of their peculiar humor. She flushed; but she made herself laugh. Then she began tentatively to say something of Old Chester; and—and what did he think? "That old man, who lives up on the hill, called, and—"

But he interrupted her. "You are very beguiling, Nelly, but I am afraid I must be thinking of the stage —it is after three. Before I go I just want to say—" then he broke off. "Come in! Well? What is it?" he demanded impatiently.

"Please, ma'am," said Sarah, standing in the doorway, her face puckered almost to tears, "David's woke up, and he's crying, and I can't do nothing with him. He wants you, ma'am."

"Oh, poor darling! Tell him I'll come right up," Mrs. Richie said, rising in quick distress.

"Nonsense!" said Lloyd Pryor, sharply. "Sarah, tell the boy to behave himself. Mrs. Richie can't come now."

Sarah hurried up-stairs, but Helena stood in painful indecision. "Oh, Lloyd, I *must* go! I'll just sit with him a minute!"

"You'll just sit with me a minute," he said calmly. "Be sensible, Helena. I want to speak to you about something."

But she did not hear him; she was listening for David's voice. A little whimpering cry reached her, and the tears sprung to her eyes. "Lloyd! I must! He is crying."

"Let him cry."

"He's takin' on so, please come up, ma'am," came Sarah's entreating voice from over the banisters in the upper hall.

"Oh, Lloyd, I must!" She turned; but he, springing up, caught her wrist and pulled her to him.

"Don't be a fool."

"Let me go! Oh, how cruel you are!" She tried to wrench her wrist from his grasp. "I hate you!"

"Hate me, do you?" He laughed, and catching her in his arms, kissed her again and again. Then he put his hands in his pockets and stepped back, leaving her free. "Will you go?"

She stood, vibrating between surprised affection and anguished longing for the child. "Lloyd!" she said faintly; she put her hands over her face, and came towards him slowly, shivering a little, and murmuring "*Lloyd!*" Then, with a sudden gasp, she turned and fled up-stairs. "David—I am coming—"

Lloyd Pryor stood dumfounded; in his astonishment he almost laughed. But at that instant he heard the crunch of wheels drawing up at the gate. "The stage!" he said to himself, and called out, angrily, "Helena!"

But it was not the stage; it was William King's shabby old buggy standing in the shadow of the big locust by the roadside; and there was the doctor himself coming up the path.

Lloyd Pryor swore under his breath.

The front door was open to the hot June afternoon, and unannounced the doctor walked into the hall. As he took off his hat, he glanced into the parlor, and for a second of consternation stood staring with angry eyes. Then he nodded stiffly. "I will be obliged if you will let Mrs. Richie know I am here."

"She is with that boy," said Lloyd Pryor. He made no motion of civility; he stood where Helena had left him, his hands still in his pockets. "Will you be so good as to tell her to come down here to me? The stage is due, and I must see her before I go."

William King, red and stolid, nodded again, and went up-stairs without another look into the parlor.

While he waited Lloyd Pryor's anger slowly rose. The presence of the doctor froze the tenderness that, for an idle moment, her face and voice and touch had awakened. The annoyance, the embarrassment, the danger of that call, returned in a gust of remembrance. When she came down-stairs, full of eager excuses, the touch of his rage seared her like a flame.

"If you will kindly take five minutes from that squalling brat—"

"Lloyd, he was in pain. I had to go to him. The instant the doctor came, I left him. I—"

"Listen to me, please. I have only a minute. Helena, this friend of yours, this Dr. King, saw fit to pry into my affairs. He came to Philadelphia to look me up—"

"*What!*"

"He came to my house"—he looked at her keenly through his curling eyelashes—"to my house! Do you understand what that means?"

In her dismay she sat down with a sort of gasp; and looking up at him, stammered, "But why? Why?"

"Why? Because he is a prying suspicious jackass of a country doctor! He came at exactly six o'clock;

it was perfectly evident that he meant to give me the pleasure of his company at dinner."

At that she sprang to her feet, her impetuous hands upon his arm. "Then he was not—suspicious! Don't you see? He was only friendly!" She trembled with the reaction of that instant of dismay. "He was not suspicious, or he wouldn't have been—been willing—" Her voice trailed into shamed silence.

Lloyd Pryor pushed her hand away, impatiently. "I'm not anxious for his friendship or even his acquaintance. You will please consider what would have happened if I had not come home just as he arrived!" He paused, his voice hardening: "My daughter saw him."

Helena stepped back, wincing and silent.

"You will be so good as to consider the result of such tomfoolery—to me."

"And what about me?" she said. "Your 'daughter'—I suppose you mean Alice—is not the only person in the world!"

But Lloyd Pryor, having dealt his blow, was gracious again. "My dear, you needn't begin recriminations. Of course, I speak on your account as much as on my own. It would have been—well, awkward, all round. You must see that it does not occur again. You will not get on terms with these people that will encourage them to look me up. You understand?"

She looked at him, terror-stricken. In all their squabbles and differences—and there had been many in the last few years—he had never spoken in this extraordinary tone. It was not anger, it was not the courteous brutality with which she was more or less familiar; it was superiority. The color swept into her face; even her throat reddened. She said stammering, "I don't know why you speak—in—in this tone—"

"I am not going to speak any more in any tone," he said lightly; "there's the stage! Good-by, my dear. I trust your boy may recover rapidly. Tell him I was prepared for his sling and the 'smooth stone out of the brook'! Sorry I couldn't have seen more of you." As he spoke he went into the hall; she followed him without a word. He picked up his hat, and then, turning, tipped her chin back and kissed her. She made no response.

When he had gone, she went into the parlor and shut the door.

CHAPTER XIX

DAVID was quite a personage in Old Chester for a few days. Mrs. Richie was his slave, and hardly left him day or night; Dr. King came to see him five times in one week; Mrs. Barkley sent him some wine jelly in a sheaf-of-wheat mould; Dr. Lavendar climbed the hill on two afternoons, to play dominoes with him, though, as it happened, Mrs. Richie was not present either day to watch the game. The first time she had just gone to lie down, Sarah said; the second time she had that moment started out to walk—"Why, my goodness!" said Sarah, "she must 'a' *just* gone! She was here not a minute ago. I should 'a' thought she'd 'a' seen you tyin' up at the gate?"

"Well, evidently she didn't," Dr. Lavendar said, "or she would have waited. Tell her I'm sorry to miss her, Sarah." Then, eagerly, he went on up-stairs to David.

William King, too, was scarcely more fortunate; he only found her at home once, so at the end of the week he was unable to tell her that David was improving. It was, of course, necessary that she should be told this; so that was why he and Jinny continued to come up the hill for another week. At any rate that was the explanation he gave his Martha.

"I must let her know just when David can go back to school," he said. And Martha, with a tightening lip remarked that she should have supposed a woman of Mrs. Richie's years could use her own judgment in such a matter.

William's explanation to Dr. Lavendar was somewhat fuller: "I make a point of calling, on the plea of seeing David, but it's really to see her. She's so high strung, that this little accident of his has completely upset her. I notice that she sort of keeps out of the way of people. I'm pretty sure that yesterday she saw me coming and slipped out into the garden to avoid me—think of that! Nervousness; pure nervousness. But I have a plan to brighten her up a little—a surprise-party. What do you say?"

Dr. Lavendar looked doubtful. "William," he said, "isn't life surprising enough? Now, here's Sam Wright's Sam's performance."

Dr. Lavendar looked care-worn, and with reason. Sam Wright's Sam had indeed provided a surprise for Old Chester. He had quietly announced that he was going to leave town.

"Going away!" repeated the senior warden. "What are you talking about?"

Sam said briefly that he wanted to try to get a drama he had written, published.

"You are out of your senses!" his father said; "I forbid it, sir. Do you hear me?"

Sam looked out of the window. "I shall go, I think, to-morrow," he said thoughtfully.

Samuel Wright stared at his wife in dumfounded silence. When he got his breath, he said in awful tones, "Eliza, he defies me! A child of mine, and lost to all sense of duty! I cannot understand it;—unless such things have happened in *your* family?" he ended with sudden suspicion.

THE AWAKENING OF HELENA RICHIE

"Never!" protested the poor mother; "but Samuel, my dear—Sammy, my darling—"

The senior warden raised a majestic hand. "Silence, if you please, Eliza." Then he thrust his right hand into his bosom, rested his left fist on the marble-topped centre-table, and advanced one foot. Standing thus, he began to tell his son what he thought of him, and as he proceeded his anger mounted, he forgot his periods and his attitudes, and his voice grew shrill and mean. But, alas, he could not tell the boy all that he thought; he could not tell him of his high ambitions for him, of his pitiful desire for his love, of his anguished fear lest he might be unhappy, or foolish, or bad. These thoughts the senior warden had never known how to speak. Instead, he detailed his grievances and his disappointments; he told Sam with ruthless candor what the world called his conduct: dishonest, idiotic, ungrateful. He had a terrifying string of adjectives, and through them all the boy looked out of the window. Once, at a particularly impassioned period, he glanced at his father with interest; that phrase would be fine in a play, he reflected. Then he looked out of the window again.

"And now," Mr. Wright ended sonorously, "what reply have you to make, sir?"

Sam looked confused. "I beg your pardon, father? I did not hear what you were saying."

Samuel Wright stared at him, speechless.

As for the boy, he said calmly, "Good night, father," and went up-stairs to his own room where he began his packing. The next morning he had gone.

"Where?" asked Dr. Lavendar, when the angry father brought him the news.

"I do not know," said the senior warden, "and I do not—"

"Yes, you do," said Dr. Lavendar; "but that's not the point. The point is that it doesn't really matter, except for our comfort, whether we know or not. Sam is a man, and our protection is an impertinence. He's taking a dive on his own account. And as I look at it, he has a right to. But he'll come up for breath, and then we'll get some information. And he'll get some sense."

But of course the Wright family was in a most distressed state. The mother was overwhelmed with anxious grief; the father was consumed with mortification and blazing with anger.

"He didn't take his second-weight flannels," moaned Mrs. Wright; "he will catch cold. Oh, where is he? And nobody knows how to cook his hominy for him but our Betsy. Oh, my boy!"

"Good riddance," said Sam senior between his teeth; "ungrateful puppy!"

Dr. Lavendar had his hands full. To reassure the mother, and tell her that the weather was so warm that Sam couldn't use the second-weight flannels if he had them, and that when he came back Betsy's hominy would seem better than ever—"Old Chester food will taste mighty good, after a few husks," said Dr. Lavendar, cheerfully—to tell Sam senior that a grateful puppy would be an abnormal monster, and to refrain from telling him that whatever a father sows he is pretty sure to reap—took time and strength. So Dr. Lavendar did not enter very heartily into William King's plans for a surprise-party. However, he did promise to come, if the doctor succeeded in getting Old Chester together.

THE AWAKENING OF HELENA RICHIE

Meantime he and Danny and Goliath went up to The Top to tell Benjamin Wright about Sam's Sam. The grandfather displayed no surprise.

"I knew he was going to clear out," he said; he was poking about among his canaries when Dr. Lavendar came in, and he stopped and sat down, panting. "These fowls wear me out," he complained. "Whiskey? No? Dear me! Your senior warden's got you to sign the pledge, I suppose? Well, I will; to drink the cub's health. He'll amount to something yet, if he doesn't eat his fatted calf too soon. Fatted calf is very bad for the digestion."

"Wright, I don't suppose you need to be told that you behaved abominably Sunday night? Do you know where Sam is?"

"I don't; and I don't want to. Behaved abominably? He wouldn't shake hands with me! Sam told me he was going, and I gave him some money—well! why do you look at me like that? Gad-a-mercy, ain't he my grandson? Besides, since our love-feast, ain't it my duty to help his father along? I've had a change of heart," he said, grinning; "where's your joy over the one sinner that repenteth? I'm helping young Sam, so that old Sam may get some sense. Lavendar, the man who has not learned what a damned fool he is, hasn't learned anything. And if I mistake not, the boy will teach my very respectable son, who won't smoke and won't drink, that interesting fact. As for the boy, he will come back a man, sir. A man! Anyway, I've done my part. I offered him money and advice—like the two women grinding at the mill, one was taken and the other was left. Yes; I've done my part. I've evened things up. I gave him his first tobie, and his first drink, and now I've given him a chance to see the world—which your senior warden once said was a necessary experience for a young man. I've evened things up!" He thrust a trembling hand down into the blue ginger-jar for some orange-skin. "He said he'd pay the money back; I said, 'Go to thunder!' As if I cared about the money. I've got him out of Old Chester; that's all I care about."

"Well," said Dr. Lavendar, "I hope you haven't got him merely out of the frying-pan."

"So you think there is no fire in Old Chester? She's a pretty creetur, Lavendar, ain't she? Poor thing!"

Dr. Lavendar did not follow the connection of ideas in the older man's mind, but he did say to himself, as he and Goliath went away, that it was queer how possessed Benjamin Wright was that Sam's love-making was dangerous. Then he sighed, and his face fell into troubled lines. For all his brave words, he wished he knew where the boy was; and though he was already late for dinner, he drew up at William King's door to ask the doctor if he had any new ideas on the subject.

But Willy was not at home. Martha was sitting under the grape-vine trellis at the back door, topping and tailing gooseberries. From the kitchen behind her came the pleasant smell of preserving. She had a big yellow earthenware bowl in her lap, and excused herself for not rising when Dr. Lavendar came round the corner of the house to find her.

"*I* am a housekeeper, Dr. Lavendar. William thinks it's pretty not to understand housekeeping; but I expect if he didn't have preserves for his supper, he wouldn't think it was so pretty. No; he isn't at home, sir. He's gone out—with the thermometer at ninety

THE AWAKENING OF HELENA RICHIE

—to see about that party he is getting up for Mrs. Richie. So long as he has time to spare from his patients, I should think he would like to take up my spare-room carpet for me. But, oh dear, no. He has to see about parties!"

"William is always doing friendly things," said Dr. Lavendar, sitting down on the door-step and helping himself to a gooseberry from Martha's bowl. "You are going to make some fool for the supper, of course?" He took off his hat, and wiped his forehead with his big red handkerchief.

"Oh, of course. I'm very tired, and I have my housekeeping to attend to; but I can make gooseberry fool. That's what I'm for."

"When is this party?" said Dr. Lavendar. "I declare, I've been so worried about Sam's Sam, I've forgotten."

"It's next week; Thursday. Yes; she can send that boy to his death, maybe; but we must have parties to cheer her up."

"Oh, come now," Dr. Lavendar remonstrated; "I don't believe a glimpse of the world will kill him. And nobody can blame Mrs. Richie for his foolishness. I suppose we are all going?"

"Everybody," Martha King said scornfully; "even Samuel Wright. He told his wife that he wouldn't have any nonsense about Sam, and she'd got to go. I think it's positively cruel; because of course everybody knows that the boy was in love with this housekeeper that doesn't know how to make soap!" Martha shook her bowl sharply, and the toppling green pyramid crumbled. Dr. Lavendar looked at her over his spectacles; instantly her face reddened, and she tossed her head. "Of course, you understand that I haven't

THE AWAKENING OF HELENA RICHIE

the slightest personal feeling about it. That's one thing about me, Dr. Lavendar, I may not be perfect, but nobody despises anything like—that, more than I do. I merely regret William's judgment."

"Regret William's judgment! Why, think of the judgment he displayed in choosing a wife," said Dr. Lavendar. But when he climbed into his old buggy he had the grace to be ashamed of himself; he admitted as much to Danny. "For she's a sensible woman, Daniel, and, at bottom, kind." Danny yawned, and Dr. Lavendar added, "Poor Willy!"

Mrs. Richie's first hint of Dr. King's proposed festivity came a week later from David, who happened to be at home to dinner, and who saw fit to mention that Lydia Wright wasn't to be allowed to come up with her father and mother.

"Come up where?" Mrs. Richie said, idly. She was leaning forward, her elbows on the table, watching the child eat. When he said, "To your party to-night," she sat up in astonished dismay.

"My *what?* David! Tell me—exactly. Who is coming? Oh, dear!" she ended, tears of distress standing in her eyes.

David continued to eat his rice pudding. "Can I sit up till nine?"

Mrs. Richie pushed her chair back from the table, and caught her lower lip between her teeth. What should she do? But even as she asked herself the question, Dr. King stood, smiling, in the French window that opened on to the lawn.

"May I come in?" he said.

The fact was, a misgiving had risen in William's mind; perhaps a complete surprise would not be pleasant. Perhaps she would rather have an idea of what

THE AWAKENING OF HELENA RICHIE

was going to happen. Perhaps she might want to dress up, or something. And so he dropped in to give a hint: "Half a dozen of us are coming in tonight to say how-do-you-do," he confessed. ("Whew! she doesn't need to dress up," he commented inwardly.) The red rose in her hair and her white cross-barred muslin with elbow sleeves seemed very elegant to William. He was so lost in admiration of her toilet, that her start of angry astonishment escaped him.

"Dr. King," said David, scraping up the sugar from his saucer, "is God good because He likes to be, or because He has to be?"

"David," said William King, "you will be the death of me!"

"Because, if He likes to be," David murmured, "I don't see why He gets praised; and if He has to be, why—"

"Dr. King," said Helena breathlessly, "I'm afraid—really, I'm not prepared for company; and—"

"Oh," said William, cheerfully, "don't bother about that. Mrs. King is going to bring up one or two little things, and I believe Mrs. Barkley has some ideas on the subject. Well, I must be going along. I hope you won't be sorry to see us? The fact is, you are too lonely up here with only David to keep you busy; though I must say, if he fires off questions like this one, I should think you would be pretty well occupied!"

When he had gone, Helena Richie sat looking blankly at David. "What on earth shall I do!" she said aloud.

"Did God make Sarah?" David demanded.

"Yes, dear, yes!"

"Did He make me, and the Queen, and my rabbits?"

"Why, of course. Oh, David, you do ask so many questions!"

"Everything has to be made," he ruminated.

She agreed, absently. David put his spoon down, deeply interested.

"Who made God?—another god, higher up?"

"I think," she said, "that I'll send word I have a headache!"

David sighed, and gave up theological research. "Dr. King didn't look at my scar, but I made Theophilus Bell pay me a penny to show it to him. Mrs. Richie, when I am a man, I'm *never* going to wash behind my ears. I tell Sarah so every morning. I'm going to see my rabbits, now. Good-by."

He slipped down from his chair and left her to her perplexity — as if she had not perplexity enough without this! For the last few days she had been worried almost to death about Mr. Benjamin Wright. She had not written to Lloyd yet of that terrible interview in the garden which would drive her from Old Chester; she had been afraid to. She felt instinctively that his mood was not hospitable to any plan that would bring her to live in the East. He would be less hospitable if she came because she had been found out in Old Chester. But her timidity about writing to him was a curious alarm to her; it was a confession of something she would not admit even long enough to deny it. Nevertheless, she did not write; "I will to-morrow," she assured herself each day. But now, on top of her worry of indecision and unacknowledged fear, came this new dismay — a party! How furious Lloyd would be if he heard of it; well, he must not hear of it. But what could she do? If she put it off with a flimsy excuse, it would only defer the descent upon her. How helpless she was! They would come, these people, they would be friendly; she could not escape them!

"Oh, I must stop this kind of thing," she said to herself, desperately

CHAPTER XX

WITH the exception of Benjamin Wright, all Old Chester lent itself to William King's project with very good grace. Mr. Wright said, gruffly, that a man with one foot in the grave couldn't dance a jig, so he preferred to stay at home. But the rest of Old Chester said that although she was so quiet and kept herself to herself so much, Mrs. Richie was a ladylike person; a little shy, perhaps—or perhaps only properly hesitant to push her way into society; at any rate it was but kind to show her some attention.

"Her modesty does her credit," Mrs. Barkley said, "but it will be gratifying to her to be noticed. I'll come, William, and bring a cake. And Maria Welwood shall tell Ezra to take three bottles of Catawba."

A little before eight, the company began to assemble, full of such cordial courtesy that Mrs. Richie's shrinking and awkward coldness only incited them to heartier friendliness. Dr. King, master of ceremonies, was ably assisted by his Martha. Mrs. King may have been, as she told all the guests, very tired, but she could be depended upon to be efficient. It was she who had engaged Uncle Davy and his fiddle; she who put the cakes and wine and fruit upon the dining-room table, already somewhat meagrely arranged by Helena's reluctant hands; she who bustled about to find card-tables, and induced Tom Dilworth to sing:

"*Thou—Thou reignest in this bosom!—*"

and got Mr. Ezra Barkley to ask statistical conundrums.

"It's well there is somebody to attend to things," she said in a dry aside to William. "Mrs. Richie just walks around as if she didn't belong here. And she lets that child sit up until this hour! I can't understand how a sensible woman can deliberately spoil a child.—I'd like to know what that perfume is that she uses," she ended frowning.

It was after supper, while the husband and wife, still oppressed with their responsibilities, were standing in the doorway looking in upon the cheerful party now in full enjoyment of its own hospitality, that Eddy Minns came up behind them and touched William King's arm.

"Dr. King," he said breathlessly, "a telegram, sir. For Mrs. Richie. And mother said it was bad news!"

"Oh, William!" said Martha; "bad news! Do you know what it is, Eddy?"

"Somebody is dead," the boy said, important and solemn.

"Her brother?" William King asked in dismay.

"Well, not the brother that comes here; his name is Lloyd, mother said. This is somebody whose name begins with 'F.' Perhaps another brother. Mother showed the despatch to me; it just said: 'F. died suddenly yesterday in Paris.' It was signed 'S. R.'"

"It isn't from Pryor, then," William commented.

"Oh, William," Martha whispered, "what shall we do? Must you give it to her *now?*—oh, William!"

Dr. King stood staring at the orange-colored envelope in silence.

"Shall I call Dr. Lavendar?" Martha asked breathlessly.

"Wait," her husband said; "let me think: it may not be anybody very near and dear; but whether it is or not, there is nothing she can do about it to-night. The telegraph-office is closed. I don't see why her evening need be spoiled. No; I won't give it to her now. When the people go—"

"Oh, dear! Dr. Lavendar says we must end up with a reel. But I'll get them off as soon as I can," Martha declared, in her capable voice, "and then I'll break it to her."

"I will tell her," the doctor said. He put the envelope in his pocket with a troubled frown.

"If she is in affliction, a woman will be more comfort to her than a man," Martha instructed him. "Look at her now, poor thing! She little thinks— No indeed; I must stay with her. I'm very tired, and she's not very friendly, but I won't shirk my duty on that account. That's one thing about me: I may not be perfect, but I don't let personal feelings interfere with duty."

"It isn't your duty," William said impatiently; "you'd better arrange about the reel." And with that he left her. But he was so uneasy at withholding the telegram that he forgot to choose a partner, and let Martha push him into place opposite Miss Maggie Jay, who was so stout that when the two large bodies went jigging down the lane, the clasping hands arched above their heads had to break apart to give them room.

"She may think I ought to have told her at once," William was saying to himself, watching Mrs. Richie with such furtive attention that he forgot to turn his partner, until Martha's sharp reminder set him shuffling his feet, and grinning in a sickly way at panting Miss Maggie. . . . "Who is 'F.'? Will 'F.'s death be a great grief? Will she suffer?" William King's kind heart began to beat thickly in his throat. If she should cry! He bowed, with stiffly swinging arms to Miss Maggie. He thought of Helena,—who was moving through the dance as a flower sways on its stalk,— as one thinks of a child in pain; with the impulse to hold out his arms. In his absorption he stood stock-still—but happily the reel was over, and the people were beginning to say good-by. He drew a long breath of relief at getting rid of them, and as he stood waiting, Martha plucked at his sleeve. "Give me the despatch; I'll break it to her."

He looked at her with absent eyes. "No; I'll see to it. Do start, Martha, and maybe that will hurry them off!"

Mrs. King drew back, affronted. "Oh, very well," she said; and made her cold adieux.

But Helena Richie was oblivious of Mrs. King's coldness; her anxiety and dismay had grown into an uncontrollable nervousness, and when at last, thinking she was alone, she threw up her arms with a gesture of relief, the sight of William King, coming gravely towards her, made her break into an angry exclamation. But before she knew it, he had taken her hand, and was holding it in his kind clasp.

"Mrs. Richie, I am afraid I must give you bad news."

"Bad—news—?"

"A telegram has come," he began, taking the envelope from his pocket; but she interrupted him, seizing it with a sort of gasp and tearing it open. A moment later she stood quite still, looking at the despatch, then with dilating eyes at the doctor, and again at the despatch. She pressed her fingers hard against her lips, and he saw that she was trembling.

"You must sit down," he said gently, and put his big, quiet hand on her shoulder. She sank under his firm touch into a chair.

"It is not—bad news."

"I am glad of that," William said. "But you are a little pale," he added smiling.

"It was a shock."

"I am glad it was nothing more."

She spread out the telegram and read it again. She did not seem to hear him. Dr. King looked at her uneasily. There was certainly no grief in her face, yet her color did not come back.

"Some one is dead," she said. "Not—a friend." William was silent. "But it startled me."

"Yes," the doctor said.

"Oh, Dr. King!" she cried violently; and put her hands over her face. He thought with relief that tears had come. "He was—an enemy," she said.

"He is dead, Mrs. Richie; forgive him."

She did not answer. It was all William King could do not to stroke the soft hair of the bent head, and say "Don't cry," as if to a child. But when she lifted her face, her eyes were quite dry; there was a flashing look in them that broke into breathless, wavering laughter.

"I beg your pardon; it is just the—the shock, you know."

"Yes," the doctor said; "I know." He could not help covering with his big, warm palm, the shaking hands that were pulling and twisting the telegram. "There, there! My dear Mrs. Richie—where is that bromide I gave you for David? I want you to take some."

"Oh, it isn't necessary; truly it isn't. I am not unhappy. I am just—"

"You are startled; and you must have a good night's sleep. Is the bromide in David's room? I'll get it."

When he came back with the medicine, she took it hurriedly — anything to get rid of him! "Is there anything I can do?" he said. "Do you want to send any reply? I can take it down to-night and send it the first thing in the morning."

"Oh!" she exclaimed, "what am I thinking of! Of course, a message—I must send a message! Will you take it? Oh, I am afraid I trouble you very much, but you are so kind. I'll go and write it."

She tried to rise, but she was still so shaken that involuntarily he put out his hand to help her. At the old mahogany desk between the windows she hunted about for paper and pencil, and when she found them, wrote for a moment, rapidly; then paused, and tore the paper up. William glanced at her sidewise; she was pressing the pencil against her lips, her left hand opening and closing with agitation. The doctor shook his head. "That won't do," he said to himself. Again she wrote; again hesitated; again tore the sheet of paper across. It seemed to him that he waited a long time. But when she brought him the message, it was very short; only: "*F. is dead*," and her initials. It was addressed to Mr. Lloyd Pryor.

"I am very much obliged to you," she said; her color was coming back, and she had evidently got control of herself. But she hardly noticed William's farewell, and he had not reached the front door before she began to pace up and down the parlor.

THE AWAKENING OF HELENA RICHIE

"Well!" said Martha, "was it a brother, or sister? How did she take it? I suppose you think she found it easier because you broke it to her. I must say, William, flatly and frankly, that I think a nice woman would rather have a woman near her when she is in trouble, than a man. I was very tired, but I was perfectly willing to remain. Well! what relation was this F.? A cousin?"

"Why, I don't know," the doctor confessed blankly; "she didn't say, and it never occurred to me to ask; and—"

"Well, upon my word!" said Martha King.

CHAPTER XXI

HELENA stood breathing quickly; it was as if she had been smothering, and suddenly felt free air. She was alone. The people—the terrible, persistently friendly, suffocating people, were gone! She could draw a full breath; she could face her own blazing fact; . . . *Frederick was dead.*

She was walking back and forth, staring with unseeing eyes at the confusion of the room—chairs pulled out from their accustomed places; two card-tables with a litter of cards and counters; the astral-lamp burning low on the rosewood table that was cluttered with old daguerreotypes belonging to the house. The dining-room door was ajar, and as she passed it she had a glimpse of the empty disorder of the room, and could hear her two women moving about, carrying off plates and glasses and talking to each other.

"Well, I like company," she heard Sarah say. "I wish she'd have somebody in every day."

And Maggie's harsh murmur: "You ain't got to cook for 'em." Then the clatter of forks and spoons in the pantry.

"Seemed to me like as if she wasn't real glad to see 'em," Sarah commented. "My! look at all this here good cake crumbled up on somebody's plate."

"Well, a widow woman don't enjoy company," Maggie explained.

THE AWAKENING OF HELENA RICHIE

A minute later Sarah came bustling in to close the parlor windows for the night, and started to find the room still occupied. "I thought you had gone upstairs, ma'am," the girl stammered, wondering nervously if she had said anything that she would not care to have overheard.

"I am going now," Mrs. Richie said, drawing a long breath, and opening and shutting her eyes in a dazed way;—"like as if she'd been asleep and was woke up, sudden," Sarah told Maggie later.

In her own room, the door locked, she sank down in a chair, her clasped hands falling between her knees, her eyes staring at the floor.

Dead.

How long he had been about dying. Thirteen years ago Lloyd had said, "He'll drink himself to death in six months; and then—!" Well; at least part of the programme was carried out: he drank. But he did not die. No; he went on living, living, living! That first year they were constantly asking each other for news of him: "Have you heard anything?" "Yes; an awful debauch. Oh, he can't stand it. He'll be in his grave before Christmas." But Christmas came, and Frederick was still living. Then it was "before spring"—"before fall"—"before Christmas" again. And yet he went on living. And she had gone on living, too. At first, joyously, except when she brooded over the baby's death; then impatiently—for Frederick would not die! Then, gradually, gradually, with weary acceptance of the situation. Only in the last two or three years had she begun to live anxiously, as she realized how easily Lloyd was accepting Frederick's lease of life. Less and less often he inquired whether Mr. Raynor had mentioned Frederick's health in the letter that came with her quarterly statement. By and by, it was she, not Lloyd, who asked, "Have you heard anything of Frederick?"

The house was quite silent now, except when Sarah trudged up the back stairs with the clanking silver-basket on her arm. The lamp on the corner of her bureau flickered, and a spark wavered up the chimney; the oil was gone and the wick charring. She got up and blew the smouldering flame out; then sat down again in the darkness. . . . Yes; Lloyd was no longer vitally interested in Frederick's health. She must make up her mind to that. But after all, what difference did that make? He loved her just the same; only men are not like women, they don't keep on saying so; —for that matter, she herself did not say so as often as in those first days. But of course she loved him just as much. She had grown a little dull, she supposed. No; she would not distrust him. She was sure he loved her. Yet behind her most emphatic assertions cowered that dumb apprehension which had struck its cold talons into her heart the day that David had hurt his hand: . . . *Suppose Frederick's death should be an embarrassment to Lloyd!*

In the darkness, with the brush of the locust branches against the closed shutters of the east window, her face blazed with angry color, and she threw her head up with a surge of pride. "If he doesn't want me, I don't want him!" she said aloud. She pulled the lace bertha from her shoulders, and began to take out her hairpins; "*I* sha'n't be the one to say 'Let us be married.'"

When she lay down in the darkness, her eyes wide open, her arms straight at her sides, it flashed into her mind that Frederick was lying still and straight, too.

His face must be white, now; sunken, perhaps; the leer of his pale eyes changed into the sly smile of the dead. *Dead.* Oh, at last, at last!—and her mind rushed back to its own affairs. . . . That horrible old Mr. Wright and his insinuations; how she had worried over them and over the difficulty of getting away from Old Chester, only that afternoon. Ah, well, she need never think of such things again, for never again could any one have an insulting thought about her; and as for her fear that Lloyd would not want her to leave Old Chester—why, he would take her away himself! And once outside of Old Chester, she would have a place in the world like other women. She was conscious of a sudden and passionate elation: *Like other women.* The very words were triumphant! Yes; like that dreadful Mrs. King; oh, how intolerably stupid the woman was, how she disliked her; but when Lloyd came and they went away together, she would be like Mrs. King! She drew an exultant breath and smiled proudly in the darkness. For the moment the cowering fear was forgotten. . . . How soon could he come? He ought to have the telegram by ten the next morning—too late to catch the express for Mercer. He would take the night train, and arrive at noon on Saturday. A day and a half to wait. And at that she realized with sudden astonishment that it was still Thursday. It seemed hours and hours since she had read that telegram. Yet it was scarcely an hour ago that she had been dancing the Virginia reel with those terrible people! A little later she had noticed William King lingering behind the departing guests; how annoyed she had been at his slowness. Then he had taken that envelope out of his pocket—she gasped again, remembering the shock of its contents.

THE AWAKENING OF HELENA RICHIE

In this tumult of broken and incoherent thought, the night passed. It was not until dawn that her mind cleared enough for consecutive thinking, and when it did she was so fatigued that she fell asleep and slept heavily till awakened by an anxious knock at her door. Had Mrs. Richie one of her headaches? Should Sarah bring her some coffee?

"Why, what time is it? Has David gone to school? What! ten o'clock!" She was broad awake at that— he must have got the despatch. Allowing for delays, his answer ought to reach her by noon.

She sprang up with the instinct to do something! to get ready! She began to plan her packing, the thrill of action tingling through her. She dressed hurriedly, looking incessantly at the clock, and then laughing to herself. What difference did it make how late it was? By no possibility could Lloyd appear on the morning stage; unless, yes, it *was* possible; Mr. Raynor might have telegraphed him. No; Mr. Raynor had never recognized the situation. Lloyd could not reach her until noon on Saturday; he could only telegraph. She sighed and resigned herself to facts, drinking the coffee Sarah brought her, and asking whether David was all right. "Poor darling, having his breakfast all alone," she said. Then she looked at the clock; Lloyd's despatch could hardly arrive for another hour.

The still, hot morning stretched interminably before her. A dozen times it was on her lips to order the trunks brought down from the garret. A dozen times some undefined sense of fitness held her back. When his answer came, when he actually said the word— then; but not till then. . . . What time was it? After eleven! She would go into the garden, where she could look down the road and have the first glimpse of Eddy

Minns climbing the hill. With her thoughts in galloping confusion, she put on her flat hat with its twist of white lace about the crown, and went out into the heat. From the bench under the big poplar she looked across at the girdling hills, blue and hot in the still flood of noon; below her was the valley, now a sea of treetops islanded with Old Chester roofs and chimneys; there was no gleam of the river through the midsummer foliage. She took her watch out of the little watch-pocket at her waist—nearly twelve! If he had got the despatch at nine, it was surely time for an answer. Still, so many things might have happened to delay it. He might have been late in getting to his office; or, for that matter, Eddy Minns might be slow about coming up the hill. Everybody was slow in Old Chester!

The empty road ran down to the foot of the hill; no trudging messenger climbed its hot slope. Twelve! "I'll not look at the road for five minutes," she told herself, resolutely, and sat staring at the watch open in her hand. Five minutes later she snapped the lid shut, and looked. Blazing, unbroken sunshine. "It ought to have been here by this time," she thought with a tightening of her lips. Perhaps he was away? Her heart sank at that; but how absurd! Suppose he was. What did a few hours' waiting amount to? She had waited thirteen years.

For another hour she watched in the heat and silence of the garden; then started to hear Sarah, at her elbow, saying that dinner was on the table.

"Very well," she answered impatiently. "I'll wait another five minutes," she said to herself. But she waited ten. When she sat down in the dining-room, she ate almost nothing. Once she asked Sarah if she knew how long it took for a despatch to come from

Philadelphia to Old Chester. Sarah gaped at the question, and said she didn't know as she'd ever heard.

In the afternoon, with covert glances out of the window, she kept indoors and tried to put her mind on practical things: the arrangements with her landlord for cancelling the lease; the packing and shipping of furniture. At last, on a sudden impulse, she said to herself that she would go and meet David as he came home from school—and call at the telegraph-office.

In the post-office, where the telegraph bound Old Chester to the outer world, Mrs. Minns, looking up from her knitting, saw the tense face at the delivery window.

"No letters for you, Mrs. Richie," she said; then she remembered the telegram that had by this time interested all Old Chester, and got up and came forward, sympathetically curious. "Well'm; I suppose there's a good deal of dyin' this time of year?"

"Have you a despatch for me?" Mrs. Richie said curtly.

"No'm;" said Mrs. Minns.

"Did Dr. King send a telegram for me this morning?" she asked in a sudden panic of alarm.

"Yes'm," the postmistress said, "he sent it."

Mrs. Richie turned away, and began to walk about the office; up and down, up and down. Once she stopped and read the names on the pigeonholes of the letter-rack; once the telegraph instrument clicked, and she held her breath: "Is that mine?"

"It ain't," Mrs. Minns said laconically.

Helena went to the open doorway, and gazed blankly out into Main Street. She might as well go home; he wasn't going to telegraph. She told herself that he was out of town, and had not received her despatch. But her explanation was not convincing; if he was away, the despatch would have been forwarded to him. It must be that as he was coming on Saturday, he had not thought it worth while to telegraph. She wandered aimlessly out into the hot street—there was no use waiting any longer; and as for meeting David, he had gone home long ago.

As she went up the street, Dr. Lavendar stopped her. He had been told that the news of the night before did not mean affliction, but Dr. Lavendar knew that there are worse things than affliction, so he stood ready to offer comfort if it was needed. But apparently it was not wanted, and after a minute's pause, he began to speak of his own affairs: "I've been wondering if you would trust David to me for two or three days in October."

"David?" she repeated, blankly; her mind was very far away from David.

"I have to go to Philadelphia then;" Dr. Lavendar was really eager; "and if you will let me take him along—I guess Rose Knight will let him off—we would have a fine time!"

"Certainly, Dr. Lavendar," she said, courteously. But she thought quickly, that she and David would not be in Old Chester in October. However, she could not explain that to Dr. Lavendar. It was easier to say yes, and be done with it. "Good evening," she added impatiently, for the old gentleman would have kept her indefinitely, talking about David.

But as she climbed the hill her mind went out to the child with the relief of one who in darkness opens a door towards the light. She found him in the parlor, curled up in a big chair by the window, looking at a picture-book. He climbed down immediately, and came and took her hand in his, a demonstration of affection so unusual that she caught him in her arms and might have cuddled him with the undesired "forty kisses," if he had not gently moved his head aside. But her eyes were so blurred with tears of fatigue and fright she did not notice the rebuff.

The next twenty-four hours were tense with expectation and fear. Helena's mind veered almost with every breath: He had not telegraphed because he had not received her despatch; because he was away from home; because he was coming on Saturday;—*because he was sorry Frederick was dead* . . .

Saturday morning she and David watched the hill road from nine o'clock until stage-time. From the green bench under the poplar, the tavern porch on Main Street could just be seen; and at a little before twelve Jonas's lean, shambling nags drew up before it. Mrs. Richie was very pale. David, fretting at the dulness of the morning, asked her some question, but she did not hear him, and he pulled at her skirt. "Does everything grow?"

"Yes, dear, yes; I suppose so."

"How big is everything when it begins to grow?"

"Oh, dear little boy, don't ask so many questions!"

"When you began to grow, how big were you? Were you an inch big?"

"If he has come," she said breathlessly, "the stage will get up here in fifteen minutes!"

David sighed.

"Oh, why don't they start?" she panted; "what *is* the matter!"

"It's starting," David said.

"Come, David, hurry!" she cried. "We must be at the gate!" She took his hand, and ran down the path

THE AWAKENING OF HELENA RICHIE

to the gate in the hedge. As she stood there, panting, she pressed her fingers hard on her lips; they must not quiver before the child. She kept her watch in her hand. "It isn't time yet to see them; it will take Jonas ten minutes to get around to the foot of the hill."

Overhead the flicker of locust leaves cast checkering lights and shadows on her white dress and across the strained anxiety of her face. She kept her eyes on her watch, and the ten minutes passed in silence. Then she went out into the road and looked down its length of noon-tide sunshine; the stage was not in sight. "Perhaps," she thought, "it would take twenty minutes to get to the foot of the hill? I'll not look down the road for ten minutes more." After a while she said faintly, "Is it—coming?"

"No'm," David assured her. "Mrs. Richie, what does God eat?"

There was no answer.

"Does he eat us?"

"No; of course not."

"Why not?"

Helena lifted her head, suddenly; "It would take twenty-five minutes—I'm sure it would."

She got up and walked a little way down the road, David tagging thoughtfully behind her. There was no stage in sight. "David, run down the hill to the turn, and look."

The little boy, nothing loath, ran; at the turn he shook his head, and called back, "No'm. Mrs. Richie, He *must*, 'cause there's nothing goes to heaven but us. Chickens don't," he explained anxiously. But she did not notice his alarm.

"I'll wait another five minutes," she said. She

waited ten; and then another ten. "David," she said, in a smothered voice, "go; tell Maggie he isn't coming —to dinner. You have your dinner, dear little boy. I—don't want any."

She went up-stairs to her own room, and shut and locked the door. All was over. . . .

Yet when, in the early afternoon, the mail arrived, she had a pang of hope that was absolute agony, for he had written.

There were only a dozen lines besides the "Dearest Nelly":

"I am just starting out West, rather unexpectedly, on business. I am taking Alice along, and she is greatly delighted at the idea of a journey—her first. I don't know just when I'll get back; not for six weeks anyhow. Probably eight. Hope you and your youngster are all right.

"Yours, L. P.

"Your despatch received. We must talk things over the next time I come to Old Chester."

She passed her hand over her eyes in a bewildered way; for a moment the words had absolutely no sense. Then she read them again: "We must talk things over—"

What things? Why, their marriage, of course! Their marriage? She burst out laughing; and David, looking at her, shrank away.

CHAPTER XXII

THE next few days were intolerable. But of course, after the first passion of disappointment, she began to hope; he would write fully in a few days. She kept calculating how soon she might expect this fuller letter. She did not write to him, for as he had given no address it was evident that he did not wish to hear from her.

That week passed, and then another, and though he wrote, he did not write "fully." In fact, he made no allusion whatever to Frederick, or the future. Helena was instant with explanation: he was absorbed with business; Alice was with him; he had no time. That these were absurd excuses she knew. But they were the best she could find, and she had to have excuses. It was at this time that she saw herself age. When still another week passed, the tension lessened; indeed, she would have broken down under the strain if she had not fallen into a sort of apathy. She told herself that after all there was no reason why she should leave Old Chester immediately. Mr. Benjamin Wright's insolence had been outrageous and he was a horrible old man; but he had said that he would not speak of her affairs. So as far as he was concerned she could perfectly well wait until that Western trip was over; she would just try not to think of him. So she played with David, and talked to him, and listened to his confidences about the journey to Philadelphia which Dr. Lavendar planned. It was more than two months off, but that did not trouble David. He and Dr. Lavendar had long talks on the subject, of which, occasionally, the little boy dropped condescending hints.

"Maybe I'll take you to Philadelphia," Helena said once, jealously; "will you like that?"

"Yes'm," said David, without enthusiasm.

At which she reproached him; "I should think you would like to go with me, to see Liberty Bell?"

Silence.

"And maybe Mr. Pryor will take you to ride on a steamboat," she lured him.

"I like Dr. Lavendar best," said David, with alarm.

It was only David with whom Helena talked in these days of waiting; Old Chester found her still unsociable, and William King was obliged to admit that his party had not accomplished much. However, he insisted upon being sociable himself, and continued to come frequently to see her on the ground that she was not very well. Before she knew it she yielded again to the temptation of friendliness, and was glad to see the big, kind figure trudging up the garden path. He told her all the news Old Chester afforded, which was not extensive, and she replied with that listening silence which is so pleasant and that gave the doctor the opportunity—so valued by us all—of hearing himself talk; an opportunity not often allowed him in his own house. The silence covered bleak anxiety and often an entire absence of mind; but William, rambling on, could not know that. He was perfectly happy to look at her, although sometimes his face sobered, for hers had changed. It was paler; the delicate oval of her cheek had hollowed;

the charming indolence had gone; the eyes had lost their sweet shallowness, something cowered in their depths that he could not clearly see—fear, perhaps, or pain. Or perhaps it was her soul. Sometimes when the body relaxes its grip a little, the convict soul within struggles up to look with frightened bewilderment out of the windows of its prison. Dr. King watching the childlike droop of Helena's lip, admitted reluctantly that she had changed. "Depressed," he told himself. So he did his best to cheer her with Old Chester's harmless gossip; and one day—it was in September—she did show a quick and even anxious interest.

"Sam Wright's Sam has come back," the doctor said, "the young man arrived on the noon stage. I wonder what monkey-shines he'll be up to next!"

"*Oh!*" she said, and he saw her hands clasp in her lap; "I wonder if his grandfather knows?"

The color was hot in her face, and William said to himself that the cub ought to be thrashed! "Maybe he's got some sense by this journey in search of a publisher," he announced comfortingly.

In her consciousness of old Mr. Wright's dismay, she hardly heard what the doctor said; but she asked vaguely if Sam had found a publisher.

"Perhaps; I don't know. There are fools in every profession—except medicine, of course! But I believe he has not imparted any information on that point. His father merely told me he had come back." In spite of himself, William's face fell into its own kind lines. "His father is hard on him," he said; and then he began to tell her stories of the three generations of Wrights; ending with the statement that, in a dumb sort of fashion, Samuel loved his son like the apple of his eye. "But he has always taken hold of him the wrong way," William said.

Certainly the doctor's opinion was borne out by the way in which Sam senior took hold of his son on his return. Reproaches were perhaps to be expected; but, alas, the poor, sore-hearted father tried sneers as well. A sneer is like a flame; it may occasionally be curative because it cauterizes, but it leaves a bitter scar. Of his dreadful anxiety in these seven or eight weeks of absence, of his sleepless nights, of his self-accusings, of his anguished affection, the senior warden could find nothing to say; but for anger and disappointment and contempt he had fluent and searing words. Such words were only the recoil from anxiety; but Sam could not know that; he only knew that he was a disgrace to his family. The information left him apparently unmoved. He did not betray—very likely he really did not recognize in himself—the moral let-down that is almost always the result of such upbraiding. He was silent under his father's reproaches, and patient under his mother's embraces. He vouchsafed no information beyond, "I had to come back," which was really no information at all. Mr. Wright sneered at it, but Mrs. Wright was moved; she said, her mild eyes swimming in tears, "Of course, Sammy, dear. Mother understands. I knew you couldn't stay away from us."

Sam sighed, submitting to be kissed, and turned to go up-stairs; but something made him hesitate,—perhaps his mother's worn face. He came back, and bending down kissed her cheek. Mrs. Wright caught her breath with astonishment, but the boy made no explanation. He went on up to his own room and standing listlessly at the window, said again to himself, "I had to come back." After a while he added, "But I won't bother her." He had already forgotten the two sore hearts down-stairs.

The next morning he hurried to church; but Mrs. Richie was not there, and in his disappointment he was as blind to Old Chester's curious glances as he was deaf to Dr. Lavendar's sermon.

The long morning loitered past. After dinner the Wright family dispersed for its customary Sunday afternoon nap. The senior warden, with *The Episcopalian*, as large as a small blanket, spread over his face, slept heavily in the library; Mrs. Wright dozed in her bedroom with one finger marking her place in a closed volume of sermons; the little girls wandered stealthily about the garden, memorizing by their father's orders their weekly hymn. The house was still, and very hot. All the afternoon young Sam lay upon his bed turning the pages of *The Wealth of Nations*, and brooding over his failures: he could not make Mrs. Richie love him; he could not write a great drama; he could not add up a column of figures; he could not understand his father's rages at unimportant things; "and nobody cares a continental whether I am dead or alive!—except mother," he ended; and his face softened. At five o'clock he reminded himself that he must go up to The Top for supper. But it was nearly six before he had energy enough to rise. The fact was, he shrank from telling his grandfather that the drama was no longer in existence. He had been somewhat rudely rebuffed by the only person who had looked at his manuscript, and had promptly torn the play up and scattered the fragments out of the window of his boarding-house. That was two days ago. The curious lassitude which followed this *accès* of passion was probably increased by the senior warden's reproaches. But Sam believed himself entirely indifferent both to his literary failure, and to his father's scolding. Neither was in his mind as he climbed the hill, and halted for a wistful moment at the green gate in the hedge; but he had no glimpse of Mrs. Richie.

He found his grandfather sitting on the veranda behind the big white columns, reading aloud, and gesticulating with one hand:

> "'But if proud Mortimer do wear this crown,
> Heaven turn it to a blaze of quenchless fire!
> Or like the snaky wreath of Sisiphon—'"

He looked up irritably at the sound of a step on the weedy driveway, then his eyes snapped with delight.

"Hullo—hullo! what's this?"

"I had to come back, grandfather," Sam said.

"Well! Well!" said Benjamin Wright, his whole face wrinkling with pleasure. "'Had to come back?' Money gave out, I suppose? Sit down, sit down! Hi, Simmons! Damn that nigger. Simmons, here's Master Sam. What have you got for supper? Well, young man, did you get some sense knocked into you?" He was trembling with eagerness. Marlowe, in worm-eaten calf, dropped from his hand to the porch floor. Sam picked the book up, and sat down.

"If you wanted some more money, why the devil didn't you say so?"

"I had money enough, sir."

"Well—what about the drama?" his grandfather demanded.

"He said it was no good."

"Who said it was no good?" Mr. Wright pulled

off his hat, fiercely, and began to chew orange-skin. Sam, vaguely turning over the leaves of the book upon his knee, mentioned the name of a publisher. "Fool!" said Benjamin Wright; "what does he know? Well; I hope you didn't waste time over him. Then who did you send it to?"

"Nobody."

"Nobody! What did you do with it?"

"Oh, tore it up," Sam said patiently.

His grandfather fell back in his chair, speechless. A moment later, he told Sam he was not only a fool, but a d——

"Supper's ready, suh," said Simmons. "Glad you're back, Master Sam. He ain't lookin' peart, suh?" Simmons added confidentially to Mr. Wright.

"Well, you get some of that Maderia—'12," commanded the old man, pulling himself up from his chair. "Sam, you are a born idiot, aren't you? Come and have some supper. Didn't I tell you you might have to try a dozen publishers before you found one who had any sense? Your experience just shows they're a fool lot. And you tore up your manuscript! Gad-a-mercy!" He grinned and swore alternately, and banged his hat on to his head so that his ears flattened out beneath the brim like two red flaps.

They sat down at either end of the dining-room table, Simmons standing at one side, his yellow eyes gleaming with interested affection and his fly-brush of long peacock feathers waving steadily, even when he moved about with the decanter.

"I had to come back," Sam repeated, and drank his glass of '12 Maderia with as much appreciation as if it had been water.

"I've got a new family," Mr. Wright declared.

"Simmons, unhook that second cage, and show him the nest. Look at that. Three of 'em. Hideous, ain't they? Simmons, you didn't chop that egg fine enough. Do you want to kill 'em all? A nigger has no more feeling for birds than a cat."

"I done chop it, as—"

"Hold your tongue!" said Mr. Wright, amiably. "Here; take that." He fumbled in his vest pocket, and the peacock feathers dipped dangerously as Simmons caught the expected cigar. "Come, come, young man, haven't you had enough to eat? Give him another glass of wine, Simmons, you freckled nigger! Come out on the porch, and tell me your wanderings, Ulysses."

The boy was faintly impressed by his grandfather's attentions; he felt that he was welcome, which gave him a vague sort of pleasure. On the porch, in the hot dusk, Benjamin Wright talked; once or twice, apropos of nothing, he quoted some noble stanza, apparently for the joy of the rolling numbers. The fact was, he was full of happiness at his grandson's return, but he had had so little experience in happiness that he did not know how to express it. He asked a good many questions, and received apathetic answers.

"Have you got any notes of the drama?"

"No, sir."

" Doggone your picter!—

"'Then sing, ye birds, sing, sing a joyous song,
  And let the young lambs bound
  As to the tabor's sound!'

So you made up your mind to come home?"

"I had to come back," Sam said.

There was a pause. Benjamin Wright was reminding himself that in handling a boy, one must be careful not to say the wrong thing; one must express one's self with reserve and delicacy; one must weigh one's words —boys were such jackasses.

"Well;" he said, "got over your fool falling in love with a female old enough to be your mother?"

Sam looked at him.

"I hope your trip has put sense into you on that subject, anyhow?"

"I love Mrs. Richie as much as I ever did, if that's what you mean, sir," Sam said listlessly.

Upon which his grandfather flew into instant rage. "As much in love as ever! Gad-a-mercy! Well; I give you up, sir, I give you up. I spend my money to get you out of this place, away from this female, old enough to be your grandmother, and you come back and say you are as much in love with her as ever. I swear, I don't believe you have a drop of my blood in you!" He flung his cigar away, and plunged his hand down into the ginger-jar on the bench beside him; "A little boy like you, just in breeches! Why, your mother ought to put you over her knee, and—" he stopped. "You have no sense, Sam," he added with startling mildness.

But Sam's face was as red as his grandfather's. "She is only ten years older than I. That is nothing. Nothing at all. If she will overlook my comparative youth and marry me, I—"

"Damnation!" his grandfather screamed. "*She* overlook? *She?*"

"I am younger," the boy said; "but love isn't a matter of age. It's a matter of the soul."

"A matter of the soul!" said Benjamin Wright; "a matter of—of a sugar-tit for a toothless baby! Which

is just about what you are. That female, I tell you
could have dandled you on her knee ten years ago."

Sam got up; he was trembling all over.

"You needn't insult me," he said.

Instantly his grandfather was calm. He stopped
chewing orange-skin, and looked hard at his ridgy
finger-nails.

"I shall ask her again," Sam said. "I said I
wouldn't, but I will. I must. That was why I came
back. And as for my age, that's her business and
mine."

"You've drunk too much," said his grandfather.
"Sit down. I've something to say to you. You can't
marry that woman. Do you understand me?"

"You mean she doesn't care for me?" Sam laughed
noisily. "I'll make her. Old—young—what does it
matter? She must!" He flung up his arms, and then
sank down and hid his face in his hands.

"Sammy," said the old man, and stopped. "Sam,
it can't be. Don't you understand me? She isn't fit
to marry."

The young man gaped at him, blankly.

"She's—bad," Benjamin Wright said, in a low voice.

"How dare you!" cried the other, his frowning
bewilderment changing slowly to fury; "how dare
you? If she had a relative here to protect her, you
would never dare! If her brother was here, he would
shoot you; but she has me, and I—"

"Her *brother!*" said Benjamin Wright; "Sam, my
boy, he isn't her brother."

"Isn't he?" Sam flung back at him, "well, what of
that? I'm glad of it; I hate him." He stood up, his
hands clenched, his head flung back. "What difference does it make to me what he is? Her cousin, her

friend—what do I care? If she marries me, what do I care for her relations?"

His grandfather looked up at him aghast; the young, insulted innocence of love blazed in the boy's face. "Gad-a-mercy," said Mr. Wright, in a whisper, "*he doesn't understand!*" He pulled himself on to his shaking legs, and laid his hand on the young man's shoulder. "Sam," he said very gently, "he is her lover, my boy."

Sam's lips fell apart; he gasped heavily; his hands slowly opened and shut, and he swayed from side to side; his wild eyes were fixed on that old face, all softened and moved and pitying. Then, with a discordant shriek of laughter, he flung out his open hand and struck his grandfather full in the face.

"You old fool! You lie! You lie! Do you hear me?"

Benjamin Wright, staggering slightly from the blow, tried to speak, but the boy, still laughing shrilly, leaped down the porch steps, and out into the darkness.

"I'll ask her!" he screamed back; "you liar!"

CHAPTER XXIII

HELENA had gone up-stairs to put David to bed. There was some delay in the process, because the little boy wished to look at the stars, and trace out the Dipper. That accomplished however, he was very docile, and willing to get into bed by shinning up the mast of a pirate-ship—which some people might have called a bedpost. After he had fallen asleep, Helena still sat beside him in the darkness, her absent eyes fixed on the little warm body, where, the sheets kicked off, he sprawled in a sort of spread-eagle over the bed. It was very hot, and she would have been more comfortable on the porch, but she could not leave the child. When she was with David, the sense of aching apprehension dulled into the comfort of loving. After a while, with a long sigh she rose, but stopped to draw the sheet over his shoulders; then smiled to see how quickly he kicked it off. She pulled it up again as far as his knees, and to this he resigned himself with a despairing grunt.

There was a lamp burning dimly in the hall; as she passed she took it up and went slowly down-stairs. Away from David, her thoughts fell at once into the groove of the past weeks. Each hour she had tormented herself by some new question, and now she was wondering what she should do if, when Lloyd came to fulfil his promise, she should see a shade, oh, even the faintest hint, of hesitation in his manner. Well; she would meet it! She threw her head up, and came down with a quicker step, carrying the lamp high, like a torch. But as she lifted her eyes, in that gust of pride, young Sam Wright stood panting in the doorway. As his strangled voice fell on her ear, she knew that he knew.

"I have—come—"

Without a word she put the lamp down on the table at the foot of the stairs, and looked at him standing there with the darkness of the night behind him. Instantly he was across the threshold and at her side. He gripped her wrist and shook it, his eyes burning into hers.

"You will tell me that he lied! I told him he lied. I didn't believe him for a second. I told him I would ask you."

"Please let go of my arm," she said, faintly. "I don't know what you are—talking about."

"Did he lie?"

"Who?" she stammered.

"My grandfather. He said your brother was not your brother. He said he was your lover. My God! Your lover! Did he lie?" He shook her arm, worrying it as a dog might, his nails cutting into her flesh; he snarled his question out between shut teeth. His fury swept words from her lips.

She stepped back with a spring of terror, trying to pull her wrist from his grasp; but he followed her, his dreadful young face close to hers. She put her other hand behind her, and clutched at the banister-rail of the stairs. She stared at him in a trance of fright. There was a long minute of silence.

Then Sam said slowly, as though he were reading it word by word, aloud, from the open page of her face, "He—did—not—lie." He dropped her wrist; flung it from him, even, and stood motionless. Again neither of them spoke. Then Sam drew a long breath. "So, *this* is life," he said, in a curiously meditative way. "Well; I have had enough of it." He turned as he spoke, and went quietly out into the night.

Helena Richie sat down on the lowest step of the stairs. She breathed in gasps. Suddenly she looked at her arm on which were four deep red marks; in two places the skin was broken. Upon the fierce pangs of her mind, flayed and stabbed by the boy's words, this physical pain of which she had just become conscious, was like some soothing lotion. She stroked her wrist tenderly, jealous of the lessening smart. She knew vaguely that she was really wincing lest the smart should cease and the other agony begin. She looked with blind eyes at the lamp, then got up and turned the wick down; it had been smoking slightly and a half-moon of black had settled on the chimney. "Sarah doesn't half look after the lamps," she said aloud, fretfully—and drew in her lips; the nail-marks stung. But the red was dying out of them. Yes; the other pain was coming back. She paled with fright of that pain which was coming; coming; had come. She covered her face with her hands. . . .

"Who," demanded a sleepy voice, "was scolding?"

Helena looked around quickly; David, in his little cotton night-drawers, was standing at the head of the stairs.

"Who scolded? I heard 'em," he said, beginning to come down, one little bare foot at a time; his eyes blinked drowsily at the lamp. Helena caught him in her arms, and sank down again on the step. But he struggled up out of her lap, and stood before her. "It's too hot," he said; "I heard 'em. And I came down. Was anybody scolding you?"

"Yes, David," she said in a smothered voice.

"Were you bad?" David asked with interest.

Helena dropped her forehead on to his little warm shoulder. She could feel his heart beating, and his breath on her neck.

"Your head's pretty heavy," said David patiently; "and hot."

At that she lifted herself up, and tried to smile; "Come, dear precious; come up-stairs. Never mind if people scold me. I—deserve it."

"Do you?" said David. "Why?"

He was wide awake by this time, and pleaded against bed. "Tell me why, on the porch; I don't mind sitting on your lap out there," he bribed her; "though you are pretty hot to sit on," he added, truthfully.

She could not resist him; to have him on her knee, his tousled head on her breast, was an inexpressible comfort.

"When I go travelling with Dr. Lavendar," David announced drowsily, "I am going to put my trousers into the tops of my boots, like George does. Does God drink out of that Dipper?"

Her doubtful murmur seemed to satisfy him; he shut his eyes, nuzzling his head into her breast, and as she leaned her cheek on his hair—which he permitted because he was too sleepy to protest—the ache of sobs lessened in her throat. After a while, when he was sound asleep again, she carried him up-stairs and laid him in his bed, sitting beside him for a while lest he should awake. Then she went down to the porch and faced the situation. . . .

Sometimes she got up and walked about; sometimes sat down, her elbows on her knees, her forehead in her hands, one foot tapping, tapping, tapping. Her first idea was flight: she must not wait for Lloyd; she must take David and go at once. By to-morrow, everybody would know. She would write Lloyd that she would await him in Philadelphia. "I will go to a hotel" she told herself. Of course, it was possible that Sam would keep his knowledge to himself, as his grandfather had done, but it was not probable. And even if he did, his knowledge made the place absolutely unendurable to her; she could not bear it for a day—for an hour! Yes; she must get off by to-morrow night; and—

Suddenly, into the midst of this horrible personal alarm, came, like an echo, Sam's last words. The memory of them was so clear that it was almost as if he uttered them aloud at her side: "Well; I have had enough of it." Enough of what? Of loving her? Ah, yes; he was cured now of all that. But was that what he meant? "So this is life. . . . I have had enough of it."

Helena Richie leaped to her feet. It seemed to her as if all her blood was flowing slowly back to her heart. There was no pain now in those nail-marks; there was no pain in her crushed humiliation. "*I have had enough of it.*". . .

Good God! She caught her skirts up in her hand and flew down the steps and out into the garden. At the gate, under the lacey roof of locust leaves, she stood motionless, straining her ears. All was still. How long ago was it that he had rushed away? More than an hour. Oh, no, no; he could not have meant—! But all the same, she must find him: "*I have had enough of it.*" Under her breath she called his name. Silence. She told herself distractedly that she was a fool; but a moment later she fled down the hill. She must find Dr. King; he would know what to do.

She was panting when she reached his gate, and after she had rung and was beating upon the door with the palm of her hand, she had to cling to the knob for support.

"Oh come; oh, hurry! Hurry!" she said, listening to Mrs. King's deliberate step on the oilcloth of the hall.

"Where is Dr. King?" she gasped, as the door opened; "I want Dr. King!"

Martha, in her astonishment at this white-faced creature with skirts draggled by the dew and dust of the grass-fringed road, started back, the flame of the lamp she carried flickering and jumping in the draught. "What is the matter? Is David—"

"Oh, where is Dr. King? Please—please! I want Dr. King—"

William by this time was in the hall, and when he saw her face he, too, said:

"David?"

"No. It's— May I speak to you a moment? In the office? I am alarmed about—something."

She brushed past Mrs. King, who was still gaping at the suddenness of this apparition from the night, and followed the doctor into the little room on the left of the passage. Martha, deeply affronted, saw the door shut in her face.

As for Mrs. Richie, she stood panting in the darkness of the office:

"I am very much frightened. Sam Wright has just left me, and—"

THE AWAKENING OF HELENA RICHIE

William King, scratching a match under the table and fumbling with the lamp chimney, laughed. "Is that all? I thought somebody had hung himself."

"Oh, Dr. King," she cried, "I'm afraid, I'm afraid!"

He put out his friendly hand and led her to a chair. "Now, Mrs. Richie," he said in his comforting voice, "sit down here, and get your breath. There's nothing the matter with that scalawag, I assure you. Has he been making himself a nuisance? I'll kick him!"

At these commonplace words, the tension broke in a rush of hysterical tears, which, while it relieved her, maddened her because for a moment she was unable to speak. But she managed to say, brokenly, that the boy had said something which frightened her, for fear that he might—

"Kill himself?" said the doctor, cheerfully. "No indeed! The people who threaten to kill themselves, never do. Come, now, forget all about him." And William, smiling, drew one of her hands down from her eyes. "Gracious! what a wrist! Did David scratch you?"

She pulled her hand away, and hid it in the folds of her skirt. "Oh, I do hope you are right; but Dr. King, he said something—and I was so frightened. Oh, if I could just know he had got home, all safe!"

"Well, it's easy to know that," said William. "Come, let us walk down to Mr. Wright's; I bet a hat we'll find the young gentleman eating a late supper with an excellent appetite. Love doesn't kill, Mrs. Richie—at Sam's age."

She was silent.

William took his lantern out of a closet, and made a somewhat elaborate matter of lighting it, wiping off the oozing oil from the tank, and then shutting the frame with a cheerful snap. It would give her time to get hold of herself, he thought.

"I must apologize to Mrs. King," Helena said. "I was so frightened, that I'm afraid I was abrupt."

"Oh, that's all right," said Martha's husband, easily, and opened the outer door of the office. "Come."

She followed him down the garden path to the street; there in the darkness, broken by the gay zigzag of the lantern across the flagstones of the sidewalk, William found it easier to speak out:

"I hope you don't mind my referring to Sam's being in love, Mrs. Richie? Of course, we have all known that he had lost his heart. Boys will, you know. And, honestly, I think if ever a boy had excuse for—that sort of thing, Sam had. But it has distressed me to have you bothered. And to-night is the climax. For him to talk like a—a jack-donkey, because you very properly snubbed him—you mustn't mind my speaking plainly; I have understood the whole thing from the beginning—makes me mad. You're really worn out. Confound that boy! You are too good, Mrs. Richie, that's the trouble. You let yourself be imposed upon."

Her broken "no—no" seemed to him a lovely humility, and he laughed and shook his head.

"Yes, yes! When I see how gentle women are with us clods of men, I really, I—you know—" William had never since his courting days got into such a bog of sentiment, and he stammered his way out of it by saying that Sam was a perfect nuisance.

When they reached the gateway of the senior warden's place, Mrs. Richie said that she would wait. "I'll stand here in the road; and if you will make some excuse, and find out—"

THE AWAKENING OF HELENA RICHIE

"Very well," he said. "I'll come back as quickly as I can, and tell you he's all right. There isn't a particle of reason for anxiety, but it's a better sedative for you than bromide. That's the why I'm doing it," said William candidly. He gave her the lantern, and said he did not like to leave her. "You won't be frightened? You can see the house from here, and can call if you want me. I'll have to stay about ten minutes, or they wouldn't understand my coming in."

She nodded, impatient at his delay, and he slipped into the shadow of the maples and disappeared. For a minute she could hear the crunch of his footsteps on the gravel of the driveway. She sat down on the grass by the roadside, and leaned her head against the big white gate-post. The lantern burned steadily beside her, casting on the ground a shower of yellow spots that blurred into a widening circle of light. Except for the crickets all was still. The cooler air of night brought out the heavy scents of damp earth and leaves, and over in the deep grass a late May-apple spilled from its ivory cup the heavy odor of death. A bob-white fluted in the darkness on the other side of the road.

Her acute apprehension had ceased. William King was so certain, that, had the reality been less dreadful she would have been ashamed of the fuss she had made. She wanted only this final assurance that the boy was at home, safe and sound; then she would think of her own affairs. She watched the moths fly about the lantern, and when one poor downy pair of wings touched the hot, domed top and fell fluttering into the road, she bent forward and looked at it, wondering what she could do for it. To kill it would be the kindest thing, —to put it out of its pain. But some obscure connection of ideas made her shudder back from death, even a moth's death; she lifted the little creature gently, and laid it in the dewy grass.

Down the Wrights' carriage road she heard a footstep on the gravel; a step that grew louder and louder, the confident, comforting step of the kind friend on whom she relied as she had never relied on any human being.

"What did I tell you?" William called to her, as he loomed out of the darkness into the circle of light from the lantern.

"He is all right?" she said trembling; "you saw him?"

"I didn't see him, but—"

"Oh," she said blankly.

"I saw those who had, ten minutes before; won't that do?" he teased her. "I found the Wright family just going to bed—where you ought to be this minute. I said I had just stopped in to say how-do-you-do. Samuel at once reproved me, because I hadn't been to evening church."

"And he—Sam? Was he—"

"He was in the house, up-stairs, his mother said. I asked about him sort of casually, and she said he had just come in and gone up to his room. His father made some uncomplimentary remarks about him. Samuel oughtn't to be so hard on him," William said thoughtfully; "he said he had told Sam that he supposed he might look forward to supporting him for the rest of his life—'as if he were a criminal or an idiot.' Imagine a father saying a thing like that!" William lifted his lantern and turned the wick up. "Now, I'm only hard on him when he is a goose; but his father— *What was that?*"

William King stood bolt upright, motionless, his

lips parted. Mrs. Richie caught at his arm, and the lantern swinging sharply, scattered a flying shower of light; they were both rigid, straining their ears, not breathing. There was no sound except the vague movement of the leaves overhead, and faintly, from across the meadow—"*Bob-white! bob-white!*"

"I thought—I heard—" the doctor said in a whisper. Helena, clutching at his arm, reeled heavily against him.

"Yes. It was. That was what it was."

"No! Impossible!" he stammered. And they stood listening breathlessly; then, just as the strain began to relax, down through the darkness from the house behind the trees came a cry:

"Dr. King—"

An instant later the sound of flying steps on the gravel, and a girl's shrill voice: "Dr. King!"

"Here, Lydia!" William said, running towards the little figure; "what's the matter!"

Helena, in the shadow of the gate-post, only caught a word:

"Sam—"

And the doctor and the child were swallowed up in the night.

When William King came out of that house of confusion and death, he found her huddled against the gate-post, haggard, drenched with dew, waiting for him. He started, with a distressed word, and lifted her in his arms. "Oh, you ought not to be here; I thought you had gone home long ago!"

"*Dead?*"

"Yes."

"He—shot—?"

"Yes. Poor boy; poor, foolish, crazy boy! But it wasn't your fault. Oh, my poor child!"

She shivered away from him, then without a word turned towards Old Chester. The doctor walked at her side. It was nearly three, and very dark. No one saw them as they went through the sleeping streets; at William's house, she stopped, with a silent gesture of dismissal.

"I am going to take you home," he said gently. And a few minutes later he began to tell her about it. "He was dead when I got there. They think it was an accident; and it is best they should. I am afraid I'll have to explain to my wife, because she saw your apprehension. But nobody else need know. Except —I must tell Dr. Lavendar, of course; but not until after the funeral. There is no use complicating things. But other people can just think it was an accident. It was, in one way. He was insane. Everybody is, who does—that. Poor Samuel! Poor Mrs. Wright! I could not leave them; but I thought you had gone home, or I would have come. Mrs. Richie, promise me one thing: promise me not to feel it was your fault."

She dropped her face in her hands. "Not my fault! . . . I killed him."

CHAPTER XXIV

"HE was cleaning his father's pistol, and it went off—" the poor, dazed mother said, over and over. The father said nothing. He sat, his elbow on his knee, his forehead resting in the palm of his hand. Sometimes his heavy eyes glanced up, but he did not lift his head. He had hardly spoken since the accident. Then, he had said to William King:

"I suppose he undertook to clean my revolver. He always did things at queer times. I suppose it went off. It had a tricky hammer. It went off. By accident—not . . . He hadn't any reason to . . . He said, only yesterday, when he got back, that he couldn't stay away from home any longer. He said he *had* to come home. So, you see, there isn't any reason to think . . . He was cleaning it. And it went off. The hammer was tricky."

The slow, bewildered words were spoken with his eyes fixed blindly on the floor. At the sight of his dreadful composure, his wife's loud weeping died into a frightened whimper. He did not repeat the explanation. Dr. Lavendar heard it from Mrs. Wright, as she knelt beside the poor, stony father, patting his hand and mothering him.

"It was an accident, Dr. Lavendar. Sammy took a notion to clean his father's pistol. And it went off. And oh, he had just come back to us again. And he was so glad to get home. He went to church yesterday morning. I didn't have to urge him. He wanted to go. I feel sure he had begun to think of his Saviour. Yes; and he wanted to go back to the bank, and write up his ledgers; he was so happy to be among us again. Oh, Dr. Lavendar, he said to me, 'I just had to come home, mother, to you and father.' And I kissed him, and I said, 'Yes, my darling; home is the best place.' And he kissed me, Dr. Lavendar. Sammy was not one to do that—a big boy, you know. Oh, I am so glad he *wanted* to come home. And now the Lord has taken him. Oh, Samuel, try, try to say: 'Blessed be the name of the Lord!'"

The senior warden stared in silence at her plump hand, shaking and trembling on his knee. Dr. Lavendar did not urge any word of resignation. He sat beside the stricken pair, hearing the mother's pitiful babble, looking at the father's bent gray head, saying what he could of Sam—his truthfulness, his good nature, his kindness. "I remember once he spent a whole afternoon making a splint for Danny's leg. And it was a good splint," said Dr. Lavendar. Alas! how little he could find to say of the young creature who was a stranger to them all!

Dr. Lavendar stayed with them until noon. He had been summoned just as he was sitting down to breakfast, and he had gone instantly, leaving Mary wringing her hands at the double distress of a dreadful calamity and Dr. Lavendar's going without his breakfast. When he saw William King he asked no questions, except:

"Who will tell his grandfather?"

But of course there was only one person to tell Mr.

Benjamin Wright, and Dr. Lavendar knew it. "But you must come with me, William; Benjamin is very frail."

"Yes;" said William King; "only you've got to have something to eat first."

And that gave Dr. Lavendar the chance to ask Mrs. Wright for some breakfast, which made her stop crying, poor soul, for a little while.

As Goliath pulled them slowly up the hill, William told part of his part of the story. He had dropped in to the Wrights' the night before to say how-do-you-do. "It was nearly ten. I only stayed a few minutes; then I went off. I had got as far as the gate, and I was—was fixing my lantern, and I thought I heard a shot. And I said—'*What's that?*' And I stood there, sort of holding my breath, you know; I couldn't believe it was a shot. And then they called. When I got to the house, it was all over. It was instantaneous. Samuel told me that Sam had been fooling with his revolver, and—"

"Yes;" said Dr. Lavendar; "that's what Eliza told me."

Both men were silent. Then Dr. Lavendar said "Will it kill Benjamin?"

"I don't know. I don't know;" the doctor said, sighing. "Oh, Dr. Lavendar, why does the Lord hit the innocent over the guilty's shoulder? The boy is out of it; but his father and mother and grandfather, and—and others, they have got to bear it."

"Why, Willy, my boy," said Dr. Lavendar, "that's where the comfort of it is. It means we're all one—don't you see? If we suffer in the boy's suffering or wrong-doing, it is because we and he are one in Christ Jesus."

"Yes, sir," said William respectfully. But he did not understand.

When they reached The Top, it seemed to take them a long time to hitch Goliath. It was Dr. Lavendar who got himself together first and said calmly, "Come, William."

The front door was open, and the two bearers of heavy news entered unannounced. Benjamin Wright was in the dining-room, where the shutters were bowed to keep out the heat. He had taken off his hat, and was pottering about among his canaries, scolding Simmons and swearing at the weather. Dr. Lavendar and William, coming from the white glare of sunshine, could hardly distinguish him as he shuffled back and forth among the shadows, except when he crossed the strip of dazzling green light between the bowed shutters. Dr. Lavendar stopped on the threshold; William stood a little behind him.

Mr. Wright was declaiming sonorously:

> "—Did you ever see the Devil,
> With his wooden leg and shovel,
> A-scratching up the gravel—"

He paused to stick a cuttlefish between the bars of a cage, and catching sight of the first figure, instantly began to snarl a reproach:

"I might have been in my grave for all you know, Edward Lavendar; except you'd have had to 'give hearty thanks for the good example' of the deceased. What a humbug the burial service is—hey? Same thing for an innocent like me, or for a senior warden. Come in. Simmons! Whiskey"—

He stopped short; William had moved in the shadows. "Why, that's Willy King," he said; and dropped the cuttlefish. "Something's wrong. Two black coats at this hour of the day mean something. Well! Out with it! What's happened?"

"Benjamin," said Dr. Lavendar, coming into the room, "Sam's Sam—"

"Keep Willy King out!" commanded the very old man in a high, peevish voice. "I'm not going to die of it. He's—killed himself? Well; it's my fault. I angered him." He took up his hat, clutching the brim with shaking hands and pulling it fiercely down over his eyes. "Keep Willy off! I'm not—I'm not—"

Simmons caught him as he lurched back into a chair, and Dr. Lavendar bent over him, his old face moving with tears.

"It was an accident, Benjamin, either of the body or the soul—it doesn't matter which."

William King, standing behind the chair that held the forlorn and quivering heap, ventured gently: "Samuel says that Sam was cleaning his pistol, and—"

But Dr. Lavendar held up his hand and William was silent.

"Hold your tongue;" said Benjamin Wright. "Lavendar knows I don't like lies. Yes; my fault. I've done it again. Second time. Second time. Simmons! Get these—gentlemen some—whiskey."

Simmons, his yellow jaws mumbling with terror, looked at Dr. Lavendar, who nodded. But even as the old man got himself together, the brain flagged; William saw the twist come across the mouth, and the eyes blink and fix.

It was not a very severe shock, and after the first moments of alarm, the doctor said quietly:

"He is not dying."

But he was, of course, perfectly helpless and silenced;

his miserable eyes seemed to watch them, fixedly, as they carried him to his bed, and did what little could be done; but he could make no demand, and offer no explanation.

It was not until late in the afternoon that William King had time to go to the Stuffed Animal House. He had had a gravely absorbing day; not only because of the Wrights' pitiful demands upon his time, but because of the necessary explanations and evasions to Old Chester. To his wife evasions were impossible; he gave her an exact statement of the facts as he knew them. Martha, listening, and wiping her eyes, was shocked into fairness and sympathy.

"But, William, she was not to blame!"

"That's what I told her."

"Poor thing!" said Martha; "why, I feel as if I ought to go right up and comfort her."

"No, no; it isn't necessary," William said. "I'll go, on my way to The Top."

Mrs. King drew back, coldly, and sympathy wavered into common sense. "Well, perhaps it's just as well you should. I'm afraid I couldn't make her feel that she had no responsibility at all,—as you seem to think. That's one thing about me, I may not be perfect, but I am sincere; I think she ought to have stopped Sam's love-making months ago!—Unless perhaps she returned it?" Martha ended, in a tone that made William redden with silent anger. But he forgot his anger and everything else when he came into the long parlor at the Stuffed Animal House, late that afternoon.

"I've thought of you all day," he said, taking Helena's hand and looking pitifully into her face. It was strangely changed. Something was stamped into it that had never been there before. . . . Weeks ago, a hurricane of anger had uprooted content and vanity and left confusion behind it. But there was no confusion now; it had cleared into terror.

William found her walking restlessly up and down; she gave him a look, and then stood quite still, shrinking a little to one side, as if she expected a blow. Something in that frightened, sidewise attitude made him hesitate to tell her of Benjamin Wright; she hardly knew the old gentleman, but it would startle her, the doctor reasoned. And yet, when very carefully, almost casually, he said that Mr. Wright had had a slight shock—"his life is not in danger just now," said William, "but he can't speak;"—she lifted her head and looked at him, drawing a full breath, as if eased of some burdening thought.

"Will he ever speak?" she said.

"I don't know; I think so. But probably it is the beginning of the end; poor old man!"

"Poor old man," she repeated mechanically; "poor old man!"

"I haven't told Dr. Lavendar about—last night," William said; "but if you have no objection I would like to just hint at—at a reason. He would know how entirely blameless you were."

"Oh, no! please, please, don't!" she said. And William King winced at his own clumsiness; her reticence made him feel as if he had been guilty of an impropriety, almost of an indelicacy.

After a pause he said gently, that he hoped she would sit with Mrs. King and himself at the funeral on Wednesday.

Helena caught her hands together convulsively; "*I* go? Oh, no, no! I am not going."

The doctor was greatly distressed. "I know it is hard for you, but I'm afraid Samuel and his wife will be so hurt if you don't come. They know the boy was fond of you—you were always so good to him. I don't like to urge you, because I know it pains you; but—"

"Oh, I can't—I can't!"

She turned so white that William had not the heart to say anything more. But that same kind heart ached so for the father and mother, that he was grateful to her when he saw her on Wednesday, among the people gathering at the church. "Just like her unselfishness!" he said to himself.

All Old Chester, saddened and awed, came to show its sympathy for the stricken parents, and its pity, if nothing more, for the dead boy. But Helena, ghastly pale, had no room in her mind for either pity or sympathy. She heard Mr. Dilworth's subdued voice directing her to a pew, and a few minutes afterwards found herself sitting between Dr. and Mrs. King. Martha greeted her with an appropriate sigh; but Mrs. Richie did not notice her. There was no sound in the waiting church, except once in a while a long-drawn breath, or the faint rustle of turning leaves as some one looked for the burial service. The windows with their little borders of stained glass, were tilted half-way open this hot morning, and sometimes the silence was stirred by the brush of sparrows in the ivy under the sills. On the worn carpet in the chancel the sunshine lay in patches of red and blue and purple, that flickered noiselessly when the wind moved the maple leaves outside; it was all so quiet that Helena could hear her own half-sobbing breaths. After a while, the first low note of the organ crept into the stillness, and as it deepened into a throbbing chord, there was the grave rustle of a rising congregation. Then from the church door came the sudden shock of words:

"*I am the Resurrection and the Life, saith the Lord.*"

Helena, clutching at the back of the next pew, stood up with the rest. Suddenly she swayed, as though the earth was moving under her feet . . . The step of the bearers came heavily up the aisle. Her eyes fled from what they carried—("oh, was he so tall?")—and then shuddered back again to stare.

Martha King touched her arm; "We sit down now."

Helena sat down. Far outside her consciousness words were being said: "Now is Christ risen—" but she did not hear them; she did not see the people about her. She only saw, before the chancel, that long black shape. After a while the doctor's wife touched her again; "Here we stand up." Mechanically, she rose; her lips were moving in a terrified whisper, and Martha King, glancing at her sidewise, looked respectfully away. "Praying," the good woman thought; and softened a little.

But Helena was far from prayer. As she stared at that black thing before the chancel, her selfishness uncovered itself before her eyes and showed its nakedness.

The solid ground of experience was heaving and staggering under her feet, and in the midst of the elemental tumult, she had her first dim glimpse of responsibility. It was a blasting glimpse, that sent her cowering back to assertions of her right to her own happiness. Thirteen years ago Lloyd had made those assertions, and she had accepted them and built them into a shelter against the assailing consciousness that she was an outlaw, pillaging respect and honor from her community. Until now nothing had ever shaken that shelter. Nor had its dark walls been pierced by the disturbing light of any heavenly vision declaring that when personal happiness conflicts with any great human ideal, the right to claim such happiness is as nothing compared to the privilege of resigning it. She had not liked the secrecy which her shelter involved; no refined temperament likes secrecy. But the breaking of the law, in itself, had given her no particular concern; behind her excusing platitudes she had always been comfortable enough. Even that whirlwind of anger at Benjamin Wright's contempt had only roused her to buttress her shelter with declarations that she was not harming anybody. But sitting there between William King and his wife, in the midst of decorously mournful Old Chester, she knew she could never say that any more; not only because a foolish and ill-balanced youth had been unable to survive a shattered ideal, but because she began suddenly and with consternation to understand that the whole vast fabric of society rested on that same ideal. And she had been secretly undermining it! Her breath caught, strangling, in her throat. In the crack of the pistol and the crash of ruined family life she heard for the first time the dreadful sound of the argument of her life to other lives; and at that sound the very foundation of those excuses of her right to happiness, rocked and crumbled and left her selfishness naked before her eyes.

It was so unbearable, that instantly she sought another shelter: obedience to the letter of the Law—Marriage. To marry her fellow outlaw seemed to promise both shelter and stability—for in her confusion she mistook marriage for morality. At once! Never mind if he were tired of her; never mind if she must humble what she called her pride, and plead with him to keep his word; never mind anything— except this dreadful revelation: that no one of us may do that which, if done by all, would destroy society. Yes; because she had not understood that, a boy had taken his own life. . . . Marriage! That was all she thought of; then, suddenly, she cowered—the feet of the bearers again.

"I will be married," she said with dry lips, "oh, I will— I *will!*" And Martha King, looking at her furtively, thought she prayed.

It was not a prayer, it was only a promise. For with the organic upheaval into her soul of the primal fact of social responsibility, had come the knowledge of guilt.

But the Lord was not in the earthquake.

CHAPTER XXV

BENJAMIN WRIGHT lay in his great bed, that had four mahogany posts like four dark obelisks. ... He had not spoken distinctly since the night of his seizure, though in about a fortnight he began to babble something which nobody could understand. Simmons said he wanted his birds, and brought two cages and hung them in the window, where the roving, unhappy eyes could rest upon them. He mumbled fiercely when he saw them, and Simmons cried out delightedly; "There now, he's better—he's swearin' at me!" The first intelligible words he spoke were those that had last passed his lips: "M-m-my f-f—," and from his melancholy eyes a meagre tear slid into a wrinkle and was lost.

Dr. Lavendar, sitting beside him, put his old hand over the other old hand, that lay with puffed fingers motionless on the coverlet. "Yes, Benjamin, it was your fault, and mine, and Samuel's. We were all responsible because we did not do our best for the boy. But remember, his Heavenly Father will do His best."

"M-m-my f—" the stammering tongue began again, but the misery lessened in the drawn face. Any denial of the fact he tried to state would have maddened him. But Dr. Lavendar never denied facts; apart from the question of right and wrong, he used

252

to say it was not worth while. He accepted old Mr. Wright's responsibility as, meekly, he had accepted his own, but he saw in it an open door.

And that was why he went that evening to the Wright house. It was a melancholy house. When their father was at home, the little girls whispered to each other and slipped away to their rooms, and when they were alone with their mother, they quivered at the sight of her tears that seemed to flow and flow and flow. Her talk was all of Sam's goodness and affection and cleverness. "He read such learned books! Why, that very last afternoon, when we were all taking naps, he was reading a big leather-covered book from your father's library, all about the *Nations*. And he could make beautiful poetry," she would tell them, reading over and over with tear-blinded eyes some scraps of verse she had found among the boy's possessions. But most of all she talked of Sam's gladness in getting home, and how strange it was he had taken that notion to clean that dreadful pistol. No wonder Lydia and her sisters kept to themselves, and wandered, little scared, flitting creatures, through the silent house, or out into the garden, yellowing now and gorgeous in the September heats and chills.

Dr. Lavendar came in at tea-time, as he had lately made a point of doing, and sat down beside Mrs. Wright in Sam's chair.

"Samuel," said he, when supper was over and the little girls had slipped away; "you must comfort your father. Nobody else can."

The senior warden drew in his breath with a start.

"He blames himself, Samuel."

"Blames himself! What reason has *he* got to blame himself? It was my fault."

"Oh, my dear," said the poor mother, "you couldn't tell that he was going to clean your pistol."

Samuel Wright looked heavily over at Dr. Lavendar.

"Well," said the old minister, "he gave Sam the money to go away. I suppose that's on his mind, for one thing. He may think something went wrong, you know."

"Oh," broke in the mother, beginning to cry, "he was so glad to get home; he said to me the night he got back, 'Mother, I just had to come home to you and father; I couldn't stay away any longer.' I'm sure he couldn't have said anything more loving, could he? And he kissed me. You know he wasn't one to kiss much. Yes; he couldn't bear to be away from us. He said so."

"Go and see him, Samuel," urged Dr. Lavendar. "You, too, have lost a son, so you know now how he has felt for thirty-two years. His was a loss for which he knows he was to blame. It is a cruel knowledge, Sam?"

"It is," said the senior warden. "It is."

"Then go and comfort him."

Samuel went. A great experience had wiped the slate so clean of all the years of multiplications and additions of resentment and mortification, that the thought of facing his father did not stir his dull indifference to the whole dreary matter. When Simmons saw him coming up the garden path, he said under his breath, "Bless the Lawd!" Then, mindful of hospitality, offered whiskey.

"Certainly not," said Samuel Wright; and the old habit of being displeased made his voice as pompous as if he cared—one way or the other. "Can you make him understand that I'm here, Simmons? Of course, I won't go up-stairs unless he wants to see me."

"He'll want to see you, suh, he'll want to see you," said Simmons. He's right smart to-day. He kin use his left hand. He dun shuck that fist at me this mawnin'. Oh, laws, yes, he'll want to see you."

"Go and ask him."

Simmons went, and came back triumphantly. "I tole him. He didn't say nothin'. So it's all right"

The visitor went ponderously up-stairs. On the first landing he caught his breath, and stood still.

Directly opposite him, across the window of the upper hall was a horsehair-covered sofa, with great, shiny, slippery mahogany ends. Samuel Wright put his hand up to his throat as if he were smothering. . . . He used to lie on that sofa on hot afternoons and study his declensions. It had no springs; he felt the hardness of it in his bones, now, and the scratch of the horsehair on his cheek. Instantly words, forgotten for a generation, leaped up:

> Stella
> Stellæ
> Stellæ
> Stellam—

Mechanically his eyes turned to the side wall; an old secretary stood there, its glass doors curtained within by faded red rep. He had kept his fishing-tackle in its old cupboard; the book of flies was in a green box on the second shelf, at the left. Samuel looked at those curtained doors, and at the shabby case of drawers below them where the veneer had peeled and blistered under the hot sun of long afternoons, and the sudden surge of youth into his dry, middle-aged mind, was suffocating. Something not himself impelled him on up the half-flight from the landing, each step creaking under his heavy tread; drew him across the hall, laid his hand on the door of the secretary. . . . Yes; there they were: the green pasteboard box, the flannel book to hold the flies. He put out his hand stealthily and lifted the book;— rust and moth-eaten rags.

The shock of that crumbling touch and the smell of dust made him gasp—and instantly he was back again in middle age. He shut the secretary quietly, and looked around him. On the right side of the hall was a closed door. *His* door. The door out of which he had rushed that windy March night thirty-two years ago. How hot with passion he had been then! How cold he was now. On the other side of the hall a door was ajar; behind it was his father. He looked at it with sombre indifferent eyes; then pushed it open and entered. He saw a little figure, sunk in the heap of pillows on the big bed; a little shrunken figure, without a wig, frightened-eyed, and mumbling. Samuel Wright came forward with the confidence of apathy. As he stood at the foot of the bed, dully looking down, the thick tongue broke into a whimpering stammer:

"M-m-my f—"

And at that, something seemed to melt in the poor locked heart of the son.

"*Father!*" said Samuel Wright passionately. He stooped and took the helpless fingers, and held them hard in his own trembling hand. For a moment he could not speak. Then he said some vague thing about getting stronger. He did not know what he said; he was sorry, as one is sorry for a suffering child. The figure in the bed looked at him with scared eyes.

One of the pillows slipped a little, and Samuel pulled it up, clumsily to be sure, but with the decided touch of pity and purpose, the touch of the superior. That fixing the pillow behind the shaking helpless head, swept away the last traces of the quarrel. He sat down by the gloomy catafalque of a bed, and when Benjamin Wright began to say again, "M-m-my f—" he stopped him with a gesture.

"No, father; not at all. He would have gone away anyhow, whether you had given him the money or not. No; it was my fault," the poor man said, dropping back into his own misery. "I was hard on him. Even that last night, I spoke harshly to him. Sometimes I think that possibly I didn't entirely understand him."

He dropped his head in his hand, and stared blankly at the floor. He did not see the dim flash of humor in the old eyes.

CHAPTER XXVI

THE day that Sam Wright was buried Helena had written to Lloyd Pryor. She must see him at once, she said. He must let her know when he would come to Old Chester—or she would come to him, if he preferred. "It is most important," she ended, "*most* important." She did not say why; she could not write of this dreadful thing that had happened. Still less could she put down on paper that sense of guilt, so alarming in its newness and so bewildering in its complexity. She was afraid of it, she was even ashamed of it; she and Lloyd had never talked about— things like that. So she made no explanation. She only summoned him with a peremptoriness which had been absent from their relations for many years. His answer, expected and despaired of, came three weeks later.

It was early in October one rainy Friday afternoon. Helena and David were in the dining-room. She had helped him with his lessons,—for it was Dr. Lavendar's rule that Monday's lessons were to be learned on Friday; and now they had come in here because the old mahogany table was so large that David could have a fine clutter of gilt-edged saucers from his paint-box spread all around. He had a dauby tumbler of water beside him, and two or three *Godey's Lady's Books* awaiting his eager brush. He was very busy putting

THE AWAKENING OF HELENA RICHIE

gamboge on the curls of a lady whose petticoats, by a discreet mixture of gamboge and Prussian blue, were a most beautiful green.

"Don't you think crimson-lake is pretty red for her lips?" Helena asked, resting her cheek on his thatch of yellow hair.

"No, ma'am," David said briefly; and rubbed on another brushful. Helena put an eager arm about him and touched his ear with her lips; David sighed, and moved his head. "No; I wasn't going to," she reassured him humbly; it was a long time since she had dared to offer the "forty kisses." It was then that Sarah laid the mail down on the table; a newspaper and—Lloyd Pryor's letter.

Helena's start and gasp of astonishment were a physical pang. For a long time afterwards she could not bear the smell of David's water-colors; gamboge, Chinese white and Prussian blue made her feel almost faint. She took up the letter and turned it over and over, her pallor changing into a violent rush of color; then she fled up-stairs to her own room, tearing the letter open as she ran.

Her eyes blurred as she began to read it, and she had to stop to wipe away some film of agitation. But as she read, the lines cleared sharply before her. The beginning, after the "Dear Nelly," was commonplace enough. He was sorry not to have answered her letter sooner; he had been frightfully busy; Alice had not been well, and letter-writing, as she knew, was not his strong point. Besides, he had really expected to be in Old Chester before this, so that they could have talked things over. It was surprising how long Frederick had hung on, poor devil. In regard to the future, of course—here the page turned. Helena gasped, folding it back with trembling fingers: "Of course, conditions have changed very much since we first considered the matter. My daughter's age presents an embarrassment which did not exist a dozen years ago. Now, if we carried out our first arrangement, some kind friend would put two and two together, and drop a hint, and Alice would ask questions. Nevertheless"—again she turned a page—nevertheless, Lloyd Pryor was prepared to carry out his promise if she wished to hold him to it. She might think it over, he said, and drop him a line, and he was, as ever, hers, L. P.

Helena folded the letter, laying the edges straight with slow exactness.... He would carry out his promise if she held him to it. She might drop him a line on the subject.... While her dazed mind repeated his words, she was alertly planning her packing: "Can Sarah fold my skirts properly?" she thought; but even as she asked herself the question, she was saying aloud, "Marry him? Never!" She slapped the letter across her knee. Ah, he knew that. He knew that her pride would come to his rescue! The tears stung in her eyes, but they did not fall.... Sarah must begin the next morning; but it would take a week to close everything up.... Well; if he had ceased to want her, she did not want him! What a letter she would write him; what indifference, what assurances that she did not wish to hold him to that "first arrangement"; what anger, what reproach! Yes; she would "drop him that line"! Then it came over her that perhaps it would be more cutting not to write to him at all. She raised her rag of pride but almost instantly it fell shuddering to the dust—*Sam Wright*....

She sat up in her chair, trembling. Yes; she and David would start on Monday; she would meet Lloyd in Philadelphia on Tuesday, and be married that morning. Her trunks could follow her; she would not wait for the packing. George must do up the furniture in burlap; a railroad journey across the mountains would injure it very much, unless it was carefully packed.

She rose hurriedly, and taking her travelling-bag out of the wardrobe, began to put various small necessities into it. Suddenly she stopped short in her work, then went over to the mantel-piece, and leaning her arms upon it looked into the mirror that hung lengthwise above it. The face that gazed back at her from its powdery depths was thinner; it was paler; it was—not so young. She looked at it steadily, with frightened eyes; there were lines on the forehead; the skin was not so firm and fresh. She spared herself no details of the change, and as she acknowledged them, one by one, the slow, painful red spread to her temples. Oh, it was horrible, it was disgusting, this aging of the flesh! The face in the mirror looked back at her helplessly; it was no weapon with which to fight Lloyd Pryor's weariness! Yet she must fight it, somehow. It was intolerable to think that he did not want her; it was more intolerable to think that she could not match his mood by declaring that she did not want him. "But that's only because of Sam Wright," she assured herself, staring miserably at the white face in the glass; "if it wasn't for that—! But I must get more sleep; I mustn't let myself look so worn out."

In such cross-currents of feeling, one does not think consecutively. Desires and motives jumbled together until Helena said to herself desperately, that she would not try to answer Lloyd's letter for a day or two. After all, as he had so clearly indicated, there was no hurry; she would think it over a little longer.

But as she thought, the next day and the next, the wound to her affection and her vanity grew more unbearable, and her feeling of responsibility waned. The sense of guilt had been awakened in her by her recognition of a broken Law; but as the sense of sin was as far from her consciousness as ever, she was able to argue that if no one knew she was guilty, no further harm could be done. So why kill what lingering love there might be in Lloyd's heart by insisting that he keep his promise? With that worn face of hers, how could she insist! And suppose she did not? Suppose she gave up that hungry desire to be like other people, arranged to leave Old Chester—on that point she had no uncertainty—but did not make any demand upon him? It was perfectly possible that he would be shamed into keeping his promise. She said to herself that, at any rate, she would wait a week until she had calmed down and could write with moderation and good humor.

Little by little the purpose of diplomacy strengthened, and with it a determination to keep his love—what there was of it—at the price of that "first arrangement." For, after all, the harm was done; Sam Wright was dead. She was his murderer, she reminded herself, sullenly, but nothing like that could ever happen again, so why should she not take what poor happiness she could get?

Of course this acceptance of the situation veered every day in gusts of misery and terror; but, on the whole, the desire for peace prevailed. Yet the week she had allowed herself in which to think it over, lengthened to ten days before she began to write her letter. She sat down at her desk late in the afternoon, but by tea-time she had done nothing more than tear up half a dozen beginnings. After supper David rattled the backgammon-board significantly.

"You are pretty slow, aren't you?" he asked, as she loitered about her desk, instead of settling down to the usual business of the evening.

"Don't you think, just to-night, you would rather read a story?" she pleaded.

"No, ma'am," said David, cheerfully.

So, sighing, she opened the board on her knees. David beat her to a degree that made him very condescending, and also extremely displeased by the interruption of a call from William King.

"Nobody is sick," David said politely; "you needn't have come."

"Somebody is sick further up the hill," William excused himself, smiling.

"Is Mr. Wright worse?" Helena said quickly. She lifted the backgammon-board on to the table, and whispered a word of manners to David, who silently stubbed his copper-toed shoe into the carpet.

"No," the doctor said, "he's better, if anything. He managed to ask Simmons for a poached egg, which made the old fellow cry with joy; and he swore at me quite distinctly because I did not get in to see him this morning. I really couldn't manage it, so I went up after tea, and he was as mad as—as David," said William, slyly. And David, much confused, kicked vigorously.

"Do you think he will ever be able to talk?" she said.

William would not commit himself. "Perhaps; and perhaps not. I didn't get anything clear out of him to-night, except—a bad word."

"Damn?" David asked with interest.

William chuckled and then remembered to look

proper. But David feeling that he was being laughed at, hid his face on Helena's shoulder, which made her lift him on to her knee. There, in the drowsy warmth of the little autumn fire, and the quiet flow of grown people's meaningless talk, he began to get sleepy; gradually his head slipped from her shoulder to her breast, and when she gathered his dangling legs into her lap, he fell sound asleep.

"It isn't his bedtime yet," she excused herself. She rested her cheek on the child's head and looked over at the doctor. She wore a dark crimson silk, the bosom filled with sheer white muslin that was caught together under her soft chin by a little pearl pin; her lace undersleeves were pushed back so that William could see the lovely lines of her white wrists. Her parted hair fell in soft, untidy waves down over her ears; she was staring absently across David's head into the fire.

"I wish," William said, "that you would go and call on old Mr. Wright some time. Take David with you. It would cheer him up." It seemed to William King, thinking of the forlorn old man in his big four-poster, that such a vision of maternity and peace would be pleasant to look upon. "He wouldn't use David's bad word to you, I am sure."

"Wouldn't he?" she said.

For once the doctor's mind was nimble, and he said in quick expostulation: "Come, come; you mustn't be morbid. You are thinking about poor Sam and blaming yourself. Why, Mrs. Richie, you are no more responsible for his folly than I am."

She shook her head. "That day at the funeral, I thought how they used to bring the murderer into the presence of the man he had killed."

THE AWAKENING OF HELENA RICHIE

William King was really displeased. "Now, look here, you must stop this sort of thing! It's not only foolish, but it's dangerous. We can none of us play with our consciences without danger; they cut both ways."

Mrs. Richie was silent. The doctor got up and planted himself on the hearth-rug, his back to the fire, and his hands under his coat tails.

"Let's have it out: How could you help it because that poor boy fell in love? You couldn't help being yourself—could you? And Sam couldn't help being sentimental. Your gentleness and goodness were like something he had never seen before. But you had to stop the sentimentality, of course; that was just your duty. And I know how wisely you did it—and kindly. But the boy was always a self-absorbed dreamer; the mental balance was too delicate; it dipped the wrong way; his mind went. To feel it was your fault is absolute nonsense. Now there! I've never been so out of patience with you before," he ended smiling; "but you deserve it."

"I don't deserve it," she said; "I wish I did."

"When I spoke about goodness," the doctor amended, "I didn't mean to reflect on his father and mother. Mrs. Wright is one of the best women in the world. I only meant—" William sat down and looked into the fire. "Well; just plain goodness isn't necessarily—attractive. A man—at least a boy like Sam, admires goodness, of course; but he does sort of hanker after prettiness;" William's eyes dwelt on her bent head, on the sheer muslin under David's cheek, on the soft incapable hands that always made him think of white apple-blossoms, clasped around the child's yielding body;—"Yes; something pretty, and pleasant, and sweet; that's what a man—I mean a boy, Sam was only a boy; really wants. And his mother, good as she is, is not,—well; I don't know how to express it."

Helena looked over at him with a faint smile. "I thought goodness was the finest thing in the world; I'm sure I used to be told so," she ended dully.

"Of course, *you* would feel that," the doctor protested; "and it is, of course it is! Only, I can understand how a boy might feel. Down at the Wrights' there was just nothing but plain goodness, oh, very plain, Mrs. Richie. It was all bread-and-butter. Necessary; I'm the last person to say that bread-and-butter isn't necessary. But you do want cake, once in a while; I mean when you are young. Sam couldn't help liking cake," he ended smiling.

"Cakes and ale," Helena said.

But the connection was not clear to William. "At home, there was just plain, ugly goodness; then he met you. And he saw goodness, and other things!"

Helena's fingers opened and closed nervously. "I wish you wouldn't call me good," she said; "I'm not. Truly I'm not."

William laughed, looking at her with delighted eyes. "Oh, no; you are a terrible sinner!"

At which she said with sudden, half-sobbing violence, "Oh, *don't;* I can't bear it. I am not good."

The doctor sobered. This really was too near the abnormal to be safe; he must bring her out of it. He must make her realize, not only that she was not to blame about Sam Wright, but that the only shadow on her goodness was this same morbid feeling that she was not good. He got up again and stood with his back to the fire, looking down at her with good-natured determination.

"Now lock here!" he said, "conscience is a good thing; but conscience, unrestrained by common sense, does a fine work for the devil. That isn't original, Dr. Lavendar said it; but it's true. I wish Dr. Lavendar knew of this morbid idea of yours about responsibility —he'd shake it out of you! Won't you let me tell him?"

"Oh, no! no! Please don't!"

"Well, I won't; but he would tell you that it was wrong not to see straight in this matter; it's unfair to your—to Providence," William said. He did not use religious phrases easily, and he stumbled over "unfair to your Heavenly Father," which was what Dr. Lavendar had said in some such connection as this: "Recognize your privileges and be grateful for the help they have been in making you as good as you are. To deny what goodness you have is not humility, it's only being unfair to your Heavenly Father." But William could not say a thing like that; so he blundered on about Providence, while Helena sat, trembling, her cheek on David's hair.

"You are as good as any mortal of us can be," William declared, "and better than ninety-nine mortals in a hundred. So there! Why Mrs. Richie"—he hesitated, and the color mounted slowly to his face; "your loveliness of character is an inspiration to a plain man like me."

It was intolerable. With a breathless word, she rose, swaying a little under the burden of the sleeping child; then, moving swiftly across the room, she laid him on a sofa. David murmured something as she put him down, but she did not stop to hear it. She came back and stood in front of William King, gripping her hands together in a passion of denial.

"Stop. I can't bear it. I can't sit there with David in my arms and hear you say I am good. It isn't true! I can't bear it—" She stopped short, and turned away from him, trembling very much.

The doctor, alarmed at this outbreak of hysteria, and frowning with concern, put out his kind protesting hands to take hers. But she cringed away from him.

"Don't," she said hoarsely; and then in a whisper: "He is not—my brother."

William, his hand still outstretched, stared at her, his mouth falling slowly open.

"I told you," she said, "that I wasn't—good."

"*My God!*" said William King. He stepped back sharply, then suddenly sat down, leaning his head on his clenched hand.

Helena, turning slightly, saw him. "I always told you I wasn't," she cried out angrily; "why would you insist on saying I was?"

He did not seem to notice her, though perhaps he shrank a little. That movement, even if she only imagined it, was like the touch of flame. She felt an intolerable dismay. It was more than anger, far more than terror; it seemed to envelop her whole body with a wave of scarlet. It was a new, unbearable, burning anguish. It was shame.

She had an impulse to tear it from her, as if it were some tangible horror, some blazing film, that was covering her flesh. With a cry, she broke out:

"You don't understand! I am not wicked. Do you hear me? I am not wicked. You must listen!"

He made no answer.

"I am not wicked—the way you think. My husband killed my baby. I told you that, long ago.

And I could not live with him. I couldn't! Don't you see? Oh, listen, please! Please listen! And Lloyd loved me, and he said I would be happy. And I went away. And we thought Frederick would divorce me, so we could be married. But he didn't. Oh, he didn't *on purpose!* And we have been waiting for him to die. And he didn't die—he wouldn't die!" she said with a wail. "But now he is dead, and—"

And what? Alas, what? She waited a second, and then went on, with passionate conviction. "And now I am to be married. Yes, you see, I am not as wicked as you think. I am to be married; you won't think me wicked then, will you? Not when I am married? I couldn't have you say those things while I sat and held David. But now I am to be married." In her excitement she came and stood beside him, but he would not look at her. Silence tingled between them. Over on the sofa, David stirred and opened his eyes.

"The child!" William King said; "be careful." He went and lifted David to his feet. "Go up-stairs, my boy." He did not look at Mrs. Richie, who bent down and kissed David, mechanically.

"I dreamed," the little boy mumbled, "'at my rabbits had earrings; an'—"

"Go, dear," she said; and David, drowsily obedient, murmured good-night. A minute later they heard him climbing up-stairs.

Helena turned dumb eyes towards the silent figure on the hearth-rug, but he would not look at her. Under his breath he said one incredulous and tragic word:

"*You?*"

Then he looked at her.

THE AWAKENING OF HELENA RICHIE

And at his look she hid her face in her bent arm. That new sensation, that cleansing fire of shame, swept over her again with its intolerable scorch.

"No! No! I am going to be married; I—"

The front door closed behind him. Helena, alone, crouched, sobbing, on the floor.

But the Lord was not in the fire.

CHAPTER XXVII

"IS old Mr. Wright worse?" Martha called downstairs, when the doctor let himself in at midnight. "No."

"Well, where on earth have you been?" Mrs. King demanded. She was leaning over the banisters in her gray flannel dressing-gown, her candle in its hooded candlestick, throwing a flickering light on her square, anxious face.

William, locking the front door, made no answer. Martha hesitated, and then came down-stairs.

"I must say, William, flatly and frankly, that you—" she paused. "You look tired out, Willy?"

William, fumbling with the guard-chain, was silent.

"Come into the dining-room and I'll get you something to eat," said his wife.

"I don't want anything to eat."

Martha glanced at him keenly. His face was white and haggard, and though he looked at her, he did not seem to see her; when she said again something about food, he made no answer. "Why, William!" she said in a frightened voice. Then with quick common sense, she put her alarm behind her. "Come up-stairs, and go to bed. A good night's sleep will make a new man of you." And in a sort of cheerful silence, she pushed him along in front of her. She asked no more questions, but just as he got into bed she brought him a steaming tumbler of whiskey and water. "I guess you have taken a little cold, my dear," she said.

William looked at her dumbly; then realizing that there was no escape, drank his whiskey, while Martha, her candle in one capable hand, waited to make sure that he drained the last drop. When he gave the glass back to her, she touched his shoulder gently and bade him go to sleep. As she turned away, he caught that capable hand and held it in both of his for a moment.

"Martha," he said, "I beg your pardon."

"Oh, well," said Martha, "of course, a doctor often has to be out late. If you only don't come down with a cold on your lungs, it's all right."

"I sha'n't come down with a cold on my lungs," said William King.

The letter Helena wrote Lloyd Pryor after she had picked herself up, sobbing, from the floor, had no diplomacy about it. Things had happened; she would not go into them now, she said, but things had happened which made her feel that she must accept his offer to carry out their original plan. "When I got your letter, last week, I did hesitate," she wrote, "because I could not help seeing that you did not feel about it as you used to. But I can't hesitate any longer. I must ask you—"

Lloyd Pryor read as far as that, and set his teeth. "Lloyd, my friend," he said aloud, "it appears you have got to pay the piper."

Swearing quietly to himself he tore the letter into many small pieces, and threw them into the fire. "Well," he said grimly, "I have never repudiated yet; but I propose to claim my ninety days,—if I can't squeeze out of it before that!" He sat a long time in his inner office, thinking the thing over: if it had to be, if the piper was inexorable, if he could not squeeze out, how should he safeguard Alice? Of course, a girl of nineteen is bound to resent her father's second marriage; her annoyance and little tempers Lloyd Pryor could put up with, if only she need never know the truth. But how should the truth be covered? They could all three go to Europe for a year. If there was going to be any gossip—and really the chance of gossip was rather remote; very few people had known anything about Frederick Richie or his affairs, and Helena had absolutely no relatives,—but if they went to Europe for a year, any nine days' wonder would have subsided before they got back. As for the offensiveness of presenting Helena to his daughter as a stepmother, Pryor winced, but admitted with a cold impartiality, that she was not intrinsically objectionable. It was only the idea which was unpleasant. In fact, if things were not as they were, she would make an admirable stepmother—"and she is good-looking still," he thought, with an effort to console himself. But, of course, if he could squeeze out of it— And so his answer to Helena's letter was a telegram to say he was coming to Old Chester.

William King, driving down the hill in the October dusk, had a glimpse of him as the stage pulled up at the gate of the Stuffed Animal House, and the doctor's face grew dully red. He had not seen Helena since that black, illuminating night; he had not seen Dr. Lavendar; he had scarcely seen his own wife. He devoted himself to his patients, who, it appeared, lived back among the hills. At any rate, he was away from home from morning until night. William had many things to face in those long drives out into the country, but the mean self-consciousness that he had been fooled was not among them. A larger matter than mortification held him in its solemn grip. On his way home, in the chill October twilights, he usually stopped at Mr. Benjamin Wright's. But he never drew rein at the green gate in the hedge; as he was passing it the night that Pryor arrived, he had to turn aside to let the stage draw up. A man clambered out, and in the dull flash of the stage lanterns, William saw his face.

"Lloyd?" some one said, in a low voice; it was Mrs. Richie, waiting for him inside the gate. William King's face quivered in the darkness.

"That you, Nelly?" Mr. Pryor said;—"no, no; I'll carry my own bag, thank you. Did a hamper come down on the morning stage? Good! We'll have something to eat. I hope you haven't got a sick cook this time. Well, how are you?"

He kissed her, and put his arm around her; then withdrew it, reminding himself not to be a fool. Yet she was alluring! If only she would be sensible, there was no reason why things should not be as pleasant as ever. If she obliged him to pay the piper, Lloyd Pryor was coldly aware that things would never be pleasant again.

"So many dreadful things have happened!" she burst out; but checked herself and asked about his journey; "and—and Alice?"

"Oh, pleasant enough, rather chilly. She's well, thank you." And then they were at the door, and in the bustle of coming in, and taking off his coat, and saying "Hullo, David! Where's your sling?" disagreeable topics were postponed. But in the short twilight before the parlor fire, and at the supper-table, the easy commonplaces of conversation tingled with the consciousness of the inevitable reappearance of those same topics. Once, at the table, he looked at her with a frown.

"What's the matter, Nelly? You look old! Have you been sick?"

"Things have happened," she said with an effort; "I've been worried."

"What things?" he said; but before she could reply, Sarah came in with hot waffles, and the subject was dropped.

"You need more cinnamon with this sugar," Mr. Pryor said with annoyance. And Helena, flushing with anxiety, told the woman to add some cinnamon at once. "Oh, never mind now," he said.—"But you ought to look out for things like that," he added when Sarah had left the room. And Helena said quickly, that she would; she was so sorry!

"Dr. Lavendar," David announced, "he won't let you say you don't like things. He says it ain't polite. But I don't like—"

"Dry up! dry up!" Mr. Pryor said irritably; "Helena, this young man talks too much."

Helena whispered to David to be quiet. She had already arranged with him that he was not to come into the parlor after supper, which was an agreeable surprise to him; "For, you know, I don't like your brother," he said, "nor neither does Danny." Helena was too absorbed to remonstrate; she did, however, remember to tell Mr. Pryor that David had asked if she was coming up to hear him say his prayers.

"I told him I couldn't to-night; and what do you suppose he said? He said, 'Does God like ladies better than gentlemen? I do.'"

It made him laugh, as she had hoped it would. "I

fancy that is a reflection upon me," he said. "The young man has never liked me." And when he had clipped off the end of his cigar and struck a match under the mantelpiece, he added, "So you hear him say his prayers? I didn't know you were so religiously inclined."

"I'm not religiously inclined; but, of course, one has to teach a child to say his prayers."

"Oh, I don't object to religion," Mr. Pryor assured her; "in fact, I like it—"

"In other people?" she interrupted gayly.

"Well, yes; in other people. At any rate in your charming sex. Alice is very religious. And I like it very much. In fact, I have a good deal of feeling about it. I wouldn't do anything to—to shock her, you know. I really am perfectly sincere about that, Helena."

He was sincere; he looked at her with an anxiety that for once was quite simple.

"That's why I wrote you as I did about the future. I am greatly embarrassed about Alice."

She caught her breath at the suddenness of his reference, but she knew him well enough not to be much surprised. If a disagreeable topic was to be discussed, the sooner it was taken up and disposed of, the better. That was Lloyd's way.

"Of course," he went on, "if Alice knew of our—ah, acquaintance, it would shock her. It would shock her very much." He paused. "Alice's great charm is her absolute innocence," he added thoughtfully.

That comment was like a blow in the face. Helena caught her breath with the shock of it. But she could not stop to analyze its peculiar terror. "Alice needn't know," she began—but he made an impatient gesture.

"If we married, it would certainly come out."

THE AWAKENING OF HELENA RICHIE

He was standing with his back to the fire, one hand in his pocket, the other holding his cigar; he blew three smoke rings, and smiled. "Will you let me off, Nelly?"

"I know you don't love me," she broke out passionately—

"Oh, now, Helena, not a scene, please! My dear, I love you as much as ever. You are a charming woman, and I greatly value your friendship. But I can love you just as much, not to say more, if you are here in your own house in Old Chester, instead of being in my house in Philadelphia. Why, it would be like sitting on a volcano!"

"I cannot stay in Old Chester any longer," she said; "dreadful things have happened, and—"

"What things? You said that before. Do explain these mysterious allusions."

"Mr. Wright's son," she began—and then her voice broke. But she told him as well as she could.

Mr. Pryor gave a frowning whistle. "Shocking! Poor Nelly!"

"You see, I must go away," she said, wringing her hands; "I can't bear it!"

"But, my dear," he protested, "it wasn't your fault. You were not to blame because a rash boy—" Then a thought struck him; "but how the devil did he discover—?"

When Helena explained that she supposed old Mr. Wright had told his grandson, Pryor's anger broke out: "He knew? How did *he* find out?"

Helena shook her head; she had never understood that, she said. Lloyd's anger always confused her, and when he demanded furiously why she had not told him about the old fool—"he'll blazon the whole thing!"

—she protested, quivering, that Mr. Wright would not do that.

"I meant to tell you, but I—I forgot it. And anyway, I knew he wouldn't; he said he wouldn't; besides, he had a stroke when he heard about Sam, and he hasn't spoken since. And Dr. King—" she winced—"Dr. King says it's the beginning of the end."

"Thank God!" Lloyd said profoundly relieved. He stood frowning for a minute, then shrugged his shoulders, "Well, of course, that settles it; you can't stay here; there's no question about that. But there's a very pleasant little town, on the other side of Mercer, and—"

"It isn't just the going away," she broke in; "it's being different from people. I never thought about it before; I never really minded. But now, I can't help seeing that if you are—different, I mean just to please yourself, you know, it—it hurts other people, somehow. Oh, I can't explain," she said, incoherently, "and I don't want to trouble you, or talk about right and wrong, and religion, and—that sort of thing—"

"No; please don't," he said, dryly.

"But you promised—you promised!"

"I promised," he said, "and I have a prejudice in favor of keeping my word. Religion, as you call it, has nothing to do with it. I will marry you; I told you so when I wrote to you. But I felt that if I put the matter before you, and told you how difficult the situation was, and appealed to your generosity, for Alice's sake—"

"I appeal to *your* generosity!—for the sake of other people. It isn't only Alice who would be shocked, if it was found out. Lloyd, I don't insist on living with you. Keep the marriage a secret, if you want to;

only, I must, I must be married!" She got up and came and stood beside him, laying her hands on his arm, and lifting her trembling face to his; he frowned, and shrugged her hands away.

"Go and sit down, Nelly. Don't get excited. I told you that I had a prejudice in favor of keeping my word."

She drew back and sat down on the sofa, cowering a little in the corner. "Do you suppose I have no pride?" she breathed. "Do you suppose it is easy for me to—*urge?*" He saw her fingers tremble as, with elaborate self-control, she pleated the crimson silk of her skirt in little folds across her knee. For a moment they were both silent.

"Secrecy wouldn't do," he said. "To get married, and not tell, is only whipping Satan round the stump as far as Alice is concerned. Ultimately it would make double explanations. The marriage would come out, somehow, and then the very natural question would be: 'Why the devil were they married secretly?' No; you can't keep those things hidden. And as for Alice, if she didn't think anything else, she'd think I had fibbed to her. And that would nearly kill her; she has a perfect mania about truth! You see, it leads up to the same thing: Alice's discovery that I have been—like most men. No; if it's got to be, it shall be open and aboveboard."

She gasped with relief; his look of cold annoyance meant, just for the moment, nothing at all.

I shall tell her that I have met a lady with whom I was in love a long time ago—"

"*Was* in love? Oh, Lloyd!" she broke in with a cry of pain; at which intrusion of sentimentality Lloyd Pryor said with ferocity: "What's that got to do with it? I'm going to pay the piper! I'll tell Alice that, or any other damned thing I please. I'll tell her I'm going to be married in two or three months; I shall go through the form of an engagement. Alice won't like it, of course. No girl likes to have a stepmother; but I shall depend on you, Helena, to make the thing go as well as possible. That's all I have to say."

He set his teeth and turning his back on her, threw his half-smoked cigar into the fire. Helena, cowering on the sofa, murmured something of gratitude. Mr. Pryor did not take the trouble to listen.

"Well," he said, "the next thing is to get you away from this place. We've got to stage the drama carefully, I can tell you."

"I can go at once."

"Well; you had better go to New York;—what will you do with your youngster?" he interrupted himself. "Leave him on Dr. Lavendar's doorstep, I suppose?"

"My youngster?" she repeated. "Do you mean David?"

Mr. Pryor nodded absently; he was not interested in David.

"Why," Helena said breathlessly, "you didn't suppose I was going to leave David?"

At which, in spite of his preoccupation, Pryor laughed outright. "My dear Helena, even you can hardly be so foolish as to suppose that you could take David with you?"

She sat looking at him, blankly. "Not take David! Why, you surely didn't think that I would give up David?"

"My dear," said Lloyd Pryor, "you will either give him up, or you will give me up."

"And you don't care which!" she burst out passionately.

He gave her a deadly look. "I do care which."

And at that she blenched but clung doggedly to his promise. "You must marry me!"

"There is no *must* about it. I will. I have told you so. But I did not suppose it was necessary to make your giving up David a condition. Not that I mean to turn the young man out, I'm sure. Only, I decline to take him in. But, good Heavens, Helena," he added, in perfectly genuine astonishment, "it isn't possible that you seriously contemplated keeping him? Will you please consider the effect upon the domestic circle of a very natural reference on his part, to your *brother?* You might as well take your servants along with you —or your Old Chester doctor! Really, my dear Nelly," he ended banteringly, "I should have supposed that even you would have had more sense."

Helena grew slowly very white. She felt as if caught in a trap; and yet the amused surprise in Lloyd Pryor's face was honest enough, and perfectly friendly. "I cannot leave David here," she said faintly. And as terror and despair and dumb determination began to look out of her eyes, the man beside her grew gayly sympathetic.

"I perfectly understand how you feel. He is a nice little chap. But, of course, you see it would be impossible?"

"I can't give him up."

"I wouldn't," he said amiably. "You can go away from Old Chester—of course you must do that—and take him with you. And I will come and see you as often as I can."

He breathed more freely than he had for weeks;

more freely than since the receipt of that brief despatch:—"F. is dead," and the initials H. R. So far from having used a sling and a smooth stone from the brook, the boy had been a veritable armor-bearer to the giant! Well; poor Nelly! From her point of view, it was of course a great disappointment. He hated to have her unhappy; he hated to see suffering; he wished they could get through this confounded interview. His sidewise, uneasy glance at her tense figure, betrayed his discomfort at the sight of pain. What a pity she had aged so, and that her hands had grown so thin. But she had her old charm yet; certainly she was still an exquisite creature in some ways—and she had not grown too fat. He had been afraid once that she would get fat. How white her neck was; it was like swan's-down where the lace fell open in the front of her dress. For a moment he forgot his prudent resolutions; he put his arm around her and bent his head to touch her throat with his lips.

But she pushed him away with a flaming look. "David saves you, does he? Well; he will save me!"

Without another word she left him, as she had left him once before, alone in the long parlor with the faintly snapping fire, and the darkness pressing against the uncurtained windows. This time he did not follow her to plead outside her closed door. There was a moment's hesitation, then he shook his head, and took a fresh cigar.

"No," he said, "it's better this way."

CHAPTER XXVIII

"IF it was *me* that was doin' it," said Sarah, "I'd send for the doctor."

"Well, but," Maggie protested, "she might be mad."

"If it was me, I'd let her be mad."

"Well, then, why don't you?" Maggie retorted.

"Send for him?" Sarah said airily impersonal. "Oh, it's none of my business."

"Did you even it to her?" Maggie asked in a worried way.

"I did. I says, 'You're sick, Mrs. Richie,' I says.—She looked like she was dead.—'Won't I tell George to run down and ask Dr. King to come up?' I says."

"An', what did she say?" Maggie asked absently. She knew what Mrs. Richie had said, because this was the fourth time she and Sarah had gone over it.

"'No,' she says, 'I don't want the doctor. There's nothing the matter.' And she like death! An' I says, 'Will you see Mr. Pryor, ma'am, before he goes?' And she says, 'No,' she says; 'tell Mr. Pryor that I ain't feelin' very well.' An' I closed the shutters again, an' come down-stairs. But if it was me, I'd send for Dr. King. If she ain't well enough to see her own brother—and him just as kind!"—Sarah put her hand into the bosom of her dress for a dollar bill—

"Look at that! And you had one, too, though he's hardly ever set eyes on you. If she ain't well enough to see him, she's pretty sick."

"Well," said Maggie, angrily, "I guess I earned my dollar as much as you. Where would his dinner be without me? That's always the way. The cook ain't seen, so she gets left out."

"You ain't got left out this time, anyhow. He's a kind man; I've always said so. And she said she wasn't well enough to see him! Well; if it was me, I'd send for Dr. King."

So the two women wrangled, each fearful of responsibility, until at last, after Maggie had twice gone up-stairs and listened at that silent door, they made up their minds.

"David," Maggie said, "you go and wait at the gate, and when the butcher's cart comes along, you tell him you want on. An' you go down street, an' tell him you want off at Dr. King's. An' you ask Dr. King to come right along up here. Tell him Mrs. Richie's real sick."

"If it was me, I'd let him wait till he goes to school," Sarah began to hesitate; "she'll be mad."

But Maggie had started in and meant to see the matter through: "Let her be mad!"

"Well, it's not my doin'," Sarah said with a fine carelessness, and crept up-stairs to listen again at Mrs. Richie's door. "Seemed like as if she was sort of—*cryin'!*" she told Maggie in an awed whisper when she came down.

David brought his message to the doctor's belated breakfast-table. William had been up nearly all night with a very sick patient, and Martha had been careful not to wake him in the morning. He pushed his plate back, as David repeated Maggie's words, and looked blankly at the table-cloth.

"She's never really got over the shock about Sam Wright's Sam, has she?" Martha said. "Sometimes I almost think she was—" Mrs. King's expressive pantomime of eyebrows and lips meant "in love with him"—words not to be spoken before a child.

"Nonsense!" said William King curtly. "No; I don't want any more breakfast, thank you, my dear. I'll go and hitch up."

Martha followed him to the back door. "William, maybe she's lonely. I'm very tired, but perhaps I'd better go along with you, and cheer her up?"

"Oh, no," he called back over his shoulder; "it isn't necessary." Then he added hastily, "but it's very kind in you, Martha, to think of it."

"I'd just as lieves," she insisted flushing with pleasure.

He tried to get his thoughts in order as he and Jinny climbed the hill. He knew what, sooner or later, he must say to Mrs. Richie, and he thought with relief, that if she were really ill, he could not say it that day. But the sight of David had brought his duty home to him. He had thought about it for days, and tried to see some way of escape; but every way was blocked by tradition or religion. Once he had said stumblingly to Dr. Lavendar, that it was wonderful how little harm came to a child from bad surroundings, and held his breath for the reply.

"An innocent child in a bad home," said Dr. Lavendar cheerfully, "always makes me think of a water-lily growing out of the mud."

"Yes!" said the doctor, "the mud doesn't hurt it."

"Not the lily; but unfortunately, Willy, my boy,

every child isn't a lily. I wouldn't want to plant one in the mud to see how it would grow, would you?"

And William admitted that he would not.

After that he even put the matter to his wife. "Martha, you're a sensible woman; I'd like to ask you about a case."

"Oh, well," said Martha simpering, "I don't pretend to any very great wisdom, but I do know something about sickness."

"This isn't sickness; it's about a child. Do you think a child is susceptible to the influence of an older person who is not of the highest character? If, for instance, the mother was—not good; do you suppose a child would be injured?"

"Not good?" said Martha, horrified. "Oh, William! Somebody in Upper Chester, I suppose?"

"But she is a devoted mother; you couldn't be more conscientious yourself. So do you think her conduct could do any harm to a child?"

"Oh, Willy! A child in the care of a bad woman? Shocking!"

"Not bad—not bad—" he said faintly.

"Most shocking! Of course a child would be susceptible to such influences."

William drew arabesques on the table-cloth with his fork. "Well, I don't know—" he began.

"*I* know!" said Martha, and began to lay down the law. For if Martha prided herself upon anything, besides her common sense, it was the correctness of her views upon the training of children. But she stopped long enough to say, "William, please! the table-cloth." And William put his fork down.

He thought of his wife's words very often in the next few days. He thought of them when David

THE AWAKENING OF HELENA RICHIE

stood rattling the knob of the dining-room door, and saying "Maggie says please come and see Mrs. Richie." He thought of them as Jinny pulled him slowly up the hill.

Sarah was lying in wait for him at the green gate; Maggie had sent for him, she said; and having put the responsibility where it belonged, she gave him what information she could. Mrs. Richie wasn't well enough to see her brother before he went away on the stage; she wouldn't eat any breakfast, and she looked like she was dead. And when she (Sarah) had given her a note from Mr. Pryor, she read it and right afterwards kind of fainted away like. An' when she come to, she (Sarah) had said, "Don't you want the doctor?" An' Mrs. Richie said "No." "But Maggie was scared, Dr. King; and she just sent David for you."

"Quite right," said William King. "Let Mrs. Richie know I am here."

He followed the woman to Helena's door, and heard the smothered dissenting murmur within; but before Sarah, evidently cowed, could give him Mrs. Richie's message that she was much obliged, but did not wish —William entered the room. She was lying with her face hidden in her pillows; one soft braid fell across her shoulder, then sagged down and lay along the sheet, crumpled and wrinkled with a restless night. That braid, with its tendrils of little loose locks, was a curious appeal. She did not turn as he sat down beside her, and he had to lean over to touch her wrist with his quiet fingers.

"I did not send for you," she said in a muffled voice; "there is nothing the matter."

"You haven't had any breakfast," said William King. "Sarah, bring Mrs. Richie some coffee."

"I don't want—"

"You must have something to eat."

Helena drew a long, quivering breath; "I wish you would go away. There is nothing the matter with me."

"I can't go until you feel better, Mrs. Richie."

She was silent. Then she turned a little, gathering up the two long braids so that they fell on each side of her neck and down across her breast; their soft darkness made the pallor of her face more marked. She was so evidently exhausted that when Sarah brought the coffee, the doctor slipped his hand under her shoulders and lifted her while she drank it.

"Don't try to talk; I want you to sleep."

"Sleep! I can't sleep."

"You will," he assured her.

She lay back on her pillows, and for the first time she looked at him. "Dr. King, he has quarrelled with me."

William flinched, as though some wound had been touched; then he said, "Don't talk of it now."

She turned her face sharply away from him, burying it in her pillow.

"Mrs. Richie, you must try to eat something. See, Maggie has sent you some very nice toast."

"I won't eat. I wish you would go."

There was silence for a moment. Then, suddenly, she cried out, "Well? What are you going to do, all of you? What did Dr. Lavendar say?"

"Dr. Lavendar doesn't know anything about it."

"I don't know why I told you! I was out of my head, I think. And now you despise me."

"I don't despise you."

She laughed. "Of course you do."

"Mrs. Richie, I'm too weak myself to despise anybody."

"I wish you would go away," she repeated.

"I will; but you must have a sedative first."

"David's bromide?" she said sarcastically. "A broken finger, or a broken—well, anything. Dr. King—you won't tell Dr. Lavendar?"

"Tell? What kind of a man do you suppose I am! I wish you would tell him yourself, though."

"Tell him myself?" she gave him another swift look that faltered as her eyes met his. "You are crazy! He would take David away."

"Mrs. Richie," said William miserably, "you know you can't keep David."

"Not keep David!"

She sat up in bed, supported on each side by her shaking hands; she was like a wild creature at bay; she looked him full in the face. "Do you think I would give him up, just to please you, or Dr. Lavendar, when I quarrelled with Lloyd, to keep him? Lloyd wouldn't agree that I should have him. Yes; if it hadn't been for David, you wouldn't have the right to despise me! Why, he's all I've got in the world."

William King was silent.

"You think I am wicked! But what harm could I possibly do him?" Her supporting arms shook so that the doctor laid a gentle hand on her shoulder.

"Lie down," he said, and she fell back among her pillows.

"Who could do more for him than I can? Who could love him so much? He has everything!" she said faintly.

"Please take this medicine," William interposed, and his calm, impersonal voice was like a blow.

"Oh, you despise me! But if you knew—"

"I don't despise you," he said again. And added, "I almost wish I did."

But this she did not hear. She was saying desperately, "I will never give David up. I wish I hadn't told you; but I will never give him up!"

"I am going now," the doctor said. "But sometime I am afraid I must tell you how I feel about David. But I'll go now. I want you to try to sleep."

When he had gone, she took from under her pillow that letter which had made her "faint like." It was brief, but conclusive:

"The matter of the future has seemed to settle itself—I think wisely; and I most earnestly hope, happily, for you. The other proposition would have meant certain unhappiness all round. Keep your boy; I am sure you will find him a comfort. I am afraid you are a little too excited to want to see me again immediately. But as soon as you decide where you will go, let me know, and let me be of any service in finding a house, etc. Then, when you are settled and feel equal to a visit, I'll appear. I should certainly be very sorry to let any little difference of opinion about this boy interfere with our friendship. L. P."

Sitting up in bed, she wrote in lead-pencil, two lines:

"I will never see you again. I never want to hear your name again."

She did not even sign her name.

CHAPTER XXIX

TO have David go away for the long-anticipated trip with Dr. Lavendar, was a relief to Helena struggling up from a week of profound prostration. Most of the time she had been in bed, only getting up to sit with David at breakfast and supper, to take what comfort she might in the little boy's joyous but friendly unconcern. He was full of importance in the prospect of his journey; there was to be one night on a railroad-car, which in itself was a serious experience; another in an hotel; hotel! David glowed at the word. In Philadelphia they were to see the sights in the morning; in the afternoon, to be sure, Dr. Lavendar had warned him that it would be necessary to sit still while some one talked. However, it is never necessary to listen. After the talking, they would go and see the ships at the wharves, and Liberty Bell. Then—David's heart sank; bed loomed before him. But it would be an hotel bed;—there was some comfort in that! Besides, it is never necessary to sleep. The next day going home on the cars they would see the Horseshoe Curve; the very words made his throat swell with excitement.

"Did the locomotive engine ever drop off of it?" he asked Helena.

"No, dear," she said languidly, but with a smile. She always had a smile for David.

THE AWAKENING OF HELENA RICHIE

After the Horseshoe Curve there would be a night at Mercer. Mercer, of course, was less exciting than Philadelphia; still, it was "travelling," and could be boasted of at recess. But as David thought of Mercer, he had a bleak revelation. For weeks his mind had been on this journey; beyond it, his thought did not go. Now, there rushed upon him the staggering knowledge that after the night in Mercer, *life would still go on!* Yes, he would be at home; in Miss Rose Knight's school-room; at supper with Mrs. Richie. It is a heavy moment, this first consciousness that nothing lasts. It made David feel sick; he put his spoon down and looked at Mrs. Richie. "I shall be back," he said blankly.

And at that her eyes filled. "Yes, darling! Won't that be nice!"

And yet his absence for the next few days would be a relief to her. She could think the whole thing out, she said to herself. She had not been well enough to think clearly since Lloyd had gone. To adjust her mind to the bitter finality meant swift oscillations of hate and the habit of affection—the spirit warring with the flesh. She would never see him again;— she would send for him! she despised him;—what should she do without him? Yet she never wavered about David. She had made her choice. William King's visit had not shaken her decision for an instant; it had only frightened her horribly. How should she defend herself? She meant to think it all out, undisturbed by the sweet interruptions of David's presence. And yet she knew she should miss him every minute of his absence. Miss him? If Dr. King had known what even three days without David would mean to her, he would not have wasted his

breath in suggesting that she should give him up!
Yet the possibility of such a thing had the allurement
of terror; she played with the thought, as a child,
wincing, presses a thorn into its flesh to see how long
it can bear the smart. Suppose, instead of this three
days' trip with Dr. Lavendar, David was going away
to stay? The mere question made her catch him in
her arms as if to assure herself he was hers.

The day before he started, Helena was full of maternal preoccupations. The travelling-bag that she had
begun to pack for herself—for so different a journey!—
had to be emptied of its feminine possessions, and
David's little belongings stowed in their place. David
himself had views about this packing; he kept bringing
one thing or another—his rubber boots, a cocoon, a
large lump of slag honeycombed with air-holes; would
she please put them into the bag?

"Why, but darling, you will be back again on Saturday," she consoled him, as each treasure was rejected.
—("Suppose he was *not* coming back! How should I
feel?")

He was to spend the night before the journey at the
Rectory, and after supper Helena went down the hill
with him. "I wish I hadn't consented to it," she said
to herself; "do you like to go and leave me, David?"
she pleaded.

And David jumping along at her side, said joyously,
"Yes, ma'am."

At the Rectory he pushed the door open and bounded
in ahead of her. "I'm here!"

Dr. Lavendar put down his *Spirit of Missions*, and
looked over his spectacles. "You don't say so! And
you're here, too, Mrs. Richie? Come in!"

Helena, hesitating in the hall, said she had only come

to leave David. But Dr. Lavendar would not listen to that.

"Sit down! Sit down!" he commanded genially.

David, entirely at home, squatted at once upon the rug beside Danny.

"Dr. Lavendar," she said, "you'll bring him back to me on Saturday?"

"Unless I steal him for myself," said Dr. Lavendar, twinkling at David, who twinkled back, cozily understanding.

Helena stooped over him and kissed him; then took one of his reluctant hands from its clasp about his knees and held it, patting it, and once furtively kissing it. "Good-by, David. Saturday you'll be at home again."

The child's face fell. His sigh was not personal; it only meant the temporariness of all human happiness. Staring into the fire in sudden melancholy, he said, "'By." But the next minute he sparkled into excited joy, and jumped up to hang about her neck and whisper that in Philadelphia he was going to buy a false-face for a present for Dr. Lavendar; "or else a jew's-harp. He'll give it to me afterwards; and I think I want a jew's-harp the most," he explained.

"David," Helena said in a whisper, putting her cheek down against his, "Oh, David, won't you please, give me—'forty kisses'? I'm so—lonely."

David drew back and looked hard into her face that quivered in spite of the smile she had summoned to meet his eyes. It was a long look, for a child; then suddenly, he put both arms around her neck in a breathless squeeze. "One—two—three—four—" he began.

William King, coming in for his evening smoke, saw

that quick embrace; his face moved with pain, and he stepped back into the hall with some word of excuse about his coat. When he returned, she was standing up, hurrying to get away. "Saturday," she repeated to Dr. Lavendar; "Saturday, surely?"

"Why," the old man said smiling, "you make me feel like a thief. Yes; you shall have him Saturday night. Willy, my boy, do you think Mrs. Richie ought to go up the hill alone?"

"Oh, it will be bright moonlight in a few minutes," she protested nervously, not looking at the doctor.

"I will walk home with Mrs. Richie," William said.

"No! oh, no; please don't!" The dismay in her voice was unmistakable.

Dr. Lavendar thrust out a perplexed lower lip. "If she'd rather just go by herself, Willy, there are no highwaymen in Old Chester, and—"

But William King interrupted him gently. "I wish to speak to Mrs. Richie." And Dr. Lavendar held his tongue.

"I am sorry to bother you," William said, as he held the gate open for her; "but I felt I must speak to you."

Helena made no reply. All the way down the street, almost to the foot of the hill, Old Chester's evening stillness was unbroken, except for the rustle of fallen leaves under their feet. Suddenly the great disk of the hunter's moon lifted slowly up behind the hills, and the night splintered like a dark crystal; sheets of light spread sharply in the open road, gulfs of shadow deepened under trees and beside walls. It was as abrupt as sound. William King broke into hurried words as though he had been challenged: "I knew you didn't want me to walk home with you, but indeed you ought not to go up the hill alone. Please take my arm; the flagging is so uneven here."

"No, thank you."

"Mrs. Richie, please don't feel that I am not your friend, just because— Indeed, I think I am more your friend than I ever was. You will believe that, won't you?"

"Oh, I suppose so; that is the way saints always talk to sinners."

"I am far enough from being a saint," William King said with an awkward effort to laugh; "but—"

"But I am a sinner?" she interrupted.

"Oh, Mrs. Richie, don't let us talk this way! I have nothing but pity, and—and friendship. The last thing I mean to do, is to set myself as a judge of your actions; God knows I have no right to judge anybody! But this matter of David, that's what I wanted to speak to you about. My responsibility," he stopped, and drew in his breath. "Don't you see, my responsibility—"

Helena did not speak; she was marshalling all her forces to fight for her child. How should she begin? But he did not wait for her to begin.

"I would rather lose my right hand than pain you. I've gone all over it, a hundred times. I've tried to see some way out. But I can't. The only way is for you to give him up. It isn't right for you to have him! Mrs. Richie, I say this, and it is hard and cruel, and yet I never felt more"—William King stopped short—"friendly," he ended brokenly.

He was walking at a pace she found hard to follow. "I can't go quite so fast," she said faintly, and instantly he came to a dead stop.

"Dr. King, I want to explain to you—"

She lifted her face, all white and quivering in the moonlight, but instead of explanations, she broke out: "Oh, if you take him away from me, I shall die! I don't care very much about living anyhow. But I can't live without David. Please, Dr. King; oh, please; I will be good! I will be good," she repeated like a child, and stood there crying, and clinging to his arm. All her reasons and excuses and pleadings had dropped out of her mind. "Don't take him away from me; I will be good!" she said.

William King, with those trembling hands on his arm, looked down at her and trembled too. Then roughly, he pushed her hands away. "Come on. We mustn't stand here. Don't you suppose I feel this as much as you do? I love children, and I know what it means to you to let David go. But more than that, I—have a regard for you, and it pains me inexpressibly to do anything that pains you. You can't understand how terrible this is to me, and I can't tell you. I mustn't tell you. But never mind, it's true. It isn't right, no, it isn't right! that a woman who—you know what I mean. And even if, after all, you should marry him, what sort of a man is he to have charge of a little boy like David? He has deceived us, and lied to us; he is a loose liver, a—"

"Wait," she panted; "I am not going to marry him. I thought you understood that."

He drew away from her with a horrified gesture. "And you would keep an innocent child—"

"No! No! I've broken with him—on account of David!"

"Broken with him!" said William King; he caught her by the wrist, and stared at her. Then with a breathless word that she could not hear, he dropped her hand and turned his face away.

Again, in their preoccupation, they stood still; this time in a great bank of shadow by the wall of the graveyard half-way up the hill.

"So you won't take him from me?" she said; "I will leave Old Chester. You need never see me again."

"Good God!" said William King, "do you think that is what I want?"

She tried to see his face, but he had turned his back on her so that she stood behind him. Her hands were clasping and unclasping and her voice fluttering in her throat. "You won't take him?"

"Mrs. Richie," he said harshly, "do you love that man still?"

But before she could answer, he put the question aside. "No! Don't tell me. I've no right to ask. I—don't want to know. I've no right to know. It's—it's nothing to me, of course." He moved as he spoke out into the moonlight, and began to climb the pebbly road; she was a step or two behind him. When he spoke again his voice was indifferent to the point of contempt. "This side is smoother; come over here. I am glad you are not going to marry Mr. Pryor. He is not fit for you to marry."

"Not fit for—*me!*" she breathed.

"And I am glad you have broken with him. But that has no bearing upon your keeping David. A child is the most precious thing in the world; he must be trained, and—and all that. Whether you marry this man or not makes no difference about David. If you have lived—as you have lived—you ought not to have him. But I started the whole thing. I made Dr. Lavendar give him to you. He didn't want to, somehow; I don't know why. So don't you see? I *can't* leave him in your care. Surely you see that? I am responsible. Responsible not only to David, but to Dr. Lavendar."

"If Dr. Lavendar is willing to let me have him, I don't see why you need to feel so about it. What harm could I do him? Oh, how cruel you are—how cruel you are!"

"Would Dr. Lavendar let you have him, if — he knew?"

"But that's over; that's finished," she insisted, "oh, I tell you, it's over!"

The doctor's silence was like a whip.

"Oh, I know; you think that he was here last week. But there has to be a beginning of everything—that was the beginning. I told him I would not give David up to marry him; and we quarrelled. And—it's over."

"I can't go into that," the doctor said. "That's not my business. David is my business. Mrs. Richie, I want you quietly, without any explanation, to give the boy back to Dr. Lavendar. If you don't, I shall have no choice. I shall have to tell him."

"But you said you wouldn't tell him! Oh, you break your word—"

"I won't tell him your affairs," said William King. "I will never do that. But I'll tell him my own—some of them. I'll say I made a mistake when I advised him to let you have David, and that I don't think you ought to be trusted to bring up a little boy. But I won't say why."

"Dr. King, if I tell him just what you've said; that you think you made a mistake, and you think I am not to be trusted;—if I tell him myself, and he consents to let me keep him, will you interfere?"

William reflected heavily. "He won't consent," he said; "he'll know I wouldn't say a thing like that without reason. But if he does, I shall be silent."

There was a despairing finality in his words. They were at her own gate now; she leaned her head down on it, and he heard a pitiful sound. William King's lips were dry, and when he spoke the effort made his throat ache. What he said was only the repetition of his duty as he saw it. "I'd rather lose my right hand than make you suffer. But I've no choice. I've no choice!" And when she did not answer, he added his ultimatum. "I'll have to tell Dr. Lavendar on Sunday, unless you will just let me settle it all for you by saying that you don't want David any long—"

"*Not want David!*"

"I mean, that you've decided you won't keep him any longer. I'll find a good home for him, Mrs. Richie," he ended in a shaking voice.

She gave him one look of terror; then opened the gate and shut it quickly in his face, drawing the bolt with trembling fingers. As she flew up the path, he saw her for an instant as she crossed a patch of moonlight; then the darkness hid her.

CHAPTER XXX

IT was incredible to David as he thought it over afterwards, but he actually slept away that wonderful night on the railroad! When he climbed on to the shutting-up shelf behind red and green striped curtains, nothing had been further from his mind than sleep. It was his intention to sit bolt upright and watch the lamps swinging in the aisle, to crane his neck over the top of the curtains and look out of the small hinged window at the smoke all thick with sparks from the locomotive engine, and at the mountains with the stars hanging over them, and—at the Horseshoe Curve! But instead of seeing all these wonders that he and Dr. Lavendar had talked about for the last few weeks, no sooner had he been lifted into his berth than, in a flash, the darkness changed to bright daylight. Yes; the dull, common, everynight affair of sleep, had interfered with all his plans. He did not speak of his disappointment the next morning, as he dressed—somehow—in the jostling, swaying little enclosure where the washstands were; but he thought about it, resentfully. Sleep! "When I'm a man, I'll never sleep," he assured himself; then cheered up as he realized that absence from Sarah had brought at least one opportunity of manhood— he would not have to wash behind his ears! But he brooded over his helplessness to make up for that other loss. He was so silent at breakfast in the station that Dr. Lavendar thought he did not like his food.

"You can have something else, David. What do you want?"

"Ice-cream," David said, instantly alert.

"At breakfast!" David nodded, and the ice-cream appeared. He ate it in silence, and when he had scraped the saucer, he said,

"Can you ever get back behind, sir?"

"Behind what?" Dr. Lavendar asked. He was looking at David and wondering what was different about the child; he did not have quite his usual aspect. "I must have left off some of his clothes," Dr. Lavendar thought anxiously, and that question about getting back behind suggested buttons. "Are your braces fastened?" he asked.

"And do it over again," David said. "Is there any way you can get back behind, and do it over again?"

"Do what over again?" Dr. Lavendar said. "If they've come unfastened—"

"I don't like sleeping," said David. "If I could get behind again, I wouldn't."

Dr. Lavendar gave it up, but he fumbled under David's little coat and discovered that the buttons were all right. "There seems to be something different about you, David," he said, as they pushed their chairs from the table. David had no explanation to offer, so Dr. Lavendar consulted the waitress: "Is there anything wrong about this little boy's clothing? He doesn't look just right—"

"I guess he hasn't had his hair brushed, sir," said the smiling young woman, and carried the child off to some lair of her own, whence he emerged in his usual order.

"Thank you, my dear," said Dr. Lavendar. He took David's hand, and out they stepped into the world! For a moment they stood still on the sidewalk to get their breaths in the rush and jostle of the crowd that surged along the street; a simple, happy pair—an old man in a blue muffler and broad-brimmed felt hat, a child in a little surtout and visored cap. David gripped Dr. Lavendar's hand tight, and looked up into his face; its smile beaming upon all these hurrying people, reassured the child, and he paced along beside the old gentleman in grave content. They stopped at the first shop-window, and gazed at a row of fish bedded in ice—beautiful iridescent mackerel, fat red pompoms, and in the middle, in a nest of seaweed, green-black creatures, with great claws that ended in pincers and eyes that looked like pegs stuck into their heads. David stared, open-mouthed; then he put a hand into his pocket.

"How much would one cost, sir?"

"I don't know," said Dr. Lavendar.

"I think I will buy one, and take it home and keep it in a cage."

At which Dr. Lavendar said gravely, that he feared the creatures would not be happy in a cage—"And besides, people eat them, David."

David was silent; then, in a suppressed voice, he said, "Are they happy when people eat them? I think they'd rather be in a cage; I would hang it in my window."

But Dr. Lavendar only said, "Dear me! What have we here?" and drew him to the next shop, at the door of which stood a wooden Indian, a tomahawk in one hand, and a cigar-box in the other. Dr. Lavendar bade David wait outside while he went into this shop, which the little boy was perfectly willing to do, for it isn't every day you get the chance to examine a wooden Indian, even to climbing up on his pedestal and feeling his tomahawk with respectful fingers. When Dr. Lavendar came out, David took his kind old hand, and burst into confidences.

"When I'm big I'm going to fight Indians. Or else I'll drive fast horses. I don't know which. It's hard to decide, ain't it, sir?"

"Very hard. If you choose the horses, I'll give you Goliath."

David was silent; then he sighed: "I guess I'll fight Indians, sir," he said.

But a moment later he was cheerfully confidential: he had thirty cents to spend! "Dear, dear," said Dr. Lavendar, "we mustn't do anything rash. Here, let's look in this window."

Oh, how many windows there were, and all of them full of beautiful things! Dr. Lavendar was willing to stop at every one; and he joined in David's game of "mine," with the seriousness that all thoughtful persons give to this diversion.

"That's *mine!*" David would cry, pointing to a green china toad behind the plate glass; and Dr. Lavendar would say gravely,

"You may have it, David; you may have it."

"Now it's your turn!" David would instruct him.

"Must I take something in this window?" Dr. Lavendar would plead. And David always said firmly that he must. "Well, then, that's *mine*," Dr. Lavendar would say.

"Why, that's only a teacup! We have thousands

of them at our house!" David boasted. "I should think you would rather have the toad. I'll—I'll give you the toad, sir?"

"Oh, dear me, no," Dr. Lavendar protested; "I wouldn't rob you for the world." And so they sauntered on, hand in hand. When they came to a book-store, Dr. Lavendar apologized for breaking in upon their "game." "I'm going to play *mine*, in here," he said.

David was quite content to wait at the door and watch the people, and the yellow boxes full of windows, drawn by mules with bells jingling on their harness. Sometimes he looked fearfully back into the shop; but Dr. Lavendar was still playing "mine," so all was well. At last, however, he finished his game and came to the door.

"Come along, David; this is the most dangerous place in town!"

David looked at him with interest. "Why did you skip with your eye when you said that, sir?" he demanded.

At which the clerk who walked beside them laughed loudly, and David grew very red and angry.

But when Dr. Lavendar said, "David, I've got a bone in my arm; won't you carry a book for me?" he was consoled, and immediately began to ask questions. It seemed to Dr. Lavendar that he inquired about everything in heaven and earth and the waters under the earth, and at last the old gentleman was obliged, in self-defence, to resort to the formula which, according to the code of etiquette understood by these two friends, signified "stop talking."

"What is—" David began, and his companion replied glibly:

"Layovers for meddlers and crutches for lame ducks."

And David subsided into giggles, for it was understood that this remark was extremely humorous.

After that they went to dinner with a gentleman who wore a long black coat and no shirt; at least, David could not see any shirt. Dr. Lavendar called him Bishop, and they talked a great deal about uninteresting things. David only spoke twice: His host took occasion to remark that he did not finish all his mashed potato—"Some poor child would be glad of what you waste," said the Bishop. To which David replied, "If I ate it, what then, for the poor child?" And the gentleman with no shirt said in a grave aside to Dr. Lavendar that the present generation was inclined to pertness. His second remark was made when the clergymen pushed their chairs back from the table. But David sat still. "We haven't had the ice-cream yet," he objected, gently. "Hush! Hush!" said Dr. Lavendar. And the gentleman laughed very hard, and said that he had to send all his ice-cream to the heathen. David, reddening, looked at him in stolid silence. In the afternoon there was a pause; they went to church, and listened to another gentleman, who talked a long, long time. Sometimes David sighed, but he kept pretty quiet, considering. After the talk was over, Dr. Lavendar did not seem anxious to get away. David twitched his sleeve once or twice to indicate his own readiness, but it appeared that Dr. Lavendar preferred to speak to the talking gentleman. And the talking gentleman patted David's head and said:

"And what do you think of foreign missions, my little boy?"

David did not answer, but he moved his head from under the large white hand.

"You were very good and quiet," said the talking

THE AWAKENING OF HELENA RICHIE

gentleman. "I saw you, down in the pew with Dr. Lavendar. And I was very much complimented; you never went to sleep."

"I couldn't," said David, briefly; "the seats are too hard." The talking gentleman laughed a little, and you might have thought Dr. Lavendar skipped with his eye;—at any rate, he laughed.

"They don't always tell us why they keep awake," he said. And the talking gentleman didn't laugh any more.

At last, however, they stopped wasting time, and took up their round of dissipation again. They went to see Liberty Bell; then they had supper at a marble-topped table, in a room as big as a church!

"Ice-cream, suh?" suggested a waiter, and David said "Yes!" Dr. Lavendar looked doubtful, but David had no doubts. Yet, half-way through that pink and white and brown mound on his saucer, he sighed, and opened and shut his eyes as if greatly fatigued.

"Finished?" Dr. Lavendar asked.

"No, sir," David said sadly, and started in with a spurt; but the mound did not seem to diminish, and suddenly his chin quivered. "If you have to pay for what I don't eat, I'll try," he said; "but my breast is cold." Reassured on this point, and furtively rubbing his little chilly stomach, David put down his spoon and slipped out of his chair, ready to make a night of it. For, supper over, they went to see a magician!

"I don't know what Mrs. Richie will say to me," said Dr. Lavendar. "You won't get to bed before ten o'clock!"

"She'll say 'all right,'" said David. Then he added, "The gentleman at dinner tells lies, or else he's foolish. It would melt before the heathen got it."

THE AWAKENING OF HELENA RICHIE

Dr. Lavendar, singing to himself—

Hither ye faithful, haste with songs of triumph,—

did not hear the morals of his bishop aspersed. He took David's hand, and by and by they were sitting staring open-mouthed at a man who put eggs in a pan, and held it over a fire, and took out live pigeons! Oh, yes, and many other wonders! David never spoke once on his way back to the hotel, and Dr. Lavendar began to be worried for fear the child was overtired. He hustled him to bed as quickly as possible, and then sat down under the far-off chandelier of the hotel bedroom, to glance at a newspaper and wait until David was asleep before he got into his own bed. He did not have to wait long for the soft breathing of childish sleep. It had been poor David's intention to go over in his mind every single thing he saw the magician do, so that he wouldn't leave out anything at recess on Monday. Alas, before he could begin to think, the sun was shining again!

It was Dr. Lavendar who did the thinking before the sunlight came. Twice, in his placid, wakeful night, he rose to make sure the child was all right, to pull up an extra blanket about the small shoulders or to arrange the pillow, punched by David's fist to the edge of the bed. In the morning he let the little boy look out of the window while he packed up their various belongings; and when it was time to start, David could hardly tear himself away from that outlook, which makes such a mystical appeal to most of us—huddling roofs and chimneys under a morning sky. But when he did turn to look at Dr. Lavendar, tucking things into his valise and singing to himself, it was to realize again the immutable past. "No," he said slowly, "you can't get back behind, and begin again." Dr. Lavendar, understanding, chuckled.

"Can God?" said David.

At that Dr. Lavendar's face suddenly shone. "David," he said, "the greatest thing in the world is to know that God is always beginning again!"

But David had turned to the window to watch a prowling cat upon a roof; and then, alas, it was time to start.

"Well," said Dr. Lavendar, as, hand in hand, they walked to the big, roaring place where the cars were, "Well, David, to-morrow we shall be at home again! You sit down here and take care of my bag while I go and get the tickets."

David slid sidewise on to the slippery wooden settee. He had nothing to say; again he felt that bleak sinking right under his little breast-bone; but it stopped in the excitement of seeing Mrs. Richie's brother coming into the waiting-room! There was a young lady at his side, and he piloted her across the big, bare room, to the very settee upon which David was swinging his small legs.

"I must see about the checks, dear," he said, and hurried off without a glance at the little boy who was guarding Dr. Lavendar's valise.

The sun pouring through the high, dusty window, shone into David's eyes. He wrinkled his nose and squinted up at the young lady from under the visor of his blue cap. She smiled down at him, pleasantly, and then opened a book; upon which David said bravely, "You're nineteen. I'm seven, going on eight."

"What!" said the young lady; she put her book

down, and laughed. "How do you know I am nineteen, little boy?"

"Mrs. Richie's brother said so."

She looked at him with amused perplexity. "And who is Mrs. Richie's brother?"

David pointed shyly at the vanishing figure at the end of the waiting-room.

"Why, no, dear, that's my father."

"*I* know," said David; "he's Mr. Pryor, Mrs. Richie's brother. He comes and stays at our house."

"Stays at your house? What on earth are you talking about, you funny little boy! Where is your house?"

"O' Chester," said David.

The young lady laughed and gave him a kind glance. "You've made a mistake, I think. My father doesn't know Mrs. Richie."

David had nothing to say, and she opened her book. When Mr. Pryor returned, hurrying to collect the bags and umbrellas, David had turned his back and was looking out of the window.

It was not until they were in the train that Alice remembered to speak of the incident. "Who in the world is Mrs. Richie?" she demanded gayly, "and where is Old Chester?"

The suddenness of it was like a blow. Lloyd Pryor actually gasped; his presence of mind so entirely deserted him, that before he knew it, he had lied—and no one knew better than Lloyd Pryor that it is a mistake to lie hurriedly.

"I—I don't know! Never heard of either of them."

His confusion was so obvious that his daughter gave him a surprised look. "But I'm told you stay at Mrs. Richie's house, in Old Chester," she said laughing.

THE AWAKENING OF HELENA RICHIE

"What are you talking about!"

"Why, father," she said blankly; his irritation was very disconcerting.

"I tell you I never heard of such a person!" he repeated sharply; and then realized what he had done. "Damn it, what did I lie for?" he said to himself, angrily; and he began to try to get out of it: "Old Chester? Oh, yes; I do remember. It's somewhere near Mercer, I believe. But I never went there in my life." Then he added in his own mind, "Confound it, I've done it again! What the devil has happened? Who has told her?" Aloud, he asked where she had heard of Old Chester.

She began to tell him about a little boy, who said—"it was too funny!" she interrupted herself, smiling—"who said that *you* were 'Mrs. Richie's brother,' and you stayed at her house in Old Chester, and—"

"Perfect nonsense!" he broke in. "He mistook me for some one else, I suppose."

"Oh, of course," she agreed, laughing; upon which Mr. Pryor changed the subject by saying that he must look over some papers. "Don't talk now, dear," he said.

Alice subsided into her novel; but after a while she put the book down. No; the little boy had not mistaken him for somebody else; "he's Mr. Pryor," the child had said. But, of course, the rest was all a funny mistake. She took the book up again, but as she read, she began to frown. Old Chester: Where had she heard of Old Chester? Then she remembered. A gentleman who came to call,—King? Yes; that was his name; Dr. King. He said he had come from Old Chester. And he had spoken of somebody—now, who was it? Oh, yes, Richie; Mrs. Richie. And once last

311

spring when her father went to Mercer he said he was going to Old Chester; yet now he said he had never heard of the place.—Why! it almost seemed as if she had blundered upon a secret! Her uneasy smile faded involuntarily into delicate disgust; not because the nature of the secret occured to her, but because secrecy in itself was repugnant to her, as it is to all nobler minds. She said to herself, quickly, that her father had forgotten Old Chester, that was all. Of course, he had forgotten it!—or else— She did not allow herself to reach the alternative which his confusion so inevitably suggested:—secrecy, protected by a lie. In the recoil from it she was plunged into remorse for a suspicion which she had not even entertained. Truth was so much to this young creature, that even the shadow of an untruth gave her a sense of uneasiness which she could not banish. She looked furtively at her father, sorting out some papers, his lips compressed, his eyebrows drawn into a heavy frown, and assured herself that she was a wicked girl to have wondered, even for a minute, whether he was perfectly frank. He! Her ideal of every virtue! And besides, why should he not be frank? It was absurd as well as wicked to have that uneasy feeling. "I am ashamed of myself!" she declared hotly, and took up her novel. . . .

But David had thrown the smooth stone from the brook!

It was a very little stone; the giant did not know for many a day where he had been hit; yet it had struck him in the one vulnerable point in his armor—his daughter's trust in him. How the wound widened does not belong to this story.

When Dr. Lavendar came bustling back with his tickets, David was absorbed in thought. He had very little to say on the long day's journey over the mountains. When they reached Mercer where they were to spend the night, he had nothing whatever to say; his eyes were closing with fatigue, and he was asleep almost before his little yellow head touched the pillow. In the morning he asked a question:

"Is it a Aunt if you don't know it?"

"What?" said Dr. Lavendar, winding his clean stock carefully around his neck.

But David relapsed into silence. He asked so few questions that day that crutches for lame ducks were referred to only once.

They took the afternoon stage for Old Chester. It was a blue, delicious October day. David sat on the front seat between Dr. Lavendar and Jonas, and as Jonas told them all that had happened during their long absence, the child felt a reviving interest in life. Dr. Lavendar's humming broke out into singing; he sang scraps of songs and hymns, and teased David about being sleepy. "I believe he's lost his tongue, Jonas; he hasn't said boo! since we left Mercer. I suppose he won't have a thing to tell Mrs. Richie, not a thing!"

"Well, now, there!" said Jonas, "her George gimme a letter for you, and I'll be kicked if I ain't forgot it!" He thrust his left leg out, so that his cow-hide boot hung over the dashboard, and fumbled in his pocket; then thrust out the right leg and fumbled in another pocket; then dived into two or three coat pockets; finally a very crumpled note, smelling of the stable, came up from the depths and was handed to Dr. Lavendar.

"Slow down these two-forties on a plank road, Jonas, till I get my glasses on," said Dr. Lavendar.

THE AWAKENING OF HELENA RICHIE

After he read the letter he did not sing any more; his face fell into deeply puzzled lines. "I must ask Willy what it's all about," he said to himself. Certainly the note did not explain itself:

"DEAR DR. LAVENDAR: If it will not inconvenience you, will you let David stay at the rectory to-night?—and perhaps for a few days longer. I am not sure whether I shall be able to keep him. I may have to give him back to you. Will you let him stay with you until I can decide what to do?
"HELENA R."

"I wonder if that brother has interfered?" thought Dr. Lavendar. "Something has happened; that's evident. Keep him? Well, I guess I will!" He looked down at David, his old eyes beaming with pleasure. "Mrs. Richie wants you to stay with me to-night; what do you think of that?"

"I wanted to see the rabbits," said David; "but I don't mind staying—very much."

CHAPTER XXXI

"PERHAPS she feels that it would be better for David to be—in different surroundings."

"But Willy! Wednesday night she told me that I must be sure and bring him back to her on Saturday. What has happened between Wednesday and Saturday?"

"Very likely nothing has happened between Wednesday and Saturday. But perhaps she has just made up her mind."

"Ho!" said Dr. Lavendar; and after a while he added, "'Um."

Monday morning he went up to the Stuffed Animal House. But Mrs. Richie sent word down-stairs that she wasn't well; would he be so kind as to excuse her and to keep David a little longer. Sarah, when she gave the message, looked as mystified as Dr. Lavendar felt. "I always thought she was just wrapped up in that there boy," she told Maggie; "and yet she lets him stay away two days after he gets home!" Dr. Lavendar, poking on with Goliath up the hill to Benjamin Wright's, had very much the same feeling: "Queer! I wish Willy wasn't bottled up; of course he knows what it means. Well; if I wait, she'll explain it herself."

But many days were to pass before Helena made any effort to explain. And meantime Dr. Lavendar's mind was full of something else: old Benjamin Wright was running down-hill very rapidly.

In certain ways he seemed better; he could talk—and swear—quite fluently. "He sayed to me, this mawnin'," Simmons told Dr. Lavendar, "'Simmons, you freckled nigger,' he said, 'in the name of Lot's wife, who salted my porridge?' He spoke out just as plain!" Simmons detailed this achievement of the poor dulled tongue, with the pride of a mother repeating her baby's first word. Then he simpered with a little vanity of his own: "He was always one to notice my freckles," he said.

Benjamin Wright, lying in his bed with his hat on noticed other things than Simmons's freckles, and spoke of them, too, quite distinctly. "My boy, S-Sam, is a good boy. He comes up every day. Well, Lav-Lavendar, sometimes I think I was—at fault?"

"I know you were, Benjamin. Have you told him so?"

"Gad-a-mercy! N-no!" snarled the other. "He would be too puffed up. Won't do to make young people v-vain."

He "took notice," too, Simmons said, of the canaries; and he even rolled out, stammeringly, some of his favorite verses. But, in spite of all this, he was running down-hill; he knew it himself, and once he told Dr. Lavendar that this business of dying made a man narrow. "I th-think about it all the time," he complained. "Can't put my mind on anything else. It's damned narrowing."

Yet William King said to Dr. Lavendar that he thought that if the old man could be induced to talk of his grandson, he might rally. "He never speaks of him," the doctor said, "but I am sure he is brooding over him all the time. Once or twice I have referred to the boy, but he pretends not to hear me. He's using up all his strength to bear the idea that he is to blame. I wish I could tell him that he isn't," the doctor ended, sighing.

They had met in the hall as William was coming down-stairs and Dr. Lavendar going up. Simmons, who had been shuffling about with a decanter and hospitable suggestions, had disappeared into the dining-room.

"Well," said Dr. Lavendar, "why don't you tell him? Though in fact, perhaps he is to blame in some way that we don't know? You remember, he said he had 'angered the boy'?"

"No; that wasn't it," said William.

Dr. Lavendar looked at him with sudden attention. "Then what—" he began, but a lean, freckled shadow in the dining-room doorway, spoke up:

"Maybe he might 'a' made Marster Sam's Sam mad, suh, that night; maybe he might 'a'. But that weren't no reason," said Simmons, in a quivering voice, "for a boy to hit out and give his own grandfather a lick. No, suh; it warn't. An' call him a liar!" Dr. Lavendar and William King stared at each other and at the old man, in shocked dismay. "His grandfather used words, maybe, onc't in a while," Simmons mumbled on, "but they didn't mean no mo'n skim-milk. Don't I know? He's damned me for forty years, but he'll go to heaven all the same. The Lawd wouldn't hold it up agin' him, if a pore nigger wouldn't. If He would, I'd as lief go to hell with Mr. Benjamin as any man I know. Yes, suh, as I would with you yo'self, Dr. Lavendar. He was cream kind; yes, he was! One o' them pore white-trash boys at Morison's shanty

Town, called me 'Ashcat' onc't; Mr. Wright he cotched him, and licked him with his own hands, suh! An' he was as kind to Marster Sam as if he was a baby. But Marster Sam hit him a lick. No, suh; it weren't right—" Simmons rubbed the cuff of his sleeve over his eyes, and the contents of the tilting decanter dribbled down the front of his spotted old coat.

"Simmons," said Dr. Lavendar, "what had they been quarrelling about?"

But Simmons said glibly, that 'fore the Lawd, he didn't know.

"He does know," said Dr. Lavendar, as the man again retired to his pantry. "But, after all, the subject of the quarrel doesn't make any difference. To think that the boy struck him! That must be a satisfaction to Benjamin."

"A satisfaction?" William repeated, bewildered.

But Dr. Lavendar did not explain. He went on up-stairs, and sat beside the very old man, listening to his muffled talk, and saying what he could of commonplace things. Once Benjamin Wright asked about Mrs. Richie:

"That female at the S-Stuffed Animal House—how is she? Poor cr-creeter; pretty creeter! Tell her—"

"What, Benjamin?"

"Nothing." And then abruptly, "It was my fault. I made him angry. Tell her."

He did not refer to her again; nor did he speak of the boy, except at the very end. The end came the week that David was staying at the Rectory; and perhaps Dr. Lavendar's pitying absorption in that dreary dying, made him give less thought to the pleasure as well as the perplexity of the child's presence; though certainly, when he got back from his daily visit at The Top, he found David a great comfort. Dr. Lavendar stopped twice that week to see Mrs. Richie, but each time she sent word that she was engaged, would he excuse her? "Engaged," in the sense of not wishing to see a neighbor, was a new word in Old Chester. Dr. Lavendar did not insist. He went on up the hill to that other house, where, also, there was a deep preoccupation which Benjamin Wright had called "narrowing"; but here he was not shut out. He always stopped to say a friendly word to Simmons, sniffling wretchedly about among the cages in the dining-room, and then went on up-stairs.

On this October afternoon the old servant sneaked up at his heels; and sliding into the room behind him as noiselessly as a shadow, settled down on his hunkers close to the bedside. Once he put up a lean yellow hand, and patted the bedclothes; but he made no more claim to attention than a dog might have done. Dr. Lavendar found his senior warden in the sick-room. Of late Samuel had been there every day; he had very little to say to his father, not from any lingering bitterness, but because, to poor Samuel, all seemed said—the boy was dead. When Dr. Lavendar came in he glanced at the bed, and then, with a start, at the heavy middle-aged figure sitting listlessly at the bedside. Samuel nodded solemnly.

"A matter of hours, William says. I shall not go home until it's over."

"Does he hear you?" said Dr. Lavendar, in a low voice, leaning over to look into the gray face.

"Oh, no;" said Samuel.

The dying man opened one eye and looked at his son. "How much you know!" he said, then closed it again.

"Are you comfortable, Benjamin?" Dr. Lavendar asked him. There was no reply.

Samuel's face reddened. "You can't tell when he hears," he said. It was then that Simmons put out his hand and patted the bedclothes over the old feet.

They sat there beside him for an hour before Benjamin Wright spoke again; then William King came in, and stood looking down at him.

"He'll just sleep away," he told the son.

"I hope he is prepared," said Samuel, and sighed. He turned his back on the big bed with the small figure sliding down and down towards the foot-board, and looked out of the window. The boy had not been prepared!

Suddenly, without opening his eyes, Benjamin Wright began:

> "'Animula vagula blandula,
> Hospes comesque corporis,
> Quæ nunc abibis in loca?'

What do *you* think, Lavendar?"

"It will return to God, who gave it," said Dr. Lavendar.

There was another silence; until he wakened to say, brightly, "Simmons, you freckled nigger, you'd better wring their necks, now, I guess."

"No, suh," came a murmur from the shadow on the floor, "I'm a-goin to take care of 'em fine. Yes, suh, I'll chop their eggs small; I sho'ly will."

The dying hand began to wander over the coverlet; his son took it, but was fretfully repulsed; then Dr. Lavendar made a sign, and Simmons laid his thin old hand on it, and Benjamin Wright gave a contented sigh. After a while he opened that one eye again, and looked at Dr. Lavendar; "Isn't it cus-customary on such occasions, to—admonish?" he said, peevishly; "you ain't doing your duty by me, Lavendar."

"You don't need admonition, Benjamin. You know what to do."

Silence again, and after a while a broken murmur: "'I here forget . . . cancel all grudge, repeal thee . . .'" Then distinctly and quietly he said: "Sam, will you forgive me?"

Samuel Wright nodded; he could not speak at first, and Simmons lifting his head, looked at him, fiercely; then he swallowed several times, and said, with ponderous dignity: "Certainly, father. Certainly." And Simmons fell back into the shadows.

"Of course," murmured Benjamin Wright, "if I g-get well, it needn't hold, you know."

After that he seemed to sleep a little, until, his eyes still closed, he said, "The boy slapped my face. So it's all right."

Samuel started up from his chair at the bedside, shocked and protesting.

"Gad-a-mercy!" said Benjamin Wright, fretfully, opening his eye and looking at him—"that makes us square! Don't you see?"

There was a long silence. Once Dr. Lavendar spoke to him, and once William King touched his wrist, but he seemed to sleep. Then abruptly, and quite clearly, he spoke:

"'Crito, I owe a cock to Æsculapius'. . . . Lavendar?"

"Yes, Benjamin?"

"The debt is paid. Hey? I got the receipt."

"He is wandering," said Samuel. "Father, what do you want?"

But he did not speak again.

CHAPTER XXXII

HELENA had asked Dr. Lavendar to keep David, out of abject fear of William King. The doctor had granted her until Sunday to give him up without explanations; if she had not done so then, he must, he said doggedly, "tell." In sending the child to the Rectory she had not given him up; she had only declared a truce. She had tied Dr. King's hands and gained a breathing-space in which to decide what she must do; but she used to watch the hill road every morning, with scared eyes, lest he should stop on his way up to Benjamin Wright's to say that the truce was over. David came running joyously home two or three times, for more clothes, or to see the rabbits, or to hang about her neck and tell her of his journey. Upon one of these occasions, he mentioned casually that "Alice had gone travelling." Helena's heart stood still; then beat suffocatingly in her throat while she drew the story piecemeal from the child's lips.

"She said," David babbled, "that he didn't know you. An' she said—"

"And where was he—Mr. Pryor, all this time?" she demanded, breathlessly. She opened and shut her hands, and drew in her breath, wincing as if in physical pain; across all the days since that meeting of the Innocents, she felt his anger flaying her for the contretemps. It brought home to her, with an aching sense of finality the completeness of the break between them. But it did more than that. Even while she cringed with personal dismay, she was groping blindly towards a deeper and diviner despair: Those two young creatures were the cherubims at the east of the garden, bearing the sword that turned every way! By the unsparing light of that flashing blade the two sinners, standing outside, saw each other; but the one, at least, began to see something else: the glory of the garden upon which, thirteen years ago, she had turned her back! . . .

Helena did not ask any more questions. David, lounging against her knee, chattered on, ending with a candid and uncomplimentary reference to Mr. Pryor; but she did not reprove him. When, having, as it were, displayed his sling and his bag of pebbles, he was ready to run joyously back to the other home, she kissed him silently and with a strange new consciousness of the everlasting difference between them. But that did not lessen her passionate determination that William King should never steal him from her! Yet how could she defeat her enemy?

A week passed, and still undecided, she wrote to Dr. Lavendar asking further hospitality for David: "I want to have him with me always, but just now I am a little uncertain whether I can do so, because I am going to leave Old Chester. I will come and ask you about it in a few days."

She took the note out to the stable to George and bade him carry it to the Rectory; as she went back to the empty house, she had a glimpse of Mr. and Mrs. Smith's jewel-like eyes gleaming redly upon her from the gloom of the rabbit-hutch, and a desolate longing for David made her hurry indoors. But there the silence, unbroken by the child's voice, was unendurable; it seemed to turn the confusion of her thoughts into actual noise. So she went out again to pace up and down the little brick paths between the box borders of the garden. The morning was still and warm; the frost of a sharp night had melted into threads of mist that beaded the edges of blackened leaves and glittered on the brown stems of withered annuals. Once she stopped to pull up some weed that showed itself still green and arrogant, spilling its seeds from yellowing pods among the frosted flowers; and once she picked, and put into the bosom of her dress, a little belated monthly rose, warm and pink at the heart, but with blighted outer petals. She found it impossible to pursue any one line of thought to its logical outcome; her mind flew like a shuttlecock between a dozen plans for William King's defeat. "Oh, I must decide on something!" she thought, desperately. But the futile morning passed without decision. After dinner she went resolutely into the parlor, and sitting down on her little low chair, pressed her fingers over her eyes to shut out any possible distractions. "Now," she said, "I will make up my mind."

A bluebottle fly buzzing up and down the window dropped on the sill, then began to buzz again. Through the Venetian blinds the sunshine fell in bars across the carpet; she opened her eyes and watched its silent movement,—so intangible, so irresistible; the nearest line touched her foot; her skirt; climbed to her listless hands; out in the hall the clock slowly struck three; her thoughts blurred and ran together; her very fears seemed to sink into space and time and silence. The sunshine passed over her lap, resting warm upon her bosom; up and up, until, suddenly, like a hot finger,

THE AWAKENING OF HELENA RICHIE

it touched her face. That roused her; she got up, sighing, and rubbing her eyes as if she had been asleep. No decision! . . .

Suppose she should go down into the orchard? Away from the house, she might be better able to put her mind on it. She knew a spot where, hidden from curious eyes, she could lie at full length in the grass, warm on a western slope. David might have found her, but no one else would think of looking for her there. . . . When she sank down on the ground and clasped her hands under her head, her eyes were level with the late-blossoming grass that stirred a little in an unfelt breath of air; two frosted stalks of goldenrod, nodded and swung back and nodded again, between her and the sky. With absent intentness, she watched an ant creeping carefully to the top of a head of timothy, then jolting off at some jar she could not feel. The sun poured full upon her face; there was not a cloud anywhere in the unfathomable blue stillness. Thought seemed to drown in seas of light, and personality dwindled until her pain and fright did not seem to belong to her. She had to close her eyes to shut herself into her own dark consciousness:

How should she keep her child?

The simplicity of immediate flight she had, of course, long ago abandoned; it would only postpone the struggle with William King. That inflexible face of duty would hunt her down wherever she was, and take the child from her. No; there was but one thing to do: parry his threat of confessing to Dr. Lavendar that he had "made a mistake" in advising that David should be given to her, by a confession of her own, a confession which should admit the doctor's change of mind without mentioning its cause, and at the same time hold such promises for the future that the old minister would say that she might have David. Then she could turn upon her enemy with the triumphant declaration that she had forestalled him; that she had said exactly what he had threatened to say,—no more, no less. And yet the child was hers! But as she tried to plan how she should put it, the idea eluded her. She would tell Dr. Lavendar thus and so: but even as she marshalled her words, that scene in the waiting-room of the railroad station ached in her imagination. Alice's ignorance of her existence became an insult; what she was going to say to Dr. Lavendar turned into a denunciation of Lloyd Pryor; he was vile, and cruel, and contemptible! But these words stumbled, too. Back in her mind, common sense agreed to Lloyd's silence to his daughter; and, suddenly, to her amazement, she knew that she agreed, not only to the silence, but to his objection to marrying her. It would be an offence for her to live with Alice! Marriage, which would have quieted this new tormenting sense of responsibility and made her like other people, would not have lessened that offence. It came over her with still more acute surprise, that she had never felt this before. It was as if that fire of shame which had consumed her vanity the night she had confessed to William King, had brought illumination as well as burning. By its glare she saw that such a secret as she and Lloyd held between them would be intolerable in the presence of that young girl. Lloyd had felt it—here she tingled all over:—Lloyd was more sensitive than she! Ah, well; Alice was his own daughter, and he knew how almost fanatical she was about truth; so he was especially sensitive. But Dr. King? He had felt it about David: "whether you married this man or not would make no difference about David."

THE AWAKENING OF HELENA RICHIE

She thought about this for awhile in heavy perplexity.

Then with a start she came back again to what she must say to Dr. Lavendar: "I will promise to bring David up just as he wishes; and I will tell him about my money; he doesn't know how rich I am; he will feel that he has no right to rob David of such a chance. And I will say that nobody could love him as I can." Love him! Had she not given up everything for him, sacrificed everything to keep him? For his sake she had not married! In this rush of self-approval she sat up, and looked blindly off over the orchard below her at the distant hills, blue and slumbrous in the sunshine. Then she leaned her head in her hands and stared fixedly at a clump of clover, green still in the yellowing stubble. . . . She had chosen her child instead of a convention which, less than a month ago, she had so passionately desired; a month ago it seemed to her that, once married, she could do no more harm, have no more shame. Yet she had given all this up for David! . . . Suddenly she spurred her mind back to that talk with Dr. Lavendar: she would promise—anything! And planning her promises, she sat there, gazing with intent, unseeing eyes at the clover, until the chilly twilight drove her into the house.

It was not until Saturday that she dared to go to the Rectory. It was early in the afternoon, just as the Collect Class was gathering in the dining-room. She had forgotten it, she told Mary, as she closed her umbrella on the door-step. "Can I wait in the study?" she asked, uncertainly;—there was time to go back! The task of telling part of the truth to this mild old man, whose eye was like a sword, suddenly daunted her. She would wait a few days,—she began to open her umbrella, her fingers blundering with haste,—but retreat was cut off: Dr. Lavendar, on his way to the dining-room, with Danny at his heels, saw her; she could not escape!

"Why, Mrs. Richie!" he said, smiling at her over his spectacles. "Hi, David, who do you suppose is here? Mrs. Richie!"

David came running out of the dining-room; "Did you bring my slag?" he demanded.

And she had to confess that she had not thought of it; "You didn't tell me you wanted it, dear," she defended herself, nervously.

"Oh, well," said David, "I'm coming home to-morrow, and I'll get it."

"Would you like to come home?" she could not help saying.

"I'd just as lieves," said David.

"Run back," Dr. Lavendar commanded, "and tell the children I'm coming in a minute. Tell Theophilus Bell not to play Indian under the table. Now, Mrs. Richie, what shall we do? Do you mind coming in and hearing them say their Collect? Or would you rather wait in the study? We shall be through in three-quarters of an hour. David shall bring you some jumbles and apples. I suppose you are going to carry him off?" Dr. Lavendar said, ruefully.

"Oh," she faltered in a sudden panic, "I will come some other time," but somehow or other, before she knew it, she was in the dining-room; very likely it was because she would not loosen the clasp of David's little warm careless hand, and so her reluctant feet followed him in his hurry to admonish Theophilus. When she entered, instant silence fell upon the children. Lydia Wright, stumbling through the catechism to Ellen Dale who held the prayer-book and prompted, let her voice trail off and her mouth remain open at the sight of a visitor; Theophilus Bell rubbed his sleeve over some chalk-marks on the blackboard;—"I am drawing a woman with an umbrella," he had announced, condescendingly; "I saw her coming up the path,"—but when he saw her sitting down by Dr. Lavendar, Theophilus skulked to his seat, and read his Collect over with unheeding attention.

Then the business of the afternoon began, and Helena sat and listened to it. It was a scene which had repeated itself for two generations in Old Chester; the fathers and mothers of these little people had sat on these same narrow benches without backs, and looked at the blackboard where Dr. Lavendar wrote out the divisions of the Collect, and then looked at the sideboard, where stood a dish of apples and another of jumbles. They, too, had said their catechism, announcing, in singsong chorus that they heartily thanked their Heavenly Father that He had called them to this state of salvation; and Dr. Lavendar had asked one or another of them, as he now asked their children, "What meanest thou by this word Sacrament?" "What is the inward and spiritual grace?" That afternoon, when he swooped down on David, Helen squeezed her hands together with anxiety; did he know what was the inward and spiritual grace? Could he say it? She held her breath until he had sailed triumphantly through:

"*A death unto sin, and a new birth unto righteousness,*" and so on. When he had finished, she looked proudly at Dr. Lavendar, who, to her astonishment, did not bestow a single word of praise!

THE AWAKENING OF HELENA RICHIE

"And yet," said Helena to herself, "he said it better than any of them, and he is the youngest!—David said it very well, didn't he?" she ventured, in a whisper.

Dr. Lavendar made no answer, but opened a book; on which there was a cheerful shuffling as the children jostled each other in their efforts to kneel down in the space between the benches; when all was still, Dr. Lavendar repeated the Collect. Helena dropped her face in her hands, and listened:

"Grant, we beseech Thee, merciful Lord, to Thy faithful people pardon and peace, that they may be cleansed from all their sins, and serve Thee with a quiet mind; through Jesus Christ our Lord."

"*Amen!*" said the children, joyfully; and, scrambling to their feet, looked politely at the sideboard. David, who played host on these occasions, made haste to poke the apples at Mrs. Richie, who could not help whispering to him to pull his collar straight; and she even pushed his hair back a little from his forehead. The sense of possession came over her like a wave, and with it a pang of terror that made her lips dry; at that moment she knew the taste of fear in her mouth. When Dr. Lavendar spoke to her, she was unable to reply.

"Well, now, Mrs. Richie," he said, "I expect these little people can eat their apples without us; can't you, chickabiddies?"

"Yes, sir!" said the children, in eager chorus, eying the apples.

"You and I will go into the study for a while," said Dr. Lavendar.

She followed him speechlessly . . . the time had come.

THE AWAKENING OF HELENA RICHIE

Dr. Lavendar, hospitable and fussy, drew up a horsehair-covered chair with ears on each side of the back, and bade her sit down; then he poked the fire, and put on a big lump of coal, and asked her if she was sure she was warm enough? "It's pretty chilly; we didn't have weather as cold as this in October when I was your age."

"Dr. Lavendar," said Helena;—and at the tremor in her voice he looked at her quickly, and then looked away;—"in regard to David—"

"Yes; I understand that you are not sure that you want to keep him?"

"Oh, no! I am sure. Entirely sure!" She paused, uncertain what to say next. Dr. Lavendar gave her no assistance. Her breath caught in an unsteady laugh. "You are not smoking, Dr. Lavendar! Do light your pipe. I am quite used to tobacco smoke, I assure you."

"No," said Dr. Lavendar, quietly; "I will not smoke now."

"In regard to David," she began; and gripped her hands tight together, for she saw with dismay that they were shaking. She had an instant of angry surprise at her own body. It was betraying her to the silent, watching old man on the other side of the fire. "I want him; but I mean to leave Old Chester. Would you be willing to let me take him away?"

"Why," said Dr. Lavendar, "we shall be very sorry to have you leave us; and, of course, I shall be sorry to lose David. Very sorry! I shall feel," said Dr. Lavendar, with a rueful chuckle, "as if I had lost a tooth! That is about as omnipresent sense of loss as a human critter can have. But I can't see that that is any reason for not letting you take him."

"You are very kind," she murmured.

"Where are you going, and when do you go?" he asked, easily; but he glanced at those shaking hands.

"I want to go next week. I—oh, Dr. Lavendar! I want David; I am sure nobody can do more for him than I can. Nobody can love him as I do! And I think he would be pretty homesick for me, too, if I did not take him. But—"

"Yes?"

She tried to smile; then spread her handkerchief on her knee, and folded it over and over with elaborate self-control. "Dr. King thinks—I ought not to have him. He says," she stopped; the effort to repeat William King's exact words drove the color out of her face. "He says he made a mistake in advising you to give David to me. He thinks—" she caught her breath with a gasp;—"I am not to be trusted to—to bring him up."

She trembled with relief; the worst was over. She had kept her promise, to the letter. Now she would begin to fight for her child: "You will let me have him? You will!— Please say you will, Dr Lavendar!"

"Why does Dr. King think you are not to be trusted?" said Dr. Lavendar.

"Because," she said, gathering up all her courage, "he thinks that I—that David ought to be brought up by some one more—more religious, I suppose, than I am. I know I'm not very religious. Not as good as everybody in Old Chester; but I will bring him up just as you want me to! Any way at all you want me to. I will go to church regularly; truly I will, Dr. Lavendar; truly!"

Dr. Lavendar was silent. The lump of coal in the

THE AWAKENING OF HELENA RICHIE

grate suddenly split and fell apart; there was a crackling leap of flames, and from between the bars a spurt of bubbling gas sent a whiff of acrid smoke puffing out into the room.

"You will let me have him, won't you? You said you would! If you take him away from me—"

"Well?"

She looked at him dumbly; her chin shook.

"The care of a child is sometimes a great burden; have you considered that?"

"Nothing would be a burden if I did it for David!"

"It might involve much sacrifice."

"I have sacrificed everything for him!" she burst out.

"What?"

"There was something," she said evasively, "that I wanted to do very much; something that would have made me—happier. But I couldn't if I kept David; so I gave it up."

Dr. Lavendar ruminated. "You wanted David the most?"

"Yes!" she said passionately.

"Then it was a choice, not a sacrifice, wasn't it, my dear? No doubt you would make sacrifices for him, only in this matter you chose what you wanted most. And your choice was for your own happiness I take it, —not his?"

She nodded doubtfully, baffled for a minute, and not quite understanding. Then she said, "But I would choose his happiness; I have done some things for him, truly I have. Oh, little things, I suppose you would call them; but I wasn't used to them and they seemed great to me. But I would choose his happiness, Dr. Lavendar. So you will let me keep him?"

"If you think you ought to have him, you may."

"No matter what Dr. King says?"

"No matter what Dr. King says. If you are sure that it is best for him to be with you, I, at least, shall not interfere."

Her relief was so great that the tears ran down her face. "It is best!"

"Best to be with you," Dr. Lavendar repeated thoughtfully; "Why, Mrs. Richie?"

"Why? Why because I want him so much. I have nothing in the whole world, Dr. Lavendar, but David. Nothing."

"Other folks might want him."

"But nobody can do as much for him as I can! I have a good deal of money."

"You mean you can feed him, and clothe him, and educate him? Well; I could do that myself. What else can you do?"

"What else?"

"Yes. One person can give him material care about as well as another. What else can you do?"

"Why—" she began, helplessly; "I don't think I know just what you mean?"

"My friend," said Dr. Lavendar, "are you a good woman?"

The shock of the question left her speechless. She tried to meet his eye; quailed, half rose: "I don't know what you mean! What right have you to ask me such a question—"

Dr. Lavendar waited.

"Perhaps I don't think about things, quite as you do. I am not religious; I told you that. I don't do things because of religion; I believe in—in reason, not in religion. I try to be good in—my way. I don't know that I've been what you would call 'good.'"

"What do I call 'good'?"

At which she burst out that people in Old Chester thought that people who did not live according to convention were not good. For her part, convention was the last thing she thought of. Indeed, she believed there was more wickedness in convention than out of it! "If I have done anything you would call wrong, it was because I couldn't help it; I never wanted to do wrong. I just wanted to be happy. I've tried to be charitable. And I've tried to be good—in my way; but not because I wanted to go to heaven, and all that. I—I don't believe in heaven," she ended with terrified flippancy.

"Perhaps not," said Dr. Lavendar sadly; "but, oh, my child, how you do believe in hell!"

She stared at him for one broken moment; then flung her arms out on the table beside her, and dropped her head upon them. Dr. Lavendar did not speak. There was a long silence; suddenly she turned upon him, her face quivering; "Yes! I do believe in hell. Because that is what life is! I've never had any happiness at all. Oh, it seemed so little a thing to ask— just to be happy Yes, I believe in hell."

Dr. Lavendar waited.

"If I've done what people say isn't right, it was only because I wanted to be happy; not because I wanted to do wrong. It was because of Love. You can't understand what that means! But Christ said that because a woman loved much, much was to be forgiven! Do you remember that?" she demanded hotly.

"Yes," said Dr. Lavendar; "but do you remember

Who it was that she loved much? She loved Goodness, Mrs. Richie. Have you loved Goodness?"

"Oh, what is the use of talking about it?" she said passionately; "we won't agree. If it was all to do over again, perhaps I— But life was so dreadful! If you judge me, remember—"

"I do not judge you."

"—remember that everything has been against me. Everything! From the very beginning. I never had anything I wanted. I thought I was going to be happy, but each time I wasn't. Until I had David. And now you will take him. Oh, what a miserable failure life has been! I wish I could die. But it seems you can't even die when you want to!"

For a moment she covered her face with her hands. Then she said: "I suppose I might as well tell you. Mr. Pryor is not— . . . After my baby died, I left my husband. Lloyd loved me, and I went to live with him."

"You went to live with your brother?" Dr. Lavendar repeated perplexed.

"He is not my brother."

There was silence for a full minute. Then Dr. Lavendar said quietly, "Go on."

She looked at him with hunted eyes. "Now, you will take David away. Why did you make me tell you?"

"It is better to tell me." He laid his old hand on hers, clenched upon the table at her side. The room was very still; once a coal fell from the grate, and once there was the soft brush of rain against the window.

"It's my whole life. I can't tell you my whole life. I didn't ever want to be wicked; all I wanted was to be happy. And so I went to Lloyd. It didn't seem so very wrong. We didn't hurt anybody. His wife was dead.—As for Frederick, I have no regrets!" she ended fiercely.

The room had darkened in the rainy October twilight, and the fire was low; Dr. Lavendar could hardly see her quivering face.

"But now it's all over between Lloyd and me. I sha'n't see him ever any more. He would have married me, if I had been willing to give up David. But I was not willing."

"You thought it would make everything right if you married this man?"

"Right?" she repeated, surprised; "why, of course. At least I suppose that is what good people call right," she added dully.

"And you gave up doing right, to have David?"

She felt that she was trapped, and yet she could not understand why; "I sacrificed myself," she said confusedly.

"No," said Dr. Lavendar; "you sacrificed a conviction. A poor, false conviction, but such as it was, you threw it over to keep David."

She looked at him in terror; "It was just selfishness, you think?"

"Yes," said Dr. Lavendar.

"Perhaps it was," she admitted. "Oh, how frightful life is! To try to be happy, is to be bad."

"No; to try to be happy at the expense of other people, is to be bad."

"But I never did that! Lloyd's wife was dead;— Of course, if she had been alive"—Helena lifted her head with the curious pride of caste in sin which is so strongly felt by the woman who is a sinner;—"if she had been alive, I wouldn't have thought of such a thing. But nobody knew; so I never did any harm," —then she quailed; "at least, I never meant to do any harm. So you can't say it was at anybody's expense."

"It was at everybody's expense. Marriage is what makes us civilized. If anybody injures marriage we all pay."

She was silent.

"If every dissatisfied wife should do what you did, could decent life go on? Wouldn't we all drop down a little nearer the animals?"

"Perhaps so," she said vaguely. But she was not following him. She had entered into this experience of sin, not by the door of reason, but of emotion; she could leave it only by the same door. The high appeal to individual renunciation for the good of the many, was entirely beyond her. Dr. Lavendar did not press it any further.

"Well, anyhow," she said dully, "I didn't get any happiness—whether it was at other people's expense or not. When David came, I thought, 'now I am going to be happy!' That was all I wanted: happiness. And now you will take him away."

"I have not said I would take him away."

She trembled so at that, that for an instant she could not speak. "Not take him?"

"Not if you think it is best for him to stay with you."

She began to pant with fear. "You mean something by that. I know you do! Oh, what do you mean? I cannot do him any harm!"

"Woman," said Dr. Lavendar solemnly, "*can you do him any good?*"

She cowered silently away from him.

THE AWAKENING OF HELENA RICHIE

"Can you teach him to tell the truth, you, who have lived a lie? Can you make him brave, you, who could not endure? Can you make him honorable, you, who have deceived us all? Can you make him unselfish, you, who have thought only of self? Can you teach him purity, you, who—"

"Stop! I cannot bear it."

"Tell me the truth: can you do him any good?"

That last solemn word fell into profound silence. There was not a sound in the still darkness of the study; and suddenly her soul was still, too ... the whirlwind of anger had died out; the shock of responsibility had subsided; the hiss of those flames of shame had ceased. She was in the centre of all the tumults, where lies the quiet mind of God. For a long time she did not speak. Then, by and by, her face hidden in her arms on the table, she said, in a whisper:

"No."

And after the fire, the still small Voice.

CHAPTER XXXIII

DR. LAVENDAR looked at the bowed head; but he offered no comfort. When she said brokenly, "No; I can't have him. I can't have him," he assented; and there was silence again. It was broken by a small, cheerful voice:

"Mary says supper's ready. There's milk toast, an'—"

Dr. Lavendar went as quickly as he could to the door; when he opened it he stood between the little boy and Helena. "Tell Mary not to wait for me; but ask her to give you your supper."

"An' Mary says that in Ireland they call clover 'shamrocks'; an'—"

Dr. Lavendar gently closed the door. When he went back to his seat on the other side of the table, she said faintly, "That was—?"

"Yes," said Dr. Lavendar.

"Oh," she whispered, "I knew I would have to give him up. I knew I had no right to him."

"No; you had no right to him."

"But I loved him so! Oh, I thought, maybe, I would be—like other people, if I had him."

After a while, with long pauses between the sentences, she began to tell him. . . .

"I never thought about goodness; or badness either. Only about Lloyd, and happiness. I thought I had a right to happiness. But I was angry at all the complacent married people; they were so satisfied with themselves! And yet all the time I wished Frederick would die so that I could be married. Oh, the time was so long!" She threw her arms up with a gesture of shuddering weariness; then clasped her hands between her knees, and staring at the floor, began to speak. Her words poured out, incoherent, contradictory, full of bewilderment and pain. "Yes; I wasn't very happy, except just at first. After a while I got so tired of Lloyd's selfishness. Oh—he was so selfish! I used to look at him sometimes, and almost hate him. He always took the most comfortable chair, and he cared so much about things to eat. And he got fat. And he didn't mind Frederick's living. I could see that. And I prayed that Frederick would die.—I suppose you think it was wicked to pray that?"

"Go on."

"It was only because I loved Lloyd so much. But he didn't die. And I began not to be happy. And then I thought Lloyd didn't want to talk to me about Alice. Alice is his daughter. It was three years ago I first noticed that. But I wasn't really sure until this summer. He didn't even like to show me her picture. That nearly killed me, Dr. Lavendar. And once, just lately, he told me her 'greatest charm was her innocence.' Oh, it was cruel in him to say that! How could he be so cruel!" she looked at him for sympathy; but he was silent. "But underneath, somehow, I understood; and that made me angry,—to understand. It was this summer that I began to be angry. And then I got so jealous: not of Alice, exactly; but of what she stood for. It was a kind of fright, because I couldn't go back and begin again. Do you know what I mean?"

"I know."

"Oh, Dr. Lavendar, it is so horrible! When I began to understand, it seemed like something broken—broken—broken! It could never be mended."

"No."

... Sometimes, as she went on he asked a question, and sometimes made a comment. The comment was always the same: when she spoke of marrying Frederick to get away from her bleak life with her grandmother, she said, "Oh, it was a mistake, a mistake!"

And he said, "It was a sin."

And again: "I thought Lloyd would make me happy; I just went to be happy; that was my second mistake."

"It was your second sin."

"You think I am a sinner," she said; "oh, Dr. Lavendar, I am not as bad as you think! I always expected to marry Lloyd. I am not like a—fallen woman."

"Why not?" said Dr. Lavendar.

She shrank back with a gesture of dismay. "I always expected to marry him!"

"It would have been just the same if you had married him."

"I don't understand you," she said faintly.

"From the beginning," he said, "you have thought only of self. You would not have been redeemed from self by gaining what would have made you more satisfied with yourself."

She thought about this for a few minutes in a heavy silence. "You mean, getting married would not have changed things, really?"

"It would have made the life you were living less harmful to your fellow creatures, perhaps; but it would have made no difference between you two."

THE AWAKENING OF HELENA RICHIE

"I thought I would be happier," she said.

"Happier!" said Dr. Lavendar; "what sort of happiness could there be in a marriage where the man could never respect the woman, and the woman could never trust the man!"

"I hadn't thought of it that way," she said slowly. And then she began again. . . . Once Dr. Lavendar interrupted her to light the lamp, for the study was dark except for the wink of red coals in the grate; and once he checked her, and went into the dining-room to bring her a glass of wine and some food. She protested, but he had his way, and she ate and drank before going on with her story. When she told him, brokenly, of Sam Wright, Dr. Lavendar got up and walked the length of the study. But he made no comment—none was needed. When she ended, there was a long pause. Suddenly she clasped her hands on the top of her head, and bowed her forehead almost to her knees. She seemed to speak as if to herself:

"Not worthy; not worthy.". . . Then aloud; "*I give him up,*" she said. And stretched out empty arms.

She rose, and began to feel about for her cloak that had fallen across the arm of her chair. But she was half blind with weeping, and Dr. Lavendar found it for her and gently put it over her shoulders.

"I will go away," she said, "but I may see him again, mayn't I? Just once more, to say good-by to him."

"Yes," he said.

"I'll send his little things down to you to-morrow, Dr. Lavendar. Oh,—his dear little things!"

"Very well."

He lighted a lantern for her, but made no offer to see

her home, or to send his Mary along as an escort. Yet when he let her go away into the rainy darkness, he stood in the doorway a long while, looking after her. Then he went back to the study, to pace up and down, up and down. Twice he stopped and looked out of the window, and then at the clock. But each time he put the impulse aside. He must not interfere.

It was almost midnight before he took his lamp and went up-stairs; at David's door he hesitated, and then went in. The little boy was lying curled up like a puppy, his face almost hidden in his pillow, but his cheek glowing red under the soft thatch of hair. Dr. Lavendar, shading his lamp with one hand, looked down at him a long time. On the wall behind him and half-way across the ceiling, the old man's shadow loomed wavering and gigantic, and the light, flickering up on his face, deepened the lines of age and of other people's troubles. By and by he stooped down, and gently laid his old palm upon the little head.

When he lifted himself up his face was full of peace.

CHAPTER XXXIV

"WILLIAM," said Dr. Lavendar, "you may tell me anything I ought to know about Mrs. Richie."

The doctor looked at him with a start, and a half-spoken question.

"Yes; she told me. But I want to ask you about the man. She didn't say much about him."

This was Sunday evening; David had gone to bed, and Danny had climbed up into Dr. Lavendar's chair, and been gently deposited on the hearth-rug. "No, Daniel; not to-night, sir. I've got to have my chair just this once." William had come in for his usual smoke, but he had been more than usually silent. When Dr. Lavendar gave his calm permission, the doctor's wretched perplexity of the past month could hardly find words. He said, first of all,

"David? Of course you will take him away. It will break her heart!"

"A broken heart is not such a bad thing, Willy. Our Heavenly Father does not despise it."

"Dr. Lavendar, why can't she keep him? She'll never see that scoundrel again!"

"Do you think a woman with such a story is fit to bring up a child, William?"

The doctor was silent.

"She thinks not, herself," said Dr. Lavendar.

"Does she?" William King said; and a minute afterwards fumbled in his coat tails for his pocket-handkerchief. "What is she going to do?" he asked huskily.

"She feels that she had better leave Old Chester."

"Do you think so, sir?"

Dr. Lavendar sighed. "I would like to have her here; I would like to take care of her, for a while. But I don't think she could stand it; on your account."

"My account!" William King pushed his chair back, and got on his feet; "Dr. Lavendar, I—I—"

"She would feel the embarrassment of your knowledge," said the old man.

Dr. King sat down. Then he said, "I am the last man to judge her."

"'Beginning at the eldest, even unto the last,'" murmured Dr. Lavendar. "Shame is a curious thing, William. It's like some of your medicines. The right amount cures. Too much kills. I've seen that with hard drinkers. Where a drunkard is a poor, uneducated fellow, shame gives him a good boost towards decency. But a man of education, William, a man of opportunity—if he wakes up to what he has been doing, shame gives him such a shove he is apt to go all round the circle, and come up just where he started! Shame is a blessed thing,—when you don't get too much of it. She would get too much of it here. But—" he stopped and smiled; "sin has done its divine work, I think."

"Sin?"

"Yes," said Dr. Lavendar, cheerfully; "have you ever noticed that every single human experience—except, perhaps, the stagnation of conceit; I haven't found anything hopeful in that yet; but maybe I shall some day!—but, except for conceit, I have never known any human experience of pain or sin that could not be

THE AWAKENING OF HELENA RICHIE

the gate of heaven. Mind! I don't say that it always is; but it can be. Has that ever occurred to you?"

"Well, no," the doctor confessed; "I can't say that it has."

"Oh, you're young yet," Dr. Lavendar said encouragingly. "My boy, let me tell you that there are some good folks who don't begin to know their Heavenly Father, as the sinner does who climbed up to Him out of the gutter."

"A dangerous doctrine," William ruminated.

"Oh, I don't preach it," Dr. Lavendar said placidly; "but I don't preach everything I know."

William was not following him. He said abruptly, "What are you going to do with David?"

"David is going to stay with me."

And William said again, "It will break her heart!"

"I hope so," said Dr. Lavendar solemnly. How he watched that poor heart, in the next few days! Every afternoon his shabby old buggy went tugging up the hill. Sometimes he found her walking restlessly about in the frosted garden; sometimes standing mutely at the long window in the parlor, looking for him; sometimes prostrate on her bed. When he took her hand —listless one day, fiercely despairing the next,—he would glance at her with a swift scrutiny that questioned, and then waited. The pity in his old eyes never dimmed their relentless keenness; they seemed to raid her face, sounding all the shallows in search of depths. For with his exultant faith in human nature, he believed that somewhere in the depths he should find God. It is only the pure in heart who can find Him in impurity, who can see, behind the murky veil of stained flesh, the very face of Christ declaring the possibilities of the flesh!—but this old man sought, and knew that he should find Him. He waited and watched for many days, looking for that recognition of wrong-doing which breaks the heart by its revelation of goodness that might have been; for there is no true knowledge of sin, without a divine and redeeming knowledge of righteousness! So, as this old saint looked into the breaking heart, pity for the sinner who was base deepened into reverence for the child of God who might be noble. It is an easy matter to believe in the confident soul; but Dr. Lavendar believed in a soul that did not believe in itself!

It seemed to Helena that she had nothing to live for; that there was nothing to do except shiver back out of sight, and wait to die. For the time was not yet when she should know that her consciousness of sin might be the chased and fretted Cup from which she might drink the sacrament of life; when she should come to understand, with thanksgiving, that unless she had sinned, the holy wine might never have touched her lips!

In these almost daily talks with Dr. Lavendar, the question of the future was beaten out: it was a bleak enough prospect; it didn't matter, she said, where she went, or what became of her, she had spoiled her life, she said. "Yes," Dr. Lavender agreed; "you've spoiled what you've had of it. But your Heavenly Father has the rest, in His hands, and He'll give it to you clean and sound. All you've got to do, is to keep it so, and forget the spoiled part." That was the only thing he insisted upon: no dwelling on the past!

"I wish I was one of the people who want to do things," she told him with a sort of wistful cynicism. "But I don't. I have no story-book desires. I don't want to go and nurse lepers!—but I will, if you want me to," she added with quick and touching simplicity.

Dr. Lavendar smiled, and said that nursing lepers was too easy. He had suggested that she should live in a distant city;—he had agreed at once to her assertion that she could not stay in Old Chester. "I know some nice people there," he said; "Ellen Bailey lives there; she's Ellen Spangler now. You've heard me speak of her? Spangler is a parson; he's a good fellow, but the Lord denied him brains to any great extent. But Ellen is the salt of the earth. And she can laugh. You'll like her."

"But what will I do when I get there?"

"I think Ellen may find something to keep you busy," he said cheerfully; "and, meantime, I'll make a suggestion myself: study Hebrew."

"Hebrew!"

"Or Arabic; or Russian; it doesn't matter which; your mind needs exercise."

"When you said Hebrew, I thought you meant so I could read the Bible."

"Ho!" said Dr. Lavendar, "I think King James's version is good enough for you; or anybody else. And I wouldn't want you to wait until you can read backwards, to read your Bible. No; I only meant that you need something to break your mind on. Hebrew is as good as anything else."

She meditated on this for a while; "I begin to understand," she said with her hesitating smile; and Dr. Lavendar was mightily pleased, for he had not seen that smile of late.

Sometimes they talked about David, Mrs. Richie asking questions in a smothered voice; but she never begged for him. That part of her life was over. Dr.

Lavendar sometimes brought the child with him when he and Goliath climbed the hill for that daily visit; but he always took him back again. Indeed, the Rectory was now definitely the little boy's home. Of course Old Chester knew that the Stuffed Animal House was to lose its tenant, and that David had gone to live with Dr. Lavendar. "I wonder why she doesn't take him with her?" said Old Chester; and called to say good-by and hint that Mrs. Richie must be sorry to leave the little boy behind her? Helena said briefly, yes; she was "sorry." And Old Chester went away no wiser than it came. William King, wise and miserable, did not call. His wife said that she would say good-by for him, if he was too busy to go up the hill.

"It seems to me you've been very busy lately," she told him; "I've hardly had a glimpse of you. I only hope it will show on your bills. It is very foolish, William, to take patients so far back in the country; I don't believe it pays, considering how much time it takes. But I'll tell Mrs. Richie you send your respects, and say good-by for you."

"You needn't mind," said the doctor.

Mrs. King went to make her adieux the very next day. Her manner was so cordial that Helena was faintly surprised; but, as Martha told Dr. Lavendar, cordiality did not mean the sacrifice of truth to any false idea of politeness.

"I didn't tell her I was sorry she was going," Martha said, standing by the roadside in the chill November wind, talking into the buggy, "because, to speak flatly and frankly, I am not. I don't consider that her example is very good for Old Chester. She is not a good housekeeper. I could tell you certain things — however, I won't. I never gossip. I just said, very kindly, 'Good-by, Mrs. Richie. I hope you'll have a pleasant journey.' That was all. No insincere regrets. That's one thing about me, Dr. Lavendar, I may not be perfect, but I never say anything, just to be pleasant!"

"I've noticed that," said Dr. Lavendar; "G'on, Goliath."

And Martha, in great spirits, told her William at tea, that, though Dr. Lavendar was failing, she had to admit he could still see people's good qualities. "I told him I hadn't put on any airs of regret about Mrs. Richie, and he said he had always noticed my frankness."

William helped himself to gooseberry jam in silence.

"You do leave things so catacornered!" Martha observed, laying the thin silver spoon straight in the dish. "William, I never knew anybody so incapable as that woman. I asked her how she had packed her preserves for moving. She said she hadn't made any! Think of that, for a housekeeper. Oh, and I found out about that perfumery. I just asked her. It's nothing but ground orris!"

William said he would like a cup of tea.

"I can't make her out," Martha said, touching the teapot to make sure it was hot; "I've always said she wasn't her brother's equal, mentally. But you do expect a woman to have certain feminine qualities; now the idea of adopting a child, and then deserting him!"

"She hadn't adopted him," William said.

"It's the same thing; she took him, and now she gets tired of him, and won't keep him. She begins a thing, but she doesn't go on with it."

"I suppose it's better not to begin it?" William said. And there was an edge in his voice that caused Mrs. King to hold her tongue. "Martha," the doctor said, after a while and with evident effort, "can you give me an early breakfast to-morrow morning? I've got to go back into the country, and I want to make an early start."

Helena Richie, too, meant to make an early start the next morning; it was the day that she was to leave Old Chester. The plan of going to the western city had gradually shaped itself, and while Dr. Lavendar was writing to those friends of his, and Helena corresponding with a real-estate agent, the packing-up at the Stuffed Animal House had proceeded. Now it was all done; Maggie and Sarah had had their wages, and several presents besides; the pony had been shipped from Mercer; the rabbits boxed and sent down to the Rectory; all was done;—except the saying good-by to David. But Helena told herself that she would not say good-by to him. She could not, she said. She would see him, but he should not know it was good-by. And so she asked Dr. Lavendar to send the child up to her the day before she was to go away;—by himself. "You'll trust him with me for an hour?" she said.

She meant to cuddle the child, and give him the "forty kisses" which, at last, he was ready to accept, and let him chatter of all his multitudinous interests. Then she would send him away, and begin her empty life. The page which had held a promise of joy, would be turned over; a new, dreary chapter, with no promise in it, would begin. . . .

David came in the afternoon. He was a little late, and explained his tardiness by saying that he had found a toad, and tying a string around its waist, had tried to play horse with it, up the hill. "But he wouldn't drive," David said disgustedly; "maybe he was a lady toad; I don't know."

"Perhaps the poor toad didn't like to be driven,"

"'DR. LAVENDAR,' SAID HELENA, 'IN REGARD TO DAVID'"

THE AWAKENING OF HELENA RICHIE

Helena suggested. David looked thoughtful. "David," she said, "I am going away. Will you write a little letter to me sometimes?"

"Maybe," said David. And slapped his pocket, in a great flurry; "Dr. Lavendar ga' me a letter for you!"

She glanced at it to see if it needed an answer, but it was only to ask her to stop at the Rectory before she left town the next morning.

"Tell Dr. Lavendar I will, darling," she said, and David nodded.

She was sitting before the parlor fire; the little boy was leaning against her knee braiding three blades of grass; he was deeply absorbed. Helena took his face between her hands, and looked at it; then, to hide the trembling of her lips, she hid them in his neck.

"You tickle!" said David, and wriggled out of her arms with chuckles of fun. "I'm making you a ring," he said.

She let him push the little grass circlet over her finger, and then closed her hand on it lest it should slip off. "You won't forget me, David, will you?"

"No," he said surprised; "I never forget anything. I remember everything the magician did. An' I remember when I was born."

"Oh, David!"

"I do. I remember my brother's candy horse. My brother—was—was, oh, seven or eight weeks older 'an me. Yes; I'll not forget you; not till I'm old. Not till I'm twenty, maybe. I guess I'll go now. We are going to have Jim Crow for dessert. Mary told me. You're prettier than Mary. Or Dr. Lavendar." This was a very long speech for David, and to make up for it he was silent for several minutes. He took her hand, and twisted the little grass ring round and round on her finger; and then, suddenly, his chin quivered. "I don't like you. You're going away," he said; he stamped his foot and threw himself against her knee in a paroxysm of tears. "I hate you!"

It was so unexpected, and so entirely unlike David, that Helena forgot her own pain in soothing him. And, indeed, when she had said she would send him some candy—"and a false-face?" David blubbered;—"yes, dear precious!" she promised;—he quite cheered up, and dragging at her hand, he went skipping along beside her out to the green gate in the hedge.

"I'll stop at the Rectory in the morning," she said, when she kissed him, bravely, in the twilight; "so I'll see you again, dear."

"'By!" said David. And he had gone.

She stood staring after him, fiercely brushing the tears away, because they dimmed the little joyous figure, trotting into the November dusk.

. . . . . .

The morning broke, gray and cloudy. William King had had his early breakfast; of course he had! Rather than fail in a housekeeper's duty, Martha would have sat up all night. When the doctor started for that call out into the country, Helena was just getting into the stage at the Stuffed Animal House. Once, as the coach went jolting down the hill, she lowered the misted window and looked back—then sank into her seat and put her hands over her eyes. Just for a while, there had been a little happiness in that house.

They were half-way down the hill when Jonas drew in his horses so sharply that she made a quick effort to control herself; another passenger, she thought, shrinking into her corner.

"I'll only detain you a minute or two, Jonas," William King said from the roadside. Jinny was hitched to the fence, and at the doctor's signalling hand, the stage drew up, with rattling whiffletrees. Then he opened the door and got in; he sat down on the opposite seat.

"I wanted to say good-by to you," he said; "but, most of all, I wanted to tell you that I—I have the deepest regard for you. I want you to know that. I wanted to ask you if you would allow me to call myself your friend? I have seemed unkind, but—" he took her hand in both of his, and looked at her; his face twitched. "I implore you to believe me! I must not ask anything, or say anything, more than that. But I could not let you go away without asking your forgiveness—"

"*My* forgiveness!"

"—Without asking you to pardon me, and to believe that I—have nothing but—esteem; the most—the most—friendly esteem; you will believe that, won't you?"

"You are very good to me," she said brokenly.

He was holding her hand so hard in his, that she winced with pain; instantly his harsh grasp relaxed, and he looked down at the white hand lying in his, soft, and fragrant, and useless as a flower; he said something under his breath; then bent down and kissed it. When he lifted his head, his face was very pale. "God bless you. God always bless you. Goodby!" And he was on the road again, shutting the coach door sharply. "Go on, Jonas!" he said. And Jonas gathered up the reins.

Alone, she put her hands over her eyes again; the tumult of the moment left her breathless and broken. She had hated him because he would have robbed her of David; and then, when she robbed herself of David, she had almost forgotten him; but now, when the chill of the future was settling down upon her, to have him say he was her friend brought a sudden warmth about her heart. There seemed to be some value to life, after all.

She had told Jonas to stop at the Rectory, and Dr. Lavendar met her at the front door. He explained that he wanted to have a last look at her and make sure she was taking wraps enough for the long cold ride to Mercer. He reminded her that she was to write to him the minute she arrived, and tell him all about her journey, and Ellen Bailey,—"and Spangler, of course," Dr. Lavendar added hurriedly. Then he asked her if she would take a package with her?

"Yes, with pleasure," she said, looking vaguely out into the hall. But there was no sign of David. "Where is the package, Dr. Lavendar?"

"I told Mary to give it to Jonas," he said. There was a moment's pause, and she looked at him dumbly.

"*David?*"

"He isn't here," Dr. Lavendar said gently.

"Oh, Dr. Lavendar, tell him I love him! Will you tell him? Don't let him forget me! Oh, don't let him quite forget me."

"He won't forget you," Dr. Lavendar said. He took both her hands, and looked into her face. It was a long and solemn look, but it was no longer questioning; the joy that there is in the presence of the angels, is done with questioning.

"Helena," he said, "your Master came into the world as a little child. Receive Him in thy heart by faith, with thanksgiving."

She looked up at him, trembling, and without words:

but he understood. A moment later he gave her his blessing; then he said cheerfully, "I must not keep you any longer; come!" With Danny at his heels, he walked beside her down the garden path to the coach. It had begun to rain and the leather curtains flapped sharply in the cold wind. Jonas had buttoned the big apron up in front of him, and it was already shining wet; the steaming horses were pounding restlessly in the mud.

She did not look about her. With unsteady hands she pulled her veil down; then she said faintly, "Good-by—" She hardly returned the friendly pressure of Dr. Lavendar's hand. She was so blinded by tears that she had stumbled into the stage before she saw the child, buttoned up to his ears in his first greatcoat, and bubbling over with excitement. Even when she did see him, she did not at first understand. She looked at him, and then at Dr. Lavendar, and then back at David, to whom it was all a delightful game which, the night before, Dr. Lavendar and he had got up between them. It served its purpose, for the child had no suspicion of anything unusual in the occasion.

"*I'm* the package!" said David joyously.

. . . . . .

The stage went sagging and rumbling down the road. For a long minute Dr. Lavendar stood in the rain, looking after it. Then it turned the corner and was out of sight. He drew a long breath. David had gone!

A minute later he and Danny went back to the empty house.

THE END

POPULAR COPYRIGHT BOOKS

AT MODERATE PRICES — Any of the following titles can be bought of your Bookseller at the price you paid for this volume

---

Adventures of Captain Kettle. Cutcliffe Hyne.
Adventures of Gerard. A. Conan Doyle.
Adventures of Sherlock Holmes. A. Conan Doyle.
Alton of Somasco. Harold Bindloss.
Arms and the Woman. Harold MacGrath.
Artemus Ward's Works (extra illustrated).
At the Mercy of Tiberius. Augusta Evans Wilson.
Battle Ground, The. Ellen Glasgow.
Belle of Bowling Green, The. Amelia E. Barr.
Ben Blair. Will Lillibridge.
Bob, Son of Battle. Alfred Ollivant.
Boss, The. Alfred Henry Lewis.
Brass Bowl, The. Louis Joseph Vance.
Brethren, The. H. Rider Haggard.
By Snare of Love. Arthur W. Marchmont.
By Wit of Woman. Arthur W. Marchmont.
Cap'n Erie. Joseph C. Lincoln.
Captain in the Ranks, A. George Cary Eggleston.
Cardigan. Robert W. Chambers.
Casting Away of Mrs. Lecks and Mrs. Aleshine. Frank R. Stockton.
Circle, The. Katherine Cecil Thurston (author of "The Masquerader," "The Gambler").
Conquest of Canaan, The. Booth Tarkington.
Courier of Fortune, A. Arthur W. Marchmont.
Darrow Enigma, The. Melvin Severy.
Deliverance, The. Ellen Glasgow.
Exploits of Brigadier Gerard. A. Conan Doyle.
Fighting Chance, The. Robert W. Chambers.
For a Maiden Brave. Chauncey C. Hotchkiss.
For Love or Crown. Arthur W. Marchmont.
Fugitive Blacksmith, The. Charles D. Stewart.
Heart's Highway, The. Mary E. Wilkins.
Holladay Case, The. Burton Egbert Stevenson.
Hurricane Island. H. B. Marriott-Watson.
Indifference of Juliet, The. Grace S. Richmond.
Infelice. Augusta Evans Wilson.
In the Name of a Woman. Arthur W. Marchmont.
Lady Betty Across the Water. C. N. and A. M. Williamson.
Lane That Had No Turning, The. Gilbert Parker.
Leavenworth Case, The. Anna Katharine Green.
Lilac Sunbonnet, The. S. R. Crockett.
Lin McLean. Owen Wister.
Long Night, The. Stanley J. Weyman.
Maid at Arms, The. Robert W. Chambers.
Man from Red Keg, The. Eugene Thwing.

A. L. BURT CO., Publishers, 52-58 Duane St., New York City

POPULAR COPYRIGHT BOOKS

AT MODERATE PRICES — Any of the following titles can be bought of your Bookseller at the price you paid for this volume

---

Marathon Mystery, The. Burton Egbert Stevenson.
Memoirs of Sherlock Holmes. A. Conan Doyle.
Millionaire Baby, The. Anna Katharine Green.
Missourian, The. Eugene P. Lyle, Jr.
My Friend the Chauffeur. C. N. and A. M. Williamson.
My Lady of the North. Randall Parrish.
Mystery of June 13th. Melvin L. Severy.
Mystery Tales. Edgar Allen Poe.
Nancy Stair. Elinor Macartney Lane.
None But the Brave. Hamblen Sears.
Order No. 11. Caroline Abbot Stanley
Pam. Bettina von Hutten.
Pam Decides. Bettina von Hutten.
Partners of the Tide. Joseph C. Lincoln.
Phra the Phoenician. Edwin Lester Arnold.
President, The. Alfred Henry Lewis.
Princess Passes, The. C. N. and A. M. Williamson.
Private War, The. Louis Joseph Vance.
Prodigal Son, The. Hall Caine.
Queen's Advocate, The. Arthur W. Marchmont.
Quickening, The. Francis Lynde.
Richard the Brazen. Cyrus Townsend Brady and Edward Peple.
Rose of the World. Agnes and Egerton Castle.
Sarita the Carlist. Arthur W. Marchmont.
Seats of the Mighty, The. Gilbert Parker.
Sir Nigel. A. Conan Doyle.
Sir Richard Calmady. Lucas Malet.
Speckled Bird. Augusta Evans Wilson.
Spoilers, The. Rex Beach.
Sunset Trail, The. Alfred Henry Lewis.
Sword of the Old Frontier, A. Randall Parrish.
Tales of Sherlock Holmes. A. Conan Doyle.
That Printer of Udell's. Harold Bell Wright.
Throwback, The. Alfred Henry Lewis.
Trail of the Sword, The. Gilbert Parker.
Two Vanrevels, The. Booth Tarkington.
Up From Slavery. Booker T. Washington.
Vashti. Augusta Evans Wilson.
Viper of Milan, The (original edition). Marjorie Bowen.
Voice of the People, The. Ellen Glasgow.
Wheel of Life, The. Ellen Glasgow.
When I Was Czar. Arthur W. Marchmont.
When Wilderness Was King. Randall Parrish.
Woman in Grey, A. Mrs. C. N. Williamson.
Woman in the Alcove, The. Anna Katharine Green.

A. L. BURT CO., Publishers, 52-58 Duane St., New York City

BURT'S SERIES of STANDARD FICTION.

DARNLEY. A Romance of the times of Henry VIII. and Cardinal Wolsey. By G. P. R. James. Cloth, 12mo. with four illustrations by J. Watson Davis. Price, $1.00.

As a historical romance "Darnley" is a book that can be taken up pleasurably again and again, for there is about it that subtle charm which those who are strangers to the works of G. P. R. James have claimed was only to be imparted by Dumas.

If there was nothing more about the work to attract especial attention, the account of the meeting of the kings on the historic "field of the cloth of gold" would entitle the story to the most favorable consideration of every reader.

There is really but little pure romance in this story, for the author has taken care to imagine love passages only between those whom history has credited with having entertained the tender passion one for another, and he succeeds in making such lovers as all the world must love.

WINDSOR CASTLE. A Historical Romance of the Reign of Henry VIII Catharine of Aragon and Anne Boleyn. By Wm. Harrison Ainsworth. Cloth, 12mo. with four illustrations by George Cruikshank. Price $1.00.

"Windsor Castle" is the story of Henry VIII., Catharine, and Anne Boleyn. "Bluff King Hal," although a well-loved monarch, was none too good a one in many ways. Of all his selfishness and unwarrantable acts, none was more discreditable than his divorce from Catharine, and his marriage to the beautiful Anne Boleyn. The King's love was as brief as it was vehement. Jane Seymour, waiting maid on the Queen, attracted him, and Anne Boleyn was forced to the block to make room for her successor. This romance is one of extreme interest to all readers.

HORSESHOE ROBINSON. A tale of the Tory Ascendency in South Carolina in 1780. By John P. Kennedy. Cloth, 12mo. with four illustrations by J. Watson Davis. Price, $1.00.

Among the old favorites in the field of what is known as historical fiction, there are none which appeal to a larger number of Americans than Horseshoe Robinson, and this because it is the only story which depicts with fidelity to the facts the heroic efforts of the colonists in South Carolina to defend their homes against the brutal oppression of the British under such leaders as Cornwallis and Tarleton.

The reader is charmed with the story of love which forms the thread of the tale, and then impressed with the wealth of detail concerning those times. The picture of the manifold sufferings of the people, is never overdrawn, but painted faithfully and honestly by one who spared neither time nor labor in his efforts to present in this charming love story all that price in blood and tears which the Carolinians paid as their share in the winning of the republic.

Take it all in all, "Horseshoe Robinson" is a work which should be found on every book-shelf, not only because it is a most entertaining story, but because of the wealth of valuable information concerning the colonists which it contains. That it has been brought out once more, well illustrated, is something which will give pleasure to thousands who have long desired an opportunity to read the story again, and to the many who have tried vainly in these latter days to procure a copy that they might read it for the first time.

THE PEARL OF ORR'S ISLAND. A story of the Coast of Maine. By Harriet Beecher Stowe. Cloth, 12mo. Illustrated. Price, $1.00.

Written prior to 1862, the "Pearl of Orr's Island" is ever new; a book filled with delicate fancies, such as seemingly array themselves anew each time one reads them. One sees the "sea like an unbroken mirror all around the pine-girt, lonely shores of Orr's Island," and straightway comes "the heavy, hollow moan of the surf on the beach, like the wild angry howl of some savage animal."

Who can read of the beginning of that sweet life, named Mara, which came into this world under the very shadow of the Death angel's wings, without having an intense desire to know how the premature bud blossomed? Again and again one lingers over the descriptions of the character of that baby boy Moses, who came through the tempest, amid the angry billows, pillowed on his dead mother's breast.

There is no more faithful portrayal of New England life than that which Mrs. Stowe gives in "The Pearl of Orr's Island."

BURT'S SERIES of STANDARD FICTION.

RICHELIEU. A tale of France in the reign of King Louis XIII. By G. P. R. James. Cloth, 12mo. with four illustrations by J. Watson Davis. Price, $1.00.

In 1829 Mr. James published his first romance, "Richelieu," and was recognized at once as one of the masters of the craft.

In this book he laid the story during those later days of the great cardinal's life, when his power was beginning to wane, but while it was yet sufficiently strong to permit now and then of volcanic outbursts which overwhelmed foes and carried friends to the topmost wave of prosperity. One of the most striking portions of the story is that of Cinq Mar's conspiracy; the method of conducting criminal cases, and the political trickery resorted to by royal favorites, affording a better insight into the statecraft of that day than can be had even by an exhaustive study of history. It is a powerful romance of love and diplomacy, and in point of thrilling and absorbing interest has never been excelled.

A COLONIAL FREE-LANCE. A story of American Colonial Times. By Chauncey C. Hotchkiss. Cloth, 12mo. with four illustrations by J. Watson Davis. Price, $1.00.

A book that appeals to Americans as a vivid picture of Revolutionary scenes. The story is a strong one, a thrilling one. It causes the true American to flush with excitement, to devour chapter after chapter, until the eyes smart, and it fairly smokes with patriotism. The love story is a singularly charming idyl.

THE TOWER OF LONDON. A Historical Romance of the Times of Lady Jane Grey and Mary Tudor. By Wm. Harrison Ainsworth. Cloth, 12mo. with four illustrations by George Cruikshank. Price, $1.00.

This romance of the "Tower of London" depicts the Tower as palace, prison and fortress, with many historical associations. The era is the middle of the sixteenth century.

The story is divided into two parts, one dealing with Lady Jane Grey, and the other with Mary Tudor as Queen, introducing other notable characters of the era. Throughout the story holds the interest of the reader in the midst of intrigue and conspiracy, extending considerably over a half a century.

IN DEFIANCE OF THE KING. A Romance of the American Revolution. By Chauncey C. Hotchkiss. Cloth, 12mo. with four illustrations by J. Watson Davis. Price, $1.00.

Mr. Hotchkiss has etched in burning words a story of Yankee bravery, and true love that thrills from beginning to end, with the spirit of the Revolution. The heart beats quickly, and we feel ourselves taking a part in the exciting scenes described. His whole story is so absorbing that you will sit up far into the night to finish it. As a love romance it is charming.

GARTHOWEN. A story of a Welsh Homestead. By Allen Raine. Cloth, 12mo. with four illustrations by J. Watson Davis. Price, $1.00.

"This is a little idyl of humble life and enduring love, laid bare before us, very real and pure, which in its telling shows us some strong points of Welsh character—the pride, the hasty temper, the quick dying out of wrath. . . . We call this a well-written story, interesting alike through its romance and its glimpses into another life than ours. A delightful and clever picture of Welsh village life. The result is excellent."—Detroit Free Press.

MIFANWY. The story of a Welsh Singer. By Allan Raine. Cloth, 12mo. with four illustrations by J. Watson Davis. Price, $1.00.

"This is a love story, simple, tender and pretty as one would care to read. The action throughout is brisk and pleasing; the characters, it is apparent at once, are as true to life as though the author had known them all personally. Simple in all its situations, the story is worked up in that touching and quaint strain which never grows wearisome, no matter how often the lights and shadows of love are introduced. It rings true, and does not tax the imagination."—Boston Herald.

BURT'S SERIES of STANDARD FICTION.

THE SPIRIT OF THE BORDER. A Romance of the Early Settlers in the Ohio Valley. By Zane Grey. Cloth. 12mo. with four illustrations by J. Watson Davis. Price, $1.00.

A book rather out of the ordinary is this "Spirit of the Border." The main thread of the story has to do with the work of the Moravian missionaries in the Ohio Valley. Incidentally the reader is given details of the frontier life of those hardy pioneers who broke the wilderness for the planting of this great nation. Chief among these, as a matter of course, is Lewis Wetzel, one of the most peculiar, and at the same time the most admirable of all the brave men who spent their lives battling with the savage foe, that others might dwell in comparative security.

Details of the establishment and destruction of the Moravian "Village of Peace" are given at some length, and with minute description. The efforts to Christianize the Indians are described as they never have been before, and the author has depicted the characters of the leaders of the several Indian tribes with great care, which of itself will be of interest to the student.

By no means least among the charms of the story are the vivid word-pictures of the thrilling adventures, and the intense paintings of the beauties of nature, as seen in the almost unbroken forests.

It is the spirit of the frontier which is described, and one can by it, perhaps, the better understand why men, and women, too, willingly braved every privation and danger that the westward progress of the star of empire might be the more certain and rapid. A love story, simple and tender, runs through the book.

CAPTAIN BRAND, OF THE SCHOONER CENTIPEDE. By Lieut. Henry A. Wise, U.S.N. (Harry Gringo). Cloth, 12mo. with four illustrations by J. Watson Davis. Price, $1.00.

The re-publication of this story will please those lovers of sea yarns who delight in so much of the salty flavor of the ocean as can come through the medium of a printed page, for never has a story of the sea and those "who go down in ships" been written by one more familiar with the scenes depicted.

The one book of this gifted author which is best remembered, and which will be read with pleasure for many years to come, is "Captain Brand," who, as the author states on his title page, was a "pirate of eminence in the West Indies." As a sea story pure and simple, "Captain Brand" has never been excelled, and as a story of piratical life, told without the usual embellishments of blood and thunder, it has no equal.

NICK OF THE WOODS. A story of the Early Settlers of Kentucky. By Robert Montgomery Bird. Cloth, 12mo. with four illustrations by J. Watson Davis. Price, $1.00.

This most popular novel and thrilling story of early frontier life in Kentucky was originally published in the year 1837. The novel, long out of print, had in its day a phenomenal sale, for its realistic presentation of Indian and frontier life in the early days of settlement in the South, narrated in the tale with all the art of a practiced writer. A very charming love romance runs through the story. This new and tasteful edition of "Nick of the Woods" will be certain to make many new admirers for this enchanting story from Dr. Bird's clever and versatile pen.

GUY FAWKES. A Romance of the Gunpowder Treason. By Wm. Harrison Ainsworth. Cloth, 12mo. with four illustrations by George Cruikshank. Price, $1.00.

The "Gunpowder Plot" was a modest attempt to blow up Parliament, the King and his Counsellors. James of Scotland, then King of England, was weak-minded and extravagant. He hit upon the efficient scheme of extorting money from the people by imposing taxes on the Catholics. In their natural resentment to this extortion, a handful of bold spirits concluded to overthrow the government. Finally the plotters were arrested, and the King put to torture Guy Fawkes and the other prisoners with royal vigor. A very intense love story runs through the entire romance.

BURT'S SERIES of STANDARD FICTION.

TICONDEROGA : A Story of Early Frontier Life in the Mohawk Valley. By G. P. R. James. Cloth, 12mo. with four page illustrations by J. Watson Davis. Price, $1.00.

The setting of the story is decidedly more picturesque than any ever evolved by Cooper: The frontier of New York State, where dwelt an English gentleman, driven from his native home by grief over the loss of his wife, with a son and daughter. Thither, brought by the exigencies of war, comes an English officer, who is readily recognized as that Lord Howe who met his death at Ticonderoga. As a most natural sequence, even amid the hostile demonstrations of both French and Indians, Lord Howe and the young girl find time to make most deliciously sweet love, and the son of the recluse has already lost his heart to the daughter of a great sachem, a dusky maiden whose warrior-father has surrounded her with all the comforts of a civilized life.

The character of Captain Brooks, who voluntarily decides to sacrifice his own life in order to save the son of the Englishman, is not among the least of the attractions of this story, which holds the attention of the reader even to the last page. The tribal laws and folk lore of the different tribes of Indians known as the "Five Nations," with which the story is interspersed, shows that the author gave no small amount of study to the work in question, and nowhere else is it shown more plainly than by the skilful manner in which he has interwoven with his plot the "blood" law, which demands a life for a life, whether it be that of the murderer or one of his race.

A more charming story of mingled love and adventure has never been written than "Ticonderoga."

ROB OF THE BOWL : A Story of the Early Days of Maryland. By John P. Kennedy. Cloth, 12mo. with four page illustrations by J. Watson Davis. Price, $1.00.

It was while he was a member of Congress from Maryland that the noted statesman wrote this story regarding the early history of his native State, and while some critics are inclined to consider "Horse Shoe Robinson" as the best of his works, it is certain that "Rob of the Bowl" stands at the head of the list as a literary production and an authentic exposition of the manners and customs during Lord Baltimore's rule. The greater portion of the action takes place in St. Mary's—the original capital of the State.

As a series of pictures of early colonial life in Maryland, "Rob of the Bowl" has no equal, and the book, having been written by one who had exceptional facilities for gathering material concerning the individual members of the settlements in and about St. Mary's, is a most valuable addition to the history of the State.

The story is full of splendid action, with a charming love story, and a plot that never loosens the grip of its interest to its last page.

BY BERWEN BANKS. By Allen Raine.

It is a tender and beautiful romance of the idyllic. A charming picture of life in a Welsh seaside village. It is something of a prose-poem, true, tender and graceful.

IN DEFIANCE OF THE KING. A romance of the American Revolution. By Chauncey C. Hotchkiss. Cloth, 12mo. with four illustrations by J. Watson Davis. Price, $1.00.

The story opens in the month of April, 1775, with the provincial troops hurrying to the defense of Lexington and Concord. Mr. Hotchkiss has etched in burning words a story of Yankee bravery and true love that thrills from beginning to end with the spirit of the Revolution. The heart beats quickly, and we feel ourselves taking a part in the exciting scenes described. You lay the book aside with the feeling that you have seen a gloriously true picture of the Revolution. His whole story is so absorbing that you will sit up far into the night to finish it. As a love romance it is charming.

POPULAR LITERATURE FOR THE MASSES, COMPRISING CHOICE SELECTIONS FROM THE TREASURES OF THE WORLD'S KNOWLEDGE, ISSUED IN A SUBSTANTIAL AND ATTRACTIVE CLOTH BINDING, AT A POPULAR PRICE

BURT'S HOME LIBRARY is a series which includes the standard works of the world's best literature, bound in uniform cloth binding, gilt tops, embracing chiefly selections from writers of the most notable English, American and Foreign Fiction, together with many important works in the domains of History, Biography, Philosophy, Travel, Poetry and the Essays.

A glance at the following annexed list of titles and authors will endorse the claim that the publishers make for it—that it is the most comprehensive, choice, interesting, and by far the most carefully selected series of standard authors for world-wide reading that has been produced by any publishing house in any country, and that at prices so cheap, and in a style so substantial and pleasing, as to win for it millions of readers and the approval and commendation, not only of the book trade throughout the American continent, but of hundreds of thousands of librarians, clergymen, educators and men of letters interested in the dissemination of instructive, entertaining and thoroughly wholesome reading matter for the masses.

[SEE FOLLOWING PAGES]

BURT'S HOME LIBRARY. Cloth. Gilt Tops. Price, $1.00

Abbe Constantin. By LUDOVIC HALEVY.
Abbott. By SIR WALTER SCOTT.
Adam Bede. By GEORGE ELIOT.
Addison's Essays. EDITED BY JOHN RICHARD GREEN.
Aeneid of Virgil. TRANSLATED BY JOHN CONNINGTON.
Aesop's Fables.
Alexander, the Great, Life of. BY JOHN WILLIAMS.
Alfred, the Great, Life of. By THOMAS HUGHES.
Alhambra. By WASHINGTON IRVING.
Alice in Wonderland, and Through the Looking-Glass. By LEWIS CARROLL.
Alice Lorraine. By R. D. BLACKMORE.
All Sorts and Conditions of Men. By WALTER BESANT.
Alton Locke. By CHARLES KINGSLEY.
Amiel's Journal. TRANSLATED BY MRS. HUMPHREY WARD.
Andersen's Fairy Tales.
Anne of Geirstein. By SIR WALTER SCOTT.
Antiquary. By SIR WALTER SCOTT.
Arabian Nights' Entertainments.
Ardath. By MARIE CORELLI.
Arnold, Benedict, Life of. By GEORGE CANNING HILL.
Arnold's Poems. By MATTHEW ARNOLD.
Around the World in the Yacht Sunbeam. By MRS. BRASSEY.
Arundel Motto. By MARY CECIL HAY.
At the Back of the North Wind. By GEORGE MACDONALD.
Attic Philosopher. By EMILE SOUVESTRE.
Auld Licht Idylls. By JAMES M. BARRIE.
Aunt Diana. By ROSA N. CAREY.
Autobiography of Benjamin Franklin.
Autocrat of the Breakfast Table. By O. W. HOLMES.
Averil. By ROSA N. CAREY.
Bacon's Essays. By FRANCIS BACON.
Barbara Heathcote's Trial. By ROSA N. CAREY.
Barnaby Rudge. By CHARLES DICKENS.
Barrack Room Ballads. By RUDYARD KIPLING.
Betrothed. By SIR WALTER SCOTT.
Beulah. By AUGUSTA J. EVANS.
Black Beauty. By ANNA SEWALL.
Black Dwarf. By SIR WALTER SCOTT.
Black Rock. By RALPH CONNOR.
Black Tulip. By ALEXANDRE DUMAS.
Bleak House. By CHARLES DICKENS.
Blithedale Romance. By NATHANIEL HAWTHORNE.
Bondman. By HALL CAINE.
Book of Golden Deeds. By CHARLOTTE M. YONGE.
Boone, Daniel, Life of. By CECIL B. HARTLEY.

Bride of Lammermoor. By SIR WALTER SCOTT.
Bride of the Nile. By GEORGE EBERS.
Browning's Poems. By ELIZABETH BARRETT BROWNING.
Browning's Poems. (SELECTIONS.) By ROBERT BROWNING.
Bryant's Poems. (EARLY.) By WILLIAM CULLEN BRYANT.
Burgomaster's Wife. By GEORGE EBERS.
Burn's Poems. By ROBERT BURNS.
By Order of the King. By VICTOR HUGO.
Byron's Poems. By LORD BYRON.
Caesar, Julius, Life of. By JAMES ANTHONY FROUDE.
Carson, Kit, Life of. By CHARLES BURDETT.
Cary's Poems. By ALICE AND PHOEBE CARY.
Cast Up by the Sea. By SIR SAMUEL BAKER.
Charlemagne (Charles the Great), Life of. By THOMAS HODGKIN, D. C. L.
Charles Auchester. By E. BERGER.
Character. By SAMUEL SMILES.
Charles O'Malley. By CHARLES LEVER.
Chesterfield's Letters. By LORD CHESTERFIELD.
Chevalier de Maison Rouge. By ALEXANDRE DUMAS.
Chicot the Jester. By ALEXANDRE DUMAS.
Children of the Abbey. By REGINA MARIA ROCHE.
Child's History of England. By CHARLES DICKENS.
Christmas Stories. By CHARLES DICKENS.
Cloister and the Hearth. By CHARLES READE.
Coleridge's Poems. By SAMUEL TAYLOR COLERIDGE.
Columbus, Christopher, Life of. By WASHINGTON IRVING.
Companions of Jehu. By ALEXANDRE DUMAS.
Complete Angler. By WALTON AND COTTON.
Conduct of Life. By RALPH WALDO EMERSON.
Confessions of an Opium Eater. By THOMAS DE QUINCEY.
Conquest of Granada. By WASHINGTON IRVING.
Conscript. By ERCKMANN-CHATRIAN.
Conspiracy of Pontiac. By FRANCIS PARKMAN, JR.
Conspirators. By ALEXANDRE DUMAS.
Consuelo. By GEORGE SAND.
Cook's Voyages. By CAPTAIN JAMES COOK.
Corinne. By MADAME DE STAEL.
Countess de Charney. By ALEXANDRE DUMAS.
Countess Gisela. By E. MARLITT.

BURT'S HOME LIBRARY. Cloth. Gilt Tops. Price, $1.00

Countess of Rudolstadt. By GEORGE SAND.
Count Robert of Paris. By SIR WALTER SCOTT.
Country Doctor. By HONORE DE BALZAC.
Courtship of Miles Standish. By H. W. LONGFELLOW.
Cousin Maude. By MARY J. HOLMES.
Cranford. By MRS. GASKELL.
Crockett, David, Life of. AN AUTOBIOGRAPHY.
Cromwell, Oliver, Life of. By EDWIN PAXTON HOOD.
Crown of Wild Olive. By JOHN RUSKIN'
Crusades. By GEO. W. COX, M.A.
Daniel Deronda. By GEORGE ELIOT.
Darkness and Daylight. By MARY J. HOLMES.
Data of Ethics. By HERBERT SPENCER.
Daughter of an Empress, The. By LOUISA MUHLBACH.
David Copperfield. By CHARLES DICKENS.
Days of Bruce. By GRACE AGUILAR.
Deemster, The. By HALL CAINE.
Deerslayer, The. By JAMES FENIMORE COOPER.
Descent of Man. By CHARLES DARWIN.
Discourses of Epictetus. TRANSLATED by GEORGE LONG.
Divine Comedy. (DANTE.) TRANSLATED by REV. H. F. CAREY.
Dombey & Son. By CHARLES DICKENS.
Donal Grant. By GEORGE MACDONALD.
Donovan. By EDNA LYALL.
Dora Deane. By MARY J. HOLMES.
Dove in the Eagle's Nest. By CHARLOTTE M. YONGE.
Dream Life. By IK MARVEL.
Dr. Jekyll and Mr. Hyde. By R. L. STEVENSON.
Duty. By SAMUEL SMILES.
Early Days of Christianity. By F. W. FARRAR.
East Lynne. By MRS. HENRY WOOD.
Edith Lyle's Secret. By MARY J. HOLMES.
Education. By HERBERT SPENCER.
Egoist. By GEORGE MEREDITH.
Egyptian Princess. By GEORGE EBERS.
Eight Hundred Leagues on the Amazon. By JULES VERNE.
Eliot's Poems. By GEORGE ELIOT.
Elizabeth and her German Garden.
Elizabeth (Queen of England), Life of. By EDWARD SPENCER BEESLY, M.A.
Elsie Venner. By OLIVER WENDELL HOLMES.
Emerson's Essays. (COMPLETE.) By RALPH WALDO EMERSON.
Emerson's Poems. By RALPH WALDO EMERSON.
English Orphans. By MARY J. HOLMES.

English Traits. By R. W. EMERSON.
Essays in Criticism. (FIRST AND SECOND SERIES.) By MATTHEW ARNOLD.
Essays of Elia. By CHARLES LAMB.
Esther. By ROSA N. CAREY.
Ethelyn's Mistake. By MARY J. HOLMES.
Evangeline. (WITH NOTES.) By H. W. LONGFELLOW.
Evelina. By FRANCES BURNEY.
Fair Maid of Perth. By SIR WALTER SCOTT.
Fairy Land of Science. By ARABELLA B. BUCKLEY.
Faust. (GOETHE.) TRANSLATED BY ANNA SWANWICK.
Felix Holt. By GEORGE ELIOT.
Fifteen Decisive Battles of the World. By E. S. CREASY.
File No. 113. By EMILE GABORIAU.
Firm of Girdlestone. By A. CONAN DOYLE.
First Principles. By HERBERT SPENCER.
First Violin. By JESSIE FOTHERGILL.
For Lilias. By ROSA N. CAREY.
Fortunes of Nigel. By SIR WALTER SCOTT.
Forty-Five Guardsmen. By ALEXANDRE DUMAS.
Foul Play. By CHARLES READE.
Fragments of Science. By JOHN TYNDALL.
Frederick, the Great, Life of. By FRANCIS KUGLER.
Frederick the Great and His Court. By LOUISA MUHLBACH.
French Revolution. By THOMAS CARLYLE.
From the Earth to the Moon. By JULES VERNE.
Garibaldi, General, Life of. By THEODORE DWIGHT.
Gil Blas, Adventures of. By A. R. LE SAGE.
Gold Bug and Other Tales. By EDGAR A. POE.
Gold Elsie. By E. MARLITT.
Golden Treasury. By FRANCIS T. PALGRAVE.
Goldsmith's Poems. By OLIVER GOLDSMITH.
Grandfather's Chair. By NATHANIEL HAWTHORNE.
Grant, Ulysses S., Life of. By J. T. HEADLEY.
Gray's Poems. By THOMAS GRAY.
Great Expectations. By CHARLES DICKENS.
Greek Heroes. Fairy Tales for My Children. By CHARLES KINGSLEY.
Green Mountain Boys, The. By D. P. THOMPSON.
Grimm's Household Tales. By THE BROTHERS GRIMM.
Grimm's Popular Tales. By THE BROTHERS GRIMM.
Gulliver's Travels. By DEAN SWIFT.
Guy Mannering. By SIR WALTER SCOTT.

BURT'S HOME LIBRARY. Cloth. Gilt Tops. Price, $1.00

Hale, Nathan, the Martyr Spy. By CHARLOTTE MOLYNEUX HOLLOWAY.
Handy Andy. By SAMUEL LOVER.
Hans of Iceland. By VICTOR HUGO.
Hannibal, the Carthaginian, Life of. By THOMAS ARNOLD, M. A.
Hardy Norseman, A. By EDNA LYALL.
Harold. By BULWER-LYTTON.
Harry Lorrequer. By CHARLES LEVER.
Heart of Midlothian. By SIR WALTER SCOTT.
Heir of Redclyffe. By CHARLETTE M. YONGE.
Hemans' Poems. By MRS. FELICIA HEMANS.
Henry Esmond. By WM. M. THACKERAY.
Henry, Patrick, Life of. By WILLIAM WIRT.
Her Dearest Foe. By MRS. ALEXANDER.
Hereward. By CHARLES KINGSLEY.
Heriot's Choice. By ROSA N. CAREY.
Heroes and Hero-Worship. By THOMAS CARLYLE.
Hiawatha. (WITH NOTES.) By H. W. LONGFELLOW.
Hidden Hand, The. (COMPLETE.) By MRS. E. D. E. N. SOUTHWORTH.
History of a Crime. By VICTOR HUGO.
History of Civilization in Europe. By M. GUIZOT.
Holmes' Poems. (EARLY) By OLIVER WENDELL HOLMES.
Holy Roman Empire. By JAMES BRYCE.
Homestead on the Hillside. By MARY J. HOLMES.
Hood's Poems. By THOMAS HOOD.
House of the Seven Gables. By NATHANIEL HAWTHORNE.
Hunchback of Notre Dame. By VICTOR HUGO.
Hypatia. By CHARLES KINGSLEY.
Hyperion. By HENRY WADSWORTH LONGFELLOW.
Iceland Fisherman. By PIERRE LOTI.
Idle Thoughts of an Idle Fellow. By JEROME K. JEROME.
Iliad, POPE'S TRANSLATION.
Inez. By AUGUSTA J. EVANS.
Ingelow's Poems. By JEAN INGELOW.
Initials. By THE BARONESS TAUTPHOEUS.
Intellectual Life. By PHILIP G. HAMERTON.
In the Counsellor's House. By E. MARLITT.
In the Golden Days. By EDNA LYALL.
In the Heart of the Storm. By MAXWELL GRAY.
In the Schillingscourt. By E. MARLITT.
Ishmael. (COMPLETE.) By MRS. E. D. E. N. SOUTHWORTH.
It Is Never Too Late to Mend. By CHARLES READE.

Ivanhoe. By SIR WALTER SCOTT.
Jane Eyre. By CHARLOTTE BRONTE.
Jefferson, Thomas, Life of. By SAMUEL M. SCHMUCKER, LL.D.
Joan of Arc, Life of. By JULES MICHELET.
John Halifax, Gentleman. By MISS MULOCK.
Jones, John Paul, Life of. By JAMES OTIS.
Joseph Balsamo. By ALEXANDRE DUMAS.
Josephine, Empress of France, Life of. By FREDERICK A. OBER.
Keats' Poems. By JOHN KEATS.
Kenilworth. By SIR WALTER SCOTT.
Kidnapped. By R. L. STEVENSON.
King Arthur and His Noble Knights. By MARY MACLEOD.
Knickerbocker's History of New York. By WASHINGTON IRVING.
Knight Errant. By EDNA LYALL.
Koran. TRANSLATED BY GEORGE SALE.
Lady of the Lake. (WITH NOTES.) By SIR WALTER SCOTT.
Lady with the Rubies. By E. MARLITT.
Lafayette, Marquis de, Life of. By P. C. HEADLEY.
Lalla Rookh. (WITH NOTES.) By THOMAS MOORE.
Lamplighter. By MARIA S. CUMMINS.
Last Days of Pompeii. By BULWER-LYTTON.
Last of the Barons. By BULWER-LYTTON.
Last of the Mohicans. By JAMES FENIMORE COOPER.
Lay of the Last Minstrel. (WITH NOTES.) By SIR WALTER SCOTT.
Lee, General Robert E., Life of. By G. MERCER ADAM.
Lena Rivers. By MARY J. HOLMES.
Life of Christ. By FREDERICK W. FARRAR.
Life of Jesus. By ERNEST RENAN.
Light of Asia. By SIR EDWIN ARNOLD.
Light That Failed. By RUDYARD KIPLING.
Lincoln, Abraham, Life of. By HENRY KETCHAM.
Lincoln's Speeches. SELECTED AND EDITED BY G. MERCER ADAM.
Literature and Dogma. By MATTHEW ARNOLD.
Little Dorrit. By CHARLES DICKENS.
Little Minister. By JAMES M. BARRIE.
Livingstone, David, Life of. By THOMAS HUGHES.
Longfellow's Poems. (EARLY.) By HENRY W. LONGFELLOW.
Lorna Doone. By R. D. BLACKMORE.
Louise de la Valliere. By ALEXANDRE DUMAS.
Love Me Little, Love Me Long. By CHARLES READE.

BURT's HOME LIBRARY. Cloth. Gilt Tops. Price, $1.00

Lowell's Poems. (EARLY.) By JAMES RUSSELL LOWELL.
Lucile. By OWEN MEREDITH.
Macaria. By AUGUSTA J. EVANS.
Macaulay's Literary Essays. By T. B. MACAULAY.
Macaulay's Poems. By THOMAS BABINGTON MACAULAY.
Madame Therese. By ERCKMANN-CHATRIAN.
Maggie Miller. By MARY J. HOLMES.
Magic Skin. By HONORE DE BALZAC.
Mahomet, Life of. By WASHINGTON IRVING.
Makers of Florence. By MRS. OLIPHANT.
Makers of Venice. By MRS. OLIPHANT.
Man and Wife. By WILKIE COLLINS.
Man in the Iron Mask. By ALEXANDRE DUMAS.
Marble Faun. By NATHANIEL HAWTHORNE.
Marguerite de la Valois. By ALEXANDRE DUMAS.
Marian Grey. By MARY J. HOLMES.
Marius, The Epicurian. By WALTER PATER.
Marmion. (WITH NOTES.) By SIR WALTER SCOTT.
Marquis of Lossie. By GEORGE MACDONALD.
Martin Chuzzlewit. By CHARLES DICKENS.
Mary, Queen of Scots, Life of. By P. C. HEADLEY.
Mary St. John. By ROSA N. CAREY.
Master of Ballantrae, The. By. R. L. STEVENSON.
Masterman Ready. By CAPTAIN MARRYATT.
Meadow Brook. By MARY J. HOLMES.
Meditations of Marcus Aurelius. TRANSLATED BY GEORGE LONG.
Memoirs of a Physician. By ALEXANDRE DUMAS.
Merle's Crusade. By ROSA N. CAREY.
Micah Clarke. By A. CONAN DOYLE.
Michael Strogoff. By JULES VERNE.
Middlemarch. By GEORGE ELIOT.
Midshipman Easy. By CAPTAIN MARRYATT
Mildred. By MARY J. HOLMES.
Millbank. By MARY J. HOLMES.
Mill on the Floss. By GEORGE ELIOT.
Milton's Poems. By JOHN MILTON.
Mine Own People. By RUDYARD KIPLING.
Minister's Wooing, The. By HARRIET BEECHER STOWE.
Monastery. By SIR WALTER SCOTT.
Moonstone. By WILKIE COLLINS.
Moore's Poems. By THOMAS MOORE
Mosses from an Old Manse. By NATHANIEL HAWTHORNE.
Murders in the Rue Morgue. By EDGAR ALLEN POE.
Mysterious Island. By JULES VERNE.
Napoleon Bonaparte, Life of. By P. C. HEADLEY.

Napoleon and His Marshals. By J. T. HEADLEY.
Natural Law in the Spiritual World. By HENRY DRUMMOND.
Narrative of Arthur Gordon Pym. By EDGAR ALLAN POE.
Nature, Addresses and Lectures. By R. W. EMERSON.
Nellie's Memories. By ROSA N. CAREY.
Nelson, Admiral Horatio, Life of. By ROBERT SOUTHEY.
Newcomes. By WILLIAM M. THACKERAY.
Nicholas Nickleby. By CHAS. DICKENS.
Ninety-Three. By VICTOR HUGO.
Not Like Other Girls. By ROSA N. CAREY.
Odyssey. POPE's TRANSLATION.
Old Curiosity Shop. By CHARLES DICKENS.
Old Mam'selle's Secret. By E. MARLITT.
Old Mortality. By SIR WALTER SCOTT.
Old Myddleton's Money. By MARY CECIL HAY.
Oliver Twist. By CHAS. DICKENS.
Only the Governess. By ROSA N. CAREY.
On the Heights. By BERTHOLD AUERBACH.
Oregon Trail. By FRANCIS PARKMAN.
Origin of Species. By CHARLES DARWIN.
Other Worlds than Ours. By RICHARD PROCTOR.
Our Bessie. By ROSA N. CAREY.
Our Mutual Friend. By CHARLES DICKENS.
Outre-Mer. By H. W. LONGFELLOW.
Owl's Nest. By E. MARLITT.
Page of the Duke of Savoy. By ALEXANDRE DUMAS.
Pair of Blue Eyes. By THOMAS HARDY.
Pan Michael. By HENRYK SIENKIEWICZ.
Past and Present. By THOS. CARLYLE.
Pathfinder. By JAMES FENIMORE COOPER.
Paul and Virginia. By B. DE ST. PIERRE.
Pendennis. History of. By WM. M. THACKERAY.
Penn, William, Life of. By W. HEPWORTH DIXON.
Pere Goriot. By HONORE DE BALZAC.
Peter, the Great, Life of. By JOHN BARROW.
Peveril of the Peak. By SIR WALTER SCOTT.
Phantom Rickshaw, The. By RUDYARD KIPLING.
Philip II. of Spain, Life of. By MARTIN A. S. HUME.
Picciola. By X. B. SAINTINE.

BURT'S HOME LIBRARY. Cloth. Gilt Tops. Price, $1.00

Pickwick Papers. By CHARLES DICKENS.
Pilgrim's Progress. By JOHN BUNYAN.
Pillar of Fire. By REV. J. H. INGRAHAM.
Pilot. By JAMES FENIMORE COOPER.
Pioneers. By JAMES FENIMORE COOPER.
Pirate. By SIR WALTER SCOTT.
Plain Tales from the Hills. By RUDYARD KIPLING.
Plato's Dialogues. TRANSLATED BY J. WRIGHT, M. A.
Pleasures of Life. By SIR JOHN LUBBOCK.
Poe's Poems. By EDGAR A. POE.
Pope's Poems. By ALEXANDER POPE.
Prairie. By JAMES F. COOPER.
Pride and Prejudice. By JANE AUSTEN.
Prince of the House of David. By REV. J. H. INGRAHAM.
Princess of the Moor. By E. MARLITT.
Princess of Thule. By WILLIAM BLACK.
Procter's Poems. By ADELAIDE PROCTOR.
Professor at the Breakfast Table. By OLIVER WENDELL HOLMES.
Professor. By CHARLOTTE BRONTE.
Prue and I. By GEORGE WILLIAM CURTIS.
Put Yourself in His Place. By CHAS. READE.
Putnam, General Israel, Life of By GEORGE CANNING HILL.
Queen Hortense. By LOUISA MUHLBACH.
Queenie's Whim. By ROSA N. CAREY.
Queen's Necklace. By ALEXANDRE DUMAS.
Quentin Durward. By SIR WALTER SCOTT.
Rasselas, History of. By SAMUEL JOHNSON.
Redgauntlet. By SIR WALTER SCOTT.
Red Rover. By JAMES FENIMORE COOPER.
Regent's Daughter. By ALEXANDRE DUMAS.
Reign of Law. By DUKE OF ARGYLE.
Representative Men. By RALPH WALDO EMERSON.
Republic of Plato. TRANSLATED BY DAVIES AND VAUGHAN.
Return of the Native. By THOMAS HARDY.
Reveries of a Bachelor. By IK MARVEL.
Reynard the Fox. EDITED BY JOSEPH JACOBS.
Rienzi. By BULWER-LYTTON.
Richelieu, Cardinal, Life of. By RICHARD LODGE.
Robinson Crusoe. By DANIEL DEFOE.
Rob Roy. By SIR WALTER SCOTT.
Romance of Natural History. By P. H. GOSSE.
Romance of Two Worlds. By MARIE CORELLI.

Romola. By GEORGE ELIOT.
Rory O'More. By SAMUEL LOVER.
Rose Mather. By MARY J. HOLMES.
Rossetti's Poems. By GABRIEL DANTE ROSSETTI.
Royal Edinburgh. By MRS. OLIPHANT.
Rutledge. By MIRIAN COLES HARRIS.
Saint Michael. By E. WERNER.
Samantha at Saratoga. By JOSIAH ALLER'S WIFE. (MARIETTA HOLLEY.)
Sartor Resartus. By THOMAS CARLYLE.
Scarlet Letter. By NATHANIEL HAWHORNE.
Schonberg-Cotta Family. By MRS. ANDREW CHARLES.
Schopenhauer's Essays. TRANSLATED BY T. B. SAUNDERS.
Scottish Chiefs. By JANE PORTER.
Scott's Poems. By SIR WALTER SCOTT.
Search for Basil Lyndhurst. By ROSA N. CAREY.
Second Wife. By E. MARLITT.
Seekers After God. By F. W. FARRAR.
Self-Help. By SAMUEL SMILES.
Self-Raised. (COMPLETE.) By MRS. E. D. E. N. SOUTHWORTH.
Seneca's Morals.
Sense and Sensibility. By JANE AUSTEN.
Sentimental Journey. By LAWRENCE STERNE.
Sesame and Lilies. By JOHN RUSKIN.
Shakespeare's Heroines. By ANNA JAMESON.
Shelley's Poems. By PERCY BYSSHE SHELLEY.
Shirley. By CHARLOTTE BRONTE.
Sign of the Four. By A. CONAN DOYLE.
Silas Marner. By GEORGE ELIOT.
Silence of Dean Maitland. By MAXWELL GRAY.
Sir Gibbie. By GEORGE MACDONALD
Sketch Book. By WASHINGTON IRVING.
Smith, Captain John, Life of. By W. GILMORE SIMMS.
Socrates, Trial and Death of. TRANSLATED BY F. J. CHURCH, M. A.
Soldiers Three. By RUDYARD KIPLING.
Springhaven. By R. D. BLACKMORE.
Spy. By JAMES FENIMORE COOPER.
Stanley, Henry M., African Explorer, Life of. By A. MONTEFIORE.
Story of an African Farm. By OLIVE SCHREINER.
Story of John G. Paton. TOLD FOR YOUNG FOLKS. By REV. JAS. PATON.
St. Ronan's Well. By SIR WALTER SCOTT.
Study in Scarlet. By A. CONAN DOYLE.

BURT'S HOME LIBRARY. Cloth. Gilt Tops. Price, $1.00

Surgeon's Daughter. By Sir Walter Scott.
Swinburne's Poems. By A. C. Swinburne.
Swiss Family Robinson. By Jean Rudolph Wyss.
Taking the Bastile. By Alexandre Dumas.
Tale of Two Cities. By Chas. Dickens.
Tales from Shakespeare. By Chas. and Mary Lamb.
Tales of a Traveller. By Washington Irving.
Talisman. By Sir Walter Scott.
Tanglewood Tales. By Nathaniel Hawthorne.
Tempest and Sunshine. By Mary J. Holmes.
Ten Nights in a Bar Room. By T. S. Arthur.
Tennyson's Poems. By Alfred Tennyson.
Ten Years Later. By Alexander Dumas.
Terrible Temptation. By Charles Reade.
Thaddeus of Warsaw. By Jane Porter.
Thelma. By Marie Corelli.
Thirty Years' War. By Frederick Schiller.
Thousand Miles Up the Nile. By Amelia B. Edwards.
Three Guardsmen. By Alexandre Dumas.
Three Men in a Boat. By Jerome K. Jerome.
Thrift. By Samuel Smiles.
Throne of David. By Rev. J. H. Ingraham.
Toilers of the Sea. By Victor Hugo.
Tom Brown at Oxford. By Thomas Hughes.
Tom Brown's School Days. By Thos. Hughes.
Tom Burke of "Ours." By Charles Lever.
Tour of the World in Eighty Days. By Jules Verne.
Treasure Island. By Robert Louis Stevenson.
Twenty Thousand Leagues Under the Sea. By Jules Verne.
Twenty Years After. By Alexandre Dumas.
Twice Told Tales. By Nathaniel Hawthorne.
Two Admirals. By James Fenimore Cooper.
Two Dianas. By Alexandre Dumas.
Two Years Before the Mast. By R. H. Dana, Jr.
Uarda. By George Ebers.
Uncle Max. By Rosa N. Carey.
Uncle Tom's Cabin. By Harriet Beecher Stowe.
Under Two Flags. By "Ouida."

Utopia. By Sir Thomas More.
Vanity Fair. By Wm. M. Thackeray.
Vendetta. By Marie Corelli.
Vespucius, Americus, Life and Voyages. By C. Edwards Lester.
Vicar of Wakefield. By Oliver Goldsmith.
Vicomte de Bragelonne. By Alexandre Dumas.
Views A-Foot. By Bayard Taylor.
Villette. By Charlotte Bronte.
Virginians. By Wm. M. Thackeray.
Walden. By Henry D. Thoreau.
Washington, George, Life of. By Jared Sparks.
Washington and His Generals. By J. T. Headley.
Water Babies. By Charles Kingsley.
Water Witch. By James Fenimore Cooper.
Waverly. By Sir Walter Scott.
Webster, Daniel, Life of. By Samuel M. Schmucker, LL.D.
Webster's Speeches. (Selected.) By Daniel Webster.
Wee Wifie. By Rosa N. Carey.
Westward Ho! By Charles Kingsley.
We Two. By Edna Lyall.
What's Mine's Mine. By George Macdonald.
When a Man's Single. By J. M. Barrie.
White Company. By A. Conan Doyle.
Whites and the Blues. By Alexandre Dumas.
Whittier's Poems. (Early.) By John G. Whittier.
Wide, Wide World. By Susan Warner.
William, the Conqueror, Life of. By Edward A. Freeman, LL.D.
William, the Silent, Life of. By Frederick Harrison.
Willy Reilly. By William Carleton.
Window in Thrums. By J. M. Barrie.
Wing and Wing. By James Fenimore Cooper.
Wolsey, Cardinal, Life of. By Mandell Creighton.
Woman in White. By Wilkie Collins.
Won by Waiting. By Edna Lyall.
Wonder Book. For Boys and Girls. By Nathaniel Hawthorne.
Woodstock. By Sir Walter Scott.
Wooed and Married. By Rosa N. Carey.
Wooing O't. By Mrs. Alexander.
Wordsworth's Poems. By William Wordsworth.
Wormwood. By Marie Corelli.
Wreck of the Grosvenor. By W. Clark Russell.